The Story of Cape Hope

Book One

The House

By

Barbara Ellis Conroy

Barbara Ellis Conroy

Dedication

3

For David

Acknowledgment

To Terri Zappala

As I began to pursue my dream of becoming a novelist, you made time in your hectic schedule to be my sounding board. For that, I will be forever grateful.

Table of Content

Introduction

Cape Hope was a picturesque destination renowned for its rest and recreation. Nestled on the North Shore of Boston, this small cape was famous for its jagged, weathered beaches and rocky shoreline, attracting visitors from all over the world each year. However, in the spring of 2023, the serene town was shaken when two women went missing—one a newcomer, the other a beloved social butterfly. Their disappearance prompted a desperate search by friends and family, who uncovered some answers but found themselves entangled in even more questions—and trouble—as they delved deeper.

Prologue

The interior consisted of multiple shipping containers welded together. Initially, it was dark, but as he moved, a small light at the top of the wall flickered on. Every five feet, a new light would illuminate as the one behind it dimmed, creating a tunnel that seemed to swallow the light reminiscent of a black hole.

He counted twenty lights as he walked. When he reached the end, a double metal door resembling the back of an eighteen-wheeler awaited him. He grasped the handle and pushed it down, opening the door into a dark room. Feeling along the wall, he found a button light switch.

To his surprise, the room was set up like a reception area. An elevator stood with its doors open, and another door nearby was closed. Inside that door was a cinderblock room, freshly painted. The floor bore drag marks—some old, others more recent. He closed the door and approached the elevator, noticing it had three floors. He pressed the button for the third floor, knowing that was where they had seen the covered windows.

Chapter 1

Captain Phillip Landry, Officer Lucy Finneran, and Detective Lenny Clarke sat in the diner, having breakfast and discussing the upcoming tourist season. Though it was only the beginning of April, they knew the importance of planning ahead. The police force operated comfortably from Thanksgiving until Memorial Day, but with the summer influx, their budget expanded to cover the additional demands. A retired officer, who returned each summer with his wife, usually worked the desk during the day from May through September, helping to manage the increased population.

"I got a text from Elizabeth Cook. She is moving back to town." Phil looked at Lucy "She is retired Navy, and she consults for Brock's company. She thought we may need her."

"I wonder if Trip knows she's back?" Lenny had been on the force for a long time and knew Trip well. He looked at Lucy "They have history."

Lucy wasn't a local and, at first, didn't socialize with her coworkers, so she really didn't know Trip as well as Phil and Lenny. "Is she cool?"

"She is. She is smart, and she has experience with law enforcement. I know Lenny likes her, and she is known to the longtime residents. I think she would be a good fit; besides, she is my Aunt. My mother's youngest sister."

"Are there any more relatives I don't know about?"

"Oh, probably."

"Will the Select Board approve?"

Phil leaned back. "I believe most of them know her. She is well-liked."

"May I ask? Where has she been?"

"Norfolk, Virginia. She is divorced, and her kids are scattered around the world. Three kids. Two in the service, one in California."

Lucy looked at Lenny rather inquiringly. Lenny responded, "What? We keep in touch."

"It's just that I've never heard you talk so much."

"I usually don't have much to say."

Lenny was quiet, a loner, but not in the typical keeps-to-himself way. He had friends he enjoyed spending time with, but he valued his solitude. An ex-Marine, he didn't discuss his time in Mosul with civilians, but he found camaraderie with fellow veterans at the local VFW Chapter. Lenny was a good guy, even a great guy, but he carried a serious demeanor. Shortly after joining the Cape Hope police force, Phil gave him the nickname Chuckles. Phil had a habit of bestowing pet names on those he liked, especially if they had a characteristic that he found endearing.

Lucy was a fresh hire straight out of the Academy. Initially, she was quiet and very private, but her hard work quickly impressed Phil. She was always available for special assignments and was a stickler for the law. Some saw her as unyielding, a trait she'd learned growing up. But beneath her strict exterior, Lucy had a mischievous, dry sense of humor, along with her mother's Irish temper, something she usually kept to herself most of the time. When Lucy's temper flared, it was best to steer clear. The first time Phil saw this explosion, he dubbed her Boom Boom.

"So, I'll probably like her, right?"

"I don't see how you wouldn't. You are a lot alike."

Lenny's eyes widened. "That's an incredible compliment, Boom Boom."

"Thank you, Cap."

"Take it when you can get it… whoa, speak of the devil."

"Hello, Lenny. I thought you two might be here." Elizabeth waited as Lenny stood up to hug her. "You look well." She extended her hand to Lucy "My educated guess would be you are Lucy?"

"Yes, ma'am."

"Elizabeth Cook, very nice to finally meet you. I hope they are treating you well."

Lucy looked at both men. "Most of the time." Lucy leaned across the table. "Chuckles here thinks I need to get laid."

"Do you?"

Lucy sighed. "Oh, probably."

Elizabeth laughed as she grasped Lenny's hand. "What is going on with you and Matilda?"

"Same old, same old."

"You two need to shit or get off the pot."

"Lovely visual, Lizzy."

"Phil, how is Connie?"

"Busy. All of the kids have some kind of sport they are doing now. PJ and Teresa are playing soccer again. The twins are both playing the violin, and Buddy is playing the piano."

"I was going to stop by."

"Come for dinner. I know all of us will be home. They will love to see Auntie Lizzy."

"I'd love to."

"Have you talked to Trip since the divorce?"

"Nope. Is anyone still living at home?"

"Abby, sometimes. She comes and goes. Shaw has a house near Beau and Julie. Simon and Stella are as they always have been." Phil looked toward the Pharmacy to see if Stella was busy. She saw him wave to her and excuse herself from the counter.

"You beckoned? Lizzy, when did you get back?"

"Just yesterday."

"Have you...?"

She laughed. "No, not yet. Am I wrong to assume he knows about the divorce?"

Phil joked, "Lenny is quite the gossip."

"Yes, that is the exact word I would use to describe him. Why don't the three of you decide how I should approach him, and you can let me know."

Stella clutched Lizzy's shoulder. "Tomorrow is Wednesday. Hilda is off, but she always leaves dinner for him in the refrigerator. He is a creature of habit. He is always home by six. Bring a nice Cabernet."

"What about Abby?"

"I'll make sure she stays with Coop. She usually does, but I'll give her a heads up."

"Thanks. I'm glad I stopped by. Lucy, let me know if these two give you a hard time. I have a meeting to get to with Brock."

***

Brock Hawkins hailed from a third-generation Cape Hope family, inheriting his father's financial consulting business after his untimely death last year. Brock is married to Jack Thurston, a firefighter and paramedic in town. Together, they have twin daughters, Thelma and Louise, born via surrogate. The girls were named after the characters in the movie Brock and Jack were watching when they met. As they started to talk, the girls' nicknames, Telly and Lulu, stuck and became how they referred to each other. Now, in preschool, Telly and Lulu were not only the cutest kids in the class but also the most mischievous.

Neither Brock nor Jack knew much about raising girls, so they leaned heavily on their best friends for support. Brock's closest friend was Kathryn, a childhood neighbor who became like family after a tragic loss. Kathryn's parents, both doctors with Doctors Without Borders, were killed in an attack on a small village where they were working in Africa. After that, Kathryn moved in with the Hawkins family and was eventually adopted by them.

Jack's best friend was Molly Miller, a spoiled preppy who attended a private girls' school a couple of towns away. She ultimately went on to Barnard College and later returned to Cape Hope to open a store. After some time, she reconnected with an old friend, Colton Van der Platt. Despite living in Cape Hope, Molly knew very few people her age, aside from Jack. When she graduated from college, Jack introduced her to Kathryn, who had attended the same prep school but was a year older. After their first conversation, they quickly became best friends.

Molly was both an artist and a philanthropist, while Kathryn had become an attorney. Together with Abby, Stella, Julie, and Dalton, they collaborated to raise money for several charities.

Brock stood up when he saw Elizabeth come in. "Lizzy, welcome home. Have you seen…"

"No, I haven't seen Trip. Please keep this to yourself, but I'm going there tomorrow." She sat down. "I saw Phil and Lenny at the diner. They introduced me to Lucy. She is cute."

"I know sometimes when Hilda is off, Abby drops by for dinner."

"Stella said she would keep her occupied. Does he still want me, Brock?"

"He talks about you sometimes; at least, that is what Kathryn told me."

"You are such a girl."

Brock laughed. "Yes, well… Are you going to help out Phil for the summer?"

"Yes. We haven't talked about details, but yes. Phil knows I'll be helping you, too."

"Have you stopped by to see Tim?"

"No, I just got here. Has he started dating again?"

"No."

"What about Lucy? She is funny and cute."

"She doesn't really socialize with us. I think she is still a little intimidated. Phil is her boss."

"She told me Lenny thinks she needs to get laid."

"Then she probably does."

"How are the kids?"

"Holy terrors, but they are so cute, they get away with murder."

"Has Jack's mother come around yet?"

"I don't know. She loves the twins, but I'm not the daughter-in-law she always hoped for."

"That's because she doesn't know you."

"Thanks, I've stopped worrying about it."

"Does Juice know I'm back?"

"Jack told him. He always liked you, but… He was happy to hear you lost some unwanted weight."

"My ex-husband is a racist prick."

"You moved on. You tried for the kids, but you did the right thing, and you moved on. Your kids take after you. Thank God."

"I was home. Barry was in Mosul. I still think that's the only reason they turned out so good."

"Lizzy, he met someone. Her name is Billie."

The news surprised her. "I'm happy for him."

***

Justice Mason, known as Juice, was a veteran of the Marines. He joined the Corps right out of high school and was stationed at Norfolk after completing training at Parris Island. It was there that he met Lizzy, a Navy sailor who, unbeknownst to him, was the wife of his commanding officer. Juice admired her; she was kind and helpful, but her husband ended up despising their friendship.

Juice was curious and he wanted to learn new skills, and Lizzy maintained the computer system for the Norfolk Navy Yard. When he expressed interest in taking a basic computer skills class, she readily offered to help. At that time, Elizabeth was unaware of the full extent of her husband's intolerance. Juice didn't know who Elizabeth's husband was, and she didn't know who Juice's commanding officer was. As their friendship deepened, Lizzy began to realize just how well her husband had hidden his true nature from her and the Corps.

Eventually, Juice's unit was deployed to Mosul, where he became friends with Lenny, who served as an MP there. During an altercation at the base's Officers Club between Juice and Lizzy's husband, Barry, Lenny stepped in to defend Juice. Although there were no formal charges, Barry's commanding officer issued him a verbal warning. After retiring, Lenny promised to help Juice once he was discharged. Lenny became the older brother Juice had always wanted, and Lizzy was a friend to both of them. She contacted Phil on Lenny's behalf, and together, Phil and Lenny arranged for Juice to enter firefighter training and pursue paramedic certification.

Juice and Lenny lived in a two-family home not far from the Municipal Building. Juice hoped to find a woman to fall in love with. Although his parents were African American and Mexican, he wasn't specifically looking for a woman of a particular ethnicity; he wanted someone kind and nurturing who shared his desire to have children. Most importantly, he wanted a woman who could make him laugh.

He didn't often visit local bars, but occasionally, he would go to The Pub to catch up with his friend Tim. It was during one of these visits that he met Billie Barnes.

Colton Van der Platt was a Chief in the Coast Guard and also a freelance photojournalist whom Abby occasionally employed. Colt was Billie's commanding officer, and when Juice walked in, Billie couldn't take her eyes off him.

Colt and Molly, who knew Juice, called him over to their table. Billie was athletic and enjoyed running and swimming. She had recently taken up golf, but with summer being their busiest season, she hadn't had much time to play. She also loved learning visual languages, knowing semaphore and heliography from her time in the Coast Guard, and was in the process of learning sign language. Juice was fascinated by her interests. Colt and Molly, feeling like third wheels, decided to move to the bar.

"Coast Guard. Tell me why?"

Billie understood his inquiry: "I love the water. There was something about protecting the shores of this country, of New England, that was very appealing. It may sound awful, but it was my way of serving without having to leave the States. I'm too much of a homebody. I could have been stationed anywhere, but New England is my home. I'm lucky…"

Tim watched as Juice and Billie got acquainted, feeling a pang of nostalgia as he worked through his own breakup. He still missed her; she had wanted to escape Cape Hope, but Tim was never going to leave. Eventually, she gave up on their relationship and moved to Boston. While it wasn't that far away, Tim was not a fan of the city. He refused to relocate, nor did he want to spend his days battling the hellish commute in and out of Boston.

Molly was intrigued. "Is she a new recruit?"

Colt shrugged. "Not really. I didn't want to bring her until I figured her out."

Molly snickered. "Because you are so good at that."

"Hey, I figured you out a long time ago."

Molly leaned toward Tim. "The sad thing is, he really believes that. She looked toward the door after Tim smiled and waved to someone coming through the door. "Hey, who is that?"

"I have to introduce you… Matilda, honey?"

"Timmy dearie?"

"You need to meet a friend. Matilda, Molly."

Matilda had been working for Tim Edwards at The Pub for years. She was a seasonal employee, starting as soon as school was out. During the school year, she served as the cafeteria supervisor at a local middle school and usually took a week off at the end of the school year. Since she hadn't yet discussed her schedule with Tim, she decided to walk to town during April vacation, a routine she always followed when it wasn't raining. When she worked nights, she could typically get a ride home from Tim, another employee, or one of the bar's regulars. Most people adored her, especially the men. She was funny and kind, and while some women admired Matilda's outgoing nature, others felt outright envious.

Tim was confident that Molly and Matilda would hit it off. Though they came from different worlds, he knew both women well and believed they would become good friends.

"So, Molly, what do you do for fun?"

"No, no, no." Colt laughed. "That's Matilda's subtle way of asking about me."

"Colt and I have known each other for a long time. We just reconnected a few months ago."

Matilda rested her chin on Colt's shoulder. "And where *exactly* did you *reconnect?*"

Colt's face turned bright red. "None of your business. You need to watch out for this one, Molly; she's a troublemaker."

Molly was having fun. "Does this mean you have her *figured out?*"

Colt frowned as he looked at Tim. "Thanks a lot, buddy."

***

Abby Fredericks was the only daughter of Abbott Fredricks III, known as Trip. From a young age, she dreamed of becoming a journalist. However, her father had different aspirations for her and made her the Editor in Chief of his North Shore daily, The Daily Watch. While she appreciated the faith he had in her, Abby was determined to be an investigative reporter—nothing less.

"Daddy, I love you for trusting me, but the faith you have in me is misguided. I am not the businesswoman you think I am."

"You must have someone in mind."

"You know who deserves this job."

"Cubby Edwards? He is a bit of a paradox. I have no idea where he stands on the issues."

"Daddy, he is the most open-minded, politically moderate journalist I have ever met."

"Like I said, a paradox."

"This country needs more people like him."

Trip was direct: "Is there more going on with Cooper that you have shared?"

"No, Daddy. Coop and I are as we always have been."

"You mean, in limbo?"

"I'm not talking to you about this, Daddy."

Barnaby Edwards became a close friend of Abby's when his family visited Cape Hope to see his oldest brother, Tim, who owned a pub in town. A few years prior, Tim had jumped at the chance to buy the pub when it came up for sale.

Years later, Abby and Barnaby—nicknamed Cubby—were reunited at Columbia University. The name Cubby originated during their internship together one summer in D.C. Their advisor, infatuated with Abby, resented the friendship they shared and began calling Barnaby "Cubby," a term seasoned journalists used for new reporters. The plan backfired when Barnaby embraced the name; he had always hated his given name and disliked "Barney" almost as much, so "Cubby" was a welcome change. After Barnaby returned to Cape Hope, he and Abby's boyfriend, Cooper Matthews, became best friends.

Cooper purchased a house he knew Abby wanted—a large Cape on a hill overlooking the mansions of the area's oldest money. However, the renovation was taking longer than expected.

Trip was coy. "What is going on with you two anyway? Sometimes you sleep here alone. Sometimes, you don't come home for two or three weeks in a row. The only conclusion I can draw is that you come home when you are menstruating."

"You are still talking." Abby got up from the sofa. "I love you, Daddy, but my sex life is not open for discussion."

"But mine is?"

"Well, no, mostly because you don't have one."

Trip let out a huge belly laugh. "You are your mother's daughter."

"No, I am a perfect fusion of you both… Daddy, please?"

"I'll think about it."

***

Abbott "Trip" Fredericks III was a widower and a businessman with vast holdings. In addition to owning the newspaper *The Daily Watch*, he owned four seafood restaurants strategically located along the coasts of Rhode Island, Massachusetts, New Hampshire, and Maine. He also operated real estate offices in the same towns. Trip served on the Board of Directors for two large hospitals and a philanthropic organization his late wife had started. Before she died, he promised to keep her dream alive, and raising money for hospitals and cancer research became his reason for living.

Trip held the same expectations for his friends, family, and employees: he demanded loyalty and honesty. At work, he could be a hard-nosed businessman, but when relaxing—even with his employees—he was kind and generous.

In addition to Abby, his third child and only daughter, Trip had three sons. Abbott IV, known as Beau, was the oldest. After marrying, he took charge of the real estate holdings, which included the restaurants. Beau was very much like his father, except for one glaring exception: he was a womanizer, a trait Trip would find offensive if he ever discovered it. Consequently, Beau kept his indiscretions closely guarded; he didn't want to lose his father's trust, nor did he want to jeopardize his relationship with his children and wife, Julie—a reserved woman who was a perfect hostess, wife, and mother. Above all, Beau didn't want to lose his extracurricular activities.

The second child was Shaw, named for his mother's family. He worked as an assistant D.A. and was unmarried but in a relationship with Abby's best friend, Dalton, a kindergarten teacher. Shaw was a nice guy, but his job consumed most of his time.

The baby of the family was Simon, an ER resident in Boston. His hope, upon completing his studies, was to work in a hospital closer to home. Simon's girlfriend was Stella Landry, who was close friends with Abby and Dalton. Stella worked as a pharmacist at the small family-owned Apothecary, which was evocative of an old-style penny candy store. Along with touristy items, the Landry Apothecary was the heart of Main Street. However, the big draw was the diner situated on the right side of the building. Tables and a counter ran perpendicular to the front window, with the kitchen located in the back. Open for breakfast and lunch, the longtime residents of Cape Hope frequented both the pharmacy and the diner.

Trip Fredericks was proud of his family and of the town he had always called home.

"You need to do more than think about it…"

Ding, dong, ding.

"Daddy, I'm going home. You need to decide." She kissed her father's cheek. "I'm serious, Daddy. I'll get the door on my way out." Stella called Abby when she found out Lizzy would be dropping by. Abby always liked Lizzy and she desperately wanted her father to be happy again. Abby opened the door to find Lizzy holding a bottle of wine.

"Hi, honey. How are you?"

"I'm great." She whispered, "He would never admit it to me, but he misses you. He's in the den."

"I miss him too. Wish me luck." Lizzy was nervous. Trip was watching the news. He didn't turn around. "Did you forget something?"

"Hi, Trip."

He didn't move. "How long have you been practicing the impersonation of Lizzy?"

"Since birth?"

Trip stood up. "Lizzy…"

She put the bottle down. "How've you been?"

"Busy. Lizzy, when did you get back?"

"Yesterday. I needed to speak to Phil and Brock. We had a few things to figure out for the summer."

"Oh. Does that mean you're not staying?"

"That depends. Trip, I've missed you."

Trip wasn't prepared. He hated not being prepared. "There is a casserole in the oven. Will you join me? Maybe we can open that bottle of wine."

Chapter 2

The room smelled like… Lavender.

On the first day, Maggie found herself blindfolded and naked. She wasn't an innocent woman. The moment she heard the door creak open, she understood the impending horror.

The man was silent, but she could sense his gaze penetrating her skin. He reached out to touch her, his fingers exploring her body. Initially, his touch was gentle, but she instinctively knew; she knew…

The man assaulted her. Tears streamed down her face as he shackled her ankles. She struggled violently, only to realize that her fear seemed to excite him. As she fought against the restraints, he breathed out, "There you go."

When she stopped fighting back, it enraged the man. He got off the bed but returned moments later, wielding a whip. As the lashes fell, her sobs filled the air, and he taunted, "There you go."

After the man left, she remained alone in the dim room he had abandoned her in. Time lost meaning; she couldn't tell how long she had been trapped. Eventually, someone entered, sat beside her on the bed, and started applying ointment to her wounds. Maggie whispered, "Thank you."

What unfolded next bewildered her. The hands that had gently spread the salve began to caress her skin. They felt small and delicate, leading Maggie to believe it was a woman. After tending to her injuries, this stranger kissed her breasts and ventured between her legs. Fear washed over Maggie. A moment later, she felt a soft kiss on her forehead, followed by the sound of the door softly closing behind her.

Mmm, lavender.

When she woke, she had clothes and warm socks, and she was able to move around the room.

She always sensed when visitors were on their way. The lavender scent that filled the room lulled her into a drowsy haze. She had no clue how long she had been out, but it didn't feel like long; when she finally regained consciousness, she found herself naked, blindfolded and shackled to the bed. It wasn't every day, but there were days when it happened twice daily. She suspected she had a regular clientele. Although she never spoke to them, she learned it was wise to listen and comply.

Another constant presence was the woman who came to visit. If the sessions were especially brutal—which she assumed meant the visitors paid extra—the woman would appear. She was gentle, and at first, Maggie felt horrified. Yet, she soon realized that this woman was the only thing preventing her from descending into madness.

She was also provided with exquisite meals, a television, and a plethora of books. Surprisingly, she was even trusted with toenail clippers and an emery board, leading her to believe she was expected to maintain her grooming. Her room was exceptionally comfortable; to her, this suite, which had become her new reality, felt almost luxurious. She was grateful that her captors didn't confine her to a cold cell devoid of comforts. It seemed they prioritized their clientele's comfort. After all, they were operating a business—likely a very profitable one. Though she clung to the hope of escape, there were moments when she contemplated ending it all. Maggie felt as if she were being beaten into submission, both physically and emotionally. She was fairly certain she had become a permanent inhabitant of a room without windows.

She also realized they must have been administering some form of birth control, as her period had ceased, and she wasn't pregnant. The relief washed over her, primarily because her first fear was that if she did become pregnant, her baby would be sold. That thought terrified her far more than the abuse she endured.

The next morning, Maggie awakened naked and blindfolded, with her hands shackled. A figure entered the room.

The hands that began to touch her were large. She instinctively curled her knees to her chest and began to cry. The hands then turned her over, gripping her hips as he raped her. When he finished, he secured her ankles to the bedpost and lashed her backside and the backs of her legs. His laughter echoed in her ears as he exited the room.

Maggie was unsure how long she had been sobbing into the pillow when she thought she heard footsteps. She sensed someone sitting at the edge of the bed, and relief washed over her as ointment was squeezed onto her bruised skin. The hands were small and tender, smoothing the salve over the welts adorning her body. Her ankles were uncuffed, and just as Maggie began to relax, a hand ventured between her legs. Fingers delicately rubbed and caressed her. While one hand lingered below, the other held her waist and gently turned her to her side. The woman placed her mouth on Maggie's breast. Fear gripped her, and she hated herself because, despite everything, what she felt was pleasure.

Maggie had been cycling around New England. She had stopped by the side of the road. There were trees along the edge of the two-way street. She could see houses down the incline near the water. *The water is so calm. Must be a cove.*

She was fascinated by the homes she passed. Pedaling her bike for about a mile, she marveled at the stunning estates that seemed to date back to the late eighteen hundreds. Many boasted stone walls lining the driveways, while others featured elegant wrought iron fences, each more magnificent than the last.

She was looking at her phone to confirm her next destination, and a sharp pain shot through her. The last thing she remembered was looking down to see a dart embedded in her arm. When she finally regained consciousness, she discovered she was in a room, completely naked, blindfolded, and handcuffed to the bed.

The only baseline she had for tracking time was the state of her fingernails and toenails. Based on how often she had trimmed them, she estimated she had been trapped there for roughly eight months.

***

"I'm really curious…"

"Do not tell me you are wondering if Lizzy spent the night."

"It's human nature to be curious. Speaking of curiosity, Daddy was wondering what's going on with us. I told him it was none of his business."

"I have told him I have every intention of marrying you."

"And I want to marry you too, but not yet. I'm not ready to start a family."

"This isn't the fifties, Abbs. Just because we get married doesn't mean we have to have kids right away. I want us to be together."

"Cooper, we are together, but we haven't even taken a vacation together yet."

"Because you're afraid of missing that big story, which, by the way, won't be in Cape Hope."

"Colt and I talked about the day we both won a Pulitzer."

Cooper sighed. "I'm sure even Bob Woodward took a vacation."

Abby loved Coop, but she wasn't ready.

"I bought this house for us, Abbs."

"I will move all of my things when it's done. It's not done."

***

Lizzy had gone home the night before. She and Trip talked a lot. It was after midnight. "May we pick this up here tomorrow night?"

She went home and thought about him as she lay in bed until she finally fell asleep.

In the morning, Lizzy met Brock at his office: "Don't ask... sorry. We talked until after midnight."

"When do you see him again?"

"I'm going to call him when I'm done with you. Brock, I think he's scared."

"Of you?"

19

"He worries what the boys will think."

"Oh, dear God. That is such a cop out. Shaw and Simon want Trip to be happy. Beau actually does, too… Lizzy, Kathryn told me Julie has been distant."

"Connie said she seems distracted."

"Her father left her with a huge responsibility. I'm helping her manage the Trust he left the kids, but there are things she insists on taking care of herself… That and her Interior Design business, she is running ragged."

"Her father died over a year ago. His estate should have been settled by now."

"Helloooo… Brock said you'd be here." Kathryn was looking forward to seeing Lizzy. "We have to have lunch with the girls."

"I need to meet this girl Juice is seeing."

"Their schedules are both crazy, but she finds him fascinating, and he is captivated. They see each other when they can. Tim introduced Matilda to Billie and Molly. I heard they hit it off right away. Billie is teaching Matilda Morse Code for some reason. It is a very bizarre friendship that seems to work."

"Find out when we are all available. I can't wait."

Brock interrupted, "Lizzy, what about Trip?"

"I really don't want to miss the opportunity to see if we really have something, but I worry about Beau; he was so close to his mother."

"I'll talk to him."

"Kathryn, that isn't necessary."

"Where are you staying?"

"Until my house is ready, my sisters."

***

Beau Fredericks was notorious as a womanizer. He felt that his wealth and influence within the communities served by the family businesses granted him special privileges. Beau engaged in affairs with women beyond Cape Hope, always being upfront about his lack of interest in anything lasting. For him, it was primarily about the sex; if he ever developed feelings, he would terminate the relationship immediately. Then, he encountered Trinity. He had initially hired her as a graphic designer, but then he did the unthinkable: he fell in love. He sensed a transformation within himself, which he accepted because he believed Trinity deserved far better than the old Beau.

Trinity was self-employed and new to the northeast. She had made acquaintances at the gym, and the yoga studio, and she felt content with her relocation. Leaving Chicago was necessary for her; the sheer number of people made it feel overwhelmingly claustrophobic. After vacationing in Cape Hope, she fell in love with the area. Since her job allowed her to work remotely, she sold her condo and found a fixer-upper house in Massachusetts. Resourceful and eager, she had the time and skills to do the renovations herself. She also hoped to meet someone special, which she did. He was what she'd describe as preppy, and their encounters always took place at her place. He never stayed the night and always called her first. She wondered if he would make an anonymous call when he discovered she was missing.

When she woke up, confusion engulfed her in an unfamiliar room. Her eyes were covered, but she sensed she wasn't alone. Her wrists were handcuffed to the headboard, and a pillow propped her at a slight incline. The cuffs on her ankles were pulled tightly, leaving no room for slack.

Fear enveloped her, making her feel more vulnerable than ever before. She desperately wanted to know what she had done wrong. Just when she thought it couldn't get any worse, the question echoed in her mind: "What did I do?"

Suddenly, she heard a huff followed by the door opening and slamming shut. It felt as if someone had returned, but to her, it seemed like she had been alone for hours. Then, she felt a hand grasping her breast while another hand reached for her other breast from the opposite side.

There were at least two individuals in the room with her. Her chin began to tremble as a single tear trickled down her cheek. It was a woman's hands that started to explore her body. She attempted to recite her mantra, but the overwhelming fear of what was unfolding took control. Clearing her mind became nearly impossible as the woman's hand and mouth roamed over her breast.

Trinity struggled to block out the grim reality of what she knew was happening, but the woman was incredibly skilled. Just as she felt herself beginning to yield, she sensed someone else shifting on the bed, someone larger. Although she wore a blindfold, she instinctively squeezed her eyes shut, convinced that the man would also sexually assault her.

However, the woman adjusted her position and started to stroke between Trinity's legs. That's when she felt the man position himself behind the woman, beginning to thrust violently.

The woman remained undeterred. Both of her hands moved to Trinity's breasts while her head descended between Trinity's upper thighs. At that moment, Trinity broke down, weeping uncontrollably. She fought to regain control over her emotions, gripping the bars of the headboard as her sobs escaped.

The length of the ordeal was indeterminate, but it felt like an eternity. They left her in the same state they found her. By now, her arms had gone numb, and her hands felt lifeless. The ropes binding her ankles chafed against her skin. She began to mentally recite her mantra, repeating it over and over in her mind.

Lavender, hmm, lavender. As she began to fall asleep, she dreamed about Beau.

Beau had enlisted her services for design work related to his various companies. Since her office was at home, she proposed that he meet her there. They connected immediately. Beau not only appreciated her creative concepts but was also captivated by her unique charm. She stood out from his usual types—athletic and refreshingly modest. Her sense of humor was delightful, and she refused to follow the latest fashion trends. During their first meeting, she was casually dressed in sweats.

Additionally, she had a passion for cooking. To him, she was a delightful mystery.

On their second visit to her home, she prepared lunch for him. They discussed business briefly before diving into personal stories. Naturally, Beau left out the fact that he was married. After a month of meetings, they finally crossed the line into intimacy. It didn't take long for Trinity to realize that she was falling for him. Although she suspected he was married, that reality didn't dampen her feelings. She treasured every moment they shared.

Beau and Trinity had been involved for about eight or nine months when she disappeared one night during a typical spring rainstorm. The power in her home flickered and went out. Her backup generator started but failed. She was abducted when she ventured behind her garage to find out what was wrong.

She had been missing for two weeks when anxiety gripped Beau. There was only one course of action he could take. He needed to head to the police station to speak with Phil, though he worried that his account might backfire. Losing his family was not an option, but the fear of Trinity consumed him.

***

Matilda was eager for a respite from her year-end paperwork. She kept a close eye on Lenny's schedule and knew he was off that day. The Pub was just a stone's throw away, and she was confident that if she showed up, someone—most likely Tim—would inform him of her presence.

After mingling at the bar for about half an hour, Lenny walked in, casually dressed in his civilian clothes. With her focus on school and managing her budget, they hadn't seen each other all week. He appeared relaxed. Matilda continued her chat with Tim and two other men she had met earlier. Lenny took a seat across from her, engaging with the familiar regulars who approached.

The moment Lenny arrived, Matilda moderated her drinking. She cherished her evenings with him and didn't want to go overboard. Around ten o'clock, Lenny bid farewell. A few moments later, Matilda slipped some cash into Tim's pocket, winked playfully, and headed to the restroom before making her way to the parking lot.

Matilda was in her thirties but had a youthful appearance, accentuating her stunning figure with V-neck t-shirts and snug jeans. Her flirtatious nature could easily be viewed as a potential disaster. However, that was precisely what drew Lenny to her in the first place. She embodied a free spirit, and that was what Lenny adored most about her.

Matilda beamed as Lenny swung open the door to his truck. She stepped onto the small step below the passenger seat, leaned in towards Lenny, pressed a kiss on his lips, and beamed with delight. Whenever they drove to her place, Matilda always intertwined her fingers with Lenny's. She adored his hands—large, soft, and comforting.

Lenny maneuvered his truck to park behind Matilda's compact vehicle, and together, they entered her home. He headed straight to the refrigerator for a cold beer before clicking on the television. Meanwhile, Matilda retreated to the bedroom, swapping her outfit for a roomy V-neck t-shirt and cozy, thick slouchy socks.

"I've missed you, big boy." She straddled his lap, facing him as he drank his beer.

"Do we need to talk?" He put his beer down and caressed her thighs.

"I do miss you when we're not together. What do you have in mind?"

"Move in with me?"

"Oh honey." She put her hands on his face and caressed his cheeks. "I do love you."

"Will you at least think about it?"

Matilda smiled. "Maybe a little incentive?"

Lenny moved his hands under her rear end. His hands were so soft. She really was putty in his hands, and he knew it. He kissed her cleavage and her neck and began to nibble her ear.

"That makes me crazy…"

Lenny stood up, keeping his hands under her butt. "I know."

Chapter 3

Trip had a breakfast meeting at a little diner a few towns over. He wanted to cancel, but he hated last-minute cancellations, so he wouldn't do it to someone else, even if it was his son.

"Hi, Dad, you look like you have something on your mind."

"Lizzy is back in town. I want to talk to you before I see her again. She dropped by last night."

Shaw grinned. "And?"

Trip almost laughed. "And nothing. You are just like your sister."

"Except I have a penis."

"And you both have your mother's sense of humor. I know Beau will hate the thought of me being in another relationship, so I wanted to talk to you and Simon first."

"Give Beau a chance. Is Simon coming?"

"If he can. Shaw, we talked all night."

"And?"

"Stop saying that." This time, Trip laughed.

"Dad, I'm not going to stand in your way. I don't think Simon will either."

***

"Hmm, hmm…" Trinity woke up when she smelled a fragrance. She looked under the covers and grumbled, "Thanks?"

Trinity was fuzzy about how she got there but she did know why she was there. The first few days, she was emotionally beaten into submission. What was happening to her body was unconscionable, but she had to survive, so she acquiesced, hoping it would get better. She couldn't give up hope.

During the night, someone had dressed her in a short-sleeved nightgown. The restraints and blindfold were removed. As she surveyed her surroundings, she realized she was in a beautifully decorated bedroom. She silently wished for a nearby bathroom, her fear of moving overshadowed by the urgent need to relieve herself.

Her heart raced when a tray of food slid through a slot at the bottom of the door. She was taken aback by the intense hunger gnawing at her. *How long have I been stuck here?*

Gathering her courage, she rose and made her way to the bathroom, which was just as appealing as the bedroom. In her mind, it appeared to have undergone recent renovations.

The enticing aroma of coffee and bacon filled the air. On the tray was an empty paper cup, a carafe of freshly brewed coffee, a small bowl filled with single-serving creamers, and a plate of scrambled eggs, English muffins, crispy bacon, and fried potatoes. Accompanying it were plastic utensils—a spoon, fork, and knife.

She thought *they don't trust me; well, I don't trust them either, but I'm starving.* As she ate, she scanned the room. A bookcase stocked with hardcover books. A TV. There was a laptop loaded with games but no internet. A stack of adult coloring books and crayons, a deck of cards and several notebooks with lined paper on a desk. There was a pen, but it was attached to the desk by heavy gauge wire. *So much for stabbing my kidnapper in the eye with the pen...*

She took the tray, slid it through the opening and sat in the chair by the TV. It was a satellite. *Figures, no news, current events, no way to find what day it is or to find out if anyone knows I'm missing. They don't want me to be bored, but they don't want me to have any hope, either.*

"Noooo, nooo, stop, please stop..."

Trinity pressed her ear against the door, straining to identify the source of the cries echoing through the space. They weren't emanating from this room. Desperate for clues, she searched for an air duct and found one high on the wall above the bed. She listened intently, but silence enveloped her. For a fleeting moment, she whispered, "Why? Why are you doing this? Please stop…" A sudden *crack, snap!* Interrupted her thoughts. "Help me! Please, someone help me…"

A chilling thought crossed her mind: Human traffickers? It seemed plausible. We're on the coast… Maybe they've stowed us away on a boat… Perhaps we're not even in New England anymore. Oh God… Get it together…

Gathering her resolve, she stood up, inhaled deeply, and moved toward the bookcase. A glance revealed an array of classics: Charles Dickens, Wilkie Collins, Jack London, JD Salinger, John Steinbeck, Kurt Vonnegut, Jack Kerouac, John Irving...

Determined to avoid angering her captors, she turned on the TV, allowing the flickering screen to distract her while her eyes roamed the room. There were no windows, leaving her disoriented about the time. For all she knew, they could have served her breakfast at midnight…

Suddenly, a series of sharp, high-pitched cries for help pierced the silence, coming from an unfamiliar direction. She sank back into the chair, gripping its arms tightly as the haunting shrieks continued…

***

"Tilly? Do you have to go to work?"

"I texted I would be in before the first lunch period. You do know you are the only person who is allowed to call me Tilly?"

"You've never noticed I only call you that when we're alone?"

"I have… Len, I do love you. I want to make sure you know I love you."

"Does that mean you won't be moving?"

"No, it means I am going to think about it, but I do have to get up."

Lenny rolled on top of her and kissed her ear.

"No fair, mister."

"Stop talking." He kissed her.

"No fair…"

He continued to kiss her down to her breasts, to her torso and down to her pelvis.

"No fair…"

"I'm off on Saturday at three."

Matilda hesitated. "Are we making plans?"

"Can we do something couples do?"

"Isn't that what we just did?"

"The friendship we have is so much more. I think you know that as well as I do. I'd like to spend the whole day with you. Maybe go to the North End for dinner?"

"So, you do listen to me. My first shift at the Pub is two weeks from Tuesday." She smirked, knowing what Lenny would say.

"Maybe I'll see you there."

"Maybe you will."

***

Lizzy called Trip. She had to leave a message. She thought to herself, *Maybe I came on too strong.* Lizzy was in the back room in Brock's office. She looked up when she realized someone had come through the door.

"Should I be concerned?"

Lizzy smiled. "I just left you a message."

"I know. I was on my way here. Maybe we can have lunch? Somewhere, there won't be a crowd to bother us."

"I have to finish up here. I'll call the diner and have them send some club sandwiches. We can talk while this diagnostic runs."

"Where is Brock?"

"With Jack and the girls. He won't be back. I have a key and the alarm code."

"I talked to Shaw this morning."

"Can we do this at your house later?"

Trip extended his hand, a silent gesture of reassurance. He recognized her anxiety, mirroring the unease churning within him. After sharing breakfast with Shaw, he had a candid conversation with Simon, who offered his blessing.

Lizzy stood up and as she moved closer to Trip. With a mix of reluctance and yearning, she accepted his hand.

Using his other hand, Trip gently cupped Lizzy's neck as he leaned in to kiss her. It had been nearly a decade since his wife had passed away. Until this moment, he had felt no compelling reason to move forward. The notion of a fleeting encounter had never crossed his mind; thus, kissing Lizzy felt both strange and achingly familiar. "Now that that is out of the way."

"I have really missed you."

"So where do we go from here?"

"Truthfully, that is really up to you. I've been looking forward to seeing if we might have a future. I know that is a bit presumptuous, but I do keep in touch…"

Trip kissed her again. "I wish Abby had told me you were here."

"I asked her not to. I didn't want you to come up with a reason not to see me."

Beep, beep. Lizzy started laughing. "Saved by the bell? I have to get back to this."

"I'm going to tell Hilda to leave dinner in the oven. Does that work for you?"

"What time?"

"Six, always six." He kissed Lizzy again. "I'll get out of here so you can finish up."

Trip was walking to his car when he heard "Dad!" He turned to see Beau coming across the street. "Are you free for lunch?"

"Sure, what's up?"

"Nothing, really."

"So, we're not going to talk about it? Something is on your mind."

"I feel like a graphic designer I hired is in trouble."

"Did you do something inappropriate? These days that could be anything."

"No, we have always gotten along. She was doing some work for the restaurants. It was really good, so I asked her for some ideas for the real estate offices."

"You are worried. Has she become more to you, son?"

"I like her. She is fairly new to the area. She is from Chicago. Dad, I do like her; we really hit it off. Our first meeting was at her house. She bought that fixer-upper out on Coast Road, but I didn't meet her until three or four months ago." Beau lied, "Look, let's grab that corner table."

"Beau, I know Julie has been, I don't know, depressed since Harold died, but…"

"Her mood started before that. It has been difficult, but Dad, I need your advice. I was going to go to Phil, but I don't want to get myself involved in a scandal."

"You've been to her house."

"I stopped there on my way home. That is where we have worked, so my fingerprints are there if that's what you are getting at."

"It wasn't, but I do think you should talk to Phil. Did you talk about her family at all?"

"No, but she did say she had nothing keeping her in Chicago, so I don't think she has anyone there. Dad, she gave me a house key one day…"

"Beau…"

"I went to her house. Her car was there. The clock on her stove and microwave was blinking. The last time the electricity went out here in town was last month. Dad, the last thing I want to do is disappoint you." Beau understood the consequences if Phil chose to dig into his past, but he had to take control of the situation before it spiraled out of hand. He excelled at masking his emotions, projecting whatever facade was required at the moment; however, this time, he was genuinely afraid. The thought that any harm might come to Trinity and could potentially lead back to him gnawed at his conscience, intensifying his concern for her, too. "Dad, what should I do?"

"Let's go to the station when we are done here. Beau, since we're talking."

"Dad, I know Elizabeth is back."

"We had dinner last night. We are going to see if we have a future."

"Why don't you trust me, Dad?"

"I do trust you with most things. You have never seemed open to seeing me with another woman. Your sister and brothers…"

"You talked to them first? You *don't* trust me."

"I only talked to your brothers today. Beau, you have been overprotective since your mother died. I'm not a pushover. I can tell a gold digger when I see one. Lizzy has been in my life for a long time. Your mother actually liked her."

"It's hard, Dad."

"Beau, be honest. If Phil goes into this woman's home, where will he find your fingerprints?"

Beau was ready for the question. He had considered his response carefully. "Everywhere. She's working on her own renovations, so I helped her move some furniture around."

Trip sat back, folded his arm and sighed. "Julie will not be happy if this gets out."

"Dad, nothing I do makes her happy anymore."

"I know. Abby said she is different, so I'm not sure it is just you."

"Any advice?"

"Let's have a family dinner. I'd like to invite Lizzy. I know Julie likes her. Maybe Lizzy can talk to her. What do you say?"

"I'll talk to Julie. You can have Abby figure out a date that works for everyone."

"OK. Let's get to the station and talk to Phil."

"I'll meet you there." Beau understood that if his father supported him in his conversation with Phil, he would come across as a concerned friend rather than a suspect in her disappearance. Beau was genuinely worried for her; his feelings for Trinity had grown deeper than he expected.

After the first time they slept together, Beau found himself grappling with a whirlwind of emotions. Unlike his previous flings, which he had never considered as anything more than physical, Trinity was different. He was bewildered by the strength of his feelings and felt a pang of guilt for having misrepresented their friendship. To his surprise, he realized he had disrespected her in some way.

Trip was talking to Lenny as he waited for Beau at the station. "How did I get here first?"

"I took a call in the car, Dad. Phil doesn't look busy." Beau walked right in.

Trip groaned. "Thanks, Lenny."

Beau tapped on the side of the door. "Do you have a few minutes?" Trip sat down as Beau paced and told Phil why he was worried about his friend.

Phil was leaning back in his chair, fingers pressed together in a pyramid shape. "Are you absolutely certain she is missing?"

"No, but where is she? Like I said, I went there because I was concerned… Phil, the last time I was there, I helped her move furniture. None of the work had been done, and the furniture was in the same place we left it. That was last month. She goes to yoga and the gym, but I have no idea where."

"The only thing I can suggest would be to go to the bank and see if her mortgage payment is late. You'd have that on file, right?"

Beau knew his father wouldn't go along with that, but he thought, at some point, it may be his only option. "If she has auto-pay set up… Phil, I'm concerned because if there was foul play, I've been there."

"Well, you did the right thing coming here. What is her last name?"

"Stevens, with a V."

"Beau came to me for my advice; I came for moral support…"

"Beau, I will need your prints. Your client gave you a key, so you will need to come with us. Lenny and I will meet you there, and we can dust."

"I'll have to go to the office for the key. Twenty minutes?"

"Fine." Beau left immediately.

"I'm sorry, Trip, but do you find this story a little out of character?"

"He doesn't have a lot of friends. I think he found a friend who he is worried about. Phil, I'd like to have Lizzy come to the house for dinner with the kids. Would you and Connie be available?"

"For Lizzy, of course. Getting everyone in your family in one place at the same time will be a monumental task."

"Abby will make it happen… Phil, Beau's story was suspicious to me, too, at first. I can usually tell when he is covering for something he knows I will disapprove of; he's not doing that. He seems genuine in his concern."

Phil held off until Trip exited before summoning Lenny into his office. "I suspect Beau is plotting something. I need you to accompany me to collect fingerprints while I watch Beau."

"You have good instincts."

"Lying is unacceptable. Even a sociopath has *tells* if you know what to look for."

"Your father was a good teacher."

Phil chuckled. "He was."

Beau was waiting, pondering whether Phil was late to test his patience or simply to irritate him. He maintained his composure, careful not to betray the feelings he harbored for Trinity.

Beau gave Phil the key. He watched as Lenny gathered fingerprints. "So, you've been everywhere?"

"Pretty much. Like I told Phil, I helped move some furniture." Lenny knew that was a load of crap, but he kept his mouth shut.

Lenny went into the master bedroom. "Is this the only bathroom?"

"The only full bathroom, yes. The half bath is over there. It's out of commission."

Phil fixed his attention on Beau. He was calm and not at all nervous. He didn't hesitate when Lenny asked questions. Phil didn't trust Beau, but his actions belied any preconceived notions Phil had about him.

"Where does this door go?"

"I think that is the garage. The basement door is off the kitchen."

Phil hated that he might have been mistaken about Beau's concern for this woman. This unsettling realization only intensified his suspicion, causing his distrust to fester further.

"Beau, have you ever been in the garage?"

"No. Bedroom, bathroom, kitchen. Lenny, she was going to paint that wall. That was a week before the storm that knocked out the electricity. She didn't seem like a procrastinator, and the clocks—that is what made me think something was wrong."

"Captain, a minute… Phil, the outside door to the garage was unlocked. Maybe Beau is worried for a good reason."

***

Maggie had heard the desperate screams for help echoing through the air. A wave of concern washed over her as she worried that the voice she had heard might become a burden to their captors. Her heart raced with fear that the woman might have already been silenced for good. For her own sake and that of the others, she hoped fervently that the woman was all right and had simply given in. *This isn't my life now. I will be found; I will be rescued.* Maggie clung to the belief that someone would eventually alert the authorities, yet the flicker of hope within her was dimming.

Then the screams erupted again, but this time, they carried a different tone.

At first, the screams were muffled as if stifled by a pillow. It was difficult to determine the source of the cries, but there was undoubtedly someone else in close proximity.

As the cries morphed into soft whimpers, they eventually faded into an agonizing silence. Lost in her thoughts, she was startled to hear a voice distinct from her own for the first time since she was abducted.

"Please help me."

Her instinct to protect herself eroded gradually as she surrendered to complete obedience. She became increasingly submissive, hoping it might lead to her rescue, though deep down, she feared it would more likely result in her death. Despite this, she was resolved to endure, even as the screams erupted again, only to fade away with the regularity of a cruel routine.

She wasn't sure if she was the initial captive; she estimated there were at least four other people imprisoned within the same walls she had come to view as her grim sanctuary.

Her room seemed almost luxurious—like a five-star hotel compared to her dire situation. It was bearable, if not comfortable, given the circumstances. Yet, she was a private, modest person, often perceived as naïve due to her ideals. Even after enduring countless horrors, she still felt a profound sense of shame whenever she heard a visitor in the room.

It felt like a lifetime ago when she clung to the belief that rescue was imminent. She understood it would take time before anyone would realize she was missing, but her greatest fear was that no one would know where to begin looking. That dread became a harsh reality when no one came to free her. Months of fragile hope sustained her, but she feared that her mindset might eventually shift toward Stockholm Syndrome. The thought of losing herself to her captors was what terrified her the most.

***

Abby was in her office at the newspaper, focused on crafting an article about the annual fundraiser the family hosted at the Country Club, held on the anniversary of her mother's death. Although she aimed for a sense of detachment in her writing, she needed to ensure that potential donors understood the charity's efforts without coming across as overly self-serving.

She needed to gather her thoughts. It was crucial for people to feel empathy for the cause. Her mother's charity specifically targeted lung cancer awareness. Abby felt compelled to highlight the prevalent misinformation surrounding the disease. Her mother never smoked, nor had she been exposed to secondhand smoke. Her profession hadn't put her at risk, and there was no familial history of the illness. For her, it was a perplexing anomaly, and the family was determined to push for research into this rare occurrence.

"Hey Abbs."

"Beau, what are you doing here?"

"Has Dad talked to you about dinner?"

"Yup. As usual, Simon is the monkey wrench. Shaw and Dalton will make sure they can be there. Beau, this is important to Daddy."

"I know. Has Julie talked to you at all?"

"Close the door, sit… I know she is busy at work. With all of the home renovations going on, I think she is overwhelmed, and I think you know her control issues would never allow her to hire someone. Truthfully, I think she is exhausted, but there is something else, and I have no idea what it is."

"We should take a vacation alone."

"She would never agree to that."

"She has been drifting away since before Harold died. He wasn't sick, so it wasn't like she was caring for him for a long time."

"Maybe if you were home for dinner more."

"I don't know… do you still get bulletins about missing persons for New England, even the Northeast?"

"What's going on, Beau? Is this concern for Julie a pretense?"

"Please don't do that. Turn off the friend and sister-in-law and turn on the journalist sister. Please?" Beau wasn't trying to hide behind a façade; he needed his sister's advice.

"You're my brother first. What's up?"

"Could you remember that before you start lecturing me?"

"What's going on?"

"I've actually already talked to Dad and Phil. I hired someone to do some graphic design, and she seems to have disappeared. I don't think she has family here, and I know she doesn't have family in Chicago, where she is from."

"Maybe Julie thinks you're having an affair."

"I have no idea, but she would say something, don't you think?"

"At one time, yes. Tell me the truth, Beau."

"I really like her. She is…" Beau couldn't look at Abby.

"Beau."

"You know how you and Shaw can say anything to Dad; you can talk to him about anything, no judgment, no look of disappointment in his eyes. Well, Mom and I were like that. She would know what I should do."

"I think you did the right thing going to Phil. Did he say anything about missing person's reports?"

"No. He looked at Lenny a few times when he was taking fingerprints…"

"What? Are you leaving out details again?"

"She gave me a key." Beau looked guilty. Abby knew the look. She knew him better than he knew himself.

"Beau, how could you?"

"Please, please? This has to stay between us."

"You always do this. The poor boy who nobody understands."

"Forget it." Beau got up and started to leave.

"Please stop. You are my brother first."

His head dropped as he took in a deep breath "She reminds me of Julie before."

"That won't make Julie feel better if she finds out. What did you tell Daddy and Phil?"

"They didn't ask, but if they had, I would have told them I am a friend, and she wanted a friend to have a key."

Abby and Beau stared at each other for what would be, for most people, an uncomfortably long time.

"How long, Beau?"

"I don't know. Six months?" Beau knew it was longer, but he was afraid to tell Abby the truth.

"Why me?"

"Because Julie is your friend, and I need to know what's going on with her."

"I really don't know, but she started changing before… Are you sure it's only been six months?"

"I'll show you the invoice…"

"I'm sorry. You didn't need to come to me. To answer your original question, we get Amber Alerts, Missing Persons. Phil has access to license photos. He should send out a report to the other departments in Mass."

"If there was a pattern of missing women, would they look into that?"

"You really care for this woman."

"I'm afraid for her. She is so outgoing, funny, and artistic. She talked about her friends at yoga and at the gym."

"Did she go into town, to the diner, or the Pub?"

"I don't think so."

"OK, so I don't see anything about any unsolved missing women cases."

"Maybe if we went to New York for the weekend." Beau was thinking about Julie again.

"Maybe if you sat down and asked her what was going on. Go home. Talk to her, Beau. Tell her you are worried about her. When was the last time you told her you loved her? Let Phil take care of finding your friend. Concentrate on your wife."

Beau went behind the desk and kissed Abby on the forehead. "Thank you."

Abby yelled, "If I see her tomorrow and she's smiling, I'll know how it went."

Beau turned and smiled, but his mind was far from Abby's words; he was fixated on the urgent need to find Trinity.

***

Trinity was sure she would endure. She pondered how prostitutes managed to cope with such a brutal existence. Perhaps that's why so many of them end up addicts. Well, that's not going to happen to me.

She wondered, though, why she was perpetually blindfolded. Her initial thought was that it was to prevent her from recognizing her abusers if she ever escaped. However, she also speculated whether it was because they were still in Cape Hope, fearing she might identify them. Trinity considered the possibility that the police had been compromised, but this was not Chicago anymore. She was trapped in a small seaside vacation town along the Massachusetts coast.

She was curled up in the comfy chair, reading, when she heard a voice.

"Is someone there? If you can hear me, I need to know I'm not alone."

Trinity didn't want to fall into a trap, so she waited.

"Please?"

The voice echoing in the room belonged to the woman who had been crying for help when Trinity first arrived. It was seeping through the air vent positioned above her bed. Not long ago, Trinity had scrutinized the room, searching for hidden cameras. She speculated whether her captors were filming the clientele, possibly using the footage to blackmail them for money or favors. You've been watching too many crime dramas, she scolded herself, yet she felt it was a valid concern.

She believed it was a legitimate question. She believed she checked everywhere in the room. She didn't find any tiny lenses that had caught her eye, and there were no concealed doors that swung open to reveal a hidden camera. She hadn't discovered any listening devices either. Nonetheless, she remained on high alert, unwilling to piss these people off.

The voice abruptly ceased its pleas, and the silence that followed raised her suspicions. Was the woman gagged? Had she been sedated? Trinity recalled the peculiar mist or vapor they used to sedate her. It was the only way they could dress and undress her with such ease. It was the only way they could bind her and blindfold her. She had to force herself to stop thinking about it. She had to stop clinging to the hope that someone would realize she was missing.

"If someone is there, even if you can't talk, tap on the wall, anything, I need to know I'm not alone. Please… my name is… ooh…"

Trinity was on the verge of heading to the bathroom when an unfamiliar voice caught her attention. This one was coming from behind the television. She had always been curious about both the TV and the laptop in the room. To ensure they weren't used against her, she covered the TV with a towel when it wasn't in use and kept the laptop shut. Leaning in closer, she pressed her ear against the wall behind the TV.

"What is your name? I am Maggie."

Trinity was panicked. She wanted to talk, but she was afraid.

"I think I've been here the longest. I know there are others. How long have you been here?"

Trinity was afraid to be hopeful, and she didn't want to piss anyone off, so she went to the bed and laid down. She smelled the lavender and knew she would be asleep soon.

Her eyes were covered. She found herself standing, arms raised above her head, tethered to what felt like a hook or a metal loop. A tight corset constricted her body, leaving her bare of both a bra and panties. Unsure of her surroundings, she strained to discern whether she was alone, her heart racing as she waited in the silence.

She heard a click and then something that sounded like a belt buckle.

Someone put a leather cuff around one ankle, then the other.

She closed her eyes when her feet were spread apart and secured. Then she felt the small leather whip on her backside…

When Trinity woke up, she was in soft fleece pajamas. She could feel the welts on her backside and breasts. She looked at the nightstand. There was a jar of antiseptic cream. *My friend must have left this*. She wondered if the woman who massaged the cream into her wounds was also a customer or did she work there. Was it her job to make her feel better after being whipped? She didn't know, but it was becoming a practice she had begun to welcome. She looked at the ceiling, what looked like a fire sprinkler, also had a hook *So that's how they did it. Let's not make this a habit, OK?*

It was a long three days before another customer showed up. They seemed to believe that was the time required for her to recover, as the angry welts had faded by that point.

Today, when she woke up, she was cuffed to the bedpost and blindfolded. The man who was with her seemed different. He seemed like he wanted to have sex and nothing else. Up until now, no one had tried to kiss her. That would make the whole situation too personal, but this man kissed her, caressed her, and had sex with her without hurting her.

Trinity remained silent. The man slipped off the bed, headed to the bathroom, and turned on the shower. Trinity felt a strange mix of confusion and relief. For the first time, she didn't feel assaulted. She hoped this didn't mean she was starting to accept her visitors, but if she had to endure this nightmare, she wished there would be more clients like him. Yet, deep down, she knew that was unlikely.

"Hello? Is anybody there?"

Trinity wanted to help…

"Please… please help me."

***

Beau was having dinner with his family. After they were done, he told the nanny to get the kids ready for bed, and he brought Julie to their bedroom.

"Talk to me, Jules. Tell me, what's been going on with you?"

"I'm busy."

"You've been busy before. You have help with the house and kids. Why not get help at work?"

"All the women who are qualified…"

"Oh, come on, Jules. Hire a man."

"Where is this coming from?"

"I am worried about you. Would you like to take a vacation?"

"The kids are still in school. Then it gets crazy."

Beau sat on the loveseat next to her. "I love you. I hope you know that."

"What?"

"I've been busy too. I think we need to let the people we have hired do their jobs so we have time for each other." Beau kissed her.

She hesitated to respond to his overture, but not for long. "Oh Beau, I've missed you…"

Beau kissed Julie on the forehead. Her head rested on his shoulder.

"We do need to make more time for each other."

"I'll make sure I'm home for dinner. We need a night just for us, too."

"I do love you, Beau."

"Me too, honey." Beau kept his arms around his wife, but he was thinking about Trinity.

***

Lucy made the bold choice to step outside her comfort zone and visit the Pub. She was aware that she didn't know many locals, and with her hair down and makeup on, she doubted anyone would recognize her without her uniform.

Phil and Lenny had been discussing Tim, suggesting that Lucy should meet him. However, she felt hesitant about being set up. It was Saturday, and she was enjoying her day off. In just a few weeks, the town would overflow with tourists, and she would be working grueling twelve-hour shifts six days a week. Deep down, she realized Lenny had a point—she needed to get laid. So, after letting her hair down and slipping into a pair of jeans paired with a peasant blouse that accentuated her upper arms, she stepped confidently into the Pub.

"Hello, I'm Tim, the proprietor. Are you new to town?"

She giggled, "No, not really. I live in Essex, but I work here. I just don't get out a lot." She reached her hand toward Tim. "I'm Lucy."

Tim grinned. "*The* Lucy."

"Oh, dear God…"

"Shh, don't worry, I'll keep your secret."

"Lenny teases me because I never go out. He said he comes here on occasion. I wanted him to see I'm not the fuddy duddy he thinks I am."

"He doesn't think that, but he is kind of, sort of…"

"Taken? I know. She sounds great. Cap said we are total opposites, and he thinks we would be good friends. I was feeling brave, so I decided to drop by."

"What's your poison?"

"Well, I have to drive home, so something that won't kick my butt."

"Have you had dinner?"

"No. I hear your club sandwich is amazing."

"Great, turkey club and a Guinness." Tim whispered, "Low alcohol."

"Great, thanks."

"It can get busy in here, so don't hesitate to scream if you need something."

Tim and Lucy were engaged in a conversation, getting to know one another, when Matilda walked in. The only vacant bar stool available was on the side where Lucy sat, so Tim politely approached a few patrons and asked if they could shift to create space for Matilda to join Lucy.

"Timmy, you didn't need to do that."

"Yes I did. Lucy is here to keep you out of trouble."

Matilda smiled. "*The* Lucy?"

"I wish you people would stop saying that. I sound like I have a reputation."

Tim admitted, "You have a reputation for not having a reputation."

Lucy looked at Matilda and groaned, "Great. I'm going to have to have a talk with Lenny. For someone who doesn't talk a lot, he certainly does talk a lot."

"He thinks you need to get laid."

Tim burst out laughing and walked away.

Lucy turned bright red. "He is a dead man."

Matilda grasped Lucy's hand. "Lenny really likes you. He thinks you are lonely. Is he wrong?"

"Yes, well, no, he's not wrong. I guess he does know me. He kind of took me under his wing when I started. He told me I needed to loosen up. Coming from him, that was pretty funny."

"I think you are a lot alike. He takes his job seriously. He said you would never look the other way. He admires that."

Lucy took a sip of her beer. "So, what is Tim's story?"

"He needs to get laid, too."

Lucy laughed. "Hmm, interesting. He lives in town, right?"

"He has a house near the beach, but he spends the night upstairs sometimes. It's actually really cute…"

"So, you and Lenny use it for a quickie?"

"He doesn't know the meaning, but no. It's Tim's sanctuary… He hasn't taken his eyes off you."

"He seems really nice."

"That's because he is."

"So, if I hang out here till closing?"

"Like I said, he hasn't taken his eyes off you."

"So, I hear you work at the Middle School?"

"Ya. Next week is my busy time. We have to make sure everything is steam cleaned, and I have to go over my budget with the Principal. Just a lot of minutiae. Then a week after next I am here four, five days a week. Lenny is working next weekend, so I probably won't be around. May I put my number in your phone?"

"Yes… Uh oh. Will he even recognize me?"

"He never sits with me unless there isn't another free barstool. At first, we were mysterious, but then it just became our thing. He really is amazing."

"I hope you don't mind me saying it seems you have something special."

"It took us a long time to go from *friends with benefits* to saying those three little words."

"I'm hoping to find someone that makes me smile like that." Lucy looked at Lenny, staring at Matilda. "Is this part of your to and fro?"

"Something like that. You and Tim seem to be talking without words."

Lucy blushed again. "He does have a special way about him…"

"Ladies, can I get you anything else?"

Matilda leaned over the bar and whispered something to Tim before she put some cash in his pocket. "I probably won't be back until my first shift."

"I think I may find a way to manage without you."

"Timmy, you always make me feel so special. Lucy, I look forward to getting to know you better."

Tim wiped down the bar and then spoke to the other bartender. He also spoke to one of the servers and then went back to Lucy. "Would you like to take a walk?"

"I would like that, yes."

It was a perfect night for a walk on the beach. The moon was full, there was no wind, and the temperature was perfect. Lucy and Tim walked and talked for a couple of hours. At some point, they began holding hands. After they turned back toward town, Lucy wondered if Tim would ask her inside. As they neared the Pub, Lucy took a chance, which was something she never did. She caressed his cheek and kissed him. "Are you interested in seeing where this can go?"

Tim kissed her again. "Absolutely. Am I wrong to assume Matilda told you about my loft?"

"She called it your *sanctuary*."

"It is. The stairs are on the side." Tim followed Lucy and then unlocked the door.

"This is nice, Tim. Matilda was right; it is cute."

"Don't tell him, but Lenny was right about you too."

Lucy put her arms around Tim's waist. "I'm not usually this quick to jump into a relationship, but Lenny and Phil have been talking about you for some time."

Tim leaned his head down and kissed her again. "I was wondering if you really existed. They made you sound too good to be true."

"Well, there is only one way for you to find out." Lucy held Tim's hand and moved toward the bed. She unbuckled his belt and pulled his shirt over his head.

He unzipped her pants and kissed her just above the top of her peasant blouse. "Did you wear this hoping you would get lucky?"

"Hmm, I think you will be the lucky one."

"Oh, really. Is that why Lenny calls you Boom Boom?"

"Maybe." Lucy sat and boosted herself backward to the middle of the bed. She leaned forward, hooked her forefinger to the waistband of his boxer shorts and pulled him toward her. She took her blouse off and then reached her hand to the back of his neck. "Show me what you've got…"

Tim touched his forehead to Lucy's. "I won't expose your secret."

"What's that?"

"I was led to believe you're shy."

"Well, I was told you are a gentleman."

"I won't tell if you won't tell. I hope you don't need to go home."

Lucy laced her fingers through his hair. "You will have to drag me out of this bed."

"Not gonna happen. I'm looking forward to getting to know everything about you."

"Me too, me too."

Chapter 4

Phil and Lenny had a tradition of meeting at the diner every Monday morning, regardless of whether they were on the clock. Although Lucy was on duty that day, she felt unprepared to discuss her budding relationship with Tim. She wanted to keep him to herself for as long as she could. Entering the diner, she ordered a cup of coffee to go. While waiting, she glanced at a text from Matilda: *Lenny saw your car on the road near the Pub. For future reference, park in one of the small lots or walk from the station. If any of the others on the force spot your car there, you'll never hear the end of it. I hope I'm happy for you.*

She texted back *You are, thanks. Hope to see you when school is out.*

"Officer, excuse me, officer?"

Lucy looked toward the table. "Since you two are here, someone has to work."

"How was your weekend, Officer Finneran?"

"Pretty good. I met Matilda. She is a hoot." Lucy wouldn't look at Lenny. "It was nice to get out."

"That's all you did?" Lenny was curious.

"I'll tell you what I did if you tell me what you did."

Phil laughed. "Uh oh, Lenny, she's got you."

"I have to get back to work."

Lenny chuckled. "OK now that we've had our fun teasing Boom Boom, what do we do about the Beau situation?"

"I'm going to say what you won't say. They were having an affair, and Beau ended it. I know he wouldn't hurt anyone because, well, let's face it, he's a coward."

Lenny grunted and nodded.

"I don't think he hurt her either, but she's gone. Her car is there. I checked the airlines. Even if she met someone she would have taken clothes with her. There was laundry in the washer and in the dryer. Since Trip knows, maybe he will look into the mortgage carrier…"

"Beau gave it to me. Trip is supposed to ask if her payments have been late. I told him we would be here."

"Cap, I asked Matilda to move in with me."

"You did? What brought that on?"

"It's time."

"She is such a free spirit and she's not going to be able to turn off the flirt. Are you going to be able to live with that?"

"I do now. She hasn't said yes. She wants to think about it. She says she loves me."

"That, my friend, is obvious…"

Trip came into the diner. "Gentlemen, may I join you?"

Phil moved over. "Do you have information?"

"Beau's friend seems to be missing. The mortgage is late. Looking at her credit and past mortgage payments she has never been late with anything. Her credit score is high. She pays her credit card balance every month. I asked that she not be reported for the mortgage yet. I explained she seemed to be missing. This woman is not irresponsible, Phil."

"He seemed concerned, not because he was scared because he did something wrong, but because he seemed to be concerned for a friend."

"I haven't told Beau yet. Phil, what is the next step?"

"We need to find the yoga studio and the gym…"

Trip handed Phil a piece of paper. "Here you go. I asked to look at her debit charges."

"I hope you don't do this kind of thing on a regular basis because…"

"No, You should know me better than that. Beau wouldn't have come to me if he weren't worried. Oh, and Abby has everyone confirmed for dinner at the house on Thursday. Simon has the night off."

***

"Beau?"

"Abbs, why are you here?"

"Julie was smiling today."

"She's been smiling for a few days now. You were right. I think I needed to let her know I still love her."

"Please don't lead her on."

"I wasn't. I do love her. Sometimes… why are you here?"

"Have you heard anything about your friend?"

"Dad is making some inquiries at the bank. If her mortgage is late, or anything else is not in order, between Dad and Phil they will figure something out. I did the right thing going to Dad, right? I did, right?"

"I'm not going to lecture you about why she may have disappeared, especially if you hurt her emotionally. Sometimes, even if a person seems completely normal, a broken heart can set them down a dark path."

"I never led her on. We had fun. She made me laugh. She never asked if I was married."

"You need to get another wedding band, Beau."

"You know, at first, that's what I thought it was. It wasn't like I broke my hand on purpose. I didn't want them to cut my ring off in the ER. Besides, Julie looked. She couldn't find the same one. She wanted the same one."

"There was something going on. I just worry she is feeling euphoric…"

"Oh, come on, I don't think she has ever felt that good. That is part of the problem. It was something more than a night of mind blowing sex…"

"Oh, dear God!"

Beau was laughing. "You know what I mean. Saying *I love you* was not what changed her mood. Sex wasn't what changed her mood."

"It really is the little things, Beau. Don't dismiss her mood change. She was happy again."

"Beau? Oh, you're here." Trip could be serious even in a room full of laughter.

"I love you too, Daddy."

"Hi honey. Beau, what's going on?"

"I talked to Abby; she knows. Did you and Phil come up with a solution?"

"Promise me, Beau. Promise me you didn't do something to cause this woman to run."

"We became friends. The last time I talked to her, she was putting together a new look for the individual real estate offices that were tied together with an updated logo. She had really good ideas, Dad."

"Daddy, were you able to get any information from the bank?"

"Yes. Phil is sending Lenny to the yoga studio and to the gym. We were given access to the debit history and got the names. The mortgage is late, but nothing else. She pays her bills, and except for the house, she has no debt."

"Dad, it scares the hell out of me that I was the last person she saw."

"Lenny is going to take care of talking to neighbors…"

"She didn't have neighbors."

"Phil and Lenny know what they're doing; you need to trust them."

***

Harlow was crying again. Mr. Smith, the boss, sought specific types for their operation. With her shy demeanor, sophisticated appearance, and lack of experience, she epitomized innocence, which was precisely how she was advertised.

The choice to bring her on board came after months of careful observation, similar to the scrutiny placed on the other women in the house. However, Harlow had one distinguishing feature: she was a crier.

Unfortunately, this trait made her a favorite among clients, both male and female. Over time, Harlow's presence in the house became a topic of frequent discussion. Mr. Smith believed that her popularity outweighed her incessant sobbing.

At twenty-five years old, Harlow hailed from a wealthy Boston family. She did not hold a job and epitomized solitude. The lookout had labeled her a loner, a characteristic that fit the criteria but not always.

Trinity and Maggie occupied the two central bedrooms, allowing them to hear the sounds from the air vents connecting to the other rooms. They were the kind of girls that someone would proudly introduce to their mother. Although Trinity had been brought in at the last minute, Mr. Smith was still satisfied with her presence. The other three occupied rooms belonged to Harlow, the perpetual crier; Lauren, the voluptuous one with generous curves who seemed oddly content in her new role; and Macey, the enigmatic Asian girl who barely spoke any English and quickly adopted a subservient demeanor.

Mr. Smith's business strategy was straightforward: discreet word of mouth and cash-only transactions. Initially catering to mostly out-of-town businessmen, the operation soared thanks to a careful and strategic arrangement with a trusted concierge at a five-star hotel. These regular clients were responsible for spreading the word, fully aware that sharing information about the house with the wrong people could lead to its closure.

There were six rooms to fill, but only five women at their disposal. There was one woman they had their eyes on, but her abduction posed significant risks. They had determined the perfect moment to snatch her, and that moment was coming soon.

Chapter 5

The gathering at Trip's place was in full swing. It had been a while since the family spent any quality time together, so the atmosphere was light and cheerful. Phil made a silent decision to keep his suspicions about Beau and his story regarding the missing friend to himself. After all, he wasn't looking to stir up any drama, especially when he wasn't entirely certain of Beau's truthfulness. Could he be mistaken? Was Beau genuinely worried about a friend—someone he only had business ties with? Phil wasn't convinced either way. To the rest of them, everything seemed just fine.

Beau and Julie were inseparable. Julie was definitely happy again.

Simon and Stella spent as much time together as they could. Living under the same roof didn't change the fact that Simon's demanding hours at the hospital meant their moments together were rare and cherished. Stella's aunt, Lizzy, was also present at the gathering, adding to their shared happiness.

Shaw and Dalton had a history of being off and on; it seemed they were finally in it for the long haul. Dalton, a teacher by profession, had also been Abby's closest friend since they were kids. As Abby, Cooper, Shaw, and Dalton chatted, the gossip shifted to a new woman who had supposedly entered Tim's life.

"Cubby said Tim has a contented look on his face. He said Tim is playing dumb, but he said he recognizes the twinkle in his eye."

Phil heard the conversation and offered his opinion: "Maybe they want to bask in the glow for a while before they start sharing their relationship."

Abby wondered, "So you know something?"

"Speculation."

"Isn't that dangerous in your line of work?" Shaw was trying to poke the bear.

"We are not going there."

Dalton groaned. "Here we go."

Phil and Shaw had crossed paths on a couple of cases. Neither one of them ended up in the courtroom, but they butted heads nonetheless.

"I'm not the evil win-at-all-costs prosecutor you think I am."

"You can be a little too passionate…"

Shaw looked at Dalton. "That's not a bad thing, right?"

"Leave me out of this." She laughed and poured herself a glass of wine.

Beau was keeping his eye on his father and Lizzy. They were friendly, mingling with ease, but there was no hint of intimacy between them. That reassured him that their relationship hadn't crossed into something more serious. Although he liked Lizzy, Beau wasn't eager to give his approval without seeing a longer, more committed courtship. He was well aware that he, along with his siblings, had Trust Funds, though the specifics—how much and when they'd be released—were unclear. It was a topic his father always avoided discussing. The thought of their inheritance taking a hit if his father remarried gnawed at him. He knew a prenuptial agreement would never be brought up, but the concern still loomed in his mind, especially after Julie's father died.

Julie's father, Harold, left his entire estate to her and their children. Beau suspected he didn't have the full picture of the estate's worth, but asking Julie directly was off-limits. He knew Harold had accumulated significant real estate holdings, but the details of his financial empire remained elusive to Beau. Some of those assets had already been transferred to Julie before her father's passing, likely for tax purposes, but now everything sat securely within her Trust—something Beau had no access to. He had tried to broach the subject with Julie, but she was tight-lipped about the whole matter. Initially, Beau thought her change in behavior was due to the pressure of managing her father's wealth, but that theory was shut down when she revealed that Brock and Kathryn were handling all the details. Moreover, Beau realized that Julie's shift in attitude had started long before her father's sudden passing.

Beau hoped Julie was back to being the woman he had married, but that didn't change his growing appetite for affairs outside their marriage. He was caring and attentive enough but not so over-the-top as to raise suspicions among those close to them. He had become very cautious, especially when it came to Trinity.

As Beau made himself another drink, Phil approached him. "I think you should tell Shaw what's going on. Being up front is the…"

"I know. I don't want him to be stuck in a conflict of interest."

"Tell him so he can get in front of it."

Beau made eye contact with Shaw and motioned to him.

Shaw and Beau were not close, mostly because Shaw felt Beau took what he wanted without caring about who he stepped on. Simon and Shaw worked hard for their careers, careers that weren't associated with their father's empire.

"You two look serious, what's up?"

Beau looked at Phil, then his brother. "I've already talked to Dad and Phil. You need to know too. A woman who has been doing some work for me and is a friend, *just a friend*, has disappeared."

"So, you did the right thing."

"I know how these things work. I will be the first suspect because I was the last person to see her. I hired her to do some graphic design. We worked from her house. She gave me a key because she wanted someone, a friend, to have a key. My fingerprints are all over her house because I helped her move some furniture so she could paint."

"You're worried."

"Wouldn't you be?"

"Shaw, remember that storm that knocked out power in most of the town last month? When we went in, the stove and microwave clocks were blinking. Lenny found Beau's prints in the bedroom on one of the nightstands. Where they were located confirms his claim he moved some furniture. There were prints in the master bathroom, too. He told us ahead of time about the other bath being out of commission. We verified that too. What Beau doesn't know is we found prints on the back door of the garage we can't identify. They were only on the outside knob, nowhere else."

"So, you think she was abducted?"

"Yes. Her friends at yoga and the gym said she didn't talk about her private life. They knew she loved her job, and they knew she was excited about a project she was involved with to update some marketing for some real estate offices and restaurants. That jibes with everything Beau told us. I would have had him in already if I thought he was involved in her disappearance."

"Thank you, Phil. I appreciate that. Abby looked for missing person reports…"

"You told Abby?"

"Yes. I have nothing to hide. But I can't tell Julie. She is finally coming out of that funk she was in. I should have told her we were working outside the office but her mood was so dark, I just couldn't. Now… look at her, she is happy again."

Chapter 6

"I hear you have a brother who is a Journalist."

"I hope you won't hold that against me."

"Nah. How did you get such a prime piece of real estate?"

"It was in really rough shape. It is zoned for residential, so putting a shop or restaurant there wasn't an option. My brother's boss's family is in real estate, so I heard about it before it went to auction. Before I bought the Pub I only worked nights, so I had plenty of time to fix it up."

"You seem to be a man of many talents."

"Hmm. I'm glad you noticed." Tim kissed Lucy. "I'd like you to meet him."

"So soon?"

"You have, in a very short period of time, become very important to me."

"That's good to hear. I like you too. Does your brother see anyone?"

"Have you met Molly and Kathryn? They are best friends."

"I've heard the names."

"Molly dates Colt. You must know him. Cubby sees Kathryn. I'll call him. You're off this weekend, right?"

"At night, yes… I have to say this bed is very comfortable."

"So, you don't mind staying here all day?"

"I have to be at the station by ten today."

Tim leaned over Lucy. "Can I give you a key?"

"If you must."

"Is it too soon to talk about you moving in?"

Lucy held his head with both hands. "Can we do it on a trial basis? I wouldn't want to give up my apartment and then find out you were some kind of deviant."

"I thought you liked that about me?"

"You are very charming, Mr. Edwards."

"And I am happy again. You did that."

***

Maggie woke up and immediately noticed a difference in her room. The dark brocades of her bedspread and pillows had been swapped for the bright colors of Spring and Summer. There were flowers in a vase. Maggie tapped on it. *Plastic. I could still break it and stab someone with a shard. Someone? Who is someone? One of the customers? Don't be stupid, Maggie. Someone is bound to realize you are missing; these other women are missing.*

"Maggie?"

Maggie got up.

"Maggie?"

She walked to the wall. "What is your name?"

"Harlow."

"That's a beautiful name. There was a woman there before you. Her name was Lynn."

"So, that is either good or really, really bad…" Harlow then felt herself drifting off.

She had been awake for what felt like an eternity. It could've been five minutes or the better part of the night; time had lost all meaning. She was stark naked and shackled, though her eyes remained uncovered. Her heart nearly stopped when she saw the chair—it was straight out of some twisted Frankenstein set. Just as her panic began to surge, the bathroom door opened.

A man clad only in black leather chaps and a hood that covered his face except for cutouts at the eyes, accompanied by a woman in nothing but a thong, towering black heels, and a butterfly masquerade mask.

"No, no, no…"

The woman had a small riding crop. "Look, honey, they left us a present." *Snap.*

"No, no. Please, no."

The man was quiet. He uncuffed her but held her arms behind her back. Harlow started to fight him. She dug her heels into the rug as she tried to stop the man from putting her in the chair.

"I think she needs a little discipline, honey." The woman snapped the whip.

The man and the woman worked together to secure Harlow tightly in the chair. Her legs were bound to the supports, which tilted upward when the chair reclined. Her ankles were locked into metal stirrups, immobilizing her. The apparatus seemed to pivot as the man positioned himself near her feet and forced her legs apart.

Harlow was now crying uncontrollably.

She didn't think it could get worse until she saw another woman come out of the bathroom dressed in the same garb.

Harlow started screaming, which is exactly what the threesome paid for. That seemed to get them in the mood. They all began to fondle her and prod her. Ultimately, the two women got on the bed. They didn't take their eyes off Harlow as they began to caress and kiss each other. When Harlow tried to look away, she was warned she would be whipped if she didn't watch. The man stood over her as Harlow wept. He then strapped Harlow's head to the back of the chair, placed a gag in her mouth and raped her.

When they were done with her, she got sleepy. She began to feel funny, and she closed her eyes. When she opened them, there were two large women bathing her in the shower. They dried her off, put an oversized T-shirt on her and put her to bed.

When she was finally lucid again, she didn't remember anything from the previous 24 hours.

"Maggie, Maggie? Are you still there? My name is Trinity. Could you hear the screaming… hello?"

"Hi Trinity. I can't decide if that was real or not. But the other girl, her name is Harlow; I think that was who was screaming."

"Do you know how long you've been here, Maggie?"

"Seven, eight months…"

***

Shaw spoke to a professor at his law school, presenting his dilemma as a hypothetical scenario. He stripped the question down to its bare essentials, carefully avoiding any specifics. What he wanted to know was clear: was he legally obligated to inform his boss, the District Attorney, about what he knew?

"The police don't think the man is involved?"

"No."

"Right now, it is in the hands of the local police. If it does become a missing persons case, a good police chief will get the FBI involved."

"Thank you."

"Shaw, you did the right thing by calling me. Your boss is a bastard."

"He has a reputation, yes."

"Shaw, hold on to your ethics and your values. Don't let that man force you into doing anything you know is wrong. I know plenty of law firms who would love to have someone like you in their firm."

"Thank you, Professor." Shaw then called Phil, "May I tell you about a conversation I just had?"

Phil listened… "Shaw, I appreciate your concern. I already decided to call the FBI if it comes to that. Like I said, the prints in the garage concern me."

***

Matilda was ahead of schedule with her year-end reports, so she slipped into more casual clothes and decided to stroll into town. She had been thinking about Lenny a lot lately, knowing he had the day off, and thought it'd be nice to surprise him. But there was something else on her mind—she needed to talk to Tim. The idea of moving in with Lenny had been eating at her. She longed for it but feared the dynamic between them might shift too drastically if she took that step. Tim was always a good listener, one of the reasons his pub thrived—people loved talking to him.

The road she took was quieter than usual, but then again, weekday mornings weren't her usual time for a walk into town. She was nearly halfway when the distant sound of a boat's engine drew her attention toward the cove. This wasn't one of the sleek sailboats or the fancy cabin cruisers that lined the docks near the estates. It was a pontoon boat, curtains hanging loosely around the sides and back. There was a man holding the wheel on the bow. She laughed because even from far away, he looked like Ernest Hemmingway.

She continued her walk into town when she became aware she wasn't alone on the road. She stopped and turned to see a car on the side of the road with its open trunk. She wasn't a nervous person, but she was suspicious. She turned back to continue into town when she felt something in her neck.

Mr. Smith had a motion for their upcoming monthly meeting. It was suggested that Matilda might be an ideal candidate for the house. Descriptions of her painted her as someone with a vibrant, effervescent personality that drew people in. Both men and women found her undeniably attractive due to her striking physical features. However, what the man failed to realize was the hidden connection between Matilda and Lenny. They had carefully concealed their friendship from nearly everyone, especially patrons at the Pub. Matilda's charm and vivacity were major factors in why so many patrons kept coming back.

The plan to abduct Matilda had been made on the spur of the moment when they spotted her sauntering down the street. Although they had originally intended to snatch her at a different time, they never had the chance. Finally presenting itself, they moved quickly.

Matilda wasn't expected in town so she wasn't reported missing for almost ten days.

She woke up much like the other occupants of the house when they were first taken, blindfolded, naked, in irons attached to the headboard. Matilda wasn't scared, she was pissed. That's what Mr. Smith expected when they took her. She was described as a wild woman, and she didn't disappoint.

She started yelling, "People will miss me. They won't stop until they find me." She almost laughed when she realized she sounded very *sing-songy*. When she heard movement inside the room, she immediately stopped yelling.

"This isn't going to work; people will miss me. My friends will miss me."

The man in the room held a compact suitcase in his hand. With deliberate movements, he set it down on a nearby table close to the bathroom and unfastened it. "Oh, you really think so?" he taunted, aiming to stir her emotions. His goal was to provoke her anger; she was the perfect target for his intentions. Noticing the heavy chains attached to the footboard of the bed, he seized one of her feet and forcefully pulled it toward the end of the bed. He secured it with a tight leather cuff.

Matilda was beginning to panic. She knew she wasn't going to get out unscathed when he grasped her other foot and buckled the leather strap on her ankle.

The man went into the bathroom, shedding his clothes with a deliberate calm. He rummaged through his bag until he uncovered a small whip. Gently, he traced the supple leather across her breasts. Then, leaning closer, he let his hand slip into her cleavage, savoring the moment. He relished in teasing her, deriving pleasure from her discomfort. He was fully aware that she wouldn't submit easily; in fact, he craved her to fight back.

Matilda started yelling; she knew as long as she yelled, she wouldn't start crying.

The man began to massage her breasts. Then he squeezed them hard.

"Hey! Precious cargo buster."

"Yes, yes, it is, but you are here for me. You are here for my pleasure."

"Are you so pathetic you have to pay to get your jollies?"

"Not at all. There are certain things a real lady should never do."

"Oh, dear God. You're one of those? That is laughable."

The man whipped her across her pelvis. When he stopped, he leaned over her face. "So, who's laughing now?"

Matilda decided not to play his game. She didn't respond. She turned her head to the side when she felt his breath near her face. She believed her captors wouldn't allow the client to *damage the merchandise,* so she didn't let him see any kind of emotion.

"You are here to serve me."

Matilda remained quiet and calm, unyielding in the face of his demands. The man craved an intense reaction from her, but her calm demeanor frustrated him, prompting him to escalate the situation. He rummaged through his bag and produced a collection of devices that could only be described as instruments of torment. With a firm grip, he seized her jaw, forcing her to look directly at him. "You could make this much easier on yourself if you would just play the game, but since you don't want to play, I guess I will have to make you cooperate." He let go of her jaw and pressed a switch that produced a humming sound.

Matilda screamed.

"There you go..."

Maggie and Trinity were without company, so they could hear the screams coming through the walls. They were aware it was coming from a different direction, so they both wondered if there was a new victim. It was always frightening when the cries stopped. Maggie wasn't afraid to ask, "Are you new? If you are, please tell us if you're OK. Please?"

There was no response before all the rooms were flooded with lavender mist.

The man with Matilda was the mastermind behind her abduction. He felt a sense of satisfaction regarding Matilda. Although he didn't have a personal relationship with her, he was aware of her existence. He employed a few trusted scouts who reported back to him. After thorough evaluation and hearing their detailed accounts of Matilda, he became determined to possess her.

Just like Trinity's case, the details surrounding Matilda's kidnapping shifted at the last moment. The choice to abduct Trinity had been made when the power supply failed. The men who seized her disabled her generator, forcing her to move behind the garage. When Matilda was snatched, a matron happened to spot her strolling down the street. Both women were taken during an unforeseen convergence of events.

***

"Beau, you need to tell Julie."

"She will leave me. She will take the kids and go somewhere I will never find her."

"You don't have much faith in her."

"You saw us together last week. When was the last time she was happy like that?"

"Son, if the FBI is called in, they will be tougher on you than Phil was. If you wait, Julie will believe the worst."

"I don't know how I would bring it up."

"Don't come off as guilty. Try to be very matter-of-fact. And please, whatever you do, don't talk to her like a child. Just say *'Honey, something came up at the office the other day I think you need to know about.'* If you speak to her in a hushed tone, it will seem like you are trying to seduce her. Look her in the eye and tell her what you told me and Phil. You were worried she was in trouble, so you went to her house. She gave you a key because she trusted you. If you have to, tell her she did that after you spent a meeting talking about her and the kids."

"I remember you once said *tell the truth so you don't have to remember your lies.*"

"That is a good rule to live by, but in this case, you don't want to hurt your wife. Tell her you will be home for lunch. Ask Paulette to take the kids somewhere."

"Jules, I'm coming home for lunch."

"The kids have already eaten."

"Good. Something came up at the office I need to talk to you about."

Beau went home. Unfortunately, Julie misread the conversation and was in bed when he got there. "Hi sweetheart. I believe this what is called a nooner?"

Beau was surprised but not too surprised to make love to his wife.

"I love you…May I tell you a secret? I wasn't expecting that."

"Oh, I thought your message was code for you were coming home for a little afternoon delight."

"Well, it is afternoon, and I am delighted, but no. Sorry, I didn't think of it first."

"I do have an imagination, Beau."

"That's what makes you such a good decorator and an even better wife and mother."

"You look sad. What happened at the office?"

"Oh honey. Do you remember me saying I was looking for a new Graphic Design firm to do some upgrades for our advertising?"

"That was a few months ago, right?"

"Yes. I found a freelance designer, someone new to the area who works from home. Her ideas were really good, not the usual proposals I was getting from the local artists. They were all the same tired coastal-themed ideas I was trying to get away from."

Julie looked scared.

"Nothing happened Jules, but we did become friends. She is from Chicago; she moved here when she got sick of the city. She does all of her work from home so she can do the renovations on her house and work at the same time. Julie, you'd like her."

"OK, why are you telling me?"

"I was on my way home, and she called. Apparently, I'm the only person she knows that could help her move some furniture. So, I stopped to help her. We ended up talking about you and the kids. She admires decorators for the patience they need to put up with picky clients. I told her that sometimes you want to wring their necks. I also told her about the kids' piano lessons. She told me she wished she had listened to her mother and continued with her lessons because she really wished she could play. Anyway, as I was leaving, she asked me if I would take her extra house key. She said she felt safer giving it to a friend than one of the corner heads at the gym."

Julie laughed. "OK so why are you telling me? Something must have happened."

"I hadn't heard from her in a while. I told her to go ahead with the mock-ups she showed me and let me know when she was done. She never called or answered any of my calls, so I went over there. The clocks on the stove and microwave were blinking…"

"The electricity went out last month."

"That was my guess. After I left there, I talked to Dad. Then we talked to Phil and Lenny. Then, the other night at Dad's, we talked to Shaw. Jules, she is missing, and I'm scared to death I will be a suspect if anything happens to her."

"Why are you telling me now? She might come home tomorrow."

"I usually don't talk to you about work, but this scared me. Everything I told Phil was confirmed when we went to the house so they could take fingerprints. Honey, I didn't want to keep this from you. I didn't want you to think I was keeping things from you."

"Well, you're right; we don't talk about work. Maybe we should. So, do you think Quint and Hal should continue their piano lessons?"

Beau chuckled. "What about Annie?"

"She loves playing; I'm not worried about her."

"Honey, thank you for not getting angry."

"I would have been if you hadn't told me. Beau, I think we need to do this more often."

"Talking or making love in the afternoon?"

"Yes." Julie embraced Beau.

Beau was worried. Julie accepted what he told her too readily, then changed the subject. He expected her to be more surprised, to ask more questions. But he was feeling guilty so he buried Julie's reaction and his skepticism.

Chapter 7

Tim kissed Lucy's forehead as he brushed the hair from her face. To the fly on the wall, it would appear, from the look on his face, that he was in love.

"Is that you?"

"It's only me, the local barkeep."

"Oh good, I thought I was dreaming again. Is it really you?"

"Open your eyes, sweetheart."

"If I open my eyes, I'll have to get up."

"Sorry, I have deliveries this morning, and you have to catch the bad guys."

Lucy looked at Tim. "Maybe I should ask to change my hours so we have more time together."

"My seasonal help starts next week. I don't have to work every night."

"The customers go there because of you. They like you. What will happen if you're not there?"

"Maybe they will think I'm in love."

"Are you?"

"I am mad about you, but I am holding back for the sake of our longevity."

Lucy leaned on her elbow. "I don't understand."

"In the grand scheme of things, I know nothing about you. I can't be hurt again."

"Before I met you, Lenny band Cap were worried about you. Cap would ask if you were OK, if you had moved on yet."

"I'm not a player. I have never let a woman pick me up before. Lenny is one of my closest friends. He said you and I would be good together."

"I picked you up? Interesting."

Tim grinned. "It is dangerous for a bar owner to fraternize. Lenny likes you. Then I saw you and Matilda together. She is a social butterfly. She likes working in the room. She likes everyone, but she stayed with you. I could tell right away you two would be friends."

"But you didn't know me."

"I have known Matilda and Lenny for a long time. If Matilda didn't like you, she wouldn't have talked to you as long as she did."

Lucy caressed Tim's face. "I'm mad about you too. I think the summer season will be a real test for us. Will our schedules be an obstacle? I think, only if we allow it."

"You understand then why I am worried about getting in too deep too soon?"

"I do. I'm scared, too. I learned so much about you that first night; at least, I thought I did. I hope, with time, you will completely open up to me."

"Maybe Cubby and Kathryn will be able to help with that. Come to the Pub tonight. You can get to know me through them."

"Tim, I would love that. Matilda gave me her number. Should I call her?"

"Make plans to do something next time you are both off, but right now, she is usually busy."

"OK, you know her best." Lucy laid on Tim. "What time do you need to leave?"

"We have time."

***

Beau had lunch with a fraternity brother visiting from New York. It had been quite some time since they last met, so they talked about their shared past for a bit. Eventually, their conversation switched gears.

"Beau, I thought we were friends. Why didn't you tell me about…?" He leaned in and whispered, "The house of ill repute. It is amazing, so I

71

know why you would want to keep it to yourself, but Beau, I wish you had told me."

"I would have told you if I had known. Are you kidding? Where is it?"

"Well, no one knows. They put a bag over your head until you are at the door of the room. You tell them what you want, and that is how they decide which woman they will give you. It's a little pricey, but it is well worth it."

"I really had no idea."

"I could smell the ocean, so it is on the coast; the rooms are all very different. They keep the girls comfortable. My guess is it is in one of those coastal mansions in your neck of the woods. Do you want to try it out?"

"It sounds very tempting. How does it work?"

"First, buy one of those burner phones; they're safer. There is a five-digit number to text to. They text back a list of preferences. There is an Asian girl who is very exotic."

"Hmm. Have you seen everyone?"

"No, there is a new one I'm seeing while I'm here. She is listed as a wild woman. We can go together. You can be my guest. But it is cash only."

"When?"

"Day after tomorrow. I'll ask for the Exotic for you."

"Sounds good to me. Then, after that I can go on my own?"

"Yup."

"Where do I meet you?"

"The hotel. I'll text you when and how much to bring."

***

"Cubby, can you hold down the fort while I do charity stuff?"

"You are the boss."

"Semantics. You run this place. I'm a figurehead, and if I get my way, you will have my job soon, very soon."

"Trip wants you in that chair… Tim wants Kathryn and I to meet Lucy."

"That's great." Abby saw a look of concern on his face. "Cub?"

"He's been out of the game for a while. I hope he's not…"

"Cubby, he is a big boy."

"You worry about Beau."

"He seems to be back on the right track. He and Julie are like newlyweds again."

"For Julie's sake, I hope that's true… Hey, what's this Missing Person's report for?"

"Oh, I was researching missing women in seaside towns. I thought human trafficking would be something we should look into."

"That is something more prevalent in cities."

"Why? If no one expects it to happen in small towns, wouldn't that be the logical place to set up shop? The fishing boats in and out of here, how often are they inspected?"

"You should ask Colt if it's something you want to investigate."

"I will. I have to go."

Abby met the girls at Julie and Beau's house. Everyone was already there.

"We started without you."

"Sorry, Cubby and I were talking."

"We were talking about Tim. Cubby and I are going to the Pub tonight to spend some time with Lucy. Do you know her?"

Molly spoke up, "Up until the night she met Tim, she hadn't been inside the Pub. Juice and Lenny love her. That's good enough for me."

"I'm glad he found someone."

Julie held Abby's arm. "Before we start, may I speak to you?"

"What's up?"

"Beau told me about his friend. He didn't want to put you on the spot so he didn't tell me right away that you talked. I wanted you to know he said they were friends. I have no reason to believe it was anything more than that."

***

Matilda wasn't going to let the man's actions shatter her resolve. The man she loved was a police officer. She had faith that he would locate her, but she hoped he would do so before the man came back. There was no doubt in her mind that he was a sadist.

She remembered a time when Tim told her to steer clear of a certain bar patron. He called the man a misogynist. She knew what that meant, but she decided to research the problem in order to better deal with it. In her current predicament, she could do nothing. She prayed that he was not a regular, but she did decide not to let the men who visited know her pain or see her fear.

She spent several days without any visitors. On the first morning, she awoke unbound, dressed in a tracksuit, a T-shirt, and her own sneakers. A hearty breakfast was provided, and she took the time to familiarize herself with the surroundings. She suspected she was under surveillance, so she examined the room as if seeing it for the first time. There were books, a television with streaming options, and even a treadmill. She deduced that the person who owned the house had been watching her, so they knew she liked to walk.

She had no clue how long she had been trapped, but one thing was certain: if she detected the scent of lavender, it meant she was about to drift off to sleep. Without any reference point to tell her the time of day, she naively thought she was sleeping at night. However, she quickly realized that her sleep cycle was deliberately altered, likely to throw off her circadian rhythms, ensuring she was ready for clients whenever they wanted her. But one thing was for sure: if she woke up blindfolded, naked, and cuffed to the bed, a visitor was definitely on the way.

She felt she could withstand the abuse. Before she became exclusive with Lenny, she had a string of one-night stands. She never brought those men to her home and made it clear it was just about sex. There were instances when things got a bit rough, but she always knew how to take care of herself. That was ages ago. She regretted not telling Lenny she would move in with him.

Today, she was naked, blindfolded, with her arms over her head, handcuffed to the bed. She heard movement. A large hand grasped her thigh. It moved inside and squeezed, then moved up her torso to her breasts.

His hand stopped in her cleavage. *No, no, no, please, not again...* She cringed, but this man wasn't brutal, and he didn't talk. The other man needed to let her know he was in charge. This man seemed normal, almost tender. His approach suggested... *foreplay.*

Matilda was convinced it was some kind of trick to lull her into a false feeling of security, but this man was gentile. She felt like he was trying to seduce her, but he didn't try to kiss her, and she was OK with that.

When he was through with her, she didn't feel like she had been abused, just the opposite. Before he left, he leaned over and kissed her forehead.

Beau felt completely out of his element. When he received the text asking what he desired, he hesitated before responding. He typed, "Bondage with a subservient exotic." He wasn't entirely clear on what that actually entailed, but he was determined not to come off as a coward. Although he had no intention of causing harm to this woman, he also wanted to ensure he got his money's worth. After stepping into the bathroom, he stripped off his clothes and donned the short silk robe he had been provided.

The room exuded elegance, and the woman was absolutely breathtaking. He wore a mask that obscured his features but left his mouth exposed.

His friend had explained that part of the allure of the Asian woman's experience was showcasing her beauty; thus, his face needed to remain hidden, not hers. While Beau was not shy, he lacked experience in this kind of sex.

The woman wore a lace bustier, a garter belt, and fishnet stockings, complemented by extremely high stiletto heels. She perched on a chair that supported her only at the buttocks and hips. Her hands were locked in stocks above her head. Adjusting the chair, he secured her ankles in place and positioned himself between her legs. Aware that he only had an hour, he picked up the delicate leather whip. With a gentle touch, he began to tease her.

He was beginning to feel a surge of power. For the first time, he locked eyes with her, noticing a look that was completely unfamiliar to him. He held her chin and against the advice of his friend, he kissed her.

At first, she was unresponsive, but then, as if sensing his intentions, she was anticipating what he would do next, she responded.

Beau was surprised and aroused at her intensity; perhaps it was a hint of fear that excited him, but at that moment, he couldn't care less. The experience shifted to center around him as his primal urges took over.

***

Kathryn and Cubby were at the bar talking to Tim when Lucy walked in. She looked toward the couple as Tim casually prompted her in their direction.

Lucy held her hand to Kathryn. "Lucy Finneran."

Tim eased over to his guests. "Remember what I said. Do not, under any circumstance, believe anything this man says about me."

"You mean he doesn't idolize you?" Lucy smirked. "I got the impression you worshiped the ground he walked on."

"Delusions. The story is that Mom dropped him on his head when he was a baby." Cubby stood up. "Hi, I'm Cubby."

"Lucy, I'm glad I will have someone normal to talk to. These two have vivid imaginations."

Lucy whispered, "That's not necessarily a bad thing, right?"

Tim let out the laugh that first attracted Lucy to him. She smiled as he moved away.

"Watch out for that laugh, Lucy."

"Are you kidding? That's the hook. Did you fall for it, too?"

Kathryn looked at Cubby. "Uh-huh."

"So, I know you and Brock are best friends. I've heard Jack talk about you like you are his sister."

"Well, legally, I am Brock's sister. I kept my birth name as a tribute to my parent's memory."

"I'm sorry, what am I missing?"

"I stopped automatically explaining a long time ago. The Hawkins are my parents now."

Cubby explained without details, "I hope you have a happier story."

"For the most part. We didn't have a lot, but we made do. I have an older brother who is a firefighter. Lenny introduced me to Jack, and we started talking about the job. I like him."

"Have you met Molly?"

"No, not yet."

"Timmy, have you asked Lucy to the Gala yet?"

Tim glared at Kathryn. "No."

"Matilda told me that nickname is reserved for a select few."

"Ah yes, Matilda. She really likes you."

"Tim told me she is busy, so I'm not allowed to call her."

"She is hard to pin down sometimes. I think Lenny is probably the only person who knows her entire story. We are lucky to call her a friend."

"Well, she is the reason Tim and I connected. Would she and Lenny go to this *Gala?"*

"Probably not. They are very private."

"Well, I look forward to getting to know her better."

Chapter 8

Trip lived in one of the grand mansions on the cove, perched higher than most of the others. It was quite an impressive sight. The back lawn stretched out toward a stone slab staircase that led down to a small jetty and an unused boat dock. Annie, his late wife, had been the sailor, but since her passing, Trip hadn't touched the boat, leaving it as a quiet relic of their shared past.

Lizzy and Trip sat on the edge of the dock, talking. They had finally spent the night together, but Lizzy could sense that Trip was conflicted. Doing what came naturally to her, the way she often did with her children, she coaxed him to open up, encouraging him to talk about what was weighing on his mind.

"I'm not going to suggest you forget, but you are feeling guilty."

"Our marriages ended in different ways. You wanted to move on."

"Did Annie want you to move on?"

"Yes. You know she liked you."

"That's not good?"

"I think it is the only reason I will be able to let go. Hopefully, with time."

"Am I seeing a future in our future?"

Trip chortled, "Oh, Lizzy, you always knew how to make me laugh."

"Maybe if we go out as a couple. I can spend the night again if you want, and we can go to the diner for breakfast."

"I did want to talk to you about that. I think we should go out as a couple before the Gala."

"I'm going to the Gala?"

"Would you accompany me? I think Annie would like that."

"I would love to go with you."

"And I would like it very much if you spent the night again."

***

Beau was in his office thinking about the woman. He had been thinking about her a lot, so much so that last night Julie wondered, *What has gotten into you, Beau?*

"I love you, Jules, that's what. I don't want us drifting apart again." He really believed it when he said it, but at the same time, he was thinking about going back to the house.

On the way back to Boston, his friend talked about his liaison, over-exaggerating details to mask his embarrassment about taking the conventional approach with Matilda. Beau barely paid attention. His mind kept drifting back to the exotic woman from earlier, yet Trinity was also lingering in his thoughts…

"Beau? Beau?"

"Ya, I'm here."

"You've never been shy about your exploits before."

"It's a little weird talking to you with this hood on my head."

"No kidding. The chauffeur will buzz when we can take them off. Are you going back?"

"I'm not sure."

"The woman I was with was amazing. I sometimes feel like we settled for safe when we picked wealthy wives."

"I don't think I settled."

Buzz

"Perhaps. Well, from now on you can go on your own. You don't need me."

Beau smoothed his hair. "It was definitely an experience I won't likely forget… Thanks, Sam."

Beau looked in the locked strongbox in his desk drawer, his eyes scanning the stack of cash he always kept on hand. Explaining a large withdrawal to Julie wouldn't raise any suspicions; he was used to managing things discreetly. But as he stared at the money, he couldn't help but wonder—would he even be considering going back if Trinity hadn't disappeared?

"Where are you?"

"What?"

Julie was standing at the door in a short dress and sandals.

"Hi honey, I was just thinking about last night."

"That's sweet. Do you feel like getting lunch?"

"The diner?"

"No, I thought we'd try the Pub."

"I thought you hated that place?"

"I hated it before Cubby's brother took over. It was a dive with shady, creepy people."

"So, what changed?"

"The girls were talking about Tim's new girlfriend. Did you know Lenny has been seeing someone who works there?"

"Lenny is pretty private. The only reason I know him is because of Phil. Is she someone from town?"

"I have no idea, but the girls like her. Kathryn and Cubby met Tim's new girlfriend, too."

Beau smiled. "I haven't heard you talk like this in a long time. I'm glad you're getting reacquainted with the ladies."

"Abby said that too. So, what do you say?"

"I'd love to take you to lunch."

Beau and Julie went to the Pub. The waitress didn't know them, so she was surprised when Tim stepped in. "I will take care of these folks... I don't believe I have ever seen either of you here."

"We are broadening our horizons. Kathryn was talking about the fish and chips. I haven't had good fish and chips for a long time."

"Then you're in for a treat. Take a look at the menu. I'll send the waitress over."

"Would that be the woman Molly and Kathryn were talking about?"

"Matilda? No. She should be here Tuesday, though."

Tim was about to walk away when he saw Brock walking toward the table. "I feel like we're in the *Multiverse.*"

Julie wrinkled her brow. "What?"

Tim looked at Brock and laughed. "It is a parallel universe where people look the same but lead very different lives. You know, the Flash?"

Beau stood up to shake Brock's hand. "It's been too long. Julie said the ladies were talking about Tim the other day, so she thought it was time we came in."

"Yes, I seem to be the topic of discussion these days."

Julie asked, "Are you ready to talk about her?"

Tim whispered, "Sounds to me like Kathryn has already done that."

"She likes her."

"She's funny and smart, and she won't try to make me move."

Brock grasped Tim's shoulder. "Jack likes her. Kathryn and Cubby like her. I know Lenny likes her, and he told Jack Matilda likes her, so she has won over people who aren't pushovers."

"I guess we will have to come back next week. I'm looking forward to meeting her."

Brock was happy to see Julie smiling again. He leaned down and whispered, "I'm glad you're feeling better, honey." He smiled at Beau. "You too."

***

Billie went ashore with Colt to pick up a package at the Post Office. "Will you drop me off?"

"I will if you promise to call me when you're done."

"Don't be crude."

"OK, call me when the afterglow has waned."

"That's better."

"I have a meeting with Abby. Take your time."

"Thank you, Chief, you're a good guy."

Abby was going to be talking to one of the contractors, so she asked Colt to meet her at the house. "Hey, you've gotten quite a bit done."

"It's coming along. I wanted to talk to you about an idea I had, but I can't tell you any details."

"OK. Shouldn't you be talking to Cubby?"

"I did, but this is kind of in your wheelhouse."

"OK?"

"Do small towns like this have a problem with human trafficking and prostitution?"

"I haven't seen Cape Hope on a list. Should it be?"

"Would you be concerned if you knew there was someone missing? Someone who didn't have any ties here but was building a new business, has a new home, and suddenly she was gone?"

"You don't need to tell me how you know this, but somehow you need to tell Phil."

"He knows. I wouldn't have said anything, and maybe I'm being paranoid, but I've seen a boat on the cove. It seems out of place."

"Abby, if I had more than your paranoia to guide me, maybe. Is this something you would have brought to me if this woman hadn't gone missing or if you hadn't seen this mystery boat?"

"Cubby suggested I talk to you."

"Oh well then…"

Abby slapped his arm. "He said it is a bigger city problem."

"Actually, they tend to keep on the move. What did Phil say?"

"They are looking into it. Would you be able to tell me… no never mind, I know. Just the other day I was telling Coop we were talking about winning a Pulitzer. He said that kind of story doesn't happen here."

"I suppose. Look, I have to kill some time. Do you want to get some lunch?"

Abby told the contractor she was leaving and met Colt at his car. "So, how are Billie and Juice?"

Colt chortled, "I think Juice has finally met his match. He is mesmerized, and Billie is giddy." Colt opened the car door.

Abby was looking toward the water. "Colt, that's the boat."

He reached into his back seat and found his camera case. With a practiced hand, he focused the lens, zooming in on the scene ahead. A chuckle escaped him as he snapped a couple of pictures before he handed the camera to Abby with a grin. "Look at this," he said, still laughing, "It's the Old Man and the Sea."

She handed the camera back to Colt. "Take another picture, please. Just in case."

"I did. Do you know where it's going?"

"I've only seen it a couple of times. It's possible you are right, and I'm only seeing it now because I'm paranoid, but that kind of boat is out of place near those houses. Can you see anyone else on the boat?"

"No, not that I can see."

"Colt, can you follow it if you see it?"

"You have stirred my curiosity, but if it is doing something illegal, we don't want to spook them. Maybe I'll talk to Phil."

***

"I'd like to get together with Matilda and Lenny."

"They don't usually go out. They meet at the Pub and go on their merry way. They seem to be happy with that arrangement."

"At some point…" Billie laid her head on Juice's chest.

"What? Finish the sentence."

"At some point, those kinds of relationships either grow into something more permanent, or they fizzle out."

"I don't want us to fizzle out."

"I'm thinking I'd like to talk to the Police Captain about a job. I think I'd like to be more available for us."

"You might want to think about moving in with me."

"That didn't sound very enthusiastic."

"I wouldn't have asked if I wasn't sure. I like to save my enthusiasm for other endeavors."

"Ya, I noticed, and thanks for that, by the way. It's very much appreciated."

"Ya, I noticed, too." Juice kissed her forehead. "So, will you at least think about it?"

"Tell you what. Since Colt lives here, and I am new to the area, how about we try this on an ad hoc basis?"

"English Billie."

"For the purpose of determining the status of our relationship only, we start living together."

"Isn't that what I said?"

Bille held him closer. "Sort of. I'll hold on to my apartment, just in case."

"So, a fall back plan?"

85

"Juice, we haven't known each other very long. We're still in the *sex every chance we get phase*. That will usually ebb with time."

"Not if I can help it."

"You are so sweet."

"OK, we will try the ad hoc thing for the summer?"

"I'd have to give notice at my place anyway, so that works."

"Excellent."

***

Cooper and Cubby were at the pub when Tim returned from his break. The waitress was frantic. "I thought you said Matilda would be in today?"

Tim looked at his phone. "She was coming in at four. It's not like her to be late. Did you call or text?"

"Ya, both. Nothing."

Coop remembered, "I saw her walking to town last week. Did she change her hours?"

"No. I haven't seen her since the night I met Lucy."

Cubby was trying to lighten the mood. "Maybe you did, and you were preoccupied."

"No. You know me better than that." Cubby's comment made Tim feel guilty. "This is weird." He went outside with his phone to his ear. "Lenny, have you seen Matilda?"

"Not since we went to the North End. She's not there?"

"When have you known her to be late?"

"Never. I have a key. I'll call you back. Hey, thanks, Tim."

Lenny was at his desk when Tim called. Glancing around the squad room, he realized Lucy was out on patrol, so he called her back to the station. While waiting, he paced.

"Detective?" Phil knew Lenny, and he never lost his cool.

Lenny grabbed his arm and walked them both to Phil's office "Matilda didn't show up to her shift at the Pub."

"That doesn't sound right."

"I need to…"

"Go. I'll call Lucy."

"I did. Thanks, Cap."

Phil knew Lenny hadn't seen Matilda in over a week. That wasn't entirely out of the ordinary, but her not showing up to work definitely was. Lenny made his way around to the back of her place, and the moment he spotted her plants, his heart ached. They were wilted, lifeless. Matilda adored her plants, tending to them like they were her children. She had even named them, often talking to them. It was one of the quirks Lenny had fallen in love with. Something was definitely wrong.

Lenny called Phil. "Her car is here. Her plants haven't been watered, Phil; these plants are her babies. She hasn't been here."

"So, we now have two missing women."

"Do you know anyone at the FBI?"

"I met a man at a conference in Boston a couple of years ago. Funny guy. I have his business card. Let me see if he is still there. Come back to the station. I'll call now."

Lucy saw that Phil was on the phone. She waited until he was done to tap on the door. "Cap? Lenny sounded weird."

"Come in, close the door. Lucy, Matilda seems to be missing."

"She is supposed to be working tonight."

"Tim called Lenny. She didn't show up."

"OK, I don't know her as well as you guys, but my guess would be she never misses a shift."

"There is something that makes this more urgent. A few weeks ago, Beau Fredericks reported a woman missing. She was new to town. He had hired her to do some graphic design and apparently has disappeared. We don't have a lot to go on with her. Beau is the only one who has inquired about her."

"Is he a suspect?"

"Not really. He came to us, and everything he has told us has been checked out. We really know nothing about her, but she has excellent credit, and for the first time since she has been a homeowner, her mortgage payment is late."

"So, what do we do?"

"I called the FBI. We're going to try to keep this in-house for the time being. I will not allow this town to be turned into a media circus."

"This town could be devastated by a scandal, especially at the beginning of the summer."

"The agent I talked to said up front he doesn't want to cause a panic. He said his inquiries will be discreet."

"Tim…"

"Ya, he's concerned."

"Do you mind if I try to help him out after my shift is over? He's probably shorthanded."

"I think that is a good idea. You can also keep your ears open. I'm going to talk to Lizzy too. If anyone heard rumors, it would be there. O'Donnell is coming in early; you can get changed and help Tim. Text me if you hear anything."

***

Trinity was waiting; she wanted today's abuse to be over.

She started counting her days, using the number of dinners to estimate how long she'd been trapped—about six weeks, by her guess. Her visitors were regular, almost daily, except after she'd been whipped.

Those moments were rare but unforgettable. She had no doubt the owners of this place didn't like their girls being out of commission, but she was equally sure the scumbags who whipped her had paid extra for that particular perk.

She hadn't completely given up on being rescued; the hope of escape dwindled with each passing day. Especially after hearing the woman, she believed was named Harlow. Harlow was always crying or screaming. Trinity couldn't help but wonder if the men paid for that—the fear. But what worried her most was whether Harlow was okay.

She had just finished lunch and was about to start reading when the scent of lavender filled the air. She lay down on the bed, knowing...

When she opened her eyes, the blindfold and cuffs were securely fastened. She wasn't wearing her usual naughty garb, as she referred to it. The unpredictability of what the men—and sometimes women—did while she was clad in skimpy undergarments had led her to stop anticipating their actions and focus instead on her mantra.

Today, the man hesitated as he entered the room. He remained silent, but she thought she heard a faint gasp escape his lips. He stood still, not moving or doing anything at all. This unusual behavior was beginning to unsettle her. What bothered her the most, however, was the chilling thought that he was merely there to observe her. The idea of being looked at like that sent a shiver down her spine.

"Is someone here? Please say something." She heard movements, but she wasn't sure what she was hearing. She could feel the person near the bed. "Please, please don't hurt me."

She guessed it was about half an hour later when the door opened and closed, and Trinity began to drift off to sleep.

The man understood exactly what was expected of him. He placed the bag over his head and waited patiently for the escort to guide him to the car. The solitude was a welcome relief; he had no desire to engage in small talk with some blowhard who would only exaggerate his exploits. After a short while, he was dropped off at the hotel where he had been picked up earlier.

As soon as he got in his car, he put his head down in his hands and cried, "I will get you out of there, honey, I promise."

Beau drove home, the journey a blur. His mind was filled with the thought of Trinity lying on that bed. He wasn't positive it was her until he spotted her tattoo—a flawless depiction of Bugs Bunny etched on her hip. This revelation demanded his attention, yet urgency coursed through him; he needed to act swiftly. Time was running out, and getting her out of there became his sole priority.

***

"Thank you, sweetheart. You were a lifesaver."

"You really love Matilda."

"I do. She is special and unique. She would do anything for me, and I feel like I should be out there trying to find her."

"Does she have family?"

"Just Lenny, Cubby and me."

"Can you think of anything that would take her away? A lost love, or…"

"No. Yes, she doesn't talk about herself, but that's because she wants to forget everything that happened before she came here."

"Where do you think she is?"

"There was a time I warned her about a customer who I am still convinced is a misogynist. As much as he hated women, I think he was pissed Matilda wasn't flirting with him like she was with the other customers."

"That makes sense. Do you know his name?"

"I wrote his name down. It's on the bulletin board in my office. I'm going to tell Phil tomorrow."

"I am so sorry this is happening. Your eyes are so sad. Did you talk to Lenny again?"

"No, but Phil told him to go home." Tim laid his head on Lucy's chest. "This really can't be happening. I'm glad I'm not alone."

"Tim, you're blaming yourself. Maybe tomorrow I can get the Captain to recruit some volunteers to look for her."

"I'm afraid someone took her. I'm afraid she has a secret admirer. Oh sweetheart, I'm afraid she is somewhere being held prisoner."

Chapter 9

The man Phil spoke with at the Boston FBI office sent Special Agent Ben Malloy to the station. He arrived early to talk with Phil and Lenny. "Detective Clarke, I hesitate to let you be involved."

"I know her better than anyone."

"Is the practice of taking time at the end of the school year a habit for her?"

"Yes, but she doesn't share her private life with people outside a very small circle."

"I need those names."

Phil handed him a list.

"The man who reported the other woman missing. I read the report. You believed him?"

"He went to his father first. Then to his sister and his brother, who is the Assistant DA here, and he told his wife."

"Shaw Fredericks?"

"Yes."

"His boss is a…how do I put this?"

"A bastard? Shaw understands he may need to recuse himself, but his brother had nothing to do with the disappearance of either of these women. We did our due diligence. We spoke to his staff and his children's nanny. We spoke to her before Beau told his wife. She had her schedule on her phone. She lives with them, so she keeps a pretty extensive record of her daily activities. He was home the night of the storm that knocked out the power and that whole weekend."

"What about his wife?"

"Julie? We didn't talk to her."

"Captain, if his wife knew about this woman and thought they were having an affair."

Lenny spoke up. "Not her style."

"She is a very wealthy woman."

Lenny repeated, "Not her style."

"I'll need to talk to her since you haven't."

"She'll have her attorney with her, I'm sure. Not because she is guilty, but because she is one of her best friends."

"The problem investigating in a small town is that everyone knows everybody."

"Special Agent, That's what we have in our favor. Matilda is the most private person in this town. Everyone respects that, and everyone still loves her…"

Knock, knock.

"Phil, I have something you may need." Tim was abrupt.

"Tim Edwards owns the Pub in town where Matilda works part-time."

"Phil, there is a man who should be a person of interest." Tim handed him the man's name.

Special Agent Malloy groaned.

Tim was angry. "I have known Matilda for years. She is the best person I know."

"Are you in a relationship with her too?"

Tim looked at Lenny and laughed. "Lucy suggested we get some volunteers…"

"Mr. Edwards, let the professionals do their jobs."

"Lucy is a cop. Phil, Lenny, this guy is a piece of work, a misogynist. I told Matilda to steer clear of him, and it seemed to piss him off."

Phil stood up. "Thank you, Tim. Has he been in since the last time Matilda was in?"

"I haven't seen him, no."

Agent Malloy took a long breath. "Captain, why did you call us?"

Lenny was pissed. "Because of two missing women, possibly a serial case. Isn't that your area of expertise? We certainly wouldn't want to take on a case we are not equipped to handle. You have the resources; we have the information. If we can't work together, these women may die. Now knock off the posturing and help!"

Tim stood at the door, clapping slowly. "Thank you, Detective. Please call me."

Agent Malloy waited until Tim left. "Captain, it is my understanding that Beau Frederick's father owns the area newspaper."

"He does, and that will not be a problem. Trip doesn't involve himself in the day to day operation of the paper."

"But his daughter does. Maybe that is the real reason Beau spoke to his father and sister first."

Lenny really disliked this guy. "Do you leave this attitude at work, or do you bring it home to your wife?"

"I'm not married."

Lenny looked at Phil. "Gee, what a surprise. Cap, I'm going to take Lucy and look along the Coast Road to see if we can find any of Matilda's belongings or evidence."

"Agent, Matilda always walked along that road when she came to town. Lenny, go ahead. Stay on comms."

"Thanks, Cap."

"Captain, is this route into town common knowledge?"

"For Matilda, probably. She likes to walk."

"Would Detective Clarke mind if I looked in her house?"

"He gave me the key."

"Captain, I'm not the bad guy here. I want to find Trinity and Matilda alive, too. I will need to investigate these women's pasts. We have to go back before we can go forward."

Phil held up the piece of paper "My fear is this man is behind Matilda's disappearance."

"I will look into him, but I will need to speak to Mrs. Fredericks. She has the resources to hire someone…"

"You are really barking up the wrong tree."

"Perhaps, but I have to investigate all angles. If she believed her husband was having an affair, she may have decided to get rid of the competition."

"She would divorce him. Both families have money. She wouldn't subject their children to a scandal. Neither of them would."

"Captain…"

Kathryn and Julie walked through the front door of the station together.

"Excuse me, Agent, Mrs. Fredericks is here… Kathryn, Julie, this is Special Agent Ben Malloy."

"Phil, Tim called me. He is really upset."

Julie was confident. "Kathryn tells me you have some questions."

"Captain, do you have a room that is more private?"

***

Beau hadn't been a regular churchgoer since his wedding. He felt conflicted and wondered if he was the reason Trinity was in that place. The only person he could talk to was Father Andrew. Seeing that Andy's office door was open, Beau tapped on the door frame. "Andy?"

Andy was family—his cousin and best friend—someone Beau had known since childhood. "Beau, is the family well?" Andy asked.

"Yes, thank you. Andy, you know me better than anyone. I need your help without a lecture."

"Come in. Close the door. What happened?"

Beau rested his head in his hands. "I love Julie; I really do. But something happened. I don't know; maybe it was both of us. Even before Harold died, she changed. She was preoccupied and distant. We stopped talking."

"So, you had an affair?"

"You and I were joined at the hip before you went into the Seminary."

"If you want absolution…"

"No, I don't think there is anything I can do. Yes, I had an affair, but it's worse than that. I fell in love with her." Beau explained how he came to know Trinity.

"What aren't you telling me?"

"She is missing. I had to lie to Dad, Shaw and Phil. I told them we were friends, that's all. But I did tell Abby the truth."

"You're letting me down, Beau. Everything."

"Do you remember Sam from the fraternity?"

"Sure, he married for money. Never a good reason to get married."

"Andy… he came to town. He told me about this place. It can only be described as a high-class brothel. I went along with him. After I went, I actually reconnected with Julie. We started talking again. I told her I loved her for the first time in months. It seems that's all we needed. Everything is so much better. I do love her. Andy, I don't know what's wrong with me. I went back the other day." Beau stood up and started pacing. "Andy, the woman was Trinity, the woman I was having an affair with."

Andy, the priest, was conflicted about his role in this conversation. Andy, the cousin, was sympathetic. He embraced Beau. "Did you say anything?"

"No. I was stunned. She must have sensed there was someone in the room with her. She begged me not to hurt her. Andy, she wouldn't be there voluntarily."

"So, she didn't see you?"

Beau couldn't look at him. "She was blindfolded and handcuffed to the bed... naked. Andy, she has a Bugs Bunny tattoo; It was her. I have to get her out of there."

"So, you have no way of knowing where this place is?"

"It's about a half hour away. Or they drove us around and the brothel is actually in the hotel. But the second time, I heard water. I felt like we were sitting on the dock at the house like we did when we were kids. That is the sound I heard."

"Sloshing?"

Beau laughed but stopped abruptly. "What do I do?"

"I want to help, but I don't want to make an impetuous suggestion. I know this is a time-sensitive situation, but I need to think."

***

Ben Malloy was back in the office talking to Phil and Lenny. "Detective, I don't know you at all, but you look tired."

"Matilda and I don't live together, and we have never spent the night at my house; I haven't slept. I am afraid for her Agent. I was in a war in a foreign country on the other side of the world, and I wasn't as afraid as I am now."

"After I spoke to Mrs. Fredericks, I began to understand how private Matilda is."

"Agent, Kathryn and Matilda are friends. Did she tell you?"

"No. Attorneys usually don't volunteer information, but it was clear she wanted to find the truth. I have to say I was surprised Mrs. Fredericks didn't know her."

"Matilda is a social butterfly at the Pub only. Julie and Beau are not patrons."

"Mrs. Fredericks and her husband have solid alibi's. I hope you understand why I had to speak to her. If we don't eliminate suspects, we end up chasing our tails."

"Is Julie OK?" Lenny wondered.

"She gave me a business card and asked me to call her if I had any more questions. She was concerned that there was someone abducting women. I didn't see any deceit."

"OK, where do we go from here?"

"I need to talk to Abby Fredericks. I hesitate to make statements to the media. My boss's predecessor hated the press and used them only in extreme cases. His approach worked well. I don't want to send the residents and vacationers into a panic, but Kathryn said she is a responsible journalist. Her right hand is Tim Edwards, brother?"

"Yes. They would be good sources of information. Colton Van der Platt too. He is in the Coast Guard. He grew up here as well. I'm sure they would talk to you together."

Lenny was curious. "What about the name Tim gave you?"

Ben shook his head. "He is a business man. He is married with three kids. He is from Beverly Farms. He is squeaky clean."

"Will you talk to him?"

"No. I will look into him as much as I am allowed, but I need to be careful. Two Agents will be here. They have seen his picture. Tim has allowed me to put them in the Pub as employees. They are both experienced in undercover work.

"Agent, we have people here who want to help. Elizabeth Landry Juice Mason, both veterans. Billie Barnes is Coast Guard; she works with Colt."

"If they are locals, yes. What about that diner? Is that your family, Captain?"

"Yes. My cousin Stella is the pharmacist in the Apothecary; FYI, she dates Simon Fredericks. The diner is run by her brother Michael."

"Which one of the Fredericks does he date?"

Phil chuckled. "He stopped dating when he got married. Her name is Bethany, and she is a homebody. She stays home with the kids and she makes donuts for the diner. I can take you over there."

"I would like that. Gentlemen, I'm sorry we got off on the wrong foot."

Lenny stood up. "Hi, I'm Lenny, and this is Phil."

"Nice to meet you both. I'm Ben."

Lenny stayed at the station while Phil and Ben went to the diner. They decided to keep the story of their meeting as close to the truth as possible.

"Hey, Michael. This is Ben."

"Good to meet you. What brings you to town?"

"We met at a conference for law enforcement. I've never been here. You have a very quaint seaside village here."

"Would you like a typical homestyle breakfast?"

"I would love that."

"Phil, does Connie still have you on a diet?"

"Only at home. Bring it on, Michael."

"Phil, I came in on the Coast Road. The houses on the hill across from the cove would be a perfect lookout. Are there any homeowners there that are new or are not known to you?"

Phil leaned in and whispered, "You mean someone who may have been stalking?"

"We have to look at this from all angles, Phil."

"I know. You won't like this, but Abby and her boyfriend just bought a house up there. It's closer to the less scenic end of the cove, but the water is still visible. I'll ask if they have seen anything unusual."

"Hmm. I'll have to think about that. Does Matilda walk in inclement weather?"

"No. Sometimes, depending on the weather, we may not see her in town for a few weeks at a time. You can ask Lenny about that."

"He is definitely a man who is deeply in love."

"This isn't common knowledge, but Lenny asked Matilda to move in with him the last time she was seen in town."

"Could someone have overheard them?"

"They don't usually have personal discussions at the Pub. Lenny always drives them to her place before closing. If Lenny isn't there, Tim will drive her home. We all watch out for her."

"I am going to do everything in my power to make sure I get to meet her and Trinity. Phil, I do have a question. Would it be out of character for you to go to the Pub?"

"To get lunch, but not to sit at the bar. Regulars would notice that."

"OK. Is there a motel nearby? Commuting here daily isn't really an option."

"I have an efficiency above my garage. You are welcome to it."

"Excellent. Naomi, one of my agents, may need a place too."

"I'll talk to Tim. He has a room above the Pub."

"Thanks, I'll have her talk to him. No offense, but I hope we're not here long."

"Me too. Fair warning, I have five kids, and they're not shy."

"Either am I."

Chapter 10

Although Beau hadn't heard from Andy, it had been the weekend, so he decided to wait instead of going to the church to talk to him. He was in his office when Andy walked in. "I told your assistant you were expecting me."

"Andy, you are always welcome."

"I had some thoughts. The most prudent of those would be for you to go to Phil, tell him what you know, and bring him to an appointment with you."

"I did think of that, but the FBI has been brought in. Another woman, a very much loved woman, is missing. Do you ever go to the Pub in town?"

"Yes. I've been known to have a beer and a burger on occasion… Oh Beau. Please don't tell me it's Matilda."

"I don't know for sure, but it seems that way. The story is she had a family emergency. Although I don't know her, people are talking, and they aren't buying the reason she hasn't been to the Pub. Andy, I know you can say, but has anyone…"

"Please don't ask. You know better, but no. I have thought about that, and I spoke to the Monsignor about a hypothetical case. He said in such a case, he would hope I would remember my vows. Truthfully, I'm not sure if I could live with myself."

"I'm sorry I brought this to you."

"I'm not. Maybe Phil could make arrangements to have the car followed. I'm sure the FBI has ways to infiltrate illegal establishments."

"Right now, I have been cleared in Trinity's disappearance. If I tell Phil I have been to a brothel, I'm right back at the top of the list."

"You have to decide what is more important."

"Is the church going to allow a divorce? You don't make exceptions now based on stupidity, do you? Julie will not divorce me, but she will leave me and take the kids."

"Did you think about that before you broke your vows?"

"Julie broke her vows, too. She was… never mind. How could you possibly understand?"

"You came to me, Beau. Don't question my advice because you disagree with what I have to say. If you didn't know what you did was wrong, you never would have come to me."

Beau got up from his desk, turned his back to Andy and looked out the window.

"You know where to find me if you need me."

"Beau stayed by the window. He had to come up with a solution that would find Trinity but not end his marriage. He thought about his options again. He couldn't tell Julie that he was out. He couldn't tell Phil because he would need to tell the FBI. He thought about writing a letter, but who would he send it to?"

He stared and thought but couldn't come up with a solution. Then he sat at his desk, picked up the landline, and pressed a button.

"Hi Beau."

"Abbs, I need to talk to you. It's important."

"Is this about your friend?"

"Where can we meet?"

"Coop is in Boston. The workers at the house should be gone."

"I'm leaving now. This has to stay between us." Beau hung up.

"Beau? Beau?" Abby put her laptop in her bag and told Cubby she was leaving.

"Big story?"

"I have no idea. Family drama. I'm meeting with Phil. He wants me to meet someone. I told him tomorrow morning. I need you to be here."

Abby went straight to the house. Beau was waiting for her outside.

"You have to promise this will stay between us."

"Come on. Maybe you should be talking to Andy."

"I did, then he started getting all judgmental."

"Isn't that his job?"

"Please, this is important, but it has to stay between us."

"Like I said, I'm your sister first."

"You may need to make this a combo platter. The authorities have cleared me, but if they find out…" Beau sat on a box "Please?"

"Go ahead."

"I have a fraternity brother who called me a couple of weeks ago. He said I had to go with him to this social club, a very private social club." He couldn't look at his sister as he recounted the story of his first trip to the brothel: "Then, I don't know why, I went back." Beau stood up and walked to the window. "It was a different woman." Beau stopped talking as his head dropped. He turned around. Abby could see the tears in his eyes.

"Beau…"

"She had a Bugs Bunny tattoo on her hip. Trinity has a Bugs Bunny tattoo…"

Abby embraced her brother.

"I couldn't move, I couldn't talk. I just stood there looking at her. She doesn't want to be there. She was afraid. She begged me not to hurt her. Abby, I have to get her out of there."

"You have to tell Phil."

"That's what Andy said. Abby, he called in the FBI. How do I explain? I have no idea where this place is."

"Are you going to be able to live with yourself if you don't?"

"I end up alone either way."

"Maybe you should stop thinking about yourself." Abby shouted, "What if it had been Julie or me? Huh, what then? You know what to do."

"If I knew where this place was, but I don't. I am going to lose everything, and they may not even find her."

"Why did you tell me if you had no intention of taking my advice? You knew what I would say."

"Dad will disown me. Julie will take the kids, and I'll never see them again."

"I have nothing else to say to you except stop being a selfish prick and help this woman."

Beau was looking out the window, wiping his eyes. Abby felt sorry for him and put her arm around him.

"Beau, have you ever seen that boat in the cove before?"

"What?"

"That boat. Colt and I saw it the other day. I don't remember seeing it at any of the houses."

Beau took a deep breath. "We really don't know everyone. You know how private everyone is."

"I asked Colt if they could follow it."

Beau wiped his eyes again. "So, you're talking to me again?"

"Maybe if Cubby goes with you…"

"I love you so much."

"Hold that thought. He may say no. Kathryn wouldn't understand."

"I'm sure she has clients he wouldn't approve of."

"We have a meeting in the morning. I'll talk to him. Do me a favor. Don't do anything stupid."

"I can't make any promises."

***

Ben Malloy was a career Agent and a relentless ladder climber within the Agency. He had always adhered strictly to protocol, a tendency that occasionally blinded him to the broader implications of his work. His inability to collaborate effectively with colleagues led his former boss to assign him a female Agent as a partner. This woman was a natural charmer, capable of enlightening her teammates to view cases from multiple perspectives. Ruthless in her pursuit of the truth, she was unafraid to challenge the assumptions of her peers. She was using a confidential informant who was eventually accused of being the serial killer targeting prostitutes in Baltimore. She remained unconvinced of his guilt. She relentlessly pursued leads, putting her life on the line in the process.

Naomi was abducted and kept in a drug-induced state by the real serial killer. Ben, his team, and the local authorities were able to find her before she was given a fatal dose of heroin. The man was linked to crimes in other cities along the East Coast, where all the prostitutes were beaten and died from heroin overdoses.

Naomi's road to recovery was arduous. While the Agency psychiatrist scrutinized her mental state, she ultimately received clearance for duty. However, one nagging thought lingered in her mind regarding the case: the possibility of a female accomplice. Although there was no evidence to support this theory, her instincts wouldn't let her dismiss it. She also couldn't ignore her memory of conversations she heard while she was imprisoned, which she later shared with a compassionate new Agency therapist who provided the support she desperately needed.

Chapter 11

"OK, Abby, what is this all about?"

"Phil wants to see me, but I wanted to talk to you about something first."

"Are you running down a lead?"

"I had a talk with Colt about a possible problem with human trafficking, but I think it is more than that."

"What are you talking about?"

"Prostitution, possibly highly organized and high class, big money, but the women aren't necessarily willing."

"Abby, Matilda doesn't have a family emergency. She's missing. We were told to keep it to ourselves because the fewer the people who knew…"

"So maybe that's why Phil is coming by. Maybe he thinks I've heard something."

"Where is this coming from?"

"I really can't say. Not yet… don't look at me like that. Cub, please, I don't have time to explain. Phil is here, and he's with someone."

"Hi, Phil."

"Abby Fredericks and Cubby Edwards, Special Agent Ben Malloy."

"Cubby told me about Matilda. What can I do?"

Ben addressed Cubby, "I met your brother. He doesn't like me."

Cubby stated truthfully, "Then you must have done something to piss him off."

"I believe I did. He read me the riot act. He cares about Matilda. I want to find her. We have that in common."

"Abby, did Coop tell you he may have been the last person we know who saw her?"

"Phil, Coop and I don't talk about work a lot. When I told Cubby you were coming, he told me about Matilda. I won't jeopardize her safety for a story."

"Miss…"

"Abby, please."

"Abby, your brother told you about the woman he hired."

"Trinity, yes. The two cases have to be connected. People don't go missing here, and there is no such thing as coincidences. Please tell us how we can help?"

"Your house has a vantage point. Trinity's house is on Coast Road. Coop saw Matilda one morning, about ten days before she was reported missing. Have you seen any cars lingering on the side of the road?"

"I'm not living there yet. Did you ask Coop?"

"This just came up yesterday."

"You have my permission to put a camera in the front if you think it will help."

Phil looked at Ben. "What do you think?"

"That may not be a bad idea."

"Ben, I'm not at the house that often, but I was there a few days ago, and yesterday, both days, I saw a boat on the cove that didn't seem to belong. I've never seen it docked at any of the houses."

"Ben, Abby grew up in one of the houses on the cove. The house that is higher up, closer to the road."

"Does your father still live there?"

"Yes. Phil, he will let you put a camera in the back, I'm sure."

Ben was curt. "The less people who know we are here, the better."

"Lizzy probably told him about Matilda already. Lizzy helped Tim at the Pub. She will be filling in at the station for the summer. She is also dating Trip."

"Ben, Daddy isn't a gossip at all. If Lizzy did tell him, he kept it to himself."

"Cubby, did Tim tell you there will be two undercover agents at the Pub?"

"No, but it will be a great place to gather information. This time of year, it is so busy with tourists I'm not sure how much information can be gathered, but your agents will be in the right place. Phil, what about the diner?"

"We were there this morning. Short of reading in Michael and Stella, I'm not sure how that would work."

Ben admitted, "I don't like using civilians to gather info. It's too risky. Abby, Cubby, you both know how to do that. Would it be out of character for you to be seen there on a daily basis?"

"Cubby, no. Me yes. Stella is one of my best friends. She has been dating my youngest brother for a long time. I trust her."

Phil shared, "Ben, when she isn't busy in the pharmacy, she mingles in the diner. She is a lot like Matilda, although she doesn't flirt. She did learn to read lips when she was in college."

"Phil, it's up to you if you want to ask her to help."

Abby thought it was a good idea. "Phil, you know she would want to help."

"OK, so short of revealing a source, will you share your findings?"

Abby reached for Cubby's arm. "We will need to talk about that, but I hope so."

"I will be staying above Phil's garage." He reached for business cards. "Here is my number, call any time with anything."

Abby laughed. "Phil, have you told him Connie will expect him at dinner?"

"No, I thought that should be a surprise."

"Home cooked meals? That would be a welcome change. What time?"

"Six o'clock. Don't feel like you have to join us in saying grace."

"Not an issue. Grace was a staple growing up with my grandparents."

***

Marcus had recently joined the Boston FBI office. Although he grew up in Massachusetts, he had been dispatched to Philadelphia for an extensive undercover assignment. When vacancies in the Boston office became available, Marcus eagerly seized the opportunity to return home. While he was initially living in his childhood home, he decided to take advantage of the chance to relocate to a smaller community when the undercover position was presented. He was aware of a furnished two-bedroom house in Danvers, which offered convenient access to both Boston and Cape Hope. Traveling light, he found he didn't have much to relocate.

He was eagerly anticipating this assignment, hoping it would be a brief one. A sense of dread weighed on him regarding Trinity and Matilda. During his time working undercover in North Philadelphia, he had witnessed the darker aspects of life while attempting to gather evidence for a RICO case. Marcus effortlessly morphed into the punk persona he needed, delivering vital intelligence that helped dismantle the syndicate involved in loan sharking, drugs, and prostitution. As soon as he got the call to head back to Boston, he visited his parents then swiftly shaved his beard, trimmed his hair, and took out the brown contact lenses. Marcus was of mixed Mexican and Irish heritage. He had a Hispanic appearance and was fluent in Spanish, yet his father's striking blue eyes would have undoubtedly exposed him to the gangs.

The day before, Naomi and Marcus had met at the office to discuss their collaboration. Since they hadn't been partners for long, they felt it was essential to connect. Naomi was content to be residing above the pub. She despised the heavy traffic in the Boston area and loathed the thought of navigating the tourist congestion along the coast even more. She stood waiting at the base of the stairs when Tim arrived to meet her.

Tim had cleared out his personal belongings from the bureau and closet and showed Naomi the room. "Microwave, coffee machine, small refrigerator. You are welcome to eat in the pub or bring your meal up here."

Knock, knock. "Hi, I wanted to introduce myself before you started. I'm Lucy, Cape Hope PD."

"That explains the uniform."

Tim laughed. "You are going to fit in with us just fine. Lucy is also my girlfriend, so she will be around." He kissed the side of her head. "Have you met Marcus?"

"Yes, he's downstairs. Naomi, I'm not around here a lot, but if you want to meet at the diner for coffee call me. Phil said he gave you my number."

"Yes, thank you."

"I have to get back. Nice meeting you."

Tim walked her out to the stairs. He kissed her. "Hmm. May I do that again?"

"I insist."

"Be careful, sweetheart."

"If I'm not up when you get home, wake me gently."

"I can't wait. See you soon."

***

"Abby, tell me what you didn't tell Phil."

"This has become so much more than a missing person's case. It didn't start out as a story, but Cubby, this is going to be big." Abby was brief, "I can't tell you unless you promise."

"I won't tell a soul."

"Beau had an affair with Trinity."

"Abby…"

"I'm not done. He has an idiot fraternity brother who invited him to a high-class house of ill repute. So, my stupid brother went with him.

110

Then, a few days later, my stupid moron of a brother went back, this time with a different woman. Cubby, these women are tied up and blindfolded. They don't want to be there. They are being held against their will. Beau has no idea where this place is; he only knows how to make an appointment and where to meet the car. They have to wear bags over their heads before they are brought to the rooms."

"Abby, get to the point."

"Beau went back, this time with a different woman. Even though she was blindfolded, he recognized her. Apparently, Trinity has a Bugs Bunny tattoo on her hip. Beau said Trinity is being held at the house with the other women. Cubby, he was crying when he told me."

Cubby sat down. "I always suspected he wasn't faithful, but this? He has to tell Phil."

"Phil, Daddy and Julie know Beau hired Trinity to do work for him. Andy and I were the only people he honored with the truth."

"What aren't you telling me, Abby?"

"Beau wants to go back to the brothel. I thought it would be a good idea for you to go too."

"Are you high?"

"I think so."

"Would you be suggesting this if he were just another degenerate?"

"No. Not that it matters, but before he found her, he told me he was in love with her."

"Abby, do you think Matilda is there too?"

"If I made guesses."

"Beau was OK with you talking to me?"

"He didn't say no."

Cubby sat in the chair across from Abby's desk, elbows on his knees, his chin resting on his folded hands. "So, what do we do?"

"Maybe we can follow the car?"

"I actually thought of that too."

***

Tim was showing Naomi and Marcus the touchscreen computer ordering system. They were both quick studies; in their jobs, they had to be. The license photo of the person of interest in Matilda's disappearance was on the bulletin board in Tim's office, along with Phil's cell number below it. "I'll be here today and Friday and Saturday night. My house is only a couple of blocks over, so if you need me, scream."

Tim entered his office and fixated on the picture of the man. He had folded the sheet of paper so the man's address wasn't visible. With a push pin in hand, he turned the paper over and examined the address closely. The town was nearby—a quaint village, very upper-middle-class. Normally, this wouldn't bother Tim, but the thought of this man using his wealth and influence in the community to disrespect women made him feel nauseated.

After completing some paperwork, Tim returned to the bar. The restaurant was buzzing with activity, so he donned an apron and jumped in to help. He felt relieved and pleased that Naomi and Marcus were blending in well. Only a handful of people inquired about Matilda. News always spread quickly, so most of the regulars were already aware that she was away.

Once the dinner rush subsided, Tim prepared to head back to his office when Abby, Coop, Kathryn, and Cubby walked in. Tim recognized this as a perfect opportunity to discuss Matilda and the ongoing investigation. He informed Naomi and Marcus that he would be in the corner booth.

Cubby put his hand on his brother's shoulder. "They will find her."

"I am afraid for her. Abby, have you gotten any reports from surrounding towns? Have other coastal communities ever had this problem?"

"It's hard putting out feelers to other media outlets without sparking interest. We are going to let Phil and Ben do their jobs."

"Ben? You're friends now?"

"Cubby and I met with him the other day. I like him. Because Matilda was last seen on Coast Road and Trinity lived there, I suggested he put a camera in front of our house."

"Abby, do you know if anyone has contacted the authorities about Trinity? She must have had other clients."

"That I don't know. I can ask Phil."

"She must have had a laptop; did Phil take that so Ben could have his people look at it."

Kathryn spoke up, "They need to tread lightly. Beau reported her missing. He had a key, but he's not family or even a boyfriend."

"But Trinity gave him the key," Abby repeated.

"A defense attorney could use that against Beau, make him look guilty. Since Phil went in there without a warrant, the prosecution would have to inform the defense about the key during discovery. Beau did the right thing telling Phil, but, I don't know, I really wish we could talk to Shaw about this."

Tim suggested, "Maybe something off the record?"

Abby objected. "That really wouldn't be fair. Besides, he knows about the situation. Beau told him. I questioned his sincerity at first. Believe me, I know how he can be. We have had several discussions. He loves Julie. I have no doubt about that. But he is worried about Trinity."

Tim wanted to change the subject. "I asked Lucy to the Gala."

Kathryn put her arm around Tim. "We need to get together before then."

"Lucy wants to get to know everyone. I haven't seen Lenny. Does anyone know how he is?"

"I asked Phil when he called me the other day. He said Lenny is staying at Matilda's house. He is heartbroken."

Chapter 12

Ben was convinced that the disappearances of Matilda and Trinity were intricately linked. However, Lenny suspected something far more sinister at play. He believed there was a well-organized group orchestrating the abductions. Lenny confided his theory to Phil, who challenged his objectivity. Lenny was savvy enough to avoid pushing the issue further, and Phil was perceptive enough to recognize Lenny's determination to pursue the matter. While Phil couldn't dictate what Lenny did in his off hours, he could ensure that someone kept a watchful eye on him. So, during his time off, Juice would shadow him.

He was spending his free time visiting local bars, tuning into the chatter among patrons. He always limited himself to one beer, and he always made sure he had something to eat, even if it was only pretzels or popcorn.

He would strike up a conversation with the bartender, directly inquiring if they were the owner. Following that, he would pose innocuous questions about the area. When asked about his intentions, he would say he was interested in opening a nightclub, curious if anything similar existed nearby to attract out-of-town businessmen. *Is there something like that around here?*

Lenny had spent enough time in the detective field to identify the right channels for gathering that kind of intel. Ultimately, he discovered two promising locations. The first was an old speakeasy-style bar that exuded charm. Despite its age, it was well-maintained, featuring booths with high backs that offered a sense of privacy, seemingly designed for couples. Lenny settled himself at the bar, surveying the surroundings. The bartender was both polite and friendly. Lenny only lingered for one drink and shared his thoughts with the bartender: "Maybe on a night with a little more action."

The bartender nodded and grinned. "You are always welcome. We get a lot of transients, but a lot of them end up coming back. We're a friendly bunch here."

Lenny recognized the cheeky grin he often associated with sarcasm. "Well then, I guess I'll come back alone."

The man nodded as he smirked "As you wish."

The second place was a pub, similar to the first but lacking in warmth and charm. As he sipped his beer, Lenny pondered whether it was time to move on to another location. Just then, the bartender rolled up his sleeves, revealing a Marine insignia tattooed on his forearm. Lenny considered how best to introduce himself, weighing his options carefully. Ultimately, he decided that the most straightforward approach was often the most effective. With that in mind, he extended his hand and said, "Lenny. I was stationed in Mosul. You?"

"Pleased to meet you, Lenny. Everyone here calls me Sarge. I was in The Green Zone mostly. Kabul toward the end."

They talked about their projects until Sarge wondered, "Where did you end up?"

The backstory Lenny created proved to be helpful: "I'm in private security."

"Is that what you want to do?"

"I guess. I'm not interested in standing around looking like a target, though." Lenny recognized the look on Sarge's face and heard him mumble, "Hmm." Lenny chose to ignore the tell.

"Give me your number. If I hear of anything, I'll text. Is that good?"

"Sure."

"So, married, not married?"

"Not married. Never have been. I've been told I'm not the marrying kind."

Sarge grunted, "By a woman?"

Lenny chuckled, "Women, plural." He was well aware of the man at the pub, having constructed his profile of the likely kidnapper based on

Tim's description. If he could manage to come across as a sympathizer, perhaps he would be seen as a believer in the cause.

That night, Lenny returned to Matilda's house and did something he hadn't done since his discharge from the service: he prayed.

***

Saturday was typically the busiest day of the week at the house. However, a few months earlier, Mr. Smith received a call from a longtime client who wanted to reserve four women for a bachelor party. Reluctantly, Mr. Smith decided to make an exception for a substantial fee.

The groom was a man with a hypocritical view of life. He believed his wife should embody wholesomeness—a woman who would bear his children and remain at home. She was to be a good mother and gracious hostess, deserving of the finest things his wealth could provide. Yet, he also felt entitled to certain indulgences outside the home. The best man informed Mr. Smith that the groom preferred someone who enjoyed rough treatment. He wanted her without a blindfold and on a long leash.

The best man ordered a party bus stocked with top-shelf Scotch and bourbon. The groom-to-be had a couple of drinks on the bus before being brought to the room—not enough to be considered drunk, but just enough to be dangerous.

The ladies were served their dinner early, but Matilda's tray held a special treat that the others did not—a bowl of strawberries sprinkled with sugar. She devoured everything on her tray, savoring each bite. However, a few minutes after finishing, she began to feel strangely disoriented and woozy. Attempting to walk across the room, she collapsed to the floor before reaching the bed.

When the man entered the room, Matilda found herself completely exposed. He headed straight for the bathroom, and when he emerged, he wore only a robe.

116

Matilda was positioned in the middle of the room, with a cuff secured around one wrist. A long chain was attached to what could only be described as a stripper pole. She was utterly defenseless, ill-equipped to protect herself in this vulnerable situation.

The man had been given a suitcase with whips, thin leather gloves and a variety of leather riding crops. He picked up the slack of the chain, wrapped it around her wrists, and yanked her hands above her head, breaking her wrist. Then he threw her on the bed and raped her.

She wasn't feeling much of anything by then. The scopolamine that had been mixed in with her strawberries had taken hold. Unfortunately for her, that just pissed him off. He stood her up, took out the whip and lashed her backside. She stayed upright but stumbled backward as he slammed her against the wall. He stood in front of her and grabbed her breasts.

He was undeniably rough, but she didn't flinch. It was clear to him that she felt no pain. He picked up the whip and struck her mercilessly until blood began to flow. From her chest down to her legs, front to back, she was covered in gruesome, bloody welts.

He sat at the desk and stared at her. She was crawling on the floor when he seemed to get his second wind; he grasped her arms and threw her back on the bed, where he viciously raped her again.

Matilda's body went limp as she lay lifeless against the headboard. The man put on gloves, kneeled on the bed, and slapped her face again and again. He made a fist and punched her in the ribs, then in one eye and then the other. He had knocked her out with the first punch, but he didn't notice. He also didn't see one of the other men at the wedding party enter the room. "What is wrong with you, man?"

"She asked for it."

"You fucking moron… get dressed." He took some towels from the bathroom and covered her up before they left.

One of the matrons notified Mr. Smith immediately, "We can't use her anymore."

"Well, you know what to do. Get another firecracker before tomorrow. Take that one somewhere far away."

A few minutes after the men left, the two matrons returned to the room. They had encountered this kind of beating twice before. They placed Matilda in the shower, cleaning her inside and out. After waiting until midnight, they positioned the body where someone would find it in the morning.

***

Billie was staying with Juice for the night when he told her that he had been following Lenny. "He's going out again tonight. Please understand Lenny is my brother. I have to take care of him… Billie, I've never seen him like this."

"If anything happened to him… I'm going with you."

Juice and Billie held hands as they strolled to a nearby park, all the while keeping a watchful eye out for Lenny.

It was a Saturday night, and the town buzzed with activity. Billie enjoyed people-watching, reveling in the vibrant atmosphere. She also loved playing her favorite game, Find the Spy. Juice admired many things about Billie, but her playful nature was something he wished he could embrace as well.

"I'm going over there to get a pretzel. Do you want one?"

"No thanks." He reached into his pocket and handed her some cash. "On me."

Lenny was in a bustling tavern, seated at the bar, as he placed an order for a sandwich and a cold beer. The noise level was overwhelming, drowning out any possibility of engaging in conversation, so he resolved to call it a night. Just as he requested his check, a woman approached him. "Hi, are you alone?"

"I'm on my way home."

"That didn't answer my question."

"I have a girlfriend, but she's not here."

"So, you're alone."

"Excuse me, I am leaving."

The woman was standing on his side, holding the bar with one hand and the back of the barstool with the other. "You have no idea what you're missing."

Lenny was always a gentleman, but he was curious: "Is there a house where ladies like you congregate?"

"Excuse me?"

"Never mind. I need to leave."

"Why would you ask me that?" She stepped back.

Lenny stood up and left the bar, but the woman followed him. Once outside, she grabbed his arm and yelled, "What the hell did you mean by that?"

"Lady, leave me alone. Go back inside. Have some coffee."

The woman wouldn't let go. "What did you mean?"

Juice saw Lenny. He quickly realized that Lenny was in serious trouble. He glanced over at the pretzel cart where Billie was chatting with someone, prompting him to dash across the street.

"Hey man, I thought that was you."

"What are you doing here?"

"We're across the street." The woman disappeared into the bar. "What the hell was that all about?"

"I have no idea. She wouldn't take no for an answer."

"That's a switch."

"Billie is across the street getting a pretzel."

"Listen, brother, I know you're worried about me. I'm fine. Thank you for rescuing me. Where is Billie? I'll say hello, then go home."

Juice looked in the direction of the pretzel cart. It stood empty, save for the vendor waiting behind it. Without hesitation, they both jogged across the street to the vendor.

"The girl that was just here, with long black hair. Where did she go?"

"Sorry, I didn't notice."

"Is there a restroom somewhere?"

"Not that I know of."

Juice moved away from the cart. "I'll call her… *Hello, it's Billie, leave a message.*"

Lenny ordered, "Juice, go that way. I'll look down here." Lenny went toward the water where he saw a garbage can. There was a cord of some kind hanging out from the top. He put his hand through and tugged until a small purse came out of the trash. Lenny ran back, holding his phone to his ear. "Hi, Phil; Juice and I are together. Billie was getting a pretzel. Phil, she is gone. I found her pocketbook. Is Ben…?"

"He's here. Tell me where you are…"

***

The two men left Matilda's room and made their way back to the party bus. The second man poured himself a Scotch but chose to sit apart from the rest of the group. A sense of urgency washed over him, but he felt disoriented and unsure of their location. As he gazed at the darkened windows of the bus, something familiar caught his eye. It seemed the bus was equipped with a signal blocker, as he couldn't access navigation on his phone. He desperately needed to figure out where they had been and inform someone about the woman. With his head resting against the window, the bus suddenly lurched before it stopped. He was convinced he spotted a massive statue in the distance.

In an anonymous letter he sent to the State Police, he stated *I'm sure we were in Gloucester...*

Chapter 13

The overnight hours on the interstate were often bustling with massive trucks. Raney was driving her rig loaded with its usual cargo, making the journey from Portland to Portsmouth, then onward to Boston and Providence.

She enjoyed breakfast in Portsmouth just before dawn. True to her routine, she pulled into a rest area just a few miles from the New Hampshire border in Massachusetts. As she stepped out of her truck, she took a moment to stretch her legs and relieve the tension in her back before heading toward the door-marked woman.

An uneasy feeling washed over her as she noticed a pair of legs protruding from one of the two stalls. The door stood slightly ajar, prompting her to pull her sleeve over her hand and gently push it open. To her horror, Matilda's naked body was slumped over the toilet in the restroom stall.

"Dear God." Raney had taken first aid courses prior to embarking on her career as a trucker, primarily for her own benefit but also with the thought of being prepared for an emergency. She gently pressed two fingers to the woman's neck to find her pulse.

Raney ran back to her truck and called 911. She wanted to cover the body but hesitated, fearing she might contaminate the scene. Instead, she went inside the other stall. "I'm sorry, honey, but I have to go."

She was standing by the outside door when she heard the sirens. A State Police cruiser arrived in the vicinity a minute before the ambulance.

The two EMTs were perplexed, while the state trooper was horrified. He went to his car to get a camera, knowing they needed to get her to the hospital. He took pictures of the scene and placed yellow crime scene tape across the door before walking to the ambulance. The EMT in the back stated positively, "She has been cleaned up, then she was dumped here. There is no way this attack happened here." She was taken to Newburyport, the closest hospital in the area.

The ER doctor was more concerned with treating Matilda's injuries than identifying her. Her face was cut and bruised, and one eye was swollen shut. She had broken ribs and a fractured wrist. She was adamant with the officer, "When I'm done doing tests, I will come out, and your CSU people can come in and take your pictures, but not before."

***

Lenny and Juice were exhausted. They had been up all night. Juice told the same story over and over: "She was talking to someone. I didn't think anything of it. Phil, she was thinking about becoming a cop. My concern is that she started asking questions about Matilda. These are small, tight-knit communities. If she asked the wrong person the right question…"

"I know. We're going home. There is nothing more we can do here. Ben ordered the area cordoned off, and at sunrise, his team of agents would be there to investigate the area."

Juice was no stranger to sleepless nights, so he navigated the road home in his car. Phil took the wheel of Lenny's vehicle while Ben remained at the scene on his own. Upon returning to Cape Hope, Phil drove Lenny to his house, where Juice was already waiting. "You two are to stay out of this investigation. You both know why."

"Cap, I'm not going to argue with you, but you have to call us if they find anything."

"I'm letting Ben and his team do their jobs. I'm going to get some sleep. I suggest the two of you do the same thing."

Ben had been intently observing the pretzel vendor. The man was quite expressive, but Ben was certain he hadn't witnessed anything significant. He provided only a vague description of the woman Billie had been conversing with—she was large, somewhat butch… was the extent of his description. Lacking optimism, Ben assigned a rested officer to take charge of the investigation at the scene and headed back to Cape Hope to get some sleep.

Ben had been asleep only for a few hours when his phone rang. "Ben Malloy."

"Hi, this is Sargent Weller at the Danvers State Police. We just got a bulletin on a woman…"

"Matilda…"

"She was beaten. Her prints were in the system. She is your missing person. Special Agent Malloy, the report from the ER doctor says she was whipped, beaten and raped. Her face is a mess. The preliminary tox report says scopolamine, so as you know…"

"She won't remember. Sargent, where is she?"

"They took her to the ER in Newburyport."

"I know the hospital. Thank you, Sargent." Ben got dressed and went down to the house. Connie was in the kitchen. "Ben, good morning. Coffee?"

"May I have one to go? Phil and I need to go to Newburyport."

"Sure. I'll wake him up."

***

Billie began to awaken, sensing something was terribly wrong when she realized she couldn't move her arms. Lying on her side, her hands were cuffed together with what felt like leather straps. She found herself on a bed, completely naked, and her vision was obscured.

OK, so screaming probably isn't my best option right now. She concentrated, desperately trying to recall her surroundings. *Did that woman know more than she admitted? Am I still on the North Shore? Am I still in New England?*

She tensed at the sound of movement in the room. But when a large hand touched her breast, her instincts kicked in. Using her upper body for leverage, she bent her knees to her chest and, in one swift motion, thrust both feet out, sending the man crashing to the floor.

The loud thud echoed as her attacker fell back. Billie fell silent, feeling someone grasp her legs and secure leather straps around her ankles. They were pulled apart and fastened to the end of the bed. *This can't be good.*

She had no idea how long she had been there when she sensed movement in the room—actually, two people. Terrified, she didn't want to reveal her fear. She lay motionless as she was accosted by a man, a woman, and various implements.

When she entered the Coast Guard Academy, there had been seminars about surviving captivity at the hands of criminals, drug dealers, human traffickers, and pirates. Therapists have devised techniques designed to help one mentally escape from abuse or torture if applied correctly. Billie focused intently on blocking out the horror unfolding around her, drawing on memories of her days on the water with Colt and the time spent with Juice—especially the day they met and the first time they made love. Yet the individuals in the room with her were nothing short of sadists, pure and simple.

She couldn't withstand the pain; she let out a bloodcurdling scream.

The man tapped her on the head. "There you go."

Billie had fallen asleep. When she opened her eyes, she discovered she was clean, clothed, and free of restraints. *What kind of twisted mind would find that acceptable?* The remnants of the brutality she had endured echoed painfully both on her skin and deep within her psyche…

"Hello, hello. Are you OK?"

Billie thought she was hearing things. She sat up slowly.

"Hello? What is your name?"

Billie stood on the bed. "Billie. I was trying to find some missing women when the woman I was talking to stuck a needle in my arm."

"There was someone else in that room. I don't know what happened to her."

"I'm looking for two women. Matilda and Trinity." Billie was confused when she heard a chuckle. "Are you OK?"

"Well, Billie, you found me. I'm Trinity."

***

Phil and Ben picked up Lenny. He sat quietly in the back seat, his gaze fixed on the passing scenery outside the window. Phil broke the silence, informing him that a woman at a nearby hospital matched Matilda's description. Eventually, he reached out and placed his hand on Phil's shoulder.

"Cap, what did you mean by matching her description?"

Phil turned to the back. "She was beaten."

Lenny's face went from angry to grief-stricken in an instant. "What else."

Ben looked in the rearview mirror, then at Phil. "Go ahead."

"She was found at a rest stop in a toilet stall, naked and beaten. She has broken ribs and a broken wrist. Lenny, she had been roofied."

"And? Don't hold back. Tell me what I already suspect."

"Lenny, I can't say the word. You loved her before. You will still love her now. Right now, she is confused. She may not know you. You can talk to the doctor when we get there. Lenny, I called her Principal before we picked you up. You were listed as her in case of emergency. The form was scanned to the hospital."

"Detective, she is being well taken care of. A rape counselor has been called." Ben revealed

"She is going to need special care. I will pay for whatever she needs. I'm going to need some time to take care of her."

"Lenny, we will have time to figure that out."

"I'll drop you off at the door. She is still in the ER. The doctor will talk to you before she takes you in."

Lenny paced as he waited. Normally, he was a very patient man, but Matilda was his whole world, and he needed to see her.

He took out his badge and ordered "You need to take me to the woman that was brought in earlier."

"I'm sorry, but…"

"This badge means I can see her." He showed her his license. "I am also her emergency contact."

The nurse came out from behind the desk. "Sir, you have to wait for the doctor. She is not going to know you. The doctor will tell her who you are. You have to trust us. Unfortunately, we have experience with cases like this."

"She's not a case!" Lenny screamed.

"Sir…"

"Thank you. I'll take care of this gentleman." Dr. Monroe was the ER doctor on duty when Matilda was brought in: "Matilda has been taken to a room. She is still agitated. I told her you were here, but unfortunately, she doesn't remember you. She doesn't remember anything. She has been vomiting, which can sometimes happen with scopolamine."

"I don't care about that. I will help her. I need to be with her."

"Detective?"

Ben was talking to the State Police officer, while Phil needed to be there for Lenny. "Excuse me. Will his presence in the room hurt?"

"There is no way of knowing."

"Would you tell her Lenny is here? Tell her they have known each other for years, and they love each other very much…"

"She is confused."

"She needs to be eased back. She needs to see people who love her. Lenny and Tim Edwards are her best friends."

***

Both Tim and Lucy woke up when her phone vibrated. "Oh, sorry… Tim, it's Phil. Hi Cap, is it OK to put you on speaker?"

"Please. Tim needs to hear this… Juice and Billie followed Lenny last night. Long story short, Billie was at a pretzel cart talking to a woman while Juice and Lenny were talking across the street. Now Billie is missing, too. The feeling is the same people who took Matilda and Trinity, took Billie too."

"Phil…"

"Tim, there's more. That was Ben's conclusion after Matilda was found alive but beaten and drugged. Ben thinks Matilda was dumped, and Billie was taken to replace her."

"Where is she?"

"Tim, I need Lucy to stay in town. Lenny is, he seems like he is in mourning. The doctor said she was beaten, whipped and raped. You and Lenny know her best. You need to get to the hospital…"

"I'm on my way." Tim sprang out of bed, darted to the bathroom, and jumped into the shower, rinsing off quickly. Within five minutes, he was dressed and halfway out the door. Lucy sat on the bed, watching him rush out, her heart aching for their friends. Just as she was about to get up, Tim came back inside. Without a word, he leaned over, kissed her gently, and then stood up again, ready to leave. "I love you, sweetheart."

Lucy was stunned. "I love you too. Be careful."

"I'll call you."

Lucy waited until Tim was gone to call Phil back. "Cap, how is Juice?"

"Angry, mostly at himself for leaving her alone."

"I take it you are keeping this in-house?"

"For now, yes. I have to tell Colt."

"Should I tell Jack?"

"Yes, he's off. Juice and Lenny were up very late. Ben and I picked up Lenny. Maybe tell Jack what happened."

"What about Lizzy?"

"I'm going to call her. I'll be here for as long as it takes."

Lucy dressed for work and headed into town. As she arrived, she spotted Jack entering Brock's office with the twins. Parking at the station lot, she made her way to the office. Though Brock didn't know her well, Jack instantly recognized the expression of a cop bringing bad news "Hi girls, I need to speak to your Daddy's."

Lulu pointed at Brock, then Jack. "That's Daddy, that's Dad."

Lucy smiled. "I stand corrected."

Brock took their hands. "Can you sit here for a few minutes while Dad and I talk to Lucy?"

"OK, Daddy."

"What's wrong?"

Lucy tried to contain her emotions: "Matilda is in the hospital…"

Both Jack and Brock were in shock. "Lucy, I'll go with you to talk to Juice." Jack kissed Brock, then the girls.

"Don't worry about us. Come on, girls, we're going to the park."

Juice's back door was open. "Juice, it's Jack. Lucy and I are coming in."

Juice came out of the bathroom in a towel. "Billie?"

"Not yet. A trucker found Matilda…"

Juice sat at his kitchen table while Lucy explained, "Tim is on his way to the hospital."

"So, this is a Cape problem?"

"We don't know. Phil is calling Colt. They will discuss that, but he is more concerned about Billie right now. They are convinced Trinity and Matilda were together. She may not remember anything. Until the effects of the drug subside, even then, she may not remember."

"I know, I know. It's not likely they let her go if she knew where she was held."

"That's the current belief. I have to get to the station. I'll let you know as soon as I hear anything."

***

"Detective, Mr. Edwards, Matilda seems to be feeling better. I mentioned that she's in a long-term relationship with you, Detective and that you're one of her best friends. Unsurprisingly, she seemed somewhat ambivalent about my remarks."

"Doctor, I need to see her. I am prepared."

"Her ribs are broken on the left. One of her eyes is shut on that side, too."

"So, the monster that hit her is a lefty."

"Most likely, yes. Follow me."

Lenny went right in and sat beside her, taking her hand in his. "Tilly?" he said softly, gently caressing the top of her hand.

"Your hands are soft."

Lenny kissed her hand. "You always say that."

Matilda looked at Tim. "Are we friends too?"

"We've been friends for a long time. You waitress at my Pub sometimes."

Matilda moved her hand and grasped Lenny's hand.

"Tilly, I love you," he whispered, leaning in to kiss her cheek. Then he stood up and went to the hall.

Tim followed. "I'm going home, but I'll be back. Are you staying?"

"Ya, I'm not going anywhere."

Lenny went back into the room. Matilda's eyes were empty. He held her hand. "I love you."

***

Beau already knew from his earlier visits that the brothel used signal blockers. It explained why their phones weren't confiscated before getting into the car. After his first trip, he tried to trace the route back but couldn't—whatever they did to obscure the location worked perfectly. By the second visit, he was already looking for apps that might block the signal jammer. As he thought, he immediately felt a wave of grief hit him. *I will get you out of there.* He had bought an untraceable phone, a part of the plan he hoped wouldn't cost Trinity her life.

When he made his third appointment, it was with a purpose—to tell Trinity he had found her. When he arrived, they led him to the room where she was chained to the bed; her face turned toward the wall. She didn't react until she sensed someone was there. Slowly, she turned. Beau wanted to cry, but he forced himself to breathe in, then out, slowly and steadily.

He didn't undress. Instead, he sat down on the bed beside her, lying on his side, facing her. His hand rested on her hip for a moment as he considered his next move. It only took a few seconds before he gently moved his hand to her blindfold, lifting it up to her forehead.

Her eyes were closed, and she was cringing. He could tell she was afraid. Gently, he removed the piece of black cloth until it was completely off. Pressing his forehead against hers, he whispered, "Please, look at me. I'm not going to hurt you."

Trinity had been thinking about Beau so much that she thought she was imagining things. "Beau?" she whispered.

"Sweetheart, I don't know how, but I will get you out of here."

Beau embraced her as they lay on the bed.

"How did you find me?"

"I'm not proud of this, but a friend from college brought me here…"

"Was that you before? You didn't say anything, Beau, why?"

"I truly didn't know what to do. I'm a coward, Trinity. I didn't want to give you hope if I couldn't get you out."

"Where are we, Beau?"

"I have no idea. Have you been able to look behind the pictures and that tapestry?"

"I've looked for cameras and bugs, but no, I haven't looked behind anything on the walls."

"They use a signal blocker. I downloaded an app. I hope it will let me trace the location. Honey, I'm sorry I can't take you with me. If I could, I would schedule time with you every day, but I'm sorry, I can't." Beau couldn't look at her.

"Beau, this isn't your fault. You didn't put me here. Someone came to my house and took me. There are at least three other women here, probably more."

"There is another woman from town missing, too. I told the Police Chief you were missing. He called in the FBI. Sweetheart…"

"Beau, there are women here named Maggie, Harlow and Billie. She just got here."

"Have you seen the others?"

"No, we talked through the vent."

"Be careful, please. I can't lose you."

"Beau, I know you're married. I know you will do what you can, but I don't want you to ruin your life for me."

"I haven't been able to sleep…"

"Beau, how long have I been here?"

"About six weeks. I told the Police Chief as soon as I realized you were missing. Honey, seeing you here like this broke my heart, but I have to be careful. I don't want these people to disappear with you."

"I know, Beau, I know. Before you go, will you kiss me?"

Beau put his hands on the sides of her head. "I will get you out of here, I promise." They were both weeping as he kissed her.

"I have a phone. It has a locator. Hopefully, it can be traced. Where is a good place…?"

"See if there is room behind the books. Put it behind *The Stand*. It's pretty wide."

Beau hid the phone behind the book and headed to the bathroom. When he came out, he was drying his face with a towel. He climbed onto the bed, embraced her, and kissed her again. "Hold on to that... Phil was able to access your bank information. I paid your mortgage. I told Phil, my father, and my brother that I didn't want you to lose your house, but only my sister and my priest know the whole truth." He kissed her once more. "I'm sorry, but I have to go."

Beau was about to open the door when Trinity whispered, "Beau, I love you."

He turned back, kissed her again, and softly said, "I love you too." Then, noticing the blindfold, he gently placed it back over her eyes. "I love you too," he repeated before leaving.

***

Lucy went to the pub when she saw Tim's car parked on the side. When he wasn't at the bar, she headed to the office. "Hi, I'm afraid to ask," she said.

"She's alive, sweetheart. She's alive."

"OK, I have to get back. I'll see you at the house later?" Lucy felt a flutter of nerves; before Tim left for the hospital, he had said, "I love you," for the first time. When she responded with the same words, she meant every syllable. She hoped he truly felt the same way, too.

"Come back here, we can have dinner."

Lucy hesitated before turning around to leave. Tim knew his declaration had been sudden, but he meant it, so he stopped her ."Close the door." He got up, kissed her, and held his arms around her. He kissed her again. "I meant what I said this morning."

"Oh, did you say something?" Lucy said bashfully.

"Yes, I said I'd love to get a cat."

"Oh, me too… Tim, I meant what I said, too."

"Good. We can celebrate tonight."

"Is Matilda really going to be OK?"

"I don't think there is any way to know for sure. That animal hurt her... I can't explain, probably because I don't understand that kind of anger, but all of us together will make sure she is OK. I'm not sure what Lenny is planning, but I'm worried about him."

***

Lenny was sleeping in a chair in Matilda's room when his phone woke him up.

"Hey, Lenny, is she awake yet?"

"Hi Tim, no, she's still sleeping..."

"I'm awake, sweetie. Oh, Lenny, I knew you'd find me."

Lenny put his phone on speaker. "Matilda, we were all so worried about you."

"Hi, Timmy."

"I was there yesterday. I'll be back. I'll see you soon."

Matilda started weeping. "I knew you would bring me home."

Lenny rested his head on the pillow as Matilda lifted her hand to caress his face. "What happened to my hand?"

"Your wrist is broken." Dr. Monroe was standing in the doorway. "You have broken ribs on the left side, too. Are you hungry?"

"Lenny, would you call Timmy and ask him to bring me a frappe from the ice cream stand?"

"Sure." He kissed her forehead and started to walk out.

"Lenny, my babies."

"I've been staying there. Don't worry, they're fine. I'll be right back."

Matilda waited until Lenny was out the door. "There are other women in that place."

"What is the last thing you remember?"

"I was eating lunch."

"Do you remember what you had?"

"Um, no, not really."

"Did they feed you well?"

Matilda didn't want to think about it. "They did…You need to find the other women."

"There was a man here named Phil…"

"He is the Captain. Lenny works for him."

"He called the FBI. There was another woman who went missing the night before you were found. Do you remember any names?"

Matilda started crying. "Noooo…"

"That's OK…"

"No, it's not. They are being abused. Some of the people were cruel. I was blindfolded so…" She started crying again. "You need to find them."

"I am having the staff psychiatrist come in today. You need to talk about this."

"Lenny is the only person I need. I'm not a person who shares. Please, I need to go home."

Lenny was waiting outside the door. When he realized Matilda needed him, he went back in. "Tim is going to bring a chocolate frappe, and Lucy wants to come by. Is that okay with you?"

"I need to go home."

"Listen to me missy. You will be staying at my house. That way, the entire police and fire departments can take care of you."

"Lenny, who else is missing?"

***

Beau stood by the door to Andy's office, feeling like his world was falling apart...

Julie sensed something was wrong when he got home. "Your mood suggests you heard about Billie."

Can't be... "Billie, who?"

"She's in the Coast Guard and works with Colt. Molly is frantic. Lenny was somewhere trying to find Matilda, and Juice and Billie followed him. I don't have all the details, but Billie disappeared. Then, early yesterday, a trucker found Lenny's girlfriend in a toilet stall at a rest stop. That's all I know, except that she is in the hospital."

"Honey, I kept something from you. I don't know why. Honey, when I found out Trinity's mortgage was late, I paid it. I didn't want her to lose her house. Dad said everything else was in order. I'm sorry honey..."

"Beau?"

"Hi, Andy. I seem to be monopolizing a lot of your time."

"Have you decided to take my advice?"

"Do you want me to lose my family?"

"That's a rhetorical question, right?"

"Matilda was found. Andy..."

Andy closed the door. "I can counsel you, but your unwillingness to take my advice—Beau, what else happened?"

"One of the firefighters has a girlfriend; she is in the Coast Guard. She is missing now, too."

"Come on, Beau, you're letting me down. What else?"

"I told Julie I paid Trinity's mortgage."

"And?"

"She kissed me. She told me I was a good friend."

"And?"

"I went back to see Trinity to tell her I would get her out. She told me there were at least three other girls there. She told me their names. One of them is Billie…"

"The firefighter's girlfriend?"

"Abby's friend… Molly and Billie are friends."

"I know Molly. Beau, you know what you have to do."

"But I don't know where she is."

"You need to talk to Phil."

"Andy, I need you to go to Phil, tell him a parishioner confessed about going to the house, tell him he found Billie there…"

"You haven't changed a bit, Beau. You always have to have someone else do your dirty work…"

Beau walked out without another word.

***

Lizzy was preparing to meet with Brock when Lenny called. Matilda had flatly refused to speak with a counselor. Concerned about what might happen when Matilda returned home, her doctor asked Lenny if he had any suggestions.

"Elizabeth Cook, Lizzy."

"Would you talk to her?"

Lenny called right away. "Doc, Lizzy will be here in about an hour."

"Detective, she is in denial. She thinks she can heal on the outside and then go about her business as if nothing ever happened. Then, the next minute, she's crying uncontrollably, feeling like she's damaged goods."

"So, she is grieving. May I tell you about Matilda? She is a free spirit—confident, with a beautiful face and figure, and she knows it. When she works at Tim's Pub, she is the center of attention because everyone loves her. She's a flirt, Doctor, and she knows how to work a room. There isn't anyone who goes into that pub regularly who doesn't love her."

"Could that be what got her targeted?"

"I hope not. The other woman who is missing is in the Coast Guard— professional and analytical. She doesn't frequent bars or restaurants. Whoever took her obviously didn't know she was in the service because her CO wouldn't stop until they found her. This is a busy tourist town; haven't you had any other cases like this?"

"No. My fear is these people go after women who won't be missed; won't be reported missing."

"Well, they made a mistake with Matilda and Billie. That makes me afraid for the other women who are being held."

"The Agent seemed determined."

Lenny stepped back into Matilda's room. She stood by the window, clad in the oversized T-shirt and warm socks he had given her. He recognized that the doctor was right; she needed to speak with someone. He hoped Lizzy would be able to connect with her, but if that didn't work, Stella planned to discuss with Simon who he might recommend.

Lenny didn't say anything to Matilda; he was helpless.

"Lenny?" Lizzy whispered, "How is she?"

Lenny took Lizzy's hand. "The Matilda you know is gone. She is broken. I'm afraid I will never get her back. But what really breaks my heart is she will never get herself back."

"Oh, honey. I talked to Trip; you can bring Matilda to his house. Hilda will take care of her."

"That is very kind, but I already told her she is staying with me. Lucy, Tim, Connie, Phil, Stella, Kathryn…"

"Lizzy?" Matilda was walking toward Lizzy and Lenny. "Are you here to talk me into seeing a shrink? I don't need to talk to anyone."

"Of course, you don't. You have always known what's best for you. You don't need us."

"Elizabeth!" Lenny was surprised at Lizzy's lack of concern.

"Matilda, you don't need our help, right?"

Lenny was about to go to Matilda when a hand grasped his arm. Doctor Monroe tugged him toward her and whispered, "I don't think she wants sympathy. I believe your friend is on the right track. Come on, I'll buy you a cup of coffee."

Matilda sat in the middle of the bed. "Did I ask for this, Lizzy?"

"You know the answer to that. The best thing you can do for yourself is to move on as best you can without changing the person you were before. But I also think you need to talk about it." Lizzy tried to sit next to her. "Scooch over."

Lizzy held her hand. "I spent the night with Trip."

Matilda grinned. "I'm so happy for you." She barely finished the sentence before she started crying. "Was it wonderful?"

"Oh honey… truthfully, I think Annie was with us the first time, but I made him talk about it."

"You are very sneaky, Miss Elizabeth."

"Phil thinks someone else from town is there. She was new to town. She was doing some work for Beau. He was worried about her, so he told Trip."

"We could hear through the air vent, but I was afraid to say anything… Lizzy, have you ever thought you remembered something a certain way because that's how you wanted to remember it?"

"I don't follow?" She did, but she knew Matilda needed to talk it out.

"Tim told me about a guy that came into the bar. He said to stay away from him because he hated women, all women."

"Misogynist."

"Yes. The first man… Lizzy, the first man, I swear he was that guy. The way he was talking to me made it seem like the only thing I was good for was… he was so angry." Matilda squeezed Lizzy's hands. "I couldn't see him, but I will never forget his voice."

"Honey, Phil can use this. Tim provided the FBI agent with a photo of the man he warned you about. Honey, this is good. Matilda, look at me. This is great. Will you do me a big favor? Talk to Lenny and go home with him. I already brought your plants to his house. He is taking such good care of them."

"You think I need to talk to someone?"

"You can talk to me, Lucy, Connie, but yes, talk to a professional too."

"Lucy and Timmy?"

"Spending every free minute together, from what I hear."

"What about Juice and Billie?"

"I need to use the facility. I'm going to send Lenny back in."

"You can come in. I'm not going to fall apart."

"It's OK if you do. I'm not going anywhere." Lenny sat on the bed. "Is it OK if I hold you?"

"The only thing I had to keep me going was thinking about you holding me." She did what she always did with Lenny. She sat on his lap, facing him. She leaned forward and rested her head on his shoulder. "It's OK, you can touch me."

Lenny put his hands on her hips. Matilda put her good hand on his pec. "I'm afraid I'm never going to be the same. I'm afraid I can't be the woman you loved."

"Love Tilly. I still love you."

"Lizzy said you're taking care of my plants."

"I may be calling them by the wrong names. I think they're a little confused."

"You are such a good guy. Lenny, Lizzy didn't answer me before. How are Juice and Billie?"

Lenny caressed her hips. "I was going to different bars to listen, to see if I could hear anything. Juice was worried about me, so the other night, they followed me. Well, this woman was bothering me at one of the bars, so I left. She wouldn't take no for an answer and followed me to the sidewalk. Juice and Billie were across the street watching. Juice ran to me while Billie went to get a pretzel. Honey, we think the same people have her. We believe they already knew they couldn't keep you in the state you were in, so they needed another woman. Juice saw her talking to a woman. We think she asked the wrong questions…"

Matilda grabbed Lenny's shirt in her fist and started crying.

"I am so sorry. You needed to know the truth before I brought you home."

"Juice is going to hate me."

"You know that's not true. He was so relieved when he was told you were found."

Lenny looked at the door when Tim and Lizzy came in, followed by Doctor Monroe.

"Detective, maybe Matilda should get dressed."

Lenny glared at her, then looked down at Matilda. "Tilly, are you ready to go home?"

She was still crying. Tim squatted next to the bed. "Honey, I brought you a coffee frappe."

She looked at Tim. "Thank you. Would you tell Phil I think the bad man from the Pub was in my room? He was… he, he, he hurt me, Timmy." Tears were streaming from her eyes.

"I'll tell him, honey. I'll leave this on the table. You look tired."

"Lenny, maybe you should let Matilda take a nap before you bring her home."

"No, no, I am so comfortable." Matilda moaned. "Your hands are so soft." She closed her eyes.

Doctor Monroe whispered, "She didn't flinch when you touched her legs. That's a good sign."

"Because she trusts me. This, what we are doing now, is familiar and comfortable. She feels safe. Tim, please tell Phil…"

"I already called."

***

Beau went to the library to search for the locations of State Police barracks. After jotting down the Newbury address, he made his way to his office. Sitting at his desk, he stared blankly at his laptop, having begun to write a letter addressed "To Whom It May Concern" but struggling to formulate the next line.

His father had informed him about Matilda, which solidified his resolve to report to the authorities that he had visited the house. He needed to convey that the girl had mentioned three names: Maggie, Trinity, and Billie. Thoughts of the phone he had used for the appointment crossed his mind; he hoped they would be able to trace the phone number. He had been cautious when purchasing the phone, carefully surveying the area beforehand. Parking behind a building, he donned a baseball cap and paid cash for the device, which he had been assured could not be traced back to him.

He considered the first sentence. He didn't want the letter to be too long or too short… *you idiot, you're not Goldilocks*; *just write the damn letter…*

He used the vintage Underwood typewriter he had tucked away in his supply closet. After typing the letter, he read the finished product three times before sliding it into an envelope. The final step was to drive to a post office. He grabbed some mail he found in the outbox of his front office and set off toward Boston. He stopped at a mall, where he mailed everything together.

As he drove home, Beau couldn't shake thoughts of Andy. Should he be angry at him for expecting him to do the right thing? No, but he felt that way nonetheless. If it had been a different priest—someone who hadn't known him his entire life—would he still feel this way? Probably not.

He couldn't get Trinity out of his head. The day he met her, she was wearing yoga pants and a sports bra. At first, she was embarrassed and tried to put her jacket on, but Beau stopped her. "This is your house; you should be comfortable."

They sat at the kitchen table. At first, Beau was all business, but as Trinity began to relax, she started warming up to him. Initially, he seemed a bit too upper-crust for her taste, but as they exchanged jokes, he gradually let down his guard. Trinity was attractive even without makeup; her eyes sparkled when she smiled, making him feel special. She was charming, funny, smart, and athletic, and Beau found himself captivated. By the end of their first meeting, he was contemplating taking her to bed, but Trinity abruptly ended the conversation. "I'll have a few ideas for you in a couple of days."

Beau felt like he was getting the bum's rush, so he quickly set a date and time to meet her on his way home, thanking her for her time. This initiated a series of meetings at her home, each one lasting longer than the last. Each gathering featured food, wine, and plenty of laughter.

Beau had numerous affairs, primarily fleeting one-night stands, but Trinity was different. He felt like a college kid sowing his wild oats. While he had no interest in settling down, that decision was suddenly made for him by his father. His friend Harold had a daughter, Julie, whom he deemed perfect for Beau. She was reserved, attended prestigious private schools, and was Catholic, which mattered greatly to both of Beau's parents. Beau liked Julie and eventually grew to love her, but there was never a spark between them. With Trinity, however, he felt an undeniable chemistry.

Beau parked in front of the rectory, walked into Andy's office, and closed the door behind him. "I sent a letter to the State Police. I gave them all the information I had."

"Does this make everything all better in your mind? Beau, what about Julie?"

"You only seem to care about Julie when you can throw her in my face."

"Your ideas about marriage and trust are a bit skewed."

"Skewed? You want me to tell Julie the truth. That will end my marriage. Isn't it against the rules for a priest to recommend ending a marriage?"

"You did something that broke your vows."

"These conversations are beginning to circle. I come to you for help, and all I get is sermons. I have never professed to be perfect."

"You always have an excuse…"

"I've had time to think about all these heartwarming discussions we've been having. I needed advice. I poured my heart out to you. Everything you wanted me to do would have led to the end of my marriage. Then I remembered you entered the seminary right after Julie and I got married. You two have always been close. I never thought much of it because I knew she missed having a brother, and you were there for her…"

"You have lost your mind."

"I came to you because I loved you, and I thought you would try to help me."

"I couldn't condone what you did, Beau."

"I am going to figure out a way to tell Julie the truth, but I won't let her leave me without giving me a divorce."

"Beau, when you left Trinity, how was she?"

Beau wiped a tear from his cheek. "She was scared to death. It broke my heart to leave her there." He turned to look out the window. "I didn't put her there, but I feel responsible for her." Turning back around, he continued, "Did you know Matilda was released? They beat the crap out of her. Lizzy told Dad she is a shell of the woman she was before. I did the best I could in the midst of a very difficult situation. Julie and Trinity are two distinct women—opposites. I love them both."

"I know. I'm sorry, Beau. I'm going to call Lizzy. Maybe I can help Matilda."

"Andy, you have always been my best friend. I'm sorry."

Chapter 14

The mansion that housed the abducted women was truly grand. In its heyday, it served as the summer residence for a Gilded Age millionaire. While many tycoons of that era built their lavish homes in Newport and Long Island, a select few from Boston preferred the North Shore, just thirty minutes north of the city. This house had remained in the same family since its construction. A few years ago, a restoration team came in to redesign the interior. The third floor featured six bedrooms, each with its own private bath. The second floor housed the kitchen and storage areas, while the first floor was renovated to include two suites for the permanent staff—both women who were thoroughly vetted and required to sign rock-solid Non-Disclosure Agreements. These women were ex-cons, chosen not only for their size and strength but also for their relevant experience. One worked in hospitality, while the other was a Certified Nursing Assistant. One prepared meals, and the other maintained cleanliness throughout the house. Additionally, there was a handyman. A couple occasionally utilized a basement suite; they were used to assess the suitability of the women brought to the mansion. Outside of the mansion, they led remarkably privileged lives, complete with a home, friends, and a successful gift shop in one of the nearby seaside communities. Friends described them as the perfect couple, but they harbored a darker side as sadists.

The staff was occasionally summoned for meetings, and on this particular day, they were informed of Matilda's departure. Mr. Smith, fully aware of her background, needed to ensure her status was properly documented. Although they had never needed to eliminate a woman before, they had a contingency plan in place just in case.

It was decided that the married couple should investigate Matilda to assess whether she posed a risk to their business. They needed to travel to Cape Hope to determine Matilda's fate. However, there was one issue: they were known within their inner circle as a couple who enjoyed entertaining women. They typically avoided towns near their gift shop, not wanting to be linked to the people they associated with. So, they headed to the local pub and took a seat at the bar, where they both began to flirt with Naomi.

***

Lenny brought Matilda to his house, hoping to create a welcoming environment for her. Lizzy and Lucy joined in to help bring some of her belongings from her home, aiming to make her feel more at ease. Although Matilda wished for solitude, Lenny reassured her that Lucy, Molly, and Lizzy would take turns staying by her side.

Before they left, Lenny had discussions with the rape counselor and Dr. Monroe. The gynecologist who had treated Matilda advised her to observe a month of celibacy. While she wasn't pregnant, tests showed the presence of birth control in her system that didn't align with the prescription Lenny had found at her house. The rape counselor couldn't provide definitive advice, as Matilda refused to see her. She insisted she wouldn't bear her soul to someone who knew nothing about her, claiming that all she truly needed was Lenny.

The doctor suggested that Matilda would probably be more comfortable taking an oatmeal bath. On his way to the hospital, Lenny stopped at the drugstore to pick up something suitable for her comfort.

When Matilda went inside his house for the first time since they began their relationship, she paused in the middle of the living room, taking it all in.

"Tilly?"

"I don't know where to go."

"The doctor said you might want to take a bath."

Matilda held his arm. "I still don't know where to go."

Lenny showed her the bedroom and suggested she look around while he got the bath started. He was squatting next to the tub, pouring the oatmeal powder into the water, when she came in and put her hand on his shoulder from behind. "Will you help me so I won't fall?"

Lenny put his hand on Matilda's.

"Maybe, since we're finally alone, you should see the whole picture." She inhaled deeply and removed her shirt. Her light brown skin, once soft and flawless, had lost its luster, now marred by the brutal aftermath of a vicious, inhumane act.

Lenny stood up, turned around, and kissed her softly. "You have always been, and will always be, beautiful." He embraced her carefully, feeling the welts on her back. He didn't want to hurt her. "Please tell me if I'm hurting you."

"I have missed having you hold me. I missed your hands, your soft, gentle hands." Matilda was recalling her days in the house: "I know you would never hurt me."

Lenny kissed her forehead. "Let me help you in the tub. Do you need anything?"

As she eased her body into the water, she held Lenny's hand. "Just you." He didn't want to leave her alone; her emotional state was concerning, but he needed to let her know he trusted her. "I'll be fine. Thank you, sweetie."

"I'll be in the bedroom. Holler when you're done." He reluctantly gave her privacy. He had a vantage point from the bedroom that allowed him to watch without her awareness. Anxiety gnawed at him, fearing she might lose hope and slip into the water. He understood that her grief was legitimate and recognized her need for time, but she also needed him.

He watched as she leaned forward to drain the water. He casually walked back in. "I can run the shower gently, and you can rinse off if you'd like."

"I'd like that, thank you." She stood in the tub as Lenny rinsed the soap from her skin.

Lenny reached to the back of the door and helped her into a soft terry spa robe. "This should be more comfortable than a towel. Lizzy and I brought your clothes. I moved my things to the spare room and gave you my bureau. I'll let you decide where I'll sleep…"

Matilda looked scared. "With me, Lenny, with me." She embraced him.

"OK, I didn't want to assume."

"I need your help. I'm supposed to put this ointment on my wounds." She sighed. "Ugh, I hate that word. I wish we could call them something else."

"Next time, maybe you can ask me to grease your chassis."

Lenny was ready when Matilda began to cry. He had been informed that sadness could envelop any situation or conversation, often springing up unexpectedly. Already cradling her, he gently lifted her chin and said, "So, is that a no?"

"I'm sorry I kept so much distance between us. I've wasted too much time not spending every free minute with you."

"No regrets, honey, OK? I'll put this stuff anywhere you want."

Matilda attempted to smile as she rested her head on his chest. "If you can spackle the scrapes and sand everything down, I'm sure my chassis will eventually be as good as new."

***

"This is Ben Malloy… You're kidding. Can you scan that and send it to me at… then overnight the original to the FBI forensic lab? I'll send you the address." Ben went to the kitchen. "Good morning, folks. Phil, I have something. Can we go to the office?"

Lenny was sitting at his desk when Phil and Ben rushed in. As much as he wanted to join them, he knew he couldn't get involved. He watched as they huddled around something Phil had just printed out in the office.

"Lenny? Lenny? Detective Clarke?"

"Huh, oh, I'm sorry. What's up, Boom Boom?"

"Are you OK?"

"Have you ever seen full-body photos of a woman who has been beaten?"

"Oh, Lenny…"

"I have. I thought, *well, at least she'll heal*. I know now that was a very simpleminded attitude."

"Tim said he thinks it will be harder for her to heal emotionally."

"Tim knows her pretty well. She has lost her spirit, her confidence, her self-worth. She is suffering the loss of a loved one, the loss of herself. Lucy, she thinks it's her fault Billie is missing."

"What can I do to help?"

"At this point, I'm not sure. She insisted I come to work."

"She's been home for a few days now. She needs to get used to being alone. She also needs to get angry; she needs to feel like she has some control. Has she ever told you about her life before she came here?"

"She refuses to talk about it. I wanted a relationship with her, so I stopped asking."

"I wonder…"

"I've wondered the same thing…" Lenny looked toward the front door when he saw Beau come in. Lucy saw the anger on Lenny's face. "Detective?"

"It's nothing."

Phil and Ben called Beau in for further questioning. "The Danvers State Police received an anonymous letter," they began. "Beau, I have to ask straight out. Have you been to a brothel…"

Beau was so surprised by the question he screamed "What? Are you for real?"

Ben was terse, "Answer the question."

"No! Where is this coming from?"

"Your story never quite held water with me."

"I was told I was cleared."

"New evidence, Mr. Fredericks."

Beau looked at Phil. "What I told you is the truth whether you choose to believe it or not." Beau was scared, but he wasn't going to let this man trick him. "Agent, I went to Phil as soon as I knew Trinity was missing…"

"After you talked to your father."

"I wanted his advice. I also didn't want him hearing rumors about my visit to the station. This is a small town; my family is well-known. Phil, I didn't do whatever it is you're trying to accuse me of…" Beau hung his head then looked up at Phil. "A brothel? Really? I didn't hurt Trinity… wait, did this letter say I was there?"

"No. The person who wrote it said he was with a group of men. From the tone of the letter, it sounded as if one of the men he was with could have been the one who beat Matilda."

"So why are you wasting your time talking to me?"

"Where were you this past weekend? We are not sure when Matilda was hurt, so if you could be specific…"

"I was here. I was at the office for a while. Julie and I went to dinner. Um, what else…"

"Beau…" Shaw came in to talk to Phil and Ben after his office received a copy of the letter. "Are you charging Beau in this case?"

"No. We cleared him before we got the letter. Due diligence, Shaw."

"Beau, why didn't you call me or Kathryn?"

"It didn't cross my mind."

Phil stood up. "Oh, Shaw Fredericks, this is Special Agent Ben Malloy."

Shaw held his hand toward Ben. "My brother didn't hurt Matilda. Phil, you should know him better than that."

"Shaw, if it were anyone else, you would have been furious if we hadn't talked to him again."

Beau stood up. "It's OK."

"Agent Malloy, did your office check the postmark?"

"It has been overnighted to Boston. I asked that if anything else comes into any of the barracks, they scan it and send it to my office. They will examine it for any clues."

Beau left, and Shaw was talking to Ben when Ben got a call from his SAC in Boston… "Thanks."

"Well, the Newbury State barracks received a letter too. They scanned it to Boston, where one of the Agents, who is also a linguist, looked at both letters. She is positive they were written by different people."

"So, Beau is in the clear again."

"Mr. Fredericks, this letter mentioned the names of three women at the brothel: Maggie, Trinity and Billie."

"So, this is a bigger problem than imagined. Agent, could the second letter be someone else from the same group of men?"

"It could be, yes."

"Shaw, when I spoke to Matilda, she said she had no way of knowing the day or time while she was there. The ER doctor estimated her injuries were no more than ten to twelve hours old. She was found just after six in the morning."

"Phil, I saw Beau and Julie in their car around six on Saturday. Dalton was with me."

"Shaw, I never thought Beau hurt Trinity."

"Mr. Fredericks, your brother is in the clear. Would you mind looking into this as well?"

"I was planning on it. Thank you, Agent."

As Shaw talked to Lenny in the squad room, Ben closed the door. "Phil, there was more in the second letter. A cell phone was left behind a book in one of the rooms. The hope was it would be able to be traced. The tech couldn't get an exact location, but with information from both letters, we are hopefully able to narrow it down to a town." Ben showed

Phil his tablet. "Tell me, does the timing of the man's departure from the house and the approximate time he saw the statue, combined with the vicinity of the phone, give you an idea of where this house may be?"

Phil looked at Ben. "Are you kidding me?" He leaned against the edge of the cabinet behind his desk and rubbed his face "How long has this been going on, and why haven't we seen missing persons reports before this?"

"People who run these types of places are cagey and, unfortunately, smart. The women before now may have been outside the area of a local BOLO. We've already determined the women are solitary. If Beau hadn't reported Trinity, I'm sure we wouldn't have considered Matilda's disappearance an abduction."

"Why not?"

"Her history is incomplete, meaning she is a mystery. She has a past. We know where she was born, where she went to school and even where she worked while in college. But she had a long break after graduation before she moved to Cape Hope."

"A lot of kids take a gap year. Maybe she went to Europe. Not very unusual these days."

"No, but even you admitted she is a very private person, and no, that is not a reason to investigate her."

"Billie's abduction was a deviation. There is no way they knew she was in the service. I can't believe they had time to look at her ID before they dumped her purse, and that is only based on a sincere hope on my part."

"Do you think Matilda would talk to Naomi? She has real experience with, well, she was drugged and held by a serial killer. She is lucky to be alive."

"In this case, because she is helping Tim at the Pub, I think she might, even if it is just to catch up with what the regulars are up to."

***

Billie had an especially awful visitor before she went to sleep. He was huge, reeking of garlic and sweat, and to make matters worse, his *happy ending* wasn't happening. By the time he finally rolled off her, she desperately wanted a shower, but as always, she just drifted off to sleep instead.

When she woke, she immediately noticed she had been cleaned up, and her outfit for the day had already been laid out—casual running pants and a light shirt. About a week into her stay, a treadmill had appeared in her room, along with a pair of sneakers. She wasn't the type to sit around, so the addition had been a welcome one. She stretched, hopped on the treadmill, and began jogging. Before long, she was running, then sprinting, as if she were being chased.

As her momentum decreased, she eased into a jog before coming to a complete stop. Her eyes locked on the two pictures hanging on the wall. From her psychology classes at the Academy, she understood one thing clearly—the people who held her captive were always watching. She knew they wouldn't trust her to stay put, so she was certain every move she made was being scrutinized.

Clunk, swish. Billie had come to recognize the familiar sounds of her meals being delivered. At first, she was reluctant to eat, but the tempting smell of the food gradually encouraged her to give in. The food was good, and the accommodations were undeniably luxurious. She knew the people behind this operation had money—but why a brothel? It didn't make sense.

She had been too scared to check behind the pictures. There was nothing on the wall next to or behind the bed. The wall opposite the door led to the bathroom and housed the bookcase and TV stand. The longer wall, where the two landscape paintings hung, she assumed, must be the exterior wall. After breakfast arrived, she sat at the desk, which faced that long wall. As she ate, she contemplated what might happen if she dared to look behind the paintings. She knew there would be consequences if she got caught—she learned that lesson on her first day here. Weighing the risk of punishment against the hope of discovering a possible escape route, she hesitated.

After Billie slid her empty breakfast tray through the slot in the door, she flicked on the TV. Determined to find something reflective, she believed it might help her send out an SOS. Although she understood that this risky move could cost her life, she felt compelled to take the chance. The problem was, she had to find a window first…

"Hello? Are you there?"

Billie stood on the bed. She whispered, "Ya, I'm here."

"Are you OK?"

"I suppose. I wish I knew if Matilda was here. How many women have you talked to?"

"Three, including you."

"Do you have windows?"

"I'm afraid to look."

"Me too…"

"Gaaaaaahhhhhd… no more…. Kill me, please just kill me."

***

Lenny and Tim engaged in a serious discussion about what would be best for Matilda's state of mind. They both understood that she would despise having decisions made on her behalf, yet her mental state was deteriorating. Lenny decided to head to the pub, where they could speak to Naomi together. She had planned to bring lunch during Lenny's work hours and would do her utmost to encourage Matilda to open up. Lenny instructed her to simply knock and walk in. "I'll leave the door unlocked."

Naomi knocked twice and opened the door. "Hello, Matilda? Tim and Lenny said you like the club sandwich. Matilda?"

"Who are you?" Matilda hid in the kitchen when she heard the voice.

"I'm helping out at the Pub until you're ready to go back. A lot of people are asking about you."

Matilda stepped out of the kitchen. "How do you know Lenny?"

"Tim introduced us. He talked about you a lot. He didn't tell you why I was there?"

"No, I mean, he may have. As you can see, I've been…" She looked down. "Sorry, thank you for the sandwich."

"Matilda, I'm undercover at the Pub. I'm an FBI agent."

"So, this isn't shocking for you. I hope you haven't seen this kind of thing too much."

"Unfortunately, I have. May I come in?"

"Oh, sure." Matilda went to the couch. "Please sit… have some of the sandwich. I'm not sure I can open my mouth wide enough. Any suggestions?"

Naomi went to the kitchen and came back with two plates and some paper towels. "May I?"

"Sure."

Naomi took one wedge of the sandwich and placed it on a plate, then put another plate on top and pressed down. She removed the top plate to reveal a very flat sandwich to Matilda.

"I like your style. Thank you." Matilda took a few bites. "So why are you really here… I'm sorry that sounded really bitchy."

"I was on a case last year. There was a serial killer. I was positive the person that was suspected was innocent. The real killer took me and kept me drugged. You met Ben, right?"

"The Agent that was at the hospital? We met, but I don't remember him."

"He saved my life."

"Why did he keep you alive?"

"He liked to torture, then when he got bored, he killed. He knew I was FBI; I think he kept me for leverage, but I'm really not sure."

"Why did you go back? It's a really dangerous job."

"I learned very early in my recovery that I didn't want that man to break me. I didn't want him to win. If I didn't go back to my life as it was before that case, that man would have won."

"You know who hurt you, so you have answers. I'll never have answers."

"You may not, but there are other women who may benefit from the smallest clue, the tiniest bit of information. There may be something you could tell us that may not mean much to you but could be the clue needed to find these people."

"Don't I need time to recover before I'm questioned?"

"No one thinks you did anything wrong. You're the only person we know of that got away. Before I came here, Ben told me it was OK to tell you, but the State Police had received two letters from men who had been to the brothel. They were both concerned about the women who were there. We still have no idea where it is, but we know it is nearby."

"If those people think I knew something…"

"If those people thought you knew something, they never would have let you go. They roofied you for a reason."

"Naomi, I heard the girls screaming; one was always screaming, I don't think because they were hurting her but because she was horrified about what was being done to her." Matilda paused. "The first man in my room wanted to hurt me for the pleasure of hurting a woman. He attached clips to my nipples, then hit a switch… Naomi, that was the first time in my life I wanted to die. After that, some of the women tried to talk to me but I was so scared. I feel like if I had talked to them, I would have more information, but I couldn't go through that again."

"You had to do what was best for you. You were in survival mode. You still are. Tim told me he knew nothing about you before you got here. He said he loved and respected you too much to ask. I know people have things they are ashamed to talk about…"

"Is that why you're here?"

"No, absolutely not, but what you said made me think of what Tim told me. It made him sad. With me, since I can't talk about my work, it's hard to start a relationship. People sometimes wonder if I'm hiding some deep, dark secret."

"So, you think if I don't talk about my past, I won't recover?"

"What the hell do I know? I'm just a bartender. I'm sorry. I know, with me at least, it was easier talking to a stranger; someone who wasn't trying to shrink my head."

"Who was that?"

"It was someone from a case who became best friends with an Agent. She understood. She didn't try to read into what I was saying. She listened."

"Timmy and Lenny know me best. When I came here, I wanted to start over, not because something awful happened to me but because I wanted to be a person I liked. I didn't want to conform to what people expected me to be." Matilda sobbed.

Naomi sat next to her. "Which was what?"

"I needed to be me, but somewhere else."

"You're talking to an FBI agent. The agent hears that maybe you got mixed up with the wrong people. But me, the person who is getting to know you, hear maybe your family expected you to live up to an image, maybe? The friend also hears that maybe you don't want your friends here to know the person you were before because you're afraid they will change their opinion of you, maybe?"

"Lenny and Timmy love me."

"That is obvious."

"I'm not the person I was expected to be… I was expected to be reserved and proper and that is not me. I liked to flirt and that was unacceptable. I had friends who were considered undesirable. I went to college, got my degree, did some backpacking in Europe and I disappeared with my trust fund. When I came back, I came here and ended up at the Pub having a sandwich and flirting with Tim; we became friends right away. He asked me if I wanted a job. In a couple of hours, my life changed. I bought a house, and since I didn't have anything, I bought essentials in furniture stores. But one day at work, I asked Tim about good antique stores. He suggested I talk to his friend Lenny." Matilda started sobbing. "I love him so much. The last time I saw him, before all this, he asked me to move in with him. I was going to tell him yes, but only if he'd marry me. I can't ask him to marry me now."

"I don't know him, but I will bet you a million dollars he would marry you in a second."

Lenny was standing at the back door, not intending to snoop but reluctant to interrupt as Matilda finally began to open up. He didn't care about the specifics; what mattered most was that she was willing to talk about anything at all.

He entered just as the conversation was winding down and caught the tail end of her talking about getting married. Before her abduction, he had bought a ring, fully intending to be prepared if the opportunity presented itself.

"Helloooo." Lenny came through the kitchen.

Matilda wrapped her arms around him and whispered, "I missed you."

"I came home to check on you. Do you need anything?"

"I want to make dinner. Could you get a few things?" She knew Lenny would want to talk to Naomi, so Matilda went to the kitchen to make a list.

"Thank you for coming."

"So many people asked about her. I was intrigued. I obviously don't know her, but I think she is going to be OK." She whispered, "But she needs to talk about what happened to her in that house. Anything she remembers could be the crumb we need to get these people."

"Sweetie, get something for the grill. Will Juice come over for dinner when he's off?"

"I will ask. I have to go. I love you."

"Me too… Naomi, I just remembered something. I was walking to town the day I was taken. There was a boat on the cove. I thought it was funny because the man at the helm looked like Ernest Hemmingway…"

***

Coast Guard investigators and Ben convened with Colt at his office to strategize their next steps. Colt also requested Shaw's presence, eager to discuss the potential use of his father's dock. The proposal involved borrowing Molly's twenty-four-foot Cape Dory sailboat. Colt believed Trip's dock would provide an ideal vantage point for the female investigator, Merritt. The plan was for her to conduct surveillance from Molly's boat, with the added option of utilizing a pool house for overnight observation. Additionally, Colt would moor a skiff to the dock, giving Merritt a means to explore the surrounding houses.

Merritt was young and attractive and would draw attention in a bathing suit. She and Billie were friends from their time at the Academy, where Merritt had taught a self-defense class prior to applying to CGIS. Their friendship ran deep, and when Merritt learned of Billie's disappearance, she quickly devised this plan and presented it to her superior. Colt then proposed reaching out to his friend, the Assistant District Attorney.

The whole plan came together after Ben received a call from Naomi, who informed him that Matilda was beginning to regain memories from the day of her kidnapping. Initially, he was uncertain if her recollections were genuine until she described a man in a boat who resembled Ernest Hemingway. A corroborating account from Coop provided the necessary justification to proceed with the plan.

Merritt had resided in New London until her recent transfer to CGIS in Boston, where Billie had assisted her in finding an apartment north of the city. To Merritt, Billie was like the little sister she had always wanted. Upon Colt's call relaying the news, she immediately requested to be assigned to the case. Her boss, lovingly nicknamed Skipper, agreed.

Merritt packed her bags and met Colt and Skipper at Colt's office.

"Tell me what to do, Chief."

"Molly has to bring her rig to the cove. Once it's there, you can talk to her about the accommodations. You are welcome to stay in the pool house as well. Molly and Juice want to meet you, that is, if you want to come to the Pub with us…"

"Oh yes, that would be great. How is Juice?"

"He is crazy about Billie, so he is heartbroken. I'll call Tim to ask him to reserve the big table." Colt went outside to call Tim. Then he called Phil, "I want to keep you in the loop."

"Ben just came back from that meeting. Thank you for the call."

"How is Lenny?"

"Better. Naomi talked to Matilda today. He said she was better. With time… ah hell, I don't know if she'll ever be the same again."

Juice was sitting at the bar when Colt, Molly, Merritt, and Skipper came in. He had been talking discreetly to Naomi about Matilda. "She opened up to me. She feels responsible. I don't think there is anything soothing that could be said that would change her mind on that subject."

"I have to try. Thanks for your help." Juice went to the table. After Colt made introductions, Merritt got up. "Billie would be OK with me giving you a hug." She embraced him. He held on to her and whispered, "Thank you for coming. Please be careful."

She stepped back. "Always."

***

"Helloooo"

Lenny and Matilda looked at each other and shrugged. When Matilda saw it was Father Andy, she began to withdraw. "Tell him…"

"No, honey, you should talk to him."

"I'm afraid I'll say the wrong thing. I don't know how to talk to a priest."

"He's a regular guy Tilly… Hello Padre, come on in."

"Detective. Matilda, we met at the Pub."

Matilda had her arms around Lenny. "Thank you for coming, Father, but I'm not Catholic."

"That's OK; some of my best friends aren't Catholic or men. Uncle Trip told me what happened. I'm a really good listener."

"I'm going to talk to Phil. I won't be long. The Padre will take good care of you."

Matilda sat on the couch with her knees bent up to her chest, wrapping her arms around her lower legs.

"Your body language is screaming; you would rather be talking to anyone but me."

"I don't need to talk to anyone."

"Because you are strong enough to handle this on your own or because you are embarrassed about what happened to you?"

"I'm not a person who shares feelings."

"Well then, may I share with you what people said to me when I asked about you?"

"This isn't necessary."

"I believe it is. Everyone said you would do anything for a friend. They also all said they needed you to be well again because their lives would be incomplete without you…"

Matilda was weeping. "Why are you doing this?"

"Do you think you can go back into the Pub and be the Matilda everyone loves?"

"If I thought I could do that, I wouldn't be having such a hard time. What do I say when I'm asked where I've been? Or is Tim going to tell everyone to act like I haven't been missing? It's going to be hard."

"Ease your way back. Go in for lunch with Lizzy and Connie."

"How do I accept that I am the reason Billie is missing?"

"There are people who are kidnapping women. You, my dear, had nothing to do with that."

"Juice was watching out for his friend. I feel responsible."

"Have you talked to him?"

"I can't…"

Lenny had paused next door to have a word with Juice. Just a few moments later, Juice entered through the back door. "Hello, Padre. Hi, Matilda," he greeted warmly. He settled onto the couch and affectionately kissed her cheek. "I was so relieved when Jack and Lucy told me you were safe."

"I am so sorry…"

"For getting kidnapped?"

"I'm the reason Billie is missing."

"No. If anyone is responsible it is me for allowing her to come with me."

"I'm sorry, Father. Can I get you some coffee?"

"Hey, what about me?"

"Do you want coffee?"

"No."

"I knew that. You never drink coffee at this time of day when you're off shift. Father?"

"Please, black." Andy stood up when Matilda left the room. "Juice, she will forgive herself."

"Padre, there are so many things going on in my head. Billie is strong, but is she strong enough to survive the likes of men who go to brothels?"

"I did some research. A lot of the men are lonely; some need someone to talk to. Is thinking about what is going on there going to help Billie and the other women. No. It certainly isn't going to help you. There are people trained to find the criminals associated with this kind of activity. Let Phil and the FBI do their jobs…"

"May I say something, Father?" Matilda handed him a mug of coffee. "I've decided I was lucky someone did this to me, or I know I'd still be there. I won't repeat what some of those men and women did. They are sick, depraved people, and for you to tell Juice anything different isn't fair to him, or me, or the girls that are still there."

"I believe in hope and the power of prayer, Matilda."

"I guess I'm a little doubtful of a God who would let something like this happen."

"I don't doubt Him, Matilda, even when people get sick or there are disasters. God has a plan, and I won't question that. If I did, I would have to leave the priesthood because I would be of no help to anyone."

"Thank you for coming here. I do appreciate your concern. I'd be lying if I said I know I will recover emotionally. Maybe after my injuries heal. Maybe after I go back to the Pub, I do hope I can be the Matilda that Lenny fell in love with. He is really the only person keeping me together right now."

Juice grasped her hand. "I talked to Naomi today. She really likes you."

"Did she tell you all my secrets?"

"She said she really likes you and admires you, and she hopes you will again be the person she keeps hearing about."

"I hope I can be her too. Thank you, Father."

"Padre, I'll walk you out. Matilda, you are special to all of us. We are going to do everything in our power to help you."

Juice and Andy left by the back door. "Padre, I know you would never break the sanctity of the confessional, but if you hear anything, that could help."

"I will try to figure out a way."

Chapter 15

Dalton liked Billie, prompting her to seek out an introduction with Merritt. Given that Shaw had already met Merritt, he was going to facilitate the introductions to his father and Hilda.

As a teacher, Dalton was free for the summer, and she eagerly anticipated spending quality time with Shaw. He always made an effort to carve out time for their summer plans, but this year, their getaway was on indefinite hold due to a trial that kept getting postponed.

"Julie told me Beau was questioned again."

Shaw groaned. "I've never been a fan of Agencies swooping in to take over a case, but Phil called them in. I've never known Beau to do the right thing, maybe he's changed? I don't know. What I do know is I was pissed when I saw Beau being questioned."

"Abby said she was proud of him for stepping forward. It could have gone either way, but Julie pointed out that this woman could have come back the next day. He didn't need to tell Julie anything, but he did. Did he tell you he paid this woman's mortgage so she wouldn't lose her house?"

"No, really, and he told Julie?"

"She told me. Maybe he has changed."

"I assumed they had an affair; he broke her heart, and she took off."

"That still could be the case."

"Will you pinky swear not to breathe a word?"

"You sound like Abby. If you ask me to keep it to myself, yes, of course."

"Two State Police barracks received anonymous letters telling of a brothel somewhere in the area. Both said they were taken there by friends. Both said they were horrified by what they saw. A linguist at the FBI said they were written by different people. One of them said the woman he was with gave him three names. Maggie, Trinity, and Billie."

"Oh God. Does your boss know?"

"Ya, that's the thing, he passed it off to me…"

"Whoa, that can only mean one thing."

"That was the first thing I thought, too. He has to know something about it."

"Did you say anything?"

"No, but if he wanted to cover it up, he could have done it himself. Is he passing it off to me so I will become the fall guy?"

"To set you up?"

"Face it, he has never liked me."

"Prosecuting innocent people is not your style, Shaw."

"This guy is using his office to further his own political agenda. Sorry, don't get me started."

"Let me change the subject. You're father and Lizzy have been spending a lot of time together."

"He is happy. I'm seeing a little guilt, but I suppose that is to be expected."

"Before all of this happened, I wanted to have everyone at the house for your birthday. What do you think?"

"You've already talked to Abby?"

"And Stella. Julie was with us, too."

"Well, if you must."

"I must."

***

"Do you know who has been screaming?" Billie was afraid to ask, but she needed to know.

"I think her name is Harlow. She was here when I got here..." Billie was standing on the bed whispering into the vent when she was dosed with the lavender spray.

"Hello, hello? Damn." Trinity was afraid to get caught, so she got off the bed, smoothed out the quilt and sat in front of the TV.

Billie had spoken to Trinity about the importance of keeping a log. They both decided that maybe someone would be able to smuggle it out one day. To track the passage of time, Billie counted her days by the number of meals she received. The meal schedule was very punctual, so she knew she hadn't missed any. She used a blank journal to document her experiences. In it, she created a type of hieroglyphics that she hoped would convey meaning to Colt if someone were to find it. Each day, right after breakfast, she made a notation. She vividly remembered the day she was taken. While she had no idea how long she had been unconscious, she recalled waking up after the man assaulted her, talking to Trinity, and then having breakfast a little while later. She decided to start her entries from that day. Believing that day was a Monday, she used the Egyptian Hieroglyph alphabet to denote the day and then employed Pictionary-style symbols to convey messages about her experiences. She included details about any visitors, what they said—if anything—and whether they were big or if there was a woman present. Billie wondered if her captors ever checked to see if she was writing, so she carefully left a different clue each time she made an entry, trying to be discreet. She deemed herself safe for now, at least.

Trinity recognized the importance of recording her thoughts as well. At first, she tried to keep track of her days in captivity. Although she believed she had maintained accurate records, she often doubted whether she truly knew how long she had been there. Like Billie, she was careful in her writing. She understood the necessity of ensuring that no one was reading her thoughts, as it was vital for her sense of security.

Additionally, she wanted to transcribe her reflections about the visits with the woman. Notably, there seemed to be a pattern; the woman only appeared when the sessions had been particularly rough. Was it an attempt at sympathy from her abductors? Was she a member of the staff? It remained a mystery, yet she was the only person who showed any kindness. Was her kindness self-serving? Probably. Nevertheless, apart from her, the visits were emotionally and physically grueling.

"Aaaaahhhhh, stop, please…" Billie was being tortured, and Trinity was helpless. She whispered to herself; *Beau will figure out a way…*

Trinity went to her journal but instead of writing, she looked up at the painting and tapestry.

"Aaaaahhhhh, noooo, please, noooo."

Trinity was in tears, her heart racing as she stood against the wall, peeking cautiously behind the tapestry. She needed to maneuver the wall hanging carefully, trying not to disturb it too much. Despite her efforts, she couldn't see anything through the thick fabric, so she reluctantly returned to her journal. She thought she was in the clear, but the tension hung in the air as she waited. The staff would deal with her later, and the uncertainty gnawed at her.

***

Matilda sat bolt upright in the bed, trying to catch her breath.

"Honey…"

"I'm OK, but I remembered something. There was a man. He didn't hurt me. It was like he needed to be close. When he was done, he kissed me on the forehead… oh Lenny, I'm sorry, that sounded so callous."

"It didn't. If you want to tell me, I will listen. If you need to talk about it, who better than me."

"I told Naomi some things. I need to tell you about my life before Cape Hope."

Matilda laid her head on Lenny's shoulder and began honestly recounting her life of privilege. She felt conflicted about revealing her trust fund, but if she married him, as she hoped, she would gladly share it with him.

"Tilly, when we get married…"

She lifted her head. "We're getting married?"

"I always hoped."

"Sorry, what were you going to say?"

"Would you want to invite your family?"

"It's been a long time. I'm not sure."

"OK, no biggie. You like Naomi?"

"I do. She went through something pretty horrific during an assignment. Talking to her, even though it wasn't the same kind of brutality, I knew I felt better talking about it."

"You can talk to me."

"I know, and I probably will, but promise me; if I tell you something you think is important, please tell Phil."

"I promise."

"I hope I can be the woman you fell in love with."

"Oh, Tilly, please believe me, you already are."

Marcus knocked on the door. "May I come in?"

Lenny was in the kitchen. "Marcus, hi. Do you have news?"

"No. Does that mean I can't come in?"

Lenny laughed. "Thanks, I needed that. Come in. Coffee?"

"Great. Is Matilda here?"

"She is but I'm not sure she is ready to receive."

"Oh, stop it. You're Marcus? Naomi said she was having fun working with you."

"I've met a lot of your friends. They miss you. Lucy especially."

"Matilda is the reason Lucy is with Tim."

"Yes, I'm quite the matchmaker. I told Timmy Lucy needed to get laid, and nature took its course."

"You're kidding?"

Lenny chuckled. "She's not."

"So, Marcus, you seem to be a mix, like me."

"You're Mexican and Irish?"

"No, my mother is half black; my father is white. My maternal grandmother told me I was passing. I think the only reason she said it was because she knew how much it bothered my mother, who tended to be a little stiff."

***

Abby and Cubby were in her office when Beau walked in. Cubby sensed that Abby was keeping things from him, and he was pretty sure it had to do with Beau.

"Hi, Abbs, Cubby. Have you heard anything?"

"No, well, that's not true. You were questioned again?"

"Yeah, I'm not sure why." Beau looked at Cubby.

"On that note, I'll be in my office." Cubby wasn't Beau's biggest fan, so he left.

"You two need to play nice."

"He doesn't like me, plain and simple. Can we talk off the record?"

"I'm not going to plaster your picture all over the front page if that's what you're worried about."

"I wrote an anonymous letter and sent it to the State Police. I said the woman gave me three names: Trinity, Billie and Maggie. Abbs, you have to find out about Maggie, she must be missing from somewhere."

"Oh, Beau, where would I start? Besides, I'm sure the FBI will look into it."

"I'm worried. Have you seen Matilda?"

"No, I don't really know her. She needs to recover. I'm not going to bother her."

Beau was staring out the window.

"Beau, as much as I really abhor what you've done, they know there is a problem, and because you went back there, you were able to give them information, the police now have a jumping off point. It's a start. Beau, has anyone told you about the undercover agents?"

"Undercover? No, I've only met one agent. They called me in again after they got the letters. I guess the DA's office received copies, so Shaw came to Phil's office while I was there. Abbs, he defended me. He was pissed."

"Don't sound so surprised. Anyway, there are undercover agents at the Pub, and there will be one using Molly's boat. Daddy said they could use his dock. They have a plan, Beau. The Coast Guard agent is young and pretty. They wondered if she was seen on the boat… I don't know the details, but I thought you had the right to know why there was a strange boat on Daddy's dock."

"Thanks. Abby, I have to go back."

***

Merritt was read in on the case, and Skipper, Colt, and Ben all trusted her qualifications for the job. However, their concerns for Merritt's safety loomed large, especially after the incident involving Matilda. In response, Ben suggested implanting a micro-tracker behind her ear for added security.

As Molly and Colt docked her boat, Merritt accompanied Ben to the FBI office, where she had the tiny chip embedded in the delicate fold between her earlobe and jawline. Ben was impressed by the procedure; the incision was so minuscule it was nearly invisible.

During the short time they spent together, Merritt and Ben forged a friendship, discovering they had more in common beyond their professional lives. Both shared a passion for sports, traveling, and laughing with friends. They also admitted to putting their jobs before relationships, a truth that resonated with them both.

"Did you know Billie wanted to talk to the Chief about a job with the police department?"

"I heard something to that effect… Merritt, will you have dinner with me?"

"I'd love to, but would you mind if we made a stop? I'd like to meet Matilda."

Knock, knock. "Hi, it's Ben."

Lenny yelled, "It's open." Lenny met them in the kitchen. "Hi, you must be Merritt."

"I am. If it's not too much for her, I'd like to meet Matilda. I really shouldn't talk to her once I'm in place on the boat. I didn't want her to think she was being left out."

"You are so nice." Matilda had been waiting by the door to the kitchen. "Hi, I'm Matilda."

"Matilda, Merritt is going undercover tomorrow. Molly is bringing her boat to Trip's dock and will be observing the cove. Matilda, you are not the only person who noticed the man in the boat. He was also described as the *Old Man in the Sea.*"

"Well, I think the person in the car on the side of the road probably took me."

"Excuse me?" Ben was surprised.

"Honey, this is the first we've heard this."

"I'm sorry." She started weeping and began to leave the room. Lenny stopped her.

Ben was sympathetic. "You don't need to apologize; your memories of moments before you were taken will take a while to come back. You don't want to relive it, so you are burying everything related to your disappearance."

"I really need to accept it and move on. Ben, I thought I heard something behind me right before I saw the boat. I turned around. There was a blue car there. I'm sure it was electric because there was no grill in the front."

Lenny embraced her. "This is really good, honey."

"After I saw the boat I felt something in my neck. I should have remembered."

Merritt took Matilda's hand and sat on the couch. "I wanted to meet you so I would have the inspiration and the drive to find the people who did this…"

"What you are seeing is nothing compared to what those women are going through. It's not every day. If they hurt you…" Matilda started to sob. "Sorry, if they hurt you, they seem to give you time to recover. The room I was in was beautiful. TV with satellite, no cable, no local channels, books, things to keep you occupied. Even a laptop. It wasn't connected to anything, but I could play games. They don't want you to be aware of the outside world. The food is good. It is all very confusing because, at least for me, I was thankful for the amenities. I'm sure most of it was for the customers, but…"

"Tilly, tell her about the man you told me about."

"He was normal, kind. He didn't hurt me, and before he left, he kissed me on the forehead."

"Ben, maybe he was one of the men who wrote letters."

"Possible. Matilda, since we're talking. You couldn't see the men at all?"

"No. The blindfold felt like leather. It was thick. But I will never forget the first man's voice. I criticized him for having to pay for sex. I made fun of him. I taunted him. Then he tortured me, and he talked the whole time. I will remember that voice forever."

"My experience tells me he may be in charge. He might have acted as he did even if you hadn't provoked him. We are investigating the man from the pub that Tim warned you about. Unfortunately, he seems to be a respected member of the community. His wife is involved in the Garden Club and volunteers for the Girl Scouts. Their kids are active in sports and school activities. The man is wealthy; he plays golf and tennis and surrounds himself with people of the same status. I was able to gather information from public records, but to uncover anything more, I would need a warrant."

"Then the faster I get back to work, the better."

"Honey, he's not likely to go back…"

"Lenny, if this man is as arrogant as Tim described, he won't be able to stay away."

"Matilda, Merritt and I are having dinner at the Pub. I'll give Tim your regards."

"Thank you, Ben. Thank you both."

***

Ben and Merritt were eating when Steve and Kim walked into the Pub. They resembled a down-to-earth couple headed out for a casual dinner. Kim was makeup-free, and both of them opted for conservative attire. They settled at the bar, waiting for a table, engaging in conversation with Tim and Naomi about Cape Hope and the community of people living there.

"Are you on vacation?" was usually Tim's inquiry to new patrons.

"No, we live in Manchester. Some friends recommended your Pub. They weren't wrong."

"What was the server's name Steve? It was an unusual name."

Tim suggested, "Naomi?"

"I don't think that was it."

Naomi heard her name. "Ya, boss?"

"Oh, they were asking about an employee. I thought it might be you."

"Matilda? I think it was Matilda."

Naomi was immediately on guard. "She isn't here."

"Oh, too bad. We were told she was a lot of fun."

"She is." Naomi was abrupt.

"So…" Kim was trying to be nonchalant, "What do the year-round residents here do for fun?"

Tim snickered. "That depends on what you consider fun, I suppose." He noticed Ben and Merritt approaching the bar. "Excuse me," he said, moving over to them. He whispered, "They are asking about Matilda. I don't know them, so of course, I was suspicious."

Merritt grasped Ben's arm. "I'm going to sit next to them." As she walked to the other side of the bar, she unbuttoned her blouse to reveal her cleavage. "Is this seat taken?"

"What about your boyfriend?"

"He's cool. Tim said you were looking for some fun."

"We were wondering, that's all. There are a lot of shops and places to eat, but no clubs or nightlife. We were told to come here. But I guess the woman we heard about isn't here."

Merritt looked toward Ben. "I guess I should get back. Maybe I'll see you again."

She went to Ben's side and kissed him. "They are very interested in Matilda because they heard she was fun—whatever that means. I told them I might see them again."

Ben wrapped his arms around her and nuzzled her ear. "Well, they haven't taken their eyes off you. Maybe we can come back. I'll make sure Naomi and Tim know to call me."

Merritt smiled and then kissed him again. "It's a good thing I like you, Ben."

"I want to see if they follow us. We can take your car, but we can't go to my place."

"I'll tell Tim we are going to the boat."

"I'm pretty sure they won't approach you right away." He whispered something else, which prompted Merritt to kiss him again.

"I'm OK with that."

Tim called Marcus over. "Let Ben know if you hear anything interesting from those two at the end of the bar. I'm going to make sure they are at your station."

"Okee doke. Oh, by the way, I visited Matilda. I obviously don't know her, but she seems to be doing pretty good."

Naomi leaned in. "They asked about her, so be careful."

Merritt and Ben went to the pool house. "It's pretty nice here. I'm going to the house to let them know I'm moved in. I'll be right back. Help yourself to a beer."

Ben looked around before walking down to the boat. He approached the edge of the dock to gaze toward the far end of the cove. After taking off his shoes, he sat down.

Merritt sat next to him.

"Merritt, I can be a real bastard when I'm on assignment."

"Well, I don't work for you. Besides, I'm a big girl; I know what I'm doing."

"I wouldn't want to take advantage."

"I didn't play kissy face with you for that couple's benefit alone. I really like you."

"The feelings are mutual."

"We found out we have a lot in common. I was hoping we could learn a little more."

"You are making it very hard for me to remain professional."

"We really should stay in character. Don't we want these people to believe we are in a relationship? We really should prepare."

"Our original plan didn't include this paradigm."

"I thought we were on the same page, Ben. I'm sorry if I misread you."

"You didn't." Ben kissed her. "You didn't." He kissed her again.

Merritt stood up, took Ben's hand and tugged, "Come on. I'll be gentle." She squeezed his hand.

Ben held her hand and tried to get up, but Merritt lost her balance and fell into the water. Her head popped up just as Ben was taking off his shirt to jump in. "Are you okay?"

"I would hope so." She put her palms on the dock and lifted herself up. She used both hands to smooth her hair back.

Ben admired what he saw and smiled. "You did that on purpose." He stood, handed her one of the beers, and held her hand as they walked to the pool house.

"I suppose I should get out of these wet clothes."

Ben put on his best straight face. "I suppose you should." He sat on the daybed and drank his beer. He heard the shower running, but only for a few minutes. He sat with his forearms on his knees, holding his beer with both hands.

"Should I ask what you're thinking about?"

Ben didn't look at her. "You're pretty smart. You can probably figure that out on your own."

Merritt bent in front of him, clad only in a towel. She set his beer down on the table, leaned in to kiss him, then stood up to switch off the light and close the curtains draping the glass doors. When she turned back,

Ben was stepping into the bathroom. He emerged a couple of minutes later, a towel wrapped securely around his waist.

Merritt pulled the comforter and pillows off the daybed, taking Ben's hand as she knelt on the floor. He joined her, kneeling beside her. He kissed her softly as he gently eased her down onto the floor.

"Ben, I want you to know I'm not one who usually jumps into bed like we did."

He kissed her forehead. "I don't remember a bed."

"Am I going to have to watch out for you?"

"Oh, probably."

"May I confess something? I wanted to know you, and I was afraid if I didn't seize the moment before the assignment started I might lose the opportunity to get to know an extraordinary man. I'm not sorry; I hope you're not."

"I wouldn't say extraordinary, but if you insist."

Merritt laughed. "I knew I was right about you… but I'm scared."

"Me too." He held her closer. "This is the first time I've even considered a relationship with an Agent. When you kissed me at the Pub, I wondered which Merritt it was."

"The first time I was the Agent. After that, it was all me." Merritt lifted herself on her elbow. "I wasn't afraid of the assignment before we started talking."

"I was thinking about that. We don't know if this couple is involved. They could be *swingers;* do couples still do that?"

She laughed. "I really don't know. This is all very new to me. I know we weren't followed back here, and I would be very surprised if this couple made a move toward me without more observation. Is that a fair assessment?"

"I think so. I did think of something earlier. Phil and Connie have been talking about a Gala that the Fredericks family organizes every year. Phil thought it would be a good idea for me to be there. Would you go with me?"

"Oh, Ben, I would like that very much." Merritt moved on top of him. She put her hands under his shoulders as he rested his hands on the small of her back. "I want to make the most of our time together."

"You make it sound like we won't be able to see each other. We've already been out together."

"So, are you going to tell your boss?"

"I will. We are allowed to have relationships. You don't work for me, and I can't imagine Skipper would have a problem with us. Besides, I'd be remiss if I didn't watch out for you."

"Is that what you're doing now?"

"Right now, I can't take my eyes off of you."

***

"Billie? Are you OK? I need to know you're OK."

"Define OK. I'm alive. Have you talked to anyone else?"

"Harlow and Maggie. There was someone else, but she never told me her name. You are in the room she was in, and no, I don't know what happened to her."

"I was looking for a woman named Matilda when I was taken."

"Billie, I live in Cape Hope. Do you…"

"Trinity, are you there? Trinity?"

Billie was filled with anxiety. She picked up her notebook and began to write furiously. She sketched three small triangles to form a pyramid, followed by a plus sign, a crescent moon, and a scattering of stars. After that, she added another plus sign and a letter T. Her hope was that someone might decipher her symbols and understand her meaning.

Struggling to visualize figures for Matilda, she found herself completely stumped.

She began to cry. She went to the bed and buried her head in the pillows…

When Billie woke up, she wasn't wearing a mask, but she was cuffed to the bed frame. The sound of the door creaking open broke the silence. A woman entered, clad in a tight leather corset and garter belt, closely followed by a man dressed in leather chaps. Both figures wore leather party masks that concealed their identities. The man carried a small suitcase, which he placed on the desk, its presence looming ominously in the dimly lit room. Moments later, the door swung open once more, and another woman stepped inside, dressed much the same as the first.

The two women began to kiss. Billie averted her gaze to the ceiling, prompting the man to approach the bed. He gripped Billie's cheeks and forced her to face him. He started to caress her, but she ignored his advances, which only fueled his anger. He moved to the suitcase and pulled out a small wooden club. Gently, he pressed his lips between her breasts. She turned her head away. The women remained on the floor. She shifted back and shut her eyes, which only intensified the man's fury. He swung the club at the bottom of her foot. She wanted to scream but held it back. He struck the other foot harder, but Billie refused to show him her pain.

The man stood up, watched the woman on the floor for a minute, took something from the suitcase and went back to the bed. "Open your eyes." When Billie didn't obey, he sent a jolt of electricity through her body. "Open your eyes!"

Billie wasn't going to give in. The next jolt was excruciating, but she held her ground.

The man was getting impatient, but Billie was resolute. She thought that if she remained quiet and didn't give him what he wanted, he would get bored and move on. However, that only made him more determined.

She could hear the hum of the torture device growing louder as he held it against the bottom of her foot. When she finally screamed, the man laughed and patted Billie's head.

"There you go." He then laid over her and savagely brutalized her.

The man looked at the two women. "Go ahead." He sat in the desk chair as the women climbed onto the bed.

Billie looked up and tried to clear her mind… It was Christmas at her grandparents' house. They always had a beautiful meal, and the whole family was there. The aroma of the feast being prepared in the kitchen filled the air while children ran around, creating a lively atmosphere. It was the perfect family holiday…

"What is the matter with you? You should like this."

Billie looked at the ceiling. She had no intention of satisfying these people's sick fantasies.

The man spoke, "Give her a little incentive."

She heard the switch, then the hum and thought to herself, *Not again.*

Before they could do anything, Billie screamed as hard and loud as she could until the man silenced her by shoving a cloth into her mouth. Seizing the moment, Billie held her breath for a heartbeat, squeezed her eyes shut, allowed her head to droop to the side, choked on the fabric gagging her, and feigned passing out.

"What's wrong with her?"

"She can't breathe."

The man went to the bathroom. "This little mirror is under the toilet tank for this kind of emergency." He put the mirror under her nose to see the vapor form on the mirror. "She's fine. Well, ladies, who is going to take her place?"

"Honey, should we?"

The timid voice sounded scared. "This isn't what I paid for."

"Oh honey, you will thank us when we are done."

Billie couldn't bear to watch. Instead, she started to sing softly to herself. It was a technique she had discovered that helped her relax and clear her head. She sang the same song again and again. Again and again…

As the moans and whimpers began to fade, Billie felt a glimmer of hope that they might be leaving. It sounded as if they were gathering their things. The faint voice expressed gratitude for an extraordinary experience.

Billie opened her eyes just enough to see a woman leave the room. Once she was out the door, the couple took off their masks. Billie caught a glimpse of the man's face and quickly closed her eyes, memorizing his features. She knew she would never forget that face or the voice that said, "We have to find Matilda. Let's go. We can't be late."

***

Mr. Smith was the voice on the other side of the conference call. "Did you do as I asked?"

"Yes, we did."

"Did anyone mention the woman Matilda?"

"They said she wasn't working. Honestly, they didn't seem concerned."

"What about the other employees?"

The woman spoke up, "The man who waited on us never met her. He said the owner called her a free spirit. He wasn't surprised when she took off."

"Could she have a history of disappearing?"

"That was my thought as well." Mr. Smith seemed pleased.

"I have to bring up a possible issue."

"Then get to it!"

"The two new women seem to know each other. They have been talking through the vent. The most recent woman was heard saying she was looking for Matilda when she was taken."

The woman spoke up, "The matrons are ready to move them to different parts of the house."

"No. I have another plan. First, make sure you have replacements then these two need to be moved downstairs. Then you need to…"

Chapter 16

"Good morning, Ben."

"Good morning. It's quiet. Is that good or bad?"

Phil chuckled "In this case, good. Connie is taking the kids to see her parents. You were out late the other night."

"I was in before my curfew, Dad."

"She seems nice."

"That's because she is. She wanted to meet Matilda, so we went there first. Then we went to the Pub. There was a couple Merritt deemed persons of interest. They were there because they heard Matilda was *fun.*"

"Ben…"

"Merritt spoke to them. She said they overused the word *fun* like it was code or a prompt. She didn't overstay her welcome but expressed hope they would see each other again."

"She needs to tell Colt about your friendship."

"She is going to tell Skipper."

"And you?"

"I spoke to my boss yesterday. We are going to the Gala. Do you know when that is?"

Phil went to the calendar. He took a post-it from the stack on the counter and wrote the date and time, "Here, you'll need a tux."

"Thanks."

"May I say something as a concerned friend?"

"Can I say no?"

"Is this the best time to start a relationship?"

"She is scared. Billie is her friend. She likes Matilda. She is doing this for the women imprisoned in that house. She didn't want to pass up the chance to see if we were good together." Ben sighed. "Was it unprofessional? I'm probably the wrong person to ask. I didn't want her to go into this assignment thinking I don't care about her because I do."

"Being vulnerable is dangerous in our line of work."

"I wasn't the aggressor, Phil. I could have said no, but I really didn't want to. My boss had the same concerns, but he is cool. We are going to work as partners. The couple in the Pub saw us together as a couple, and they couldn't take their eyes off Merritt. We set a mood with them. We should see it through. They didn't follow us to Trip's, we are positive of that. Naomi and Marcus will keep an eye out for them."

"We know these people are vicious. I worry about Merritt and anyone else that may get sucked into their vortex. Do me a favor; if you stay here together, leave her car at Trip's."

"I appreciate that."

***

Trip visited Abby's office a couple of times each month, primarily to keep everyone alert and engaged. Today, he aimed to finalize the details for the Gala. He carried with him a stack of notices intended for the local businesses. While most of the tables had been sold, a few seats remained unclaimed. Trip hated seeing empty seats.

"Hello, honey. Update me on the Gala." Trip dropped the posters on Abby's desk.

"Everything is all set, Daddy. You always get so nervous."

"Will you put these in the diner and at the Pub?"

"And Molly's store, and Brock's office, and a couple of other store owners will put them up too. All the tickets will be sold."

"I trust you. Do you know about the undercover agent staying at the house?"

"Yes. This is a big story we're sitting on, Daddy."

"For the safety of those women, Abby. Lizzy has been stopping in to see Matilda. The thought that a human being could be that cruel."

"I didn't want her to think I was there for an interview, so I stayed away."

"At some point, we may need to print something; hopefully, it will be to report that all of the bastards responsible are going to jail."

"I've been keeping track of everything. We'll keep the names of the victims out of the story."

"Absolutely. Is Cubby on board?"

"He's more concerned about the victims than the story. Daddy, we need to talk about Cubby."

"Honey, if this means you can do more writing, and maybe…"

"Don't say it Daddy, no caveats."

"OK, ask him to come in. I'd like to talk to him alone."

"Mr. Fredericks."

Trip raised an eyebrow. He knew Cubby well enough to recognize when an employee was trying to suck up. Cubby was showing respect—nothing more.

"Please sit. Has Abby talked to you about her proposal regarding your promotion to Editor in Chief?"

"She isn't shy about her aversion to being in charge."

"No. She speaks her mind. I don't like deception. In our line of work, that can be dangerous. Do you agree with burying the story about the missing women?"

"I do now."

"What happened to change your stance?"

"I needed to know more before I formed an opinion. At first, truthfully, I wondered what Beau was up to. Then, as more information came to light, I realized we had a problem. In this case, keeping a lid on it is the safest and most reasonable plan."

"Isn't it important to get the story first? These days information often has multiple sources."

"I believe whoever is running this operation is cunning enough to keep the knowledge of their existence from the authorities. My brother saw Matilda the day she was found. I will not be responsible if those monsters hurt more women."

"You're not concerned about hurting our family name?"

"I don't know you as well as some, but I do know you wouldn't expect me to hold back information if it meant giving Matilda, Billie, Trinity and any other women the justice they deserve."

"Abby says you're the most politically moderate person she knows."

Cubby almost smiled. "Reporting only one side of any issue is a bit myopic, sir."

"Does my opinion count for anything?"

"Everyone's opinion matters. Mr. Fredericks, are your views more important than a single mother with two jobs, or a Veteran, or an elderly couple trying to make ends meet on Social Security?"

"No. I see your point. Abby has been singing your praises since she went to DC with you. She said you took time off to save for grad school."

"I did. I worked in the circulation department of a local paper, then became somewhat of a gofer. I learned a lot."

"Is your goal to win a Pulitzer?"

"It used to be. Abby can be very persuasive when it comes to a story, but I'm not going to go after a story for what it will mean for my career. This story about the brothel, if not reporting the story, will bring those women home safely. That is what I will do, but that doesn't preclude me from doing the research. If my legwork can help Ben and Merritt, all the better, and no, I won't reveal a source that wants to remain confidential."

"Truthfully, I'm not happy about dangling a woman as bait."

"From what I understand, it was her idea. She and Billie are friends, Molly, too. Juice is blaming himself. Sir, right now, I'm more worried about Abby or Kathryn as targets if we print anything."

"I didn't think of that. You're right. OK, thank you for your time."

"I work for you, Mr. Fredericks." Cubby passed Abby on his way to his office. He whispered, "I think he approves."

"Daddy, Ben Malloy just bought tickets to the Gala."

"Good. I was going to talk to you about security."

"I thought I should ask Phil. I don't want to go over his head straight to Ben, but I would like his advice."

"Tell him money isn't an object. If he knows people who would like to volunteer, go for it."

"Daddy, if it hadn't been for Beau, we wouldn't…"

"Abby, does Beau know about this brothel?"

"Daddy, really? He has been very honest with Julie. He even told her he paid Trinity's mortgage. I think, if anything, his friendship with Trinity made him realize how much he loves Julie."

"OK. Let me know about the security. We'll see you at Shaw's."

***

Abby went to Phil's office to discuss security with Phil and Lenny. When she saw Lucy there, she asked if she could join them.

"Phil, I asked Ben, Juice and Merritt to be here too. Can we go to the back?" She waited when she saw Juice and Ben come in.

"Daddy wants security at the Gala. I think it's a good idea too. Phil?"

Phil looked around the room. "I think we can include Jack, Colt, and Skipper if he's available. Abby, have you asked Jack?"

Juice spoke up, "I'm sure he will be on board."

Ben added, "I know the people at a security firm if needed."

"That's great. I'd like a couple of people at the door…Are we missing someone?"

Ben looked at his phone and then looked at Phil. "I'll be right back." Ben went to Phil's office. "Hi, it's me. Did you get a text from Abby Fredericks? We're having a meeting at the station about security at the Gala. Please call me."

"Ben?"

"Please don't say *I told you so.* I left her a message. I had a meeting in Boston yesterday. I stayed at my place last night. Have you seen her?"

"No. I hate to ask, but did you call her?"

"No… I'm a dope. I guess I've been out of the game too long."

"It's not a game, Ben. Go. Make sure she's OK."

Ben was furious with himself for being so careless. When he pulled up, Merritt's car was nowhere in sight, and the pool house door was locked tight. Frustrated, he hopped back into his car and made his way to the Coast Guard office, hoping to find some clues. No luck. Her car wasn't there either. Feeling the tension rise, he turned his car around, heading back to the pool house and called Phil.

"Ben, she just got here. She was on a call with Skipper…"

"Thank God."

"She didn't see the message, Ben. May I make a suggestion?"

"Do we need to talk?"

"Yes. It seems you may care for Merritt more than you're willing to admit. We're done here, but Abby would like the name of the security company."

"I'll text her… She's here. Thank you, Phil." Ben got out of his car and walked to the pool house.

Merritt didn't smile. She seemed ambivalent, "Agent Malloy." She unlocked the door. "Are you coming in?"

Ben went inside. "I'm sorry I didn't call you. I'm an idiot."

Merritt didn't say anything. She had thought he was a cad, so she was hurt. "I was thinking the worst, but I could have called you too."

Ben sat on the daybed. "This is true." Ben smiled and patted the place next to him. "I'm not one of those guys, Merritt, but I'm also not very good at relationships; at least I haven't been. I want to be better for you."

"I had this scenario in my head that yesterday morning, you would be here knocking on the door. Then I didn't hear from you all day. Then this morning… I'm not a foolish teenager, Ben, but I was hurt."

Ben kissed her. "Better?"

"Oh Ben."

"So, do you want to get some lunch?"

"You really are an idiot."

"Did you have something else in mind?"

Ben and Merritt found themselves on the floor again. Ben leaned over and kissed her. "Since we both have jobs, I suppose we should get back to work," he said, reaching toward the daybed before bursting into laughter. "Next time—and there will be a next time..." He reached under the bed and pulled out a hidden mattress. "Next time, we will use the bed." The mattress slid out and up, transforming the daybed into a double bed.

"I kind of like having the whole floor, but I wouldn't mind waking up with you in the morning."

"Oh, I almost forgot. Phil said you are welcome to spend the night at my place as long as you leave your car here. Less questions from the kids that way."

"I'd like that. I need to get into my bathing suit and get down to the boat."

"Where are you going to hide your gun?"

"I have a tote bag. I'll keep my personal weapon in the cabin. You and I should plan some sailing time. I'd like to take a look at the houses down the inlet at the end of the cove."

"Maybe we could take the skiff. I'd like to do some exploring. Phil said we could tie the boat and survey the peninsula. The house at the end is very secluded. There is a private entrance off the road. They've never had a reason to go down there, but he thought we may want to take our binoculars and a picnic."

"Do they know who owns the house?"

"No. It's a Corporate Trust out of New York. Phil thinks they run retreats out of there, but that is just a guess."

"Can you check them out?"

"Not without a reason."

Merritt picked up her phone to look at the week's weather. "Well, pick a day. We can get some cold cuts and rolls and chips and…"

Ben moved on top of her. "You're like a little kid. What did Skipper say when you told him?"

"He said he thought he saw a spark. Working together does make more sense, but he thought you should make yourself scarce during the day. What exactly is it you do, Ben?"

Ben laughed "I bought us tickets to the Gala."

"Oh, poor baby. You must be exhausted."

"I've had something on my mind. I've been worried about someone who has come to mean a lot to me. I wasn't thinking about her feelings. I know it doesn't make sense, but I am sorry."

"It's over. Maybe when we have that picnic, we can talk more."

"Does that mean we can stop talking now?"

***

Matilda was getting restless. "What are you doing today?"

"Work. Yesterday, we had a meeting about security at the Gala."

"I bought a dress just in case you asked me to go, but..." She wept, then stopped abruptly. "I have to get a grip."

Lenny sat on the couch. "Come, sit on my lap."

Matilda was still in her big T-shirt when she turned to face him, slowly settling onto his lap. Lenny's hands traced the curve of her thighs, then slid up to gently grip her rear. Matilda leaned into him, resting her head softly against his chest, allowing the quiet moment to last.

"Do you want to go to the Gala Tilly?"

"The dress is a little..."

"Little?"

"Do I flaunt my body?"

"Flaunt is the wrong word. You wear what is comfortable for you. You are a beautiful woman. You always have been, you always will be."

"Maybe Lizzy can take me shopping. I want to go with you. I want everyone to see I'm OK."

"We have time. I'm sure Lizzy will help you."

"Could you ask Naomi to come back? I really need to talk to someone."

"Do me a favor. Call Tim. He's worried about you. He'll be able to tell you when Naomi is working. You are healing, honey. I can tell you are still afraid, but you are determined, and you and I are stronger than ever."

"I want this cast off my hand. I want these marks to be gone. I need to be able to forget... OK, I'll call Timmy."

"I have to go."

"Hi Timmy."

"Hello, honey. I won't ask how you're doing."

"I'm feeling a little sorry for myself this morning. Do you think Naomi will come by?"

"She's upstairs. I know she wants to be available for you."

"Thank you."

"Anytime, honey."

As Tim went out the side door Naomi was coming down the stairs.

"Are you busy?"

"What's up?"

"Matilda needs you."

"You seem to have quite the telephone networking system here. Lenny and Phil called. Matilda may not know it right now, but she is a very lucky woman."

"She knows. She's having a hard day. Thank you. Since I have you, I've done some work with the schedule. If you and Marcus would like to go to the Gala, we'd love to have you."

"I'm not sure I'd know where to put my weapon," Naomi smirked. "I'm not sure Marcus is the Gala type, but it would be a change of pace. Thanks."

***

"Thank you for coming. I need to get out of the house. Would you take me down Coast Road?"

"Therapy?"

"Do you mind?"

"Of course not. We can talk."

Matilda stared blankly out the passenger window as Naomi guided the car along the Coast Road. Naomi couldn't help but feel concerned about her new friend's state of mind. She knew, from her own harrowing journey, how crucial it was to regain some sense of normalcy. Naomi's experience hadn't just required rehab from the drugs but from the intense terror of her captivity. Her captor had kept her drugged while he slept, allowing her moments of clarity during the day when the effects wore off. She became painfully aware of her surroundings and, more tragically, her growing dependency. Whenever she seemed close to breaking through the withdrawal, he injected her again, keeping her trapped in that torturous cycle. This hell continued for two weeks until Ben and his team finally located her, overpowering the serial killer who had held her captive.

"We can park at my house and walk." Matilda hadn't been back to her house yet. "Maybe before we go back, I can get a few things?"

"Sure." Naomi watched Matilda as they walked. Matilda was quiet but kept looking around as if searching for something. Naomi didn't want to interrupt whatever it was Matilda was seeking, but she couldn't help feeling concerned.

"I think I was right here." She turned to look back to where she saw the car. "The car was there. I remember this tree. It has a really big knot. Is there a reason they took me here?"

Naomi looked around. There was a house. It looked like… "I need to call Phil… Hi, this is Naomi. What is Trinity's address?"

"451 Coast Road, why?"

"Matilda wanted to go out. We're at the spot where she remembers being taken. There is a house across the street. Phil, could they have been using Trinity's house as a lookout? It is secluded. Is that why they took her? Was Matilda the target and Trinity was in the way?"

"I suppose. Did you ask Ben?"

"I wanted to make sure of the address. Phil, am I reading too much into this?"

"Given we think that man is behind her abduction, and he has gone to great lengths to hide his identity, I don't think you're wrong. Ben and Merritt are going to explore the peninsula. Naomi, may I speak to Matilda?"

"How are you? Is anything coming back?"

"Hi Phil. I know I didn't see anyone, but the dart in my neck could have come from that house."

"This is great. Lenny will be relieved. He is worried about you."

"I know." Matilda began to walk away. "I'm going to ask him to marry me, Phil."

"That will make him happy. Very happy."

"I bought him a watch before. I had *Marry Me* engraved on the back."

"He will like that. Honey, he isn't going anywhere, you know that."

"Remember that confidence I used to have?"

"You still have it. You just misplaced it. You will find it again."

***

Sylvie tracked down Steve and Kim at their shop in Salem, which catered to a specific clientele. Although they didn't openly advertise their niche, a subtle sign stating *Special Orders Welcome* hinted at their unique offerings. Their specialty was leather, and for certain items, special orders were handled discreetly. Customers with these requests were directed through the back door marked *Employees Only*, where a private showroom awaited behind a curtain.

Sylvie was thrilled to discover the shop. She spent over an hour there, during which Kim skillfully asked questions to gauge her preferences. It became clear that Sylvie shared the same interests as Kim and Steve. By the end of her visit, they had arranged an appointment to meet at the shop and then head to the house. The connection between them felt natural, especially after Sylvie expressed her interest in finding a new partner. She revealed that her previous partner was in jail but didn't provide any further details—and no one pressed her for more.

Sylvie did not like Billie or Trinity as regulars. She tried them both but didn't get the excitement she was seeking. Harlow, on the other hand, caught her interest—completely different, young, scared, and resistant; Harlow brought the thrill Sylvie craved.

Mr. Smith approved the shift in focus, giving Steve and Kim the task of finding two more women, specifically one to replace Matilda. They selected Naomi, who, though not biracial like Matilda, had the Mediterranean appearance they were after.

Sylvie had a specific request—she wanted to meet Naomi. With Naomi becoming a new addition to the house, Sylvie thought it might be a good idea to schedule some time together, especially since Naomi would be around regularly. Mr. Smith approved her request.

Kim suggested Sylvie meet them at the Pub in Cape Hope, mentioning that they had encountered an intriguing woman there just a few days earlier. Sylvie agreed, eager for the opportunity.

They went inside together. Naomi wasn't there, but Lucy was waiting at the bar for Tim. They were going straight from there to visit Matilda. As soon as Sylvie saw Lucy, she signaled for Steve and Kim to follow her. She sat next to Lucy and asked, "Are you here alone?"

"Me? I'm waiting for my boyfriend."

Tim was finishing up in his office, which was located at the back of the bar. He recognized the couple right away. He backed into the office and called Ben, "Hey, it's Tim. That couple just came in. There's another woman with them, and if I'm not mistaken, she's hitting on Lucy."

"We'll be there in a few minutes. Thanks, Tim."

Tim went back to the bar area to rescue Lucy. "Hi, sweetheart. Are you ready to go?"

Sylvie was brazen. "Oh, you must be the boyfriend?"

Tim didn't want to be rude, but he wanted to get Lucy out of there. "I am, and we are going to be late."

Kim spoke up, "Is the same bartender here today?"

"I'm not sure. The staff is on a rotating schedule."

"Oh. She was nice. The waiter was nice, too."

"Would you like a table?"

"Can we eat at the bar?"

Tim was distracted when Ben and Merrit came in. They were being very affectionate. "Oh, yes. I'll get you some menus."

Ben and Merritt appeared oblivious to the rest of the world as they sat at the bar and continued to kiss. Tim approached, "I'm going to pretend to tell you to get a room, but truthfully, you two are really cute."

Ben got into character. "We're not hurting anyone."

Merritt leaned back and rolled her eyes. "Now, Ben, not everyone is as open-minded as we are."

Tim whispered, "Do you want me to call anyone?"

Ben chuckled. "No. But if you could pretend to make us a couple of vodka and tonics?"

"Two vodka and tonics coming up." Tim took the bottle and tipped it with his finger over the pourer. He squeezed in two limes and made his apologies to Ben and Merritt "Jake will take care of you from here."

As soon as Lucy and Tim left, Merritt looked down the bar. "Hi again."

"So, I guess this is the place to be." Kim was taking charge of the conversation. She wondered "Do you know the bartender that was here the other day?"

Ben hung his hand over Merritt's shoulder, his fingers inside the front of her blouse, lightly stroking the top of her breast. "Not really."

"I saw a poster for a fundraiser next weekend. Sounds like it may be the only excitement here for the summer."

"We thought the same thing." Merritt licked her lips as she looked at Steve. "We always have money set aside for charity, so we bought a couple of tickets. Those kinds of events are good for networking." She leaned closer to Ben. "Right baby?"

"We have made some good contacts at those affairs."

Kim looked at Sylvie. "Would you like to go?"

"Without a date?"

Merritt spoke up, "There are always single men at those things."

To a bystander, the rest of the exchange was fairly tame, but it was filled with double meanings. Merritt took charge of the dialogue, maintaining eye contact with Steve as she talked to Kim. Prior to their arrival, they had agreed to enjoy a single drink before making their exit to attend a dinner party. Merritt discreetly squeezed his leg, a subtle gesture confirming their earlier plan.

"Well, honey, I think we need to go if we are going to get to dinner on time. It was nice seeing you again. I hope we will see you at the Gala."

Steve finally responded, "We will get the tickets when we get home. See you then."

Ben put some cash on the bar, and they left.

"You are evil."

"I figured I needed something to get them to notice. I never would have been so disrespectful if I didn't know you as well as I do."

"You think you know me, huh?"

"Not as well as I'd like to… Merritt what we were doing in there; I would never forgive myself if anything happened to you."

"Isn't that why we are teaming up?"

"Yes, still…"

"I bought everything we'll need for our picnic tomorrow. We can work and talk and eat and get to know everything about each other."

"Sounds perfect. We should have dinner. Do you have anything in mind?"

"Let's get something to take to your place. We can stop at the pool house first."

***

"So, what do you think? We can go to the Gala and pick out some new ladies, and we can take care of the other things, too. If we time it correctly, we will be at the event of the summer with hundreds of witnesses."

"What about the bartender?"

"I think if I come back late, I can probably snatch her up quickly."

Sylvie agreed, "OK, I will trust you. Can we have a little fun before I go home?"

"Sure, why not."

Steve whispered to Kim, "I'm thinking if we can't find another…"

"My thinking exactly. That's why we are so good together."

Chapter 17

Billie was determined to get herself and Trinity out of the house. She knew about the mirror, which made her curious if there were other hidden tools or gadgets stashed away. Searching every possible hiding spot, she wasn't shocked to find a window concealed behind one of the paintings. Peering through it, she was stunned to see the ocean. She didn't know her exact location, but now she knew they were near water, and with access to a mirror, she felt a spark of hope ignite.

Carefully replacing the painting, Billie decided she'd check the window again after dinner to track the sun's position. She needed a plan, but doubt crept in. *If I do this, will I endanger the others?* The thought gnawed at her. If these people think they are going to be exposed, they might dispose of the women. *Be smart, Billie. You are not the only victim here.*

Billie paced. She had to think about what was best for everyone… *no, I can't sleep now…*

She woke up feeling disoriented. The scent of lavender was unfamiliar. How did I even fall asleep? she wondered. She couldn't recall having a visitor, or at least she didn't think she did. There was a faint sense of a hangover lingering in her head. What unsettled her the most, though, was that she couldn't tell if she had been assaulted. That uncertainty gnawed at her. Breakfast hadn't arrived yet, so she decided to take a shower.

When she returned to the bedroom, two figures stood there in cowls. The hoods were drawn tightly around the neck and had mouth and eye holes.

It had been a while since she had truly felt fear, but she was determined to remain composed. She wasn't about to give in to whatever twisted game they were trying to play with her. Then, she caught sight of the whips—and that's when the panic started to creep in...

She woke up again, this time finding herself on the cold floor. Her mind was hazy, and she struggled to recall what had happened, only managing to summon a faint image of two figures dressed like executioners at the gallows. *Was it just a nightmare?* she wondered, but then flashes of reality hit her—she remembered taking a shower. The men in black hoods had been there when she stepped out of the bathroom. They had been watching her. She glanced down at her wrists. They were always sore and irritated after she was assaulted. She wasn't sore anywhere… They had whips….

She didn't understand. She started crying and fell asleep again.

"Huh? What is happening? Juice, sweetheart, where are you?" Billie was mumbling when she felt a shock that started on the bottom of her right foot. "Gaaaaaahhhhhd."

"Where do you live?"

"Whoo, whoo, whoo… um Boston."

"Who is Juice?"

"Firefighter…"

"Who is Juice?"

She felt the cold metal of the prod on her foot. "My boyfriend…"

When Billie woke up again, everything was black. *Open your eyes,* she thought, but she was so tired. Her eyes were open, yet she couldn't see a thing. She tried to move but realized she was tied down. She could sense someone standing next to her.

"I know someone is there. Just do whatever you're going to do."

The longer she waited, the more panic consumed her. Then she felt it—a hand, then lips brushing her breast, trailing down her belly, inching toward her pelvis. More hands followed, a third, then a fourth. She tried to move, but her body wouldn't respond. That familiar mechanical hum filled the air, and she cried out, her soul sinking.

Billie was being tortured, not just physically; they were breaking her mind. Mr. Smith's twisted plan was to condition her, making her doubt her own sanity so that no one would believe her if she ever escaped. They didn't kill the women they took—they stole their spirits, leaving them hollow.

Billie was nearing her breaking point. She thought of Trinity, clinging to the hope that she was still safe. What she didn't know was that Trinity was enduring the same brutal torment. Mr. Smith had a scheme for them, but first, he needed replacements. Until then, the suffering would continue.

When Billie woke up again, she was finally rested, but she still didn't know if what she experienced was real. Though she had no idea how much time had passed. She couldn't tell what had been real and what had been a nightmare. Slowly, she let herself adjust to her surroundings. Then, she cautiously stood on the bed.

"Trinity? Are you there?"

There was no response. She tried again and again, but Trinity didn't answer.

Did they punish me for looking behind the picture? She glanced around once more. Nothing had changed; everything was in its place. With growing anxiety, she stepped into the bathroom and found the mirror hidden under the toilet tank. They couldn't possibly know she knew heliography. That was her hidden advantage. But now, with everything spiraling out of control, she knew she had to take the chance. It was a slim shot, but it might be her only way out of this nightmare.

She moved the painting and looked out the window…

***

Ben and Merritt lay cozy in his bed, having talked, made love, and then talked some more before making love again. They were gradually learning each other's likes and dislikes, completely content in the moment.

When Merritt woke up, Ben was looking at her. He leaned down to kiss her, but she shielded her mouth. "Breath. I'll be right back." She got out of bed and headed to the sink to brush her teeth. Confident in her own body, she didn't bother reaching for the sheet or Ben's shirt to cover herself, which pleased him. He reached over to the nightstand and grabbed a spray bottle of breath freshener, taking a quick spritz. When Merritt stepped out of the bathroom, Ben couldn't help but smile.

"What?"

"I'm very happy you are so comfortable with me already."

She climbed into the bed. "You have made it very easy to trust you."

"I think you'll find I'm pretty easygoing."

"Do you think Phil is right about us moving too fast?"

"No. In our line of work, it is rare to find someone who understands the job. That is really half the battle. Last year, I was called into a kidnapping case. I'm not sure what would have happened if I was with someone who didn't understand what we sometimes have to do." Ben explained, "We went into a house where we were sure the woman was being held. As we were going down the basement stairs, someone shot at us. We moved back, regrouped and went back down. He shot again. I aimed and hit him in the chest. He died later in the hospital."

"Oh Ben."

"The other agent I was with went to the woman while I called for two ambulances. Merritt, what that man did to that woman. My boss at the time came in and took the crime scene photos so they could get her to the hospital. I was standing behind him before the EMT put the blanket on her. I felt remorse for shooting the man until I saw what he did to her. I had to do the mandatory counseling before I could get back in the field. I had to show remorse to him, or he would have labeled me a sociopath. I was only stuck in the office for a couple of weeks."

"How is the woman?"

"She got married. They had a baby at the end of last year. She's good."

Merritt moved on top of him. "We were warned that sometimes agents get callous. We don't have the same kind of assignments as the FBI, but there have been times I've wondered how people can be filled with so much hate." She laid her head on his shoulder.

He put his hand on the back of her head as he kissed her. "You and I are going to be OK."

After packing their lunch into the insulated knapsack Ben had borrowed from Connie, they made their way to the dock. Merritt quickly took charge, her confidence evident as she settled into the stern, grabbing hold of the rudder. Ben remained on the dock, grinning. He handed her the bag, watching with admiration as she sat at the boat, completely in control.

"Are you going to let me be the Captain?"

"You're in charge when we're on the water Chief."

"Ooh, I like the sound of that. So, I get to order you around?"

"You can try."

Merritt took the throttle as they moved slowly down the cove. Ben leaned against the bow. "I like this. Did you tell Colt we would be out here?"

"I did. I have some pretty powerful binoculars if you think we'll need them."

"I'd like to dock about halfway down, then we can walk down to the jetty. I'd like to see what's going on down there."

They dragged the boat ashore and secured it to a nearby tree. Moving inland, they kept far enough to remain hidden from the houses scattered around the cove. After roughly ten minutes of walking, they discovered a small clearing with soft grass nestled between a cluster of large boulders.

"Oh Ben, look."

"That is a perfect place for a picnic."

"Maybe we can schedule some time for a make-out session?"

Ben laughed. "How could I say no to that... I think this bag would be safe here while we explore, but we should take the binoculars. What do you say, Chief?"

"I say we're back on land, so you're in charge."

The back of the big stone house gave off an unsettling vibe. Encircled by a tall stone wall, the property felt more like a fortress. A postern gate served as a rear entrance, crafted from teak, matching the roadside gate. At the far end of the dock, a trap door was visibly distinct. Its black wrought iron hardware stood out, featuring circular pull handles on both sides of a central aperture, with sturdy hinges framing the sides.

Merritt grabbed Ben's arm. "That is very disconcerting."

"OK, so it's not just me. Colt said he and Matilda saw a pontoon boat come down here. Abby said she didn't remember seeing it at any of the docks along the cove."

"Ben, look; two dock cleats on the cove side... there has to be a watertight hatch under the dock. I wonder if we could find out if there was ever a permit pulled to install something like that."

"It wouldn't be unusual for Abby to be at her father's house. I can ask her to drop by. Maybe she has some insight or contacts that could help us."

"That would be great. I'd like to hear more about this boat. Maybe she has some history on the house."

Ben held onto Merritt's arm. "Please don't look, but there are windows that seem to be blocked. If you had a house with this view, wouldn't you want to see it?"

Merritt kissed Ben, then put her arms around him and looked at the house as she nuzzled his neck "I see what you mean. Do you think if we go back out of sight, we can use the binoculars?"

Ben put his arm around her shoulder. "Let's walk around to the other side. We are sightseers. If anyone in the house has a problem with us being here, they'll come out. The property line ends at the water line, right?"

"Well, honestly, with a property this old they could own the rocky area to the water. Usually, the property line ends at the rocks."

"What about the dock?"

"Same thing. Because the dock comes out to the end of the rocks I think they must own the dock. Maybe when we get back, I can ask Colt."

They continued walking, and when they reached the jetty, they stayed on the peninsula before heading back toward where they had left the bag. As they changed direction, Merritt suddenly stopped. "There's a reflection in one of the windows. Can you see it?"

"Yup."

"My paranoia is getting the better of me. We need to see if someone is there."

"I agree. It wouldn't bother me so much if the windows weren't covered. Is it me, or does it look like cardboard? They definitely aren't curtains… I have an idea."

Ben held her hand as he looked for a secluded spot. "This is where we have some fun." He squatted. "Assume the position."

"Really?" She put one leg over his shoulder. As he held her leg she swung the other leg over. Ben held her knees as she scanned the back of the house.

"This is more like a castle in the back. The windows along the courtyard are covered, too, except right near the door. There is a stained glass window. Let me zoom in. It can't be… wait, Ben, it looks like a family crest. Colt has some really nice cameras; maybe we can borrow one."

"Let me talk to him. I don't want to unknowingly break any Maritime laws. We have to be careful. This house could be nothing more than what Phil said, a house used for conferences and retreats."

"I'm too close, Ben. Billie is the first real friend I made in New London. I am afraid for her."

Ben kissed her leg. "What about the upper windows, anything?"

"Nothing now. Maybe we were seeing a reflection from the water. Can we come back tomorrow?"

"Maybe Colt and Skipper can get a better look from the water. Let's get back and have our picnic and maybe some extra-curricular activities?"

"You have a one-track mind, Ben Malloy."

***

Once a week, the matrons, Maude and Ellen, would come by the rooms to clean, collect laundry, and do some snooping. They weren't pleased when they entered Billie's room—it looked as if someone had gone through it. Billie had done a decent job of putting things back in place, but Maude and Ellen were detail-oriented. They noticed that the mirror, which Billie's visitors had used the other day, wasn't in its usual spot. They made a mental note of it and moved on to the next room.

The last time they were in Trinity's room, they hadn't searched thoroughly. She didn't bother hiding the book she was reading, leaving it openly on the nightstand, and her journal wasn't stashed away either. They figured she was obedient—she wasn't one to stir up trouble like some of the others. But today, they looked under the bed, behind the TV, and even checked behind the books, where they found the phone Beau had left.

"Sir, we may have a problem. The two ladies who have been talking are not behaving. One has been searching her room. The other had a cell phone hidden in the bookcase."

"Then they need to be prepared."

"We have begun the indoctrination with the first one. We will take care of this one too."

"You will need to start using the MDMA. Start dosing them about every eighteen hours. Thank you for your loyalty. Your next paychecks will reflect my appreciation."

"Thank you, sir."

Chapter 18

"Dad, when are you going to stop being such a horse's ass and find out where Maggie is?"

"As I said, you are welcome to try to find her. She left here against my wishes and began a trip that was, in my opinion, reckless. That was almost a year ago."

"She could be dead."

"Or she could be shacked up…"

"Dad, that is what started all of this. Your disapproval."

"Your sister has a mind of her own. She is unwilling to admit that she is wrong."

"No, Dad, that is you."

Maggie had left home after another fight with her father. To him, everything she did was wrong—especially her choice of friends and boyfriends. After her latest breakup, he invited a young man from his office over for dinner. He was exactly the type of man Maggie despised: stuffy, arrogant, self-absorbed, and, worst of all, completely lacking a sense of humor.

At the end of the evening, Maggie's father took it a step further, setting them up for another date, insisting they needed time alone to get to know each other better. Maggie was furious. "Dad, I have no desire to have a relationship with your humorless, stuffy lap dog."

She ran to her room, determined to take some time to rethink her life choices. As a freelance book editor between projects, she decided to finally do something she had long wanted to do. She packed a knapsack, hopped on her bike, and set out to explore New England.

She had grown up in Connecticut and had always dreamed of biking along the coast. The next day, after her father left for work, she went to her sister's room. "Clara, I'm leaving," she said

"Don't do this, please."

"I will call you every day, I promise."

Two weeks into her ride, Maggie made a decision: she would relocate. She decided to leave her father behind and use the money her mother had left her to buy a house. She had fallen in love with Marblehead, Swampscott, and Manchester-by-the-Sea. She called her sister while she was at work and left a message: "Clara, please forgive me, but I'm going off the grid for a while. I'm in a little town near Gloucester. I'm going to hang out here for a while. I love you. Bye."

That was the day before Maggie disappeared. At first, her sister was angry. Maggie missed Christmas and their father's birthday, but when she also missed Clara's birthday, Clara knew something was wrong. She decided to take some vacation time and look for her sister. Clara started by visiting the police stations in each of the coastal towns north of Boston. When she reached Cape Hope, she stopped at a pub for lunch. Tim was at the bar.

"You look like you could use a drink."

"Then I probably shouldn't have one. I'll have a Coke and a hamburger, medium rare."

"Okee doke." Tim came back with her drink. "Hi, I'm Tim. Do you want to talk about it?"

"Clara… I'm looking for my sister. I haven't heard from her since last fall. She was pissed at our father and decided to distance herself. She was biking through the Gloucester area the last time I heard from her."

"Do you have a picture?"

Clara showed Tim her photo. "Very attractive. I take it you've called."

"The phone is no longer in service. She was mad at Dad, but not me. After she didn't call on my birthday, I got worried. I've been going to the area police stations to show her picture."

"I know the police chief. Let me call him for you… Hi, there is a lady here. She has been looking for her sister… OK."

"He's just leaving his house. He is going to drop by on his way to the station."

"He didn't need to do that."

"The police station is nearby. May I ask why you waited so long?"

Clara played the voicemail… "I thought she was starting a new life. My father can be difficult. Truthfully, I thought she met someone. Then I thought she may have lost her phone. Then, I got really busy at work, and I was mad she stopped calling."

"Your voices are exactly alike…"

"Hey Tim." Phil came in and sat at the bar. "Hi, I'm Captain Phil Landry. Your sister is missing?"

"She may not be technically missing, but she missed my birthday. She wouldn't miss my birthday." She handed the photo to Phil. "I want you to recognize her, but then again, I don't. I'm making myself crazy with all the awful thoughts going through my head."

"She doesn't look familiar. Do you mind if I take a picture for my file?"

"No, please. Her name is Maggie…" Clara didn't like the way Phil and Tim looked at each other. "What was that look? Please…"

"Clara, you need to come to the station with me."

"Why? Is she dead?"

"I don't know, but I would really rather not talk to you here. Is your car nearby?"

"In the lot down the street."

Tim was sensitive. "Why don't you eat while I talk to Phil? I'll be right back…" They went to Tim's office "Phil, remember Matilda said she would never forget that man's voice? Well, she said she heard other women talking to her through the vents. Clara has a voicemail from her sister."

"OK, good to know. I'm going to call Ben and have him meet us. If that couple comes back, let me know."

Ben and Merritt were at Colt's office when Ben got the call from Phil: "You need to meet us at my office. Maggie's sister is here."

"We're on our way."

***

Abby, Kathryn, Molly, Julie, Dalton, and Stella were having lunch at the Pub, focused on finalizing the details of the Gala. Completely absorbed in the task, they were oblivious to their surroundings and didn't notice when the server seated two women at the table next to them.

Sylvie was still hoping to find a woman who could meet her wants and needs, with Kim there to guide her. They overheard the group discussing the Gala, but Kim cautioned her to stay focused. "They seem to be women who are connected. Abducting one of them may be careless."

"Then what are we doing here?"

"Listening. Sometimes these things take time… look, she is nice…" Kim saw Clara come in. She was in cut-off shorts and a tank top. She looked around then went to the bar "The bartender was here the other day, but he hasn't seen us. He seems to be busy talking to the woman. Let's eat and observe, then when she leaves we can follow her, but we have to be discreet. Tell me what you noticed about this woman."

"She is fit. She is probably a stranger. The bartender didn't seem to know her. She is alone. Women usually don't go to bars alone."

"Very good. She is the right type we are looking for, too. Let's wait outside on the benches across the street. Then we can follow her."

Kim and Sylvie put on sunglasses and took a seat across the street. When Clara stepped outside with Phil, they watched as she walked alongside him. Kim and Sylvie casually strolled on the opposite side of the street. When Clara followed Phil into the police station, they decided to split up. Kim went to retrieve the car while Sylvie entered the gift shop across the street, staying by the window, waiting for Kim.

***

Merritt and Ben parked in the lot behind the station, out of view from the street.

Phil made the introductions: "Clara, Ben is FBI, Merritt is Coast Guard Investigative Services. They are working together."

"We have had three missing women. One was found. There has been information that there are women being abducted. We have three names. Two are women who have been reported missing. The other name we have is Maggie…"

Clara looked angry, then overwhelmed with fear.

Merritt sat next to her. "We are working on finding where they are being held."

"I want to help. I'll need to find a motel and clothes, and I'll need more clothes." Clara started sobbing. "The other woman, is she alive?"

Merritt answered, "Yes." She looked at Ben.

"Clara, we believe the women who have been abducted are being held in a brothel."

"Sex slaves?"

"Unfortunately, yes."

The anger returned. "This is my father's fault. Nothing Maggie did was ever good enough…"

Merritt interrupted, "We will help you find a place to stay."

"Merritt, hold that thought." Phil left his office with his phone to his ear. He was gone for a couple of minutes. When he came back, he was smiling. "Clara, if it is OK with you…"

"I'll stay anywhere…"

"Clara, there is a firefighter in town. His girlfriend is one of the missing women. He would be happy to have you stay in his guest room. He lives on one side of a duplex. His name is Justice Mason, but he picked up the nickname Juice in the Marines. He said to come right over. Clara, the other side, is owned by one of my Detectives. His girlfriend was the woman found last week. I know she will want to talk to you. He talked to Lenny and Matilda; they want to meet you. Merritt will go with you in your car."

"Juice Mason, this is Clara."

Clara walked to him slowly. "I appreciate this." She held out her hand. "I can cook and clean. I need to do something to repay your kindness."

"You can come to the station to make dinner if you'd like?"

"Yes, absolutely. I need to stay busy. Who is the woman who got away?"

Matilda and Lenny had come in the back through the kitchen. "Hi, I'm Lenny, this is Matilda."

"You sound just like your sister."

Clara was in shock. "I am so sorry." She held her hand over her mouth as she composed herself. "Did the people who took you do this?"

"I'm not sure. This is much better than I was… Clara, when I was there, some of the other ladies tried to talk to me through the vents. You sound like one of the women. I'm really afraid your sister is there."

"You didn't talk to her?"

"The first day I was there, I challenged the man who came to my room. He got angry. He beat me and raped me. After that, I was afraid to trust anyone."

"How did you get out?"

"I don't know. I woke up in the hospital. Lenny and Phil were there. The State Police told them where they found me. I wouldn't let them tell me what happened. The doctor said I won't ever remember."

Ben added, "Clara, we know two men wrote letters to the State Police. A linguist confirmed they were written by different people. Unfortunately, they didn't know where the house was. One said it was near Gloucester." Ben looked at Merritt. "We are undercover, so if you see us in town, unless we approach you, don't approach us. As an Agent,

I never make promises, but I will do everything in my power to get the people behind this and bring the women home."

Kim and Sylvie had followed Clara's car. Ben and Phil arrived first, parking on Lenny's side of the house in the back.

Ben and Merritt were the first to leave. Matilda waved as they went to the car.

"Kim, look."

"I'm going to follow them. I'd like to see where they go."

Ben and Merritt drove to the pool house. Ben parked his SUV next to the big garage.

Kim kept driving. "Well, well. It appears our new friends have money."

***

Shaw's birthday party began as a family-only gathering, but Dalton, Kathryn, and Abby had other ideas. Abby invited Colt and Molly, Kathryn invited Jack and Brock, who in turn invited Juice and Clara. The goal was for everyone to get to know Ben and Merritt. Kathryn also asked Tim and Lucy, hoping they were available.

Trip insisted the party be held at his house, and guests began trickling in. As with previous gatherings, some of the guests had to park on the road.

Stella arrived in her own car, as she often did when Simon was running late. She parked on the road and walked in alone, paying no attention to the other cars parked along the street—just like everyone else.

But the people in the car parked across the street did take notice.

Ben and Merritt had decided that Ben should make peace with Beau. After all the introductions were made, Ben approached Beau and extended his hand. "I hope there are no hard feelings."

"I knew there would be repercussions, but I know I did the right thing."

"You did. Since you know about the letters, I can tell you that earlier today, a woman came to town looking for her sister."

"Trinity?"

"No, Maggie. We shared what we could, but she intends to stay in town. Juice offered his guest room to her."

Beau looked hopeful. "So, you are optimistic?"

"We only have an approximation. The last time Clara talked to Maggie, she said she was near Gloucester last fall."

"Ben, I didn't call Shaw the other day…"

"I know. I'd like to start over if possible."

"Dad told me he was lending his dock and pool house. I wish there was something I could do."

Andy heard the conversation and spoke up "Hi, I'm Beau's cousin Andy. I have something you may be able to use if you don't mind getting information from a priest."

"Oh, I… I don't know."

"It is hearsay at the very least, but a parishioner…"

Beau interrupted, "This is my cue to leave."

Andy continued, "He came to me because he was conflicted about something a friend told him about a brothel."

Ben groaned "I don't know."

"Agent, the information may help you with a location, nothing more. This man said he thought the location was on the water because he heard the tide slapping against a dock or rocks."

"That does help. Thank you, Father."

"Here I'm Andy. The Veteran sometimes call me Padre, but please, call me Andy. You're staying with Phil and Connie?"

"I am. I've missed being with a big family. I have three sisters. I moved here from St. Louis."

"I hope what I told you will help."

"Abby…" Beau needed to talk to his sister.

"You raced away from that conversation."

"Ben wanted us to start over." Beau whispered, "Trinity told me the name Maggie. Her sister came to town today looking for her. I don't know the details…"

"Good. I don't want you to get hurt. If you hear something, please promise you will tell Ben."

"I promise. Andy was going to tell him something. I had to get away…"

Andy went to Abby and kissed her temple. "I had to do something, Beau. I didn't give him any details, only that a parishioner's friend told him there was a brothel somewhere near the water."

"Beau, I thought you didn't know where it was."

"I don't. I guess I didn't tell you that I heard water. Andy, will it help?"

"He thinks it will."

"I really don't know how to thank you, Andy."

"It was weighing on me. I knew I wasn't breaking a vow. "

Shaw was curious about the conversations he was seeing. Sometimes, he couldn't turn off the investigator, but Dalton caught him watching "Mind your own business."

"He is always up to something."

"I thought you two were playing nice."

"I can't help it. "

"Listen to me. Julie is happier than she has been in a while. She said Beau is different. Give him a chance."

Shaw looked toward Trip and Lizzy. "Dad is happy again, too."

"Your mother wanted him to move on. Come on, cheer up. You're a year older."

Shaw laughed. "I love you. I've been thinking about something. I mean, it's been on my mind a lot more lately…. Dalton, will you marry me?"

"What? Are you kidding? I've been waiting to hear you say that since we were kids."

"You mean even when you hated me?"

"I never hated you. I was always in love with you. I don't have to think about it. Yes, yes, I'll marry you."

"Hold that thought. Don't say a word. I'll be right back."

Dalton waited as Shaw went to his father's office safe. He retrieved the ring his mother had given him. When Shaw returned, he placed the ring on her finger. "Mom hoped I would give this to you."

"Oh Shaw…" Dalton kissed him.

"Eeeek! Is that what I think it is? Abby bolted across the room and embraced her brother and best friend.

Trip put his arm around Coop. "See how happy Abby is."

"She is happy. Trip, she knows I want to marry her. You know how she gets when she thinks she is being pressured to do something. We'll get there."

Lizzy noticed Stella was still waiting for Simon to arrive. "A penny?"

"Sometimes I think Simon is more like Beau than Shaw."

"Why would you say that?"

"Are we always just going to live together? Are we ever going to get married?"

"Sweetheart, you could ask him."

"I'm afraid he'll say no. Not to change the subject, but how is Matilda?"

"Better. Go to the house. She is easing back. Friends are dropping by. She needs to get her confidence back, but Lenny is devoted to her. Right now, I think once the injuries are gone and she and Lenny are able to reconnect, well, it's going to take time…Someone is smiling."

"Hi honey, sorry I'm late." Simon loved being a doctor, but he loved Stella, too. He often wondered about their future together. They had been with each other for a long time, and he felt that getting married wouldn't change that.

Shaw and Dalton went to the back of the house by the pool. "I wish my parents were here."

"They would have been here if they knew. You know your mother can't miss one of her Garden Club events. We can go over there tomorrow. I have to ask you something. I know you'll ask Abby to be your maid of honor. I may regret this, but I think I'm going to ask Beau."

"It certainly would be a nice gesture. Simon is so busy, but you should ask him to be a groomsman."

"You do realize this will be a big affair."

"I'm OK with that. I do have a lot of friends I have to ask. You may need to hire a Rent-A-Groomsman."

"I'll manage…"

"Hey!" Abby yelled. "You two need to come back inside."

Everyone raised a glass of champagne. Abby made a toast to the birthday boy and to the newly engaged couple.

Shaw then excused himself to talk to Simon: "I think I need to ask Beau to be my best man. We are trying to be less hostile. Abby and Dalton say Julie is happy again. Besides, you're too busy to give me the bachelor party I deserve."

Simon chuckled. "I think you're right. You and Beau should try harder. I'll be happy being a groomsman. That way, I can nix whatever inappropriate party Beau plans."

"Good, but when you finally get around to proposing yourself, I will be happy to serve."

"I am always so busy. I have another year."

"Stella isn't going anywhere."

"No, I know… Go, talk to Beau."

Beau and Julie were talking to Ben and Merritt when Shaw interrupted, "May I have a word, Beau?" He walked to the backyard. "I already talked to Simon, so I was hoping you would be my best man."

"Me? Really?"

"Yes, really."

Beau was overcome. "Yes, of course. Thank you. Does Dalton know?"

Shaw chuckled. "Yes. I've noticed you and Julie are back to your old selves again."

"Something was going on even before Harold died. Abby kind of pushed me in the right direction. I still don't know what was wrong, but we talked. I guess that's all we needed to do."

"Are you going to continue paying Trinity's mortgage?"

"For the time being. I haven't seen Matilda, I don't know her, but Ben told me what happened. The whole situation scares the shit out of me."

"I saw some of the crime scene photos. You should be afraid."

***

Steve wanted to see the house Kim had described. They noticed a gathering and decided to observe from down the street. She always carried a small digital camera in her bag, mostly to take pictures of potential ladies for the house. As she scanned through the photos, "We saw some of these ladies at the Pub."

"Let's go back there. Maybe the bartender is on tonight."

It was a busy Saturday night at the Pub, but as soon as Kim and Steve walked in, Naomi texted Ben and Phil.

"Looks like it's standing room only."

"There is a single stool down here… May I get you anything?"

"Two bourbon Manhattan's. Kim likes extra cherries."

"You got it."

Naomi placed three cherries on a small spear for Kim's drink. While Steve chatted with Naomi, Kim playfully twisted the stem of one cherry in her mouth, tying it in a knot. When she was finished, she slid the knot onto the tip of her tongue and showed it to Naomi.

Naomi didn't know how to respond, so she said nothing. Instead, she just looked a little too long, blushing before walking away.

Steve whispered to Kim "Before we make our move, we need to lay low for a while, but I would like to find out where she lives."

"I have an idea we need to talk about. Why don't we go outside after we finish our drinks?"

***

"Billie, Billie, are you there?" Trinity was confused. Something was happening to her. At first, she thought she was sick, but every time she felt her mind beginning to clear, she experienced what could only be described as an episode. Terrifying nightmares, strange dreams, and lost time—at least, that's what she believed.

"Trinity?"

She stood on the bed. "Billie, are you OK?"

"I'm not sure. I feel weird. I don't feel sick, but my mind is…"

"Confused?"

Billie laid her head against the wall. "Yes. Maybe that lavender is affecting our nervous system."

"I didn't think of that. I'm having nightmares, but I don't think I'm sleeping. Like I said, it's confusing. Billie, where were you when they took you?"

"I don't think we should say too much. I think they're listening; at least, I thought they were. I'm not sure about anything anymore."

Trinity began to weep. "I'd really like to meet you someday…"

Chapter 19

After a few days of reconnaissance, Tim, Lucy, Merritt, and Ben managed to schedule a picnic on the peninsula—only after a contentious meeting with Colt, Skipper, and Phil.

Merritt had observed the pontoon boat several times. A middle-aged man wearing a floppy-brimmed Spencer Tracy hat from *The Old Man and the Sea* was often on board. She couldn't tell if anyone or anything was behind the curtains. What she did determine was that the boat never made trips after dark. After discussing their options with Ben, they decided they should spend the night camping on the peninsula. Tim and Lucy would drop them off and return the following morning to bring them home.

A full moon was expected the next night. They planned to borrow night vision binoculars and a signal lamp from Skipper. Colt and Phil didn't like the idea. Neither was comfortable leaving Ben and Merritt there without a way to escape. So, Colt decided to anchor on the mainland at a dock owned by the town. He and Molly volunteered to take the overnight shift. Only after brainstorming rescue plans did Colt and Phil agree to the plan.

"Connie has become very fond of you. Don't do anything stupid."

"Yes, Dad, geez." Ben understood the hesitation on the part of Phil and Colt; they didn't want anyone else to be hurt. Skipper trusted Merritt and he liked Ben, so he went along with their recommendation.

Colt reminded them, "We expect to see you at the Gala."

"I'm counting on Merritt to keep me safe."

"I already bought a dress, so I'm going with or without you."

Tim and Lucy met Ben and Merritt at the pool house with the food. They decided to head to the ocean side of the peninsula, where they found a spot to dock and pulled the boat ashore.

Ben and Merritt had two of Colt's cameras with them. Their plan was to try and capture pictures of the back of the house, especially close-ups of all the windows.

They walked along the shore toward the mainland, hoping to get closer to the street. While it was unlikely they'd see anything inside the house, they wanted to give it a shot.

The embankment was steep and covered in wild blackberry plants. They moved carefully through the bristly vines, but when Merritt got tangled up, Ben caught her, and they nearly toppled over. They were trying to be discreet, but it wasn't going well. After a while, they gave up and headed back.

"Well, that didn't work."

"Did you see anything?" Lucy said sarcastically.

"No, but Colt's cameras should give us a better view of those windows and the back door."

They zoomed in with the cameras, took several pictures, and then walked back to the spot they had chosen for their picnic. Merritt, never one to be shy, explained... "This area is good for a picnic, but it is also really good if you decide to get busy."

"Good to know. Lucy, maybe next time we both have the day off, we can come back."

Lucy glared at Tim, then laughed. "Ben, can you share what is going on with Clara?"

"She is spending a lot of time with Matilda. She is kicking herself for waiting so long to find Maggie. I truly don't know if we would have looked at her as a missing person given the way she left home."

"I know Juice is happy to have her at the house. He misses Billie so much."

"Well, kiddo, are you ready? I have to get to work. I know Colt and Molly will be at the dock, so I'm not as worried. See you both tomorrow. Be careful."

Ben and Merritt made their way back to the head of the peninsula, staying far enough behind the trees to remain hidden if anyone approached the dock or entered the courtyard behind the house. They spotted a van driving through the gate from the street, but it quickly disappeared behind the wall, piquing their curiosity.

They climbed the hill where the mainland met the peninsula, deliberately avoiding looking at the house. They stayed hidden behind a grove of conifers that lined the road. At the base of the driveway, they noticed a teak door, but by the time they reached it, the van had already vanished behind it.

"Well Benny, we need to find out who owns that van." Merritt saw a spot where they could lean against a tree and watch for the van. They kept their eyes on the house as they talked about their lives. But as usual, Ben did most of the talking. He missed his family. He hoped to take Merritt home with him for either Thanksgiving or Christmas. "I don't want to jump the gun, but I want you to meet my family."

"Umm." She was terrified at the thought of meeting the family. It was written all over her face: "Can we talk about it back at the campsite?"

"Sure. We have to wait a few minutes. Based on the time the van arrived, my guess is it will be another ten minutes before it heads back."

"Is this based on personal experience, or is it just a wild guess?"

"Educated guess. The appointments are probably one hour, correct?"

"I'm thinking, fifty minutes?"

"That's for a Psychiatrist, sweet cheeks."

Merritt kissed Ben. "This wasn't supposed to happen Ben."

He understood the concern. Merritt was still afraid about the assignment, and the more time they spent together, the more her fear seemed to grow. At first, he thought he was just being hopeful when he looked into her eyes. When she spoke to him, when they were intimate, he saw love. He had been in love before, but never like this. As he kissed her forehead, she bolted upright. The wooden garage door began to lift. The van rolled out, but without any license plates. Ben quickly called Phil to report the van and ask him to issue a BOLO: "It had plates when it went in the garage."

Ben and Merritt hiked back to their spot on the peninsula. Merritt spread out the blanket and glanced into the knapsack. "I'm not hungry yet, are you?"

"Not yet." Ben grasped her hand. "Come, sit."

"You want to talk?"

"Don't you think we should?"

"You know me better than anyone. I've opened up to you more than I have with anyone except maybe Billie. The day we went to Boston, we were making small talk, but you were so easy to talk to that the words were just falling out of my mouth…"

"What are you afraid of?"

"You, I'm afraid of falling in love with you."

"I'm willing to wait for you if you promise not to break my heart."

"Oh Ben, that is the last thing I want to do."

"I'm not afraid to say I love you because I do. The fact you understand my job and why people like us do what we do, removed a huge weight from my mind. The fact you came up with the assignment and brought it to Skipper not only shows you are an excellent Agent, but it showed me what a big heart you have. You are funny and smart and…"

"Stop, please stop." Merritt gently caressed Ben's face and kissed him. He wrapped his arms around her and leaned back. She lifted her shirt over her head and began to unbuckle Ben's belt. Within moments, they were both naked, lost in each other, unaware of or unconcerned with their surroundings...

Ben pecked Merritt's forehead. "You are going to get us both fired."

"Good, more time for us."

"So, there is an us? Do we have a future?"

"I do love you, Ben." Merritt knelt, straddling Ben's waist. He placed his hands on her hips, sat up, and kissed her. "But you're right, we need to talk. I'm sorry, but I'm not ready to settle down. I'm sorry."

"So, this is it? You're not ready, so we can't live together, love each other and someday…"

"What if someday never comes? I am adventurous. I'm not sure I am the marrying kind. I should have said something. Please don't hate me."

"Have you thought about anything else? I mean, after we found Naomi, I seriously thought about getting into another line of work, especially if I ever found…"

"I told you I was scared. This, you and me, is frightening because I know I will never find someone like you again. I can't ask you to wait for me. It's not fair."

"I'm not willing to give up on us or on you. Even when we're done here, we are still both based out of Boston. I hope we find Billie and Trinity soon… Oh crap, it's Phil… hey Captain, I'm with Merritt." He put the call on the speaker.

"The van is in the wind. Ben, can you see what your techs can do with enlarging those photos."

"That was my thought as well… wait a minute, Merritt?"

"Phil, do you have both sets of Trinity's house keys?"

"No, just Beau's."

"The speculation has been that Trinity was taken so they would have her house as a vantage point to eventually take Matilda. What if, since they have her keys, they are also using it as a transfer station of sorts."

"We are also pretty sure the boat isn't used at night. I would think that would be their busiest time. But, and this is a big but, they had no way of knowing Beau would report her missing. These people have to do their homework, Phil. I have an idea. What if we staked out at her house? We can put cameras on the trees in the front, both coming and going. We can see if the van is a frequent traveler along that road."

"I guess I should ask Beau. Ben?"

"I would say yes. I can't imagine he would object…"

Merritt interrupted, "Phil unless he has been playing us all along."

"Fair point, but I've known Beau for a long time. In this case, there was genuine concern… Are you two sure you want to stay there overnight?"

Merritt was adamant, "Yes!" She looked into Ben's eyes as she stroked his lower back. "Yes, we need to see this through."

"Good enough. Be safe. See you soon."

Merritt continued to sit on Ben's lap as she kissed him. "Will you be patient? Will you wait for me?"

"I will give us time, but I could decide you are a huge pain in the ass."

"Ah yes, but you love my ass."

Ben moved his hands to her rear end. "I do, and I would miss it terribly if it were gone."

"Have you always wanted a family?"

"If I found the right woman."

"If you found the right woman, but she wasn't sure about having children, what then?"

"I don't want to change anything about you, Merritt…"

"But?"

"This is your fault. You made me love you."

"Can we be happy here, in this moment? Both scenarios are scary for me. But right now, right this minute, being without you is not an option…"

***

Billie and Trinity had devices strapped to their eyelids to keep them open. They were also gagged, and their heads were secured to the backs of the chairs. A black partition separated them, so they couldn't see each other.

The wall in front of them was white. After a few minutes, a series of disturbing images flashed across the surface. The scenes were so horrifying that their minds struggled to process them.

Trinity wasn't familiar with brainwashing methods, but Billie was. It took her some time, but she managed to close her mind, not completely, but enough to dull the horrors she was witnessing. Even so, her brain was overwhelmed. Trinity's eyes were filled with tears, and those tears were the only thing preventing the horrific images from being seared into her memory.

Then the room went dark. The horrors didn't stop, though. The clasps were removed from their eyes, the gags from their mouths, and they were each assaulted by men who brutalized them without hesitation.

When Trinity woke up, she immediately curled her knees to her chest, hugging them as she cried. *No, no. Don't let them do this to you. Beau, where are you?*

Billie was confused. She was dressed in pajamas. *It can't be morning already.* How long had she been in that torture chamber?

She stood on the bed. "Trinity, are you there?"

It took Trinity a few minutes to stand on the bed. "Hi, I'm here."

"Are you OK?"

"No, I don't know if I'll ever be OK again. These people are sick."

"I was wondering if anyone else was there. I think this is some kind of indoctrination. They don't kill the ladies when they are done with them; I think they use brainwashing techniques to make us believe we are losing our minds."

Trinity started crying. "Why?"

Billie needed to change the subject. "Have you looked behind the pictures on your wall?"

"I have. Do you think we could still be in Cape Hope?"

"I don't know… hmm time to sleep…"

Chapter 20

Shaw had been driving to his father's house when a car slowed down, placed an envelope in Trip's mailbox, and sped away. Concerned, Shaw opened the mailbox to find a white envelope. It had no writing and was unsealed. Always prepared, he reached into his briefcase, took out a latex glove, and removed the envelope. Looking inside, he discovered a thumb drive, one photo, and a Post-it note that read: "Back off, or all photos will be released to the press.".

Merritt and Ben were on the peninsula, with Ben lying on the blanket. The photo was taken after Merritt had straddled his waist while Ben caressed her hips. Her face was immediately recognizable, but Ben's was not. Shaw wondered if someone from the brothel knew who Ben and Merritt were.

On the night of the party, Shaw had spent time talking to Ben and Merritt. He liked them. Merritt shared stories about the couple they met at the pub and was not shy about discussing Ben's methodology. Shaw laughed, respecting both Ben and Merritt for their honesty.

Instead of stopping in to see his father, he drove to the station. He was relieved to see Ben in Phil's office. "Ben, I'm glad you're here. A late model white Mercedes put this in my father's mailbox."

Ben opened it. At first, he looked surprised, then he smiled. "Well, this will only make Merritt more determined." He handed the picture to Phil. "I'm not ashamed, and I know she won't be, especially if this person thinks we will stop looking for Billie and Trinity and the other women."

Phil handed the picture back to Ben. "This is war."

"Gentlemen, we need to get into that house."

"What house?" Shaw was in the dark.

"Merritt and I were investigating the house at the end of the cove. There has been a boat. Colt, Cooper and Abby have seen it. Matilda also saw it the day she was abducted. We went to the peninsula to explore. We stayed on land, so unless they have high-powered listening devices on the dock or someone who reads lips, there is no way they could know what we were talking about."

Shaw was uncomfortable. "Phil, you have known me for a long time; you know I hate playing political games…"

Ben spoke up, "Your boss?"

"Yes. He gave me the letter about the brothel that was sent to our office and told me to take care of it. Ben, I think he knows something about the organization. This is something big that would be a huge boost to his plans to climb the political ladder. He thinks if the shit hits the fan and his cronies are named, he can go after me and turn the tables. The only person I told about my suspicions is Dalton. Phil knows she is the least gossipy person in town."

Ben held out the envelope. "So, Shaw, do you want a copy of this?"

He chuckled. "No, Phil, if you could put it in evidence, under lock and key. But I think you should show it to Merritt."

"I will. The problem is we were there twice. Alone the first time, then with Tim and Lucy. They left us there so we could observe at night. I just hope they don't think Tim or Lucy are involved."

"I'll speak to Lucy. Ben, I admire your composure."

"It doesn't help to get hysterical. Merritt isn't modest, and she will know this means they're scared and they will start making mistakes. I better get back to her." Ben started to leave. "Never in a million years would I have believed I would meet a woman like Merritt, especially during a case. Thank you both. We will see you at the Gala."

Ben saw Merritt on the sailboat. He jogged to the dock, stepped onto the deck, and kissed her.

"Wow, that was nice."

"You only deserve the best. I need to tell you something."

"Does this have something to do with the other night?"

"Only part of it… When we were in our spot when you were sitting on my lap?"

"And we were naked?"

"Yup. Someone took a picture and sent it here. Shaw intercepted it when he saw a car slow down at the mailbox."

"So, who has seen it besides Shaw?"

"Phil."

She laughed. "And?"

"The note said to back off, or they would send it to the press. There is a thumb drive, too."

"Is it at least my good side?"

"It is beautiful."

"Did you look at the thumb drive?"

"No. I will have to at some point. Maybe we can have some popcorn and make a night of it."

Merritt put her arm around him and laughed. "I have an idea. Maybe we should poke the bear. We would have to talk to Abby first, but if it was sent to all outlets, do you think Abby would allow us to trace the origin?"

"We need to look at the thumb drive first. We don't want Lucy and Tim caught up in this."

"I don't think either one of them would stand in the way."

"Probably not. What is your idea?"

"We leave a note on the gate. You know they've been watching, so if we leave a note, they will see it."

"What will the note say?"

"Something to tell them we're not afraid of them."

"They obviously think we live here. I think we should talk to Phil and Shaw before we do anything. I'll call Skipper; you can tell your boss."

"I did. He was in a meeting, so I had to call him back. But he said from everything he knew about you, it would only piss you off and make you more steadfast…"

"He's right... Ben, I need to talk to you about something."

"I need to stop you. I have to talk to my boss. We need to get ahead of this, but I'll be back, I promise, but you need to watch this. Then we need to talk. I love you."

"I know. I love you too."

She went to the pool house to watch the video. At first, she looked for clues about how it was recorded. To her, it appeared to be drone footage, or perhaps someone was on the edge of the clearing watching them— though a drone seemed more likely. She observed the video like an agent searching for clues, then restarted it from the beginning and tried to view it as an impartial observer.

The passion they expressed was apparent. It wasn't lust or desire. It was love, pure and simple.

She didn't realize the extent of Ben's love until she saw the video; he loved her completely. It wasn't just sex to him; he was demonstrating how deeply he cared for her. She was beginning to understand that he wanted marriage and children with the woman he loved. She had never thought about a relationship in those terms before, but watching Ben make love to her was overwhelming, and she cried.

Merritt got into the shower and wept. She had never considered a lifetime with anyone, but what she had just witnessed changed her outlook. She knew she wanted Ben in her future.

***

Matilda had her doctor's appointment a day early. She didn't tell Lenny because she really didn't want him there with her; she was nervous enough. Still, she didn't want to go alone, so Clara accompanied her.

Matilda had a plan. On the way back, they would stop at the store to buy everything needed to make Lenny's favorite meal. For dessert, she would give him the watch. She had no doubt he would agree to marry her, but she was still nervous.

The doctor she saw at the hospital was kind and very gentle. Matilda decided to see her again. She needed to talk about being intimate again, particularly about what to expect if she couldn't follow through.

"Matilda, you are doing remarkably well. You have been staying with your boyfriend?"

"He has been so patient. I need to know if I will be able to be the Matilda he fell in love with."

"You haven't been sleeping in the same bed?"

"We have. I'm still having nightmares. Even with his big arms around me all night, I'm still having nightmares."

"I'd be worried if you weren't having nightmares. You haven't talked to anyone?"

"There is an FBI agent who is working the case. We've become friends. She was abducted by a serial killer, so she understands. I'm not sure Lenny would be able to handle what those people did to me."

"He hasn't asked?"

"No, and that's OK. He knows me better than anyone. Doctor, Lenny and I were perfect together. What if I can't respond to him the way I did before?"

"I'm not going to lie to you; that may take time, just like every part of your recovery. I wish I could give you some advice, but the truth is I simply don't know. In the simplest terms, try not to think about anything except you and Lenny. I put a rush on your blood test. Everything is good. Your wrist is doing good. Please, if anything doesn't seem right, let me know."

Clara didn't ask how the appointment went; she thought it was too personal. Instead, she asked what Matilda had planned for dinner. Matilda didn't answer right away; she seemed almost sad. Clara hoped the doctor hadn't given her bad news, but she was afraid to ask and felt helpless.

After they went grocery shopping, Clara finally asked, "Do you want to talk about your appointment?"

"Oh no, but thank you. I'm actually fine. You and I have talked so much about Maggie; tell me about you. You said you don't have to get back. You don't have a job?"

"I am a book editor, like Maggie. I free-lance mostly, but technically, I work for my father."

"Is he a Publisher?"

"Yes. Can we not talk about him? He is the reason Maggie is missing."

"Have you told him?"

"No. He will twist it around and make it her fault."

"Clara, he may surprise you."

"Did you call your family?"

"I haven't spoken to them in years."

"I need to do something. I feel so helpless.

"I have an idea. There is a woman. She is a Journalist, but she is also a really good person. She has kept the story under wraps for the safety of the women. I think you should talk to her and her right hand, Cubby."

"If you trust them, then yes."

"OK, they'll be here in a few minutes. I called Ben, too. He's bringing Merritt."

"I trust you. That's good enough for me."

Abby and Cubby looked at the timetable Clara had created regarding Maggie's disappearance. Clara also let them listen to the voicemail. "She wasn't mad at me. She would have called on my birthday if she was able."

Ben saw Clara and Matilda in Abby's office. "May I come in? I have something you need to see." Ben scanned the photo and downloaded the thumb drive to his tablet. "Shaw found these in your father's mailbox. They must have been watching us.

"I know that spot. It's not visible from either shore."

Matilda looked over Abby's shoulder. "It is really refreshing to see someone not embarrassed about such an intimate photo."

"There's nothing to be embarrassed about. We walked toward that house at the end of the cove. It's weird; the back windows are covered from the inside with something like a chipboard. But after I thought about it for a while, I wondered if they were covered with large paintings."

"Matilda?"

"There were pictures. You think the brothel is in that house?"

"Speculation. But while we were in the grove by the street, a van pulled into the driveway. We tried taking pictures of the plates as it went in. When it left, the plates were gone. I called Phil, but they were nowhere to be found."

"So, they saw you?"

"Most likely."

Abby looked at the picture again. "This picture is beautiful."

Ben smiled. "They don't know who they're dealing with. My boss, Colt, Skipper, they are leaving it up to us, and neither one of us will be embarrassed if this gets out."

Abby handed the tablet back to Ben. "They are making threats because they're scared, which means they will make a mistake… Clara is feeling at loose ends. Do you think she would like to come to the Gala with us? She could borrow a dress. I think we are probably the same size."

Matilda agreed, "Yes, that is a great idea."

***

Matilda took a shower and let her curly hair hang naturally. She put on a big T-shirt and went to the kitchen, where everything was ready and staying warm in the oven.

When she saw Lenny's car pull into the driveway, she took two beers from the refrigerator and stood in the living room near the hallway leading to the back door.

"Hello Darlin.' Who might you be?"

"My name is Matilda. But you can call me Tilly."

Lenny kissed her. "That was nice. Did you go somewhere today?"

"I did. Do you want some sustenance first?"

"It smells good."

"It will keep…" She didn't want to wait. She took his hand and led him up the stairs. She put the beers on the nightstand. "I have something for you. The day I was taken, I was walking into town because I wanted to tell you I would move in with you. I pictured us going back to my place, and I was going to give this to you." She had tears in her eyes. "I'm glad I didn't have it with me that day." Matilda handed him the box.

"Tilly, this is beautiful." He was looking at the face of the watch in the package.

"Take it out; look at it."

Lenny took it out of the box. When he turned it over, his expression changed. "Oh, Tilly." He leaned toward her and kissed her. Then he got off the bed, went to his bureau, picked up the ring box, and handed it to her.

Her hands were shaking as she opened the box. She had tears in her eyes. "I asked you first."

"You did. I would love to be your husband, Tilly."

"Oh my God, Lenny. How long have you had this?"

"I bought it after we went to the North End. What do you say?"

"I would love to be your wife."

***

Merritt was at the boat in her bathing suit. It wasn't long before Ben arrived. He had gone to his place the night before because he needed to think.

Merritt held both his hands and sat on the deck chair. "Ben, I'm not sure how we ended up going our separate ways, but I didn't like it. You're not passive-aggressive or controlling in any way, so my conclusion is that you were hurt and wanted some time to reflect. I meant it when I said I don't want to break your heart, but I think I may have left it a little fractured. I'm sorry if I hurt you. I'm sorry if I made you feel like I didn't want a life with you because I do. I never want to spend another night away from you. I missed you so much… Ben, please say something."

Ben had been staring at the ground. She was right; he was hurting. He desired a family, yet his feelings for Merritt lingered. After they returned, Merritt opted to stay at the pool house while Ben headed to his own place to shower. He found himself in the kitchen, where Connie was preparing lunch for the kids. Over time, he had come to respect her and Phil, so he sought her counsel. By the time the kids wrapped up their meal and returned to their activities, Ben had resolved to spend the night reflecting on his future with Merritt.

"I know you're scared, but I love you. I think you would be a great mother, but if that isn't something you see in your future…"

"Ben, I watched the video. I never thought anyone could love me so much. I want a future with you. I want to have your children, and I never want to hurt you again." Merritt was teary eyed "I love you."

"Are you sure?" Ben smirked.

Merritt slapped his arm. "I'd like some time for us first, maybe time to travel, go to St. Louis on Thanksgiving or Christmas… or both."

"I am sorry I held back. I needed to think too. Part of being in love is thinking about a future. I don't know how it happened, but you have become the only future I can see."

"I didn't want to love you, Ben, but I do, with all my heart."

***

Abby wasn't sure what to share with Beau, but she felt he was the reason they knew about the brothel in the first place. "Hey, are you busy?"

"Yes, but I'll make time for you."

Abby closed the office door. "I asked your assistant to hold your calls."

"Is this about Trinity?"

"They haven't found her, sorry," Abby told Beau what she could while leaving out the details about the house at the end of the cove.

"Maybe it was a drone?"

"I'm not sure. From the angle, Merritt's face is clear; Ben's not so much."

"Is Dad in danger?"

"No. They believe they have seen them on the dock, on the boat and they assume they live in the house. Dad has been kept in the loop."

"Abbs, I need to go back."

"I understand, Beau, but the people behind this are scared. You don't want to be caught there if the FBI has to move in quickly."

"I didn't think of that."

"I also wanted to tell you that Maggie's sister is going to the Gala with Juice."

"I never met Maggie. Trinity told me her name, that's all."

"That is a lot, Beau. Have you talked to Andy?"

"I did. I gave him a check. I asked him to put it toward the new roof for the rectory."

"As much as I didn't like your tactics, I think Andy knew he had to say something."

"I've been a prick for so long it will be hard to change, but I think I've been scared straight.

"Beau, I understand you're worried about Trinity, but Julie is a different person. She has seen the change in you. Have you thought about what you will do when they find Trinity?"

"I can't stop thinking about it."

Chapter 21

Matilda felt happier than she could ever recall. She gazed at the ring Lenny had given her, reflecting on the previous night. Lenny admitted he was nervous, which only deepened Matilda's affection for him. She reassured him they could wait until he felt ready. He slipped into the bathroom, donned his robe, and settled against the headboard. "Come, let's do this right."

Matilda faced him as she always did, but this time it meant more. She had been given a second chance "I feel like I did the first time. You were always so quiet, but the way you looked at me, I knew I needed to know you better."

"You are still the woman I fell in love with." He caressed her hips. "You will always be that woman."

"Your hands; I've missed your hands."

He leaned forward and kissed her chest just above her cleavage, then up to her ear. He whispered, "I love you, Tilly."

"That makes me crazy."

"I know…"

Matilda smiled as she thought about Lenny. They never made it back downstairs for dinner. Instead, they reveled in each other until they fell asleep in each other's arms.

When they woke up the next morning, they made love again.

She was feeling like a woman again, which gave her the courage to go out by herself for the first time. She had to tell Tim their good news.

She saw Tim's car next to the Pub and went in the back door. The office light was on. She stood by the open door. "Well, hello there, big boy."

Tim leaped out of his chair. "You are a sight for sore eyes." He hugged Matilda, stepped back, and then hugged her again.

"Well, then, you may need to put your sunglasses on before I show you this." She held out her hand. "Did you ever think this would happen?"

"I knew Lenny would ask. I wasn't sure what your answer would be."

"I actually asked him first."

"I'll close the Pub; we can do it here."

Matilda laughed. "That would be appropriate. We're still trying to figure things out. I'm going to sell my house. I'm not sure about: I actually don't know if I can come back here."

"Oh honey, don't worry about that. Have you talked about it with Lenny?"

"No, not yet."

"Take your time. Come back for dinner."

"Maybe next week. I decided to go to the Gala. Clara is going too… So, how is Lucy?"

"Perfect. She's getting to know Kathryn and Cubby. We went to Shaw's birthday last week. She's making a lot of friends. I love her Matilda…"

"And I love him." Lucy kissed Tim, then hugged Matilda. "Look at you. I hope the grand re-opening went well?"

Tim burst into laughter. Matilda hugged Lucy. "It was wonderful. I had nothing to worry about."

"Lucy, have you noticed anything different about Matilda?"

It took a minute, but Lucy saw Matilda's ring. Lucy picked up her hand. "Was this before or after the main event?"

"Before."

"Well, I will have to talk to the ladies about a shower and a bachelorette party." Lucy hugged Matilda.

"It sounds like you have everything under control."

"Sorry, I'm excited for you, that's all. I have to go. We'll talk at the Gala."

Tim waited until the door closed. "She is in awe of you. She thinks you're the reason we're together."

"She's right. You should be thanking me, Timmy."

"Thank you, honey. Are you really OK?"

"I don't want anyone else to get hurt."

"Ben and Merritt know what they're doing."

"Abby came by with Cubby. They are being incredibly sensitive… oh, sorry."

"You mean for journalists? Yes, I agree, but you know Cubby would never hurt you."

"Did he tell you about the picture and the video?"

"He did. He wanted my advice. The ethics of journalism have always made him feel like a hypocrite. Protecting someone who may change the outcome of a case. But in this case, he and Abby are going to protect you and the other women."

"Thank you, honey. We will see you tomorrow."

***

Billie and Trinity were utterly exhausted. They hadn't been permitted to sleep and had gone without food for two days. The water they received was laced with hallucinogens, and they were also dosed with Ritalin. Their communication had dwindled as confusion engulfed them; neither Billie nor Trinity was in a sound state of mind.

The women's schedule was packed. Several regulars were incentivized to book appointments. By the time Maude and Ellen prepared Billie and Trinity for their departure, the two had been severely battered and brutalized. If there was any silver lining to their plight, it was that they felt no pain.

Trinity had surrendered, but Billie remained resolute. The intervals between their visitors leaving the bedrooms allowed Billie to regain some clarity. Although still under the drug's effects, she could concentrate better than she had earlier that day. They were confined to their rooms until all the clients had departed the house. Eventually, they were taken to the basement, where they were left on cold tables. In the space between them stood a cart filled with an array of tools…

Billie sensed she wasn't alone. She wasn't shackled or wearing a blindfold, but she hesitated to open her eyes and tried to slow her breathing…She kept her eyes closed and thought about Juice. When she thought about him, she had hope…

The door opened slowly. A man's voice asked, "Is this what you were hoping for?"

"You and your wife will join me?"

A woman?

"Absolutely."

He sounds giddy.

"How long?"

"You tell us."

As they moved out of view, she heard a *click*…

She was certain she heard a voice—a woman's voice. Cracking one eye open just a fraction, she saw two large women securing a naked figure to what resembled a birthing chair. She squeezed her eyes shut and silently pleaded *Dear God, please don't let them hurt us anymore.* Remaining still, she listened to the rustling in the room and the faint sound of a door latch clicking. She dared to peek again. This wasn't a bedroom. It was a stark cinderblock chamber painted black. High up near the ceiling, narrow windows gave it a basement-like feel. A rolling cart stood nearby, cluttered with stainless steel instruments and what looked like a car battery on the bottom shelf. Among the items, there was also a pair of hair clippers.

The woman in the chair wasn't moving…

As soon as they got the call from Steve and Kim that they were at the Gala, the plan got underway.

Two women and a man entered the room, advancing toward the other woman. She remained unresponsive, prompting the man to flip a switch and press a probe against the sole of her foot. She didn't react.

Placing two fingers on the woman's neck, the man confirmed, "She's alive." The two women unfastened the straps and transferred Trinity to the table before shifting their attention to Billie. Though she was weak, she struggled to resist but couldn't defend herself.

Billie found herself strapped into the chair. The man relinquished control to the women, who appeared unfazed by Billie's awareness; in fact, they seemed to take pleasure in it. The woman started by gently touching her. As they became absorbed in their actions, Billie's gaze shifted to Trinity. Instantly, she regretted it as the man began to fondle Trinity's breasts. It seemed he thrived on Billie's reactions, and when she averted her eyes, he reached for the prod. "Watch me, or I will send electricity through her body."

Billie twisted her head to observe as the man savagely attacked the woman on the table. His gaze remained locked on Billie, and then a sinister smile spread across his face. Fear gripped Billie; she was genuinely terrified when she heard the switch click, followed by a low hum. She recognized what that sound signified…

The man got up and walked away.

Trinity was still strapped to the table, awake but confused. Billie was forced to watch the two women again, but she felt sick and looked away. The man reached for the probe and held it between Trinity's legs. Billie screamed, "Stop, please stop…"

The man climbed on Billie, holding the probe. "Turn your head, and you'll be sorry." As he raped her, the man laughed. She felt like she was bleeding and began to weep.

The man chuckled menacingly as he grabbed the clippers. Towering over Trinity, he sheared a strip down the center of her scalp. The moment he noticed the terror etched on Billie's face, he erupted into a chilling laugh. He kept shaving until Trinity's head was left with only a coarse layer of stubble.

The man continued to laugh as he pressed a water bottle to Billie's lips, compelling her to drink. He warned her to finish every drop. Overwhelmed with fear, she complied…

***

Abby, Coop, Shaw, Dalton, Julie, Beau, Simon, and Stella, along with Trip and Lizzy, were the first to show up. Not long after, Ben, Merritt, Phil, and Connie made their entrance.

Ben introduced the two security personnel he had hired. Having previously worked with one of them reassured Trip. He wanted everything to go smoothly for the night dedicated to his late wife.

Security was positioned at the entrance, with strict ticket checks in place. Despite that, Ben and Merritt lingered in the foyer. Merritt suggested that if anyone had seen the video, it would reflect on their faces, so they opted to keep watch, ready to step in if anyone attempted to crash the event. Before the guests arrived, Ben briefed the private security team, along with Naomi, Marcus, and Merritt, sharing the names of those guests who might be armed.

Steve and Kim stood in the parking lot. They had proposed that Sylvie accompany them, but she insisted on taking her own car. While they waited, Mr. Smith called. He was furious about Sylvie's behavior towards the matron and her relentless meddling with the ladies: "I'm sorry. We thought she would be an asset. We will take care of her."

"I understand you are at a Charity Gala tonight."

"We're mixing business with pleasure. We have a plan to fill all the rooms."

"You need to be careful. No more mistakes. I am sending two gentlemen to help with the issues we have been having. I mean it, no more mistakes. There will be changes this weekend. We have to move some of the women…"

***

Lenny arrived at the Gala alongside Clara and Juice. Matilda felt a surge of panic just before they were set to leave. Frustration boiled within her; she recognized that Lenny's presence was crucial for security, not to stay home and tend to her. She firmly insisted he go, vowing to make it up to him later.

Kim, Steve, and Sylvie followed closely behind Clara, Juice, and Lenny. Sylvie quickly zeroed in on Lenny, who kindly informed her that he wasn't interested. Undeterred, she positioned herself at the small table for four with Steve and Kim, but her gaze remained fixed on Lenny—until Naomi caught her attention. "Kim, that woman in the dark green dress. She is FBI."

"What are you talking about? She is a bartender at the Pub."

Sylvie was adamant: "She was undercover, but she ended up addicted to heroin. The FBI arrested my partner. She is the reason he is in prison."

Kim and Steve looked at each other, realizing they had made a mistake with Sylvie. They would placate her for the evening, then cut ties.

"Sylvie, she probably hit rock bottom and ended up here as a bartender. Will she recognize you?"

"No, she was only there for a couple of weeks, and she was always high."

"Who is the man?" Steve wondered.

Sylvie wasn't listening. Naomi was talking to Lenny, which made her angry.

"Sylvie, honey, you need to chill."

She glared at Kim, but Kim wasn't paying attention. She saw Merritt and Ben and waved, "Steve, look at that dress."

"Very attractive. They seem to know everyone."

Kim leaned into Steve. "Sylvie is going to be in our way. We need to mingle with that couple and get some introductions."

"Listen, I have an idea…"

Sylvie was spiraling. She struck up a conversation with Marcus, catching Steve and Kim exchanging looks—they already knew how they were going to handle things. Sylvie, though, had a different plan and boldly asked Marcus to dance. Her attention made him uncomfortable, but he agreed, trying to be polite. Throughout the dance, she was overly aggressive, her comments crossing the line, but Marcus remained composed, keeping his cool. When the song ended, he quickly excused himself and headed over to Ben and Merritt. Tim soon joined the group.

"She is with that couple, Marcus. Watch out."

"Tim, she is nuts."

"Merritt and I are going to strike up a conversation. We need to find out if they are involved."

Tim was concerned. "Please be careful."

***

Matilda was at home, mad at herself for falling apart. She was thinking about going to the Gala, but she was scared. As she paced in the living room, the doorbell rang. She jumped and looked out the window to see a Cape Hope police car in front. She opened the door. "Hi, honey. Did Lenny send you?"

"Would you be mad if he did?"

"No." She hadn't changed out of her dress yet. "Would you do me a favor? Drop me at the Country Club?"

"I would be happy to." Lenny had called his friend Jimmy. He asked him to look in on Matilda. "I am going to walk you in, too. I told Lenny I would keep an eye on you, and I intend to do that until you are in his arms again."

"When did you get so romantic?"

"I always have been. But you have always only had eyes for Lenny."

She held out her hand. "Did he tell you?"

"No, but I know he has wanted to ask for a long time."

"I asked him first."

"Good for you." They pulled into the parking lot. Jimmy left the car running as he walked Matilda inside.

The two men at the door stopped them. "Ticket?"

"I'm with Detective Clarke, Cape Hope PD."

The man looked at Jimmy. "I'm sorry, but we have strict instructions not to let anyone in without a ticket."

Matilda looked melancholy until she saw Ben. "Gentlemen, this lady is with Detective Clarke. She is cool."

Matilda looked at Jimmy. "Hear that, I'm cool… Thank you so much."

Jimmy smiled. "Anytime honey. Congratulations."

Ben escorted Matilda into the ballroom. Lenny was standing at the bar when he saw Ben with his arm around Matilda. "Do you two have something to tell me?"

"I was escorting this lovely lady to her date."

Lenny looked down the bar and grabbed Juice, Phil, Jack and Brock. "Gentlemen, I would like to introduce you to my wife-to-be."

As all the men gathered around Matilda and Lenny, Kim and Steve were taken by surprise. "Steve, look!"

"I can see. There is no way she would recognize us."

"This is getting a little too close for comfort. Did you see our friend over there with his arm around her?"

"I did. I think we need to see this through."

"Normally, I'd agree with you, but Sylvie is uncontrollable; she won't stay put. You need to keep her occupied until we're ready. Ask her to dance."

Steve kissed Kim on the forehead. "Yes, dear."

Steve watched as Matilda and Lenny embraced. He tried to get close enough to overhear, but Ben was still nearby. So, he sidled up to the bar and listened.

Merritt was talking to Clara when she spotted Steve at the bar. She excused herself, stood next to Ben, and whispered, "You have a spy."

Ben kissed her ear. "I know. The friend needs a dance partner. Do you mind?"

"If it will help, go for it. I'll keep Benedict here occupied."

Ben kissed her ear again. "I love you."

Merritt stared at Steve as she replied, "Me too, baby." Merritt kept her eye on Steve as she sashayed to his side. "You look like you are pretty light on your feet. Would you like to show me your moves?"

"I could be persuaded."

Ben pretended to be disinterested in Steve and Merritt as he approached Sylvie. "You look like you could use a partner."

"I would love a new partner."

Ben struggled to keep his focus on Sylvie, especially with Steve openly caressing Merritt's lower back and nuzzling her neck. It was hard to watch, but Ben had already briefed everyone who knew he and Merritt were in an undercover situation, ensuring there wouldn't be any unwanted reactions.

Steve waited to ask Merritt about Matilda. "That woman at the bar seems to be the center of attention. Is she available?"

Merritt grinned. "You looking for a threesome?"

"Kim and I like to mix it up. Does your boyfriend play the field?"

"As long as I'm there. He is, hmm, how do I put this? Docile?"

"Good to know. Kim and I are open to new experiences… Do you know the man over there with the woman in the yellow?"

"He is the son of the woman this charity is named after. Does Kim have her eye on him?"

"Oh, probably. He looked familiar. I thought I saw his picture in the paper. What about the one in the green dress with the server from the Pub?

"She is a little shy, but from what I hear, she is definitely not a player."

Steve couldn't take his eyes off Matilda "So, that one over there. I'm getting a vibe."

"Are your vibes usually on the mark?"

"Usually. We were wrong about Sylvie, though. She is a bit of a live wire. We have to keep her harnessed.

"That's not necessarily a bad thing." Merritt winked. "Having to deal with a partner who gets too clingy or unpredictable can be a problem."

"That and finding a neutral site. Where do you and your friend usually meet?"

She didn't have a predetermined answer, so she improvised, "Our house is safe." Merritt glanced over at the bar, silently communicating with the armed men she had briefed earlier about stepping in if necessary. Juice caught Merritt's signal and quickly moved in, asking to cut in.

"I would love to dance with you, big boy."

Merritt thanked Juice. "Well, I found out they like to find a neutral site for their activities."

"The house on the cove?"

"Truthfully, we don't know."

"Lenny asked me to be his best man, but they want to wait until Billie gets back. What if she doesn't…"

"Stop thinking that way. I am here to find her. I will find her."

"Merritt, that guy is creepy. Please be careful."

"Granted, this purse won't hold my Glock, but I am still armed."

"Please?"

"I don't like the way she is hanging on Ben."

"Does Matilda know about these people?"

"No, but I hoped I would see a tell when Steve asked me about her. I don't think he knew her."

"Merritt, sociopaths don't show their evil alter egos."

"Oh honey, please don't worry about me."

"She was flirting with me and Lenny before. I'm going to give her a chance to dance with *all this.*"

She hugged him. "We are going to get Billie back. Ben will be mad for saying this, but I promise."

"I know you mean that. Let me rescue Ben; after all, that is my schtick."

Ben came back to Merritt. "Remind me to get him a bottle of Scotch."

"Steve told me she has proven to be a live wire, unpredictable. It sounded like they want to break ties with her."

"At some point, I want to go outside and see if they follow."

"Sure. I wouldn't mind hiding in the bushes for a quick make-out session."

"Did you see Matilda's ring?"

"I did. Phil told me earlier. I like your friends from the security company."

"They are actually brothers. It's a long story I'll tell you someday."

"It looks like Trip is going to say something…"

Trip was standing with Beau, Shaw, Abby and Simon. "My family would like to thank all of you for your continued support. Annie was loved and would be humbled by your continued patronage of this important research. Thank you." Trip was never a verbose man, so no one was surprised by his very succinct message.

Sylvie had her eyes on Stella. She asked Kim for her opinion, but she was more interested in dancing with Ben. "Yes, she's very nice. Excuse me."

Kim approached Ben, who was about to sit. "Would you care to dance?"

Ben whispered, "I thought you'd never ask." He tried to steer the conversation toward the house on the cove when she asked where he lived. "We are along the cove."

"That is very nice. Do you have problems with neighbors or boat traffic?"

"Not really. Although there is a house down the street that no one seems to know about."

"Hmm, that sounds mysterious."

"I hope not…" Ben noticed Simon on the phone, then talking to Stella, "The life of an ER doctor. He is always getting called into work."

"She's cute."

"And very shy." Ben was trying to protect the women as best he could.

"Well, I'm getting the eye from Steve. I think he wants to get Sylvie out of here."

"Thanks for the dance."

Kim followed Steve and Sylvie who were headed to the door.

Outside, Stella had said goodbye to Simon. She was standing next to Trip's car, looking at her phone, when she felt a pinch on her arm. Steve picked her up and put her in the back of his SUV. Sylvie was waiting by her car. As Steve reached to open the door for her, Kim stuck her with a needle, too. "Two for one."

"Ben, I want to go outside to see what they are up to; maybe we can get my shawl; it's chilly in here."

"We should go out the side door; it's less conspicuous." They watched as a large SUV drove through the gates of the Country Club. They kept walking toward Ben's SUV.

"So, what about that make-out session you talked about?"

Ben wrapped his arms around Merritt and kissed her deeply. At that moment, they were oblivious to the two men in black masks lurking nearby. Acting swiftly, Ben knocked one of the attackers to the ground. The man quickly regained his footing and lunged at Ben. They grappled fiercely until Ben managed to twist the man's arm behind his back, effectively subduing him. Just as he reached for his handcuffs, he noticed another man aiming a gun at Merritt's head.

Ben stepped back...

One of the men made a call: "We have them. We will search them and prepare them as soon as we arrive."

***

Maude and Ellen had their instructions. The two women were to be thoroughly cleansed, both inside and out, then loaded into the van for transport to a private dock. There, a boat awaited to carry them to a small dinghy nestled in a quiet inlet known for its solitude at night.

The entire operation unfolded over a couple of hours. When Kim and Steve arrived at the house, they found themselves with nothing to do. Aware that Sylvie and Stella would be occupied for hours, they left them in their respective rooms and departed for the night.

Upon their arrival, the men who had taken Ben and Merritt escorted Merritt to a room previously occupied by Billie. They left her on the bed but confiscated her purse. Their displeasure grew as they discovered the gun and Coast Guard credentials inside. Meanwhile, they brought Ben down to the basement and bound him to a chair. They rifled through his pockets, locating his gun and FBI credentials.

"We better go back upstairs and cuff that woman to the bed. Then we can call the boss and get instructions."

They went back to hear Merritt screaming and objects crashing. They wanted to wait until the noise stopped. When it finally ceased, they heard one side of a conversation.

"My name is Merritt, who are you… Maggie? Oh, Maggie, your sister is looking for you... We have been investigating this place. Do you know Billie and Trinity…? The FBI and the Coast Guard are on this. This place will be shut down…"

Maggie was worried. Merritt stopped talking. She knew what that meant.

"Sir, we have a problem. The two we were asked to abduct are Federal Agents. The woman has been talking to a woman named Maggie. Apparently, her sister came to town, and this Agent has been looking for her."

"Let me think. Are Maude and Ellen back?"

"No, we are alone. The man is in the basement, out cold."

"The woman you brought in. She needs to be taught a lesson. Can you two take care of her? She needs to be…"

"Sir, we will do what is needed. Should we leave her here?"

"No. Take her to the basement. Do it in front of the other Agent. Make him watch. Make sure you use the pre-mix to get rid of the DNA you leave. Then, throw her in a hot shower. Take the woman as far as you can. Give her a dose of Ketamine if needed, the man too." The man thought for a moment, "Leave the woman where she will be found in the morning. Use the signal blocker in your vehicle. Then take the man and the woman, Maggie. There is a motel on Route One…"

The two men, still in their balaclavas, took Merritt to the basement.

Ben was awake, gagged, and angry. He became enraged when the second man entered with Merritt over his shoulder and dropped her onto the table.

Both men started to remove her dress. They caressed her and kissed her, and once she was entirely naked, they forced her knees over the edge of the table and secured her legs to it. With her restrained, they took turns violating her.

Ben was in tears, screaming, which seemed to entertain the two men. They exited the room for a while, and when they came back, rolling the metal cart, Merritt was just starting to regain consciousness.

She began to struggle. Unable to see Ben, the man repositioned his chair so she could. They pulled instruments from the cart and commenced their methodical torment. They chose not to gag her; they wanted Ben to hear her screams.

By the time they finished, Merritt had lost consciousness. One of the men forced something into her mouth and poured water down her throat. He hoisted her over his shoulder and exited the room. While Ben remained gagged, the other man pressed a knife against his neck and forced a dose of Ketamine down his throat. Ben struggled to breathe as the man held a bottle of water in his mouth, pushing the pill further down.

When Ben was out, and Merritt was ready, they began their journey.

Before midnight, when everyone was in their expected places, one of the men, using a burner phone, contacted the State Police to report that someone was calling about a rape occurring at a motel on Route One.

The gala was almost over. Trip, Lizzy, Phil, and Connie were the last to leave, walking out with the two men from the private security firm when one of them stopped. "Excuse me, Mr. Fredericks. This is Ben's work vehicle. I know it because it used to be mine. This is the same plate."

"I'll call Hilda, Phil, call the babysitter." Trip went one way, and Phil walked away, too. After a few minutes, Trip offered, "My housekeeper checked the pool house…"

"Gentleman, they are not in Ben's apartment either. I called both cell phones. They are off."

"Excuse me. Ben would never turn his phone off. Even when we were off duty, we kept our phones on."

"When was the last time you saw them, Phil?"

"They were coming out here to follow that couple. Can you call your contacts at the FBI? We need to get ahead of this. I will call Colt and Skipper and Naomi and Marcus."

Ring, ring… "Slow down, son. I'm putting you on speaker."

"Dad, I can't find Stella. Is she with you?"

"No. Did you call Shaw and Abby?"

"Yes, Dad, I can't find her. She was supposed to get a ride home."

Phil called a patrol officer to go to Simon and Stella's house. "Trip, no one is at their house."

Phil asked to speak to the FBI agent in charge. They talked at length, and when he returned, he looked worried. "Naomi, would you mind staying with Matilda and Clara while I recruit Lenny and Juice for a search party? If someone saw Matilda, she could be in danger."

"I'll take care of them."

"Mr. Fredericks, we will stay to help with the search. We are both sorry."

"Not your fault. You will receive an excellent recommendation from me."

"Thank you, but we will stay to help."

Chapter 22

Ben's boss rolled into Cape Hope at the stroke of midnight. Before leaving home, he attempted to activate Merritt's location chip, only to find it was offline. He tried rebooting the system, but it wouldn't connect. Three possibilities crossed his mind: someone had either removed and destroyed the chip, it was out of range, or the signal was blocked. He had configured the chip to ping his phone as soon as it came back online.

Lacking a warrant, they couldn't search the house at the end of the cove, so they scoured Trinity's and Matilda's houses, along with reviewing all traffic cameras in Cape Hope and the surrounding areas.

It was almost two in the morning when Special Agent Incharge Harry Moran's phone rang. "Yes… what? You have prints to confirm?... No… Phil, where is the closest hospital?..."

Agent Moran left Phil's office and when he came back, his face was flushed. "Ben has been found in a motel on Route One, drugged, naked with a woman who is not Merritt. State Police received a call that there was a woman yelling rape. The woman had been beaten. They will bring them to Addison Gilbert."

Lucy stood up "OK, if no one else will say it, I will. Could the woman be Stella?"

Phil shook his head. "Her prints are on file…"

"She's a Pharmacist, of course."

Ping! Agent Moran's phone had Merritt's location. "This doesn't make any sense. This is saying she is in Kittery. Let me call my Portsmouth office to send someone up there…"

Colt and Skipper were the first to volunteer to go to Maine. "We're not going to sleep tonight."

"If my agent gets there and we've been sent on a wild goose chase, I will text you. Thank you both. I'm not sure what else we can do. Jeff Steve, thank you for staying. Please give my best to your father. He is missed."

"We will tell him. If possible, would you keep us updated?"

"Absolutely."

***

Marcus and Agent Moran went to the hospital. The woman looked a lot like Matilda did when they found her. Ben was agitated and confused.

The ER doctor came out, "There was a needle prick on Agent Malloy's neck, which was secobarbital. He was also given Ketamine, thus the confusion. There is no way this man raped anyone, especially this woman. They used a feminine hygiene product, my guess, to masque whoever it was that did rape her. She was also given Ketamine…"

"Dad called me. I got a swab from Clara, just in case this woman is Maggie… Oh, sorry."

"Agent Moran, this is Doctor Simon Frederick's he is an ER doctor in Boston. He is also Stella's boyfriend."

"I thought this would help." He handed the doctor the swab in an evidence bag.

"Would you mind helping?" Simon followed the other doctor through the double doors.

"Agent Moran, they were together. I saw them. They were also working with a couple they believed were involved in the brothel. They left right before Ben and Merritt. We need to get the guest list from Mr. Fredericks, maybe we can question them. We also need to find out who that other woman was. She was sitting with them. There was a car in the lot at the Country Club, but the registration doesn't match the VIN number…" Marcus respected Ben, and he considered him a friend. He was happy Ben had finally found his soulmate. Marcus was angry, and he wasn't going to sleep before he found out if Merritt was OK. "Agent Moran, do you mind if I stay here with Ben?"

"No, that's fine. I'll let you know about Merritt as soon as I do."

"Thank you, sir."

***

Colt and Skipper reached the coordinates in Maine. The FBI agent from the Portsmouth office adhered to protocol by first checking in with the local police. She and a detective arrived moments later. "Gentlemen, we believe she is on the beach over there," Agent Toni Wyatt indicated, pointing toward the water.

Navigating the slippery rocks between the road and the vacant beach, Colt switched on a large spotlight that cast a beam along the shoreline. He spotted a naked body. "Call an ambulance and grab a blanket!" he shouted. He quickly removed his shirt and sprinted across the wet sand, draping it over Merritt's body. She was alive, though visibly beaten and whipped.

Leaning over her, Colt was acutely aware that he shouldn't move her, but the coastal winds threatened to blow his shirt away. He knew Merritt wasn't one for modesty, but he felt compelled to protect her.

He saw the local authorities running across the beach. He immediately held up his badge so they would see he was on the job. "I'm going with her in the ambulance."

"The other agent filled us in. We will take care of her."

"This is how I found her. Her pulse is steady. There is bruising on her inner thighs. I'm pretty sure she's been raped."

"Sir, we need to get her to the hospital."

"Sorry, she is a friend. I need to call home… Agent Moran, Merritt is being taken to the hospital. She looks bad, really bad."

***

Carl Broderick worked weekends cleaning at a restaurant in Salisbury, Massachusetts. During the summer, he would walk home over the Chain Bridge into Newburyport. The tributaries flowing under the bridges were usually teeming with boats during the day, but this early Sunday morning was quiet. While on the Chain Bridge sidewalk, something caught his eye on the water. He looked over the side and saw what appeared to be a dinghy bobbing in the water. He thought *you're seeing things, man.* He took out his phone and tapped on the camera, zooming in on the small vessel slapping against the rocks. Panicking, he called the local police, "Hi, I'm on the Chain Bridge. There are two people in a dinghy. They look bad, man…"

The local law enforcement officers summoned the Coast Guard for the rescue operation. The two bodies were shrouded and transported by ambulance to the hospital. Skipper remained in Maine with Colt, so he reached out to Agent Moran: "Two females were found on a dinghy in Newburyport. They have been taken to the hospital. Harry, they called me because one of them is Billie. From the description I was given, they are in bad shape. If my opinion matters, I think we should wait until morning to tell Juice."

"It does. The other woman?"

"Her prints matched the ones taken at Trinity Stevens house. I asked that the dinghy be taken to your office."

"Thank you. Any news on Merritt?"

"She is still unconscious. Colt is with her. Harry, I'd like to have her brought there."

"As soon as the doctors are finished, I am going to ask that Billie and Trinity be transported to Gloucester. I'd like to keep everyone together."

"Thanks. I'll make the arrangements here. Skip, you and Colt should prepare yourselves. The bastards who are behind this have really outdone themselves this time…"

***

Stella woke up to the sound of screaming. Confused, she noticed she was wearing flannel pajamas and that her face had been washed. She yelled, "That dress was expensive; I better get it back."

"Helllpp meeeee!"

"I'm in the same pickle as you are, sister."

"I don't belong here."

"Well, neither do I." Stella was already tired of this woman.

"Help me."

"How would you like me to help you when I can't help me."

"I do not belong here."

Stella stopped talking even though the other woman was prattling on.

Stella had bigger problems to worry about. As she walked around the room, she noticed a painting and a tapestry on the wall. Without thinking twice, she looked behind them. It was dark. How long have I been here? Oh, Simon… ooh, nice, lavender.

Stella knew she was in trouble when she woke up. She was naked and cuffed to the headboard. "No, no, no."

Stella heard a maniacal laugh echoing from the bathroom. A hooded figure clad in leather chaps emerged, cracking a small riding crop against his palm. "Ooh, that hurts," he taunted.

Determined not to show fear, Stella stifled a yawn, though she wasn't sure why. The man laughed in response. His face was hidden, preventing her from seeing the anger as he approached her. Suddenly, he raised his arm and slapped her hard across the face, then lashed the whip against her pelvis. He aimed to instill fear, but rather than break down, she retorted, "Ouch?"

"Oh a funny lady." He walked to the desk and noticed a small suitcase that hadn't been there before. He opened it and took out two clamps attached by wires to a box with a switch.

She was scared, so she tried to lighten the mood. "Can't we just do this the old fashioned way?"

"What's the fun in that?"

He kneeled between her knees, grabbed her breasts and kneaded them.

"Are you planning to make bread?"

He didn't respond. Instead, he took the two clamps and attached them to her nipples. He grabbed the suitcase and placed it on the bed next to him.

"Let me see what to do, what to do?" he muttered, moving things around without taking any action. Then, he flipped the switch.

Stella screamed a silent scream.

"That's the best you can do?"

She took a few short breaths. "Sorry, I've never been able to scream."

"That sounds like a challenge."

"It's the truth."

He removed the clamps, swung his legs off the bed, and lifted the larger whip from the case, holding it high above him. But then he paused, blindfolding her before taking off his hood. He kissed and stroked her breasts, one hand sliding between her legs while the other continued to explore her body. He trailed kisses down her torso to her pelvis and further.

Stella was too terrified to feel anything. Fear gripped her, but she remained composed and silent. Once he finished accosting her, he stood up. She heard the door click shut and caught a whiff of lavender.

***

Simon was busy attending to Ben and Maggie, taking their vitals when a nurse entered the room. "Doctor Fredericks, your father is here."

Simon glanced at his watch; it was almost seven on Sunday morning. He washed his hands and went to the waiting room. "Dad, please tell me they found Stella."

Trip wasn't a demonstrative man, so Simon was terrified when his father hugged him. "No, I'm sorry. Everyone is out looking for her. Shaw has been at his office all night. Beau said Julie was up early and ran out of the house. She told him she had to do something. I think she was scared. I know Abby and Dalton are scared to death."

"Dad, this is my fault. I should have told them I wasn't available."

"You are dedicated."

"The family, Stella, last night's event, all should have come first."

262

"I already called Doctor Patel. You are being transferred here for the duration. He said it was the least he could do."

"Thank you, Dad. The woman that was found with Ben, her sister, is the woman who has been staying with Juice. She went missing last Fall. How did we not know what was going on in our own backyard?"

"We know that Ben and Merritt were investigating the peninsula and the stone house at the end of the cove. The day after they went for the second time, a note with a picture was left in my mailbox. Shaw intercepted it and showed it to Ben and Phil. The note threatened them to back off, or the naked photo of the two of them would be sent to the press. Both Ben and Merritt told Abby and Colt, and they all decided they needed to fight back."

"They did the right thing. Giving in to a threat gives them all the power."

"They are fairly sure the couple at the Gala Ben and Merritt were dancing with are involved somehow. Abby and Cooper are looking through the list of ticket holders. Cubby and Kathryn are looking through the traffic videos with the FBI agent. Everyone is looking…"

Marcus was getting coffee when he received the call about Billie and Trinity. As he was returning to Ben's room, he saw Trip and Simon. "Sir, Doctor, I have news. Billie and Trinity have been found. They are being examined in Newburyport; then, they will be transferred here. Doctor Fredericks Colt said they are in pretty bad shape. I told him you were here. He hoped you would be able to stay. He is on his way back from Maine with Merritt…"

Trip was furious. "What the hell is going on?"

Simon put his arm around his father. "Dad…"

Marcus continued, "Merritt had a chip implanted behind her ear. Colt found her on a beach in Kittery. He believes there was a signal blocker in the vehicle that brought her there. Sir, we have been trying to contact Shaw. We hoped he could help us get a warrant for that house."

"I have more contacts than he does. I'll make some calls. Tell Agent Moran I will take care of it."

***

Phil went to talk to Jack. He needed him to take Juice to the hospital. "We are going to keep Matilda in the dark for the time being. I have been told the women are in very rough shape. Ben is awake but very, very confused. Clara's sister is there too."

"I'll bring him over."

"Jack, I haven't seen them, but you may be the only person that can control Juice."

"I will take care of him."

Jack used his key to let himself into Juice's house. Lenny, hearing the car door slam, went out front, "I don't like the look on your face."

"Billie and Trinity are in the hospital. I have to take Juice. Listen, it's bad enough that the women are being brutalized, but they took it one step further. I'm afraid Juice will lose it."

Jack and Lenny went inside. Juice was in the kitchen and knew his two best friends wouldn't just be there to chat. "Just tell me."

"Jack is taking you to the hospital. I have to stay here with Matilda and try to tell her what has been going on."

"Did they find Stella?"

"No. Juice, will you knock on Clara's door? She needs to come with us, too."

Knock, knock... Lizzy walked in. "Hi guys. Trip called. He asked me to sit with Matilda. He is at the hospital. Simon is there, too. Skipper and Colt are on their way back with Merritt, Trinity and Billie are being transferred to Gloucester too..."

"Maggie?" Clara came out of the bedroom. "Is she alive?"

Lizzy answered, "Yes, but she is in pretty bad shape. Ben is there too..."

Jack drove Juice and Clara to the hospital while Lenny stayed home. Simon saw them walking through the ER doors. "I need to take Clara in to see Maggie. Then you and Jack and I will talk."

Juice argued, "Simon."

"Go over there and sit. I'll be right back." Simon explained to Clara that Maggie had been roofied: "She has also been beaten. Right now, she won't know you. I estimate it will be another three to five hours before she begins to come out of the effects of the Ketamine."

"Right now, I just want to sit with her. Thank you, Doctor."

"It's Simon. Try not to show too much emotion… Maggie, your sister is here."

Clara sat on the bed and held Maggie's hand.

"Clara, I will be next door if you need me."

Simon went to the waiting room to talk to Juice and Jack. "You both saw Matilda when Lenny brought her home. What they did to Billie and Trinity was not only barbaric, it was, I believe, an attempt to humiliate them. They were both given MDMA, along with Ketamine. They were beaten, raped, and their heads were shaved."

Juice stood up. "I need to see her. I can take care of her, Simon."

"I know you are qualified, but you are too emotional."

Jack put his hand on his shoulder and sat him down again. "She isn't going to know you."

"I know. Please, I need to see her. Jack, will you talk to Cap for me? I will need time."

"Dad offered his house for the ladies to recuperate. Hilda is a wonderful nurse, you know that. Trinity will need a place to stay. Dad thought Billie might like to stay with her. You are welcome to stay there too. Let him do this for you."

"Listen to Simon, buddy. It's a good idea."

"Can I go in?"

"Sure."

Jack put his arm around Juice's shoulder. Neither Jack nor Simon was prepared to hear Juice weep as he kissed Billie's hand.

***

After Trip left the hospital, he went to talk to Beau. "Have you talked to Julie?"

"Yes. She is frantic. She thinks if she speaks to some of Harold's old friends, they may know something about the brothel."

"Beau, let her. Maybe she had heard a conversation or a rumor. Let her follow through. It couldn't hurt. Son, there were some developments last night after I called about Stella. No one is sure how any of this happened, but Merritt and Ben were abducted. They were separated. Merritt had a location chip implanted before she started the assignment. It was blocked somehow. It went back online early this morning. Colt went to Kittery to bring her back. She had been battered and violated. Colt took her to Gloucester."

"Dad…"

"Let me finish. The State Police received a call about a possible rape in a motel on Route One. Ben was found there, drugged. The woman with him had been beaten and violated as well. The woman is Maggie. The ER doctor assured the authorities Ben, in his state, was not capable. They are at Addison as well. Simon was at loose ends, so he went there to help. I spoke to a colleague and had Simon transferred to Addison so he will be closer to home. He has been there all night." Trip sighed. "Beau, the Coast Guard was called to Newburyport for a water rescue. Two women were found in a dinghy. Simon told me as much as he could. He said they were brutalized…"

"Dad!"

"It was Billie and Trinity."

Beau looked heartbroken "Son, I know there was more going on between you and Trinity. I know you said you were friends, but you have been different."

"Julie and I had a rough patch. I talked to Abby, and Julie and I are better, much better."

"Could she have thought you were having an affair?"

"I would have been able to tell when I told her Trinity was missing. Dad, I have to go to the hospital."

"I know I have always been tougher on you than your sister and brothers. Your mother always coddled you. I know how close you were, and when she died, I may have pulled away because your relationship with her was so special."

"Dad, if I did something wrong, it's not your fault. I'm a big boy. But your example has been a lot to live up to. I never wanted to disappoint you."

Trip hugged Beau. He couldn't remember the last time he did that.

"Dad, oh God, I don't know how to tell you."

"You just did. Julie can be difficult, but you have both done the work to make things better."

"But Trinity will need me."

"I know. I have offered the house for the ladies and Ben to recuperate. Hilda wants to help. I know Trinity doesn't have family here. I've talked to Lizzy, Simon and Abby. Shaw has been at his office scouring his files, but Dalton assures me he will agree."

"Dad, yes, of course… Dad, I'm sorry."

"I know you are."

"Dad, I talked to Andy about this a lot. I gave him a check for the rectory roof as a thank you."

"I'm going to take you to the hospital. Simon would like someone to sit with her, but he needs to prepare you before you go in. Please be patient."

Beau embraced his father. "Dad, thank you."

"We will talk more when things settle down."

***

Stella stirred in her bed, clad in snug yoga pants and a cropped top. As she sat up, thoughts of the man who had invaded her space flooded her mind. Tears welled in her eyes for a brief moment before she steeled herself. No, they won't break me.

She jumped at the sound of her breakfast tray sliding through the slot in the door. Lizzy had mentioned Matilda's appreciation for the meals they provided.

Lifting the tray, she found scrambled eggs, toast slathered in jam, crispy bacon, golden home fries, a steaming cup of coffee, and a glass of orange juice. There were even condiments—salt, pepper, and a tiny bottle of hot sauce. Feeling famished, she settled at the desk and dug into her meal.

Stella was acutely aware that she was at the brothel. Her thoughts turned to Simon, Phil, and Abby; she knew they would drop everything to search for her. Anxiety crept in as she thought of her brother. The diner was his lifeblood, where he worked six days a week from six to three. He had loyal employees, but taking time off was a rarity for him.

***

Sunday mornings were always busy, so Phil waited until it was almost closing time to go in. He brought Lizzy with him.

Michael didn't like the look on Lizzy's face. "No offense, but you don't look so good. Too much to drink last night?"

"No. You left early."

"I need my sleep. What's up?"

Lizzy looked to Phil to break the news "You heard about what happened to Matilda?"

"Ya, I went by to see her last week. She looked great last night. What is going on?"

"Stella is missing. We think she was taken after she walked Simon to his car last night. She was supposed to ask one of us for a ride home."

Michael felt uneasy about the countless hours Simon spent at the hospital. While he understood the urgency, the thought of Stella being left alone gnawed at him. "Those monsters have Stella?" he muttered, worry etched on his face.

"We truly don't know, but let me tell you what has been going on." Phil explained everything that happened after the Gala."

"So Simon is working?"

"Everyone is doing their part. Right now, those women and Ben need him. They have been drugged and brutalized. Trip is calling in favors to try to get a warrant for that house. Shaw is at his office scouring his files. Simon already called someone to fill in Stella's hours. One last thing for you to worry about."

"What do I tell Dad?"

Lizzy blurted, "Nothing. He doesn't need to know. Kathleen and I will take care of your father."

"We told Mom, she agreed. He gets lost in his projects when he is in Nova Scotia for the summer. Lizzy and Mom will handle your father."

"So what do I tell people?"

"She is visiting your father. The best thing you can do is go about your business and keep your ears open."

"I swear…"

"Don't say it, Michael…"

***

Stella spent time to know her room, meticulously examining every corner for hidden cameras or listening devices. To her relief, she found none. Peering behind the painting She saw the tops of trees and water, though the location remained unfamiliar to her.

Turning on the TV, she encountered a satellite subscription screen. She left it on and shifted her attention to the laptop. Icons for games cluttered the desktop, but little else caught her eye. Clicking the start-up menu, she wondered who had occupied the room before her. Curious, she began to investigate the various programs loaded on the laptop, clicking through them in hopes of discovering a message or clue. Nothing. "Think, Stella, think. You're a highly educated woman," she urged herself.

She scrutinized the shelves lined with books, removing each one to search for hidden items. Finally, she uncovered some pieces of paper wrapped in a larger sheet. The edges appeared torn, suggesting they had been hastily removed from a table. Among them, one larger sheet bore the letters SOS and the word "soap.".

She jolted at the sound of the tray being removed. Quickly, she tidied everything up and sat in front of the TV… Lavender.

When Stella awoke, her hands were bound above her, tethered to the ceiling. A figure approached from behind, covering her eyes and groping her breasts. He began kissing down her back and reached beneath her from behind. His touch was rough, yet she remained silent. He stepped around to face her, pressing his mouth against her breasts while gripping her rear, pulling her toward him. He rubbed between her legs before thrusting into her with brutal force. Pain shot through her, but she stayed silent. To cope, she started mentally reciting the Element song—her way of recalling the periodic table from high school. It was a distraction, a means to escape the agony. The pain intensified, yet he eventually halted. With a sharp slap to her face, he turned and walked away.

Stella began taking short breaths until she heard the man talking. He must be in the bathroom.

"No, she's no good. She doesn't react, she doesn't fight back…"

"I don't know, I'm not a doctor. Maybe she's frigid…"

"She's cute, but she's too white bread. She's the baking cookies wearing an apron type…"

"No, I know, that's what some of them want, but she's, I don't know, boring…"

Stella didn't want to react, but she was smiling inside. Simon loved her imagination.

"I suppose we could hold on to her for a while. That other new one will more than make up for this one. She is crazy…"

Stella heard the water running. She had to remain lifeless. When she heard the door open, she dropped her head.

"Oh come on, honey. Tell you what, I'll leave, but I need to get my money's worth first." The man removed her mask, revealing a half-masked figure holding a large whip. He circled her, teasing as he touched and groped her. He snapped the whip, but Stella remained unfazed. He struck her a few times without eliciting any response. Moving behind her, he opened the door. Another man entered, unhooked the cuffs from the ceiling, and forcefully threw her onto the bed. He climbed on top of her and choked her as he raped her.

The other man did the same thing. Stella passed out, but the men didn't leave. They stood across the room, without their masks, talking. She couldn't hear them, but she could read their lips. All she could glean from their conversation was, "Keep her for a few days. He can make the final decision."

Stella closed her eyes. She didn't know how much longer she could endure.

***

Trip called Simon to let him know that Beau would be sitting with Trinity. Simon didn't question his father's motives. "OK Dad. I'll tell the nurse. Juice is with Billie. Merritt and Ben are in a room together. I asked for a family bed for them. I think that will be the best thing for them. Clara is still with Maggie. I think when they all wake up, they will be past the worst of it. Hopefully."

"Phil and Lizzy talked to Michael."

"I'm sure he's blaming me. Is he OK?"

"Lizzy said he understands why you work so much."

"Dad, as soon as Beau gets here, I'm going to come home. I'm going to sleep in my old room."

"I was going to suggest that. Be careful driving home."

"Thanks Dad."

Simon waited at the nurse's station until Beau came in. "I'm really sorry about Stella."

"She is strong. Did Julie find anything?"

"She's not home. Her phone keeps going to voicemail. Last time I talked to her, she was with a college friend whose father is a judge. The kids already talked to her, so she probably turned the volume down."

"Did you tell her?"

"As much as I knew."

"Does she know?"

Beau was embarrassed. "Um, what?"

"I know you pretty well. Trinity is more than a friend. It's obvious you care about her."

"Simon, what did they do to her?"

"She was beaten, raped and to add further humiliation, they shaved her head."

Beau wiped the tear that fell on his cheek.

"Beau, you need to talk to Andy."

"I already have. Please don't be mad at me. I deserve it, but right now, I can't handle it."

"You're human. Beau, she was sleeping. She may know you at this point.

Beau took a deep breath as he walked in. He grabbed Simon's arm. "She looks lost."

"That's because she is. Tell her you have been worried about her. Hold her hand; let her know she's not alone… Trinity…"

"Beau, you found me."

Simon took her pulse and checked her heart. "Billie is here too. They found you together."

"What did they do to me? She lifted her hand to her head and sobbed.

"Would you like to talk to someone?"

She looked at Beau. "Can you stay? I don't want to keep you from…" She looked at Simon.

Beau squeezed her hand. "You probably don't remember when we talked about my little brother."

"Simon? This is your baby brother, the doctor?"

"Trinity, I'm going home. Beau will stay with you."

She looked scared, so Beau held her hand. "I'm not going anywhere."

Simon checked in on Ben and Merritt. They were awake, and aside from Merritt's injuries, they looked like a normal couple in bed watching TV.

"You look comfortable. Can I get you anything?"

Ben looked at Merritt. "Honey, do you want some ginger ale?"

"Yes, please." Merritt looked at Ben. "Please don't leave me alone."

"Never."

"Ben, Dad wants you and Merritt to stay in the house while you recuperate. It will be a couple of weeks. Has anyone been in here since you woke up?"

"No, Simon, what happened?"

"Maggie, Billie and Trinity are here too. Juice is with Billie. Clara is with Maggie. They will be fine. You don't remember anything at all?"

Merritt already had her arms around Ben, and she held him tighter. "I have a pretty good idea what happened, but no, I don't remember."

"Merritt, you must have been somewhere with a signal blocker. It came back on early this morning. You were on a beach in Kittery. Ben, do you know Toni Wyatt?"

"Yes, she's from the Portsmouth office."

"She was with Colt and Skipper. Colt stayed with you until they brought you here."

"Simon, where was Ben?"

"Maggie was found at a motel on Route One. They were trying to pin her rape on you, but their plan wasn't well thought out. I'm sure Harry will fill you in more when he arrives. The State Police already handed the case to the FBI. As for Billie and Trinity—they were discovered tied together in a dinghy in Newburyport. I know you'll want to see Billie, but I have to warn you. They're both in rough shape and besides their physical injuries, their heads were shaved."

Merritt started crying. "My God, why?"

"Honey, probably so they would feel humiliated."

"I'll get the ginger ale for you. I'll see you tomorrow."

"Simon, thank you. Tell your father we would love to stay at the house."

Simon knocked on Billie's door. "Come on in, Doc."

"Hi, how are you feeling?"

"Alive. How is Trinity?"

"She is better. At some point, I think Maggie will want to see you. Dad wants you to stay at the house. Ben and Merritt are going to stay there, too. Dad said Juice is welcome to stay with you."

"Merritt is here? Who is Ben?"

Juice chuckled. "Merritt had a plan. Skipper approved, and she met the FBI agent in charge, and they fell in love. They were both taken last night, too."

"Too?"

"Honey, Stella is missing."

She started weeping. "And you're here taking care of us?"

"Juice, Dad is trying to call in some favors and get a warrant for that house."

"Simon, tell Trip we would love to stay at the house."

"Hilda is really fond of Merritt… Oh, background. Merritt was staying in the pool house at Dad's. Did Juice tell you the good news?"

"They found Matilda, yes."

"Honey, Lenny asked me to be his best man…"

Billie cried, "I can't wait to see them…"

"You mean us?" Merritt insisted on seeing Billie. Ben got a wheelchair and brought her in. Juice helped her stand up. They cried in each other's arms until Merritt laughed. "You look like a fright."

"I missed you."

"Billie, this is Ben." She held his hand "I finally found a man who will put up with me."

"Merritt and I think we poked the bear too hard."

"Ben and I were on the peninsula investigating and having a picnic. There is a spot…well, anyway, someone, or maybe a drone, took pictures and left them in Trip's mailbox with a note. Simon and Shaw found them and showed them to me and Phil. The note said to back off, or the pictures would be sent to the press. We talked to Abby and Cubby, and my boss Skipper. We think you were being held in the stone house at the end of the cove. We left a note on the gate. It must have scared them."

Billie asked, "What did the note say?"

Merritt was upset because the note was her idea: "It said, *bring it on*. We only left it the day before yesterday. They couldn't have arranged all of this in that amount of time."

Ben disagreed. "If they were scared. Like I said, we poked too hard."

Billie was wiping her eyes. "The first night I was there, I fought back. I kicked the guy across the room. He was talking to me. I will never forget his voice."

"We met a couple. They were very interested in where Matilda was. We think they have another woman working with them…"

Billie cried, "There was a man with two women… Do you know how to contact them?"

Simon had been quiet so far. "You need to rest. Listen, the FBI agent in charge of the Boston office has been here since Saturday night. He is all over this. Everyone needs to get some rest. I'm going to be at Dad's. I'm hoping Shaw has some news, but I'm going to be no good to anyone if I don't get some sleep."

Chapter 23

"Shaw, what are you doing here?" Essex County DA Edmund O'Halloran received a call from security informing him that Shaw had swiped his card just after midnight and was still in the building.

"My brother's girlfriend is missing…"

"Maybe she just…"

Shaw was pissed. "She didn't leave. You told me to handle the letters about the brothel. I'm handling it."

"You think someone took her as a sex slave?"

"Call it what you will…"

"I also received a call. It seems your father is trying to get a warrant to search a house. Why didn't you come to me?"

"You dumped this on me. If this is what we think it is, it would be a huge boost to your career. I think you wanted to steer clear of ruffling any feathers, possibly of friends who may frequent a place like that?"

"You're tired, so I'll let that pass."

"So you're not denying it?"

"Go home Shaw."

"Late last night, two Federal Agents were abducted. There were also three women who were held at that brothel who were released. They were raped and beaten and left for dead. Another woman was taken from the Gala last night. Dad is trying to help…"

"Go home, Shaw. You are obviously overwrought. I will contact the FBI and start an investigation from this office."

"The FBI has taken the lead. One of the agents was taken from the Gala and dropped on a beach in Maine. This is out of our hands."

Shaw's boss looked angry. "You should have called me."

"Why? So you could take over, set up a Task Force, pretend you care?"

"Excuse me, I am Special Agent in Charge Harry Moran." Harry held up his badge. "Shaw, Ben and Merritt are awake and lucid. We are going to give them a day to rest. They are anxious to find out who is behind this."

"Special Agent, I will be taking over. Shaw is too close."

"Mr. O'Halloran, this was a courtesy call, nothing more. There are three Federal Agents involved from two Agencies. Shaw is not wrong to believe there are people in the judiciary, politicians, and business leaders who would do anything to keep their names out of a scandal like this."

"Who let you in?"

He lifted his badge again. "This let me in!" Harry was angry. "Why are you being so confrontational?"

"Jumping into an investigation like this is foolhardy."

"This investigation started months ago. Abductions are Federal, or didn't they teach you that in law school?"

Shaw had his head resting in his hands. He looked up, trying not to smile. "Gentlemen…"

Harry addressed Shaw: "As I said, this is a courtesy call. I went to the hospital. The doctor said you could be reached here. Have you found anything?"

Shaw looked at his boss.

"Go ahead."

"The fact I haven't found anything is troubling. We have four women who were held in that house. One has given your office detailed information. I feel like the women who were found early today will have stories that are similar."

"Conjecture?"

"Mr. O'Halloran, as I said, I'm giving the women the day to rest…"

"I would like to be there for the interviews."

"Not going to happen. These women have been through enough. They have been terrorized and brutalized. How would you feel if a woman you loved was raped over and over? They don't need your condescending attitude. They need empathy. Do you even know what that is?"

"I would like to be kept in the loop."

"I will share what I can. I'd like to speak to Shaw alone."

"I'll walk you out." Shaw and Harry waited until they were in the parking lot to talk.

Harry showed Shaw the photo of the white Mercedes left in the Country Club parking lot. "Ya, it looks like the one that stopped at Dad's house."

"We think the note Ben left on the gate of that house precipitated yesterday's events."

"They would have had to move quickly."

"They are obviously scared. I take it you haven't heard any details."

"Not really. Only what they did to Ben and Maggie."

Harry explained the condition of the other ladies.

"These people are evil. They are psychopaths. They aren't going to stop. They will find another location and go about their merry way. If I'm right about Ed and his cronies, you will need to move fast. But I had a thought. What if you sent a notice to all the law offices, judiciary and state officials? Tell them you need information that can be sent anonymously."

"That might work, or it could backfire."

"That is always the case, especially if those involved believe it's a sting. Should the victims have representation?"

"My former boss consults for the Security firm…"

"I actually looked into them."

"Well, his boss, the owner of the company, is going to represent the victims."

Shaw smiled. "I know who he is. He's the best."

"You have really huge cojones talking to your boss like that."

"Ben and I have discussed him. I explained why Ed gave me the letter about the brothel. I kept Ben in the loop, though, honestly, there wasn't much to report. But now, we need to track down those people who were flirting with Ben and Merritt."

"Abby was looking through the guest list."

"Harry, thank you for advocating for me. I am tired, but I am sure he knows more than he is willing to share."

"I will be taking over for Ben. He is mourning for Merritt. That is the only way to describe his mood. I think he remembers more than he is willing to admit. Your brother is keeping busy."

"Oh, thank you for not mentioning his name. That would not have gone over well."

"Your boss has a reputation. I think you are right to believe he is protecting his friends. OK, go home. We will have a busy day tomorrow."

"Let me know what I can do from here."

"Keep your ears open. Your father's idea to keep everyone together was shrewd. Am I wrong to assume your boss won't be pleased if he finds out?"

"Not at all. They have never liked each other."

***

"Where did you go yesterday?" Kim was suspicious. When Steve got home, he was quiet. Usually, that meant he had a liaison without her.

"I had to make sure the women were secure. The matrons were otherwise occupied, and our *friend* is incommunicado."

"Where is he?"

"Not available. Sylvie is hysterical. She has been screaming at the other woman. I called one of the regulars to test the other girl out. He is not hopeful. As it turns out she may be too passive for our needs."

"So what do we do? The big man won't be happy if we have to get rid of another one."

"I went to Cape Hope. I saw the bartender coming down the stairs from above the Pub. If we take care of Sylvie, we can get the bartender."

"And Mr. Smith doesn't need to know. I'm going with you."

***

Maude and Ellen were notified that a couple would be there to see Stella. They asked that she be brought to the basement. When Stella smelled the lavender, she held her breath, hoping she would be able to identify the people who worked there when she got out because she knew she was going to get out.

Stella ran into the bathroom, turned the shower on hot, put a wet face cloth over her face, and held her breath as long as she could.

With the towel still over her nose and mouth, she opened the door and lay on the floor. When she heard the door open, she closed her eyes but kept them open just enough to see two women—two very large women. They removed her clothes, lifted her to a chair on wheels, and pushed her to an elevator. She opened her eyes to see the women behind her. The panel next to the door had numbers one through three, and the lit button was labeled B.

When the door opened, Stella saw what she could only describe as a dungeon. Black walls with stainless steel tables and carts filled with instruments. One of the women started talking, "What does the client want?"

"We're supposed to leave the full cart."

They moved Stella to the chair and fastened her ankles to the legs and her wrists behind the chair before leaving the room. The chair was next to a cart that had photographs on top. She immediately regretted looking at them—pictures of people she knew. Ben was crying, Billie was screaming, and there was a man shaving a woman's head. Hearing the door latch, she dropped her head.

"Well, well, what do we have here?"

Stella raised her head, deciding to keep her comments to herself. The man came around to the front of the chair, wearing black leather pants cut out around the crotch. She almost laughed.

The man wore a half mask, while the woman walked around the table in a bustier, garter belt and a frilly half mask. *These two have no imagination,* she thought.

The chair was reminiscent of an electric chair—very square and very wide. Stella's legs were spread apart, and the woman kneeled between them, reaching her hand between Stella's legs. Stella stayed motionless.

The woman sat back, looked at the cart, and picked up a phallus. She put it in her mouth, licked it, then pressed a switch. Standing up, she leaned forward and began kissing Stella's breasts before plunging the device between Stella's legs.

Stella had to remain still, continuing the charade that she wasn't feeling any emotion. But she was sickened at the thought of these two people touching her.

The man went behind the chair and reclined the back while his partner straddled Stella's waist, the instrument still inside her as the woman leaned forward. The man lifted his partner's hips and thrust inside her from behind. She screeched as she mauled Stella's breasts with her hands and mouth. Stella was motionless, almost catatonic, even when the woman shrieked and fell on her, panting.

Stella bit her lip, wanting to say something sarcastic but not wanting to anger them. So she lay there, unmoving, even after the woman slapped her face.

The woman moved away with the phallus and picked up another one, a much larger one, but her partner stopped her and whispered something. The woman shook her head and whispered back. Stella read their lips;

they were trying to decide what to do with her. They agreed she was probably a lost cause. Then she saw the words *Ecstasy, Scopolamine, and maybe a cocktail.* Stella knew what that meant—they were going to drug her, which might make her doubt her sanity and lead the authorities to question her stability.

The couple turned toward her. She saw the man say *Mr. Smith* and also caught words that didn't make sense: *Silvie, Chip.* They moved toward her, still whispering. She saw the man say, "No, we can't go back.".

They started by lifting the large battery onto the table. There was what looked like a cattle prod and something else, but she wasn't sure what it was. He switched the head. "Maybe a skull?" He picked up another. "Or maybe a cobra. How about this one, honey?"

A large probe was attached to the battery and inserted between her legs. He flicked the switch on and off repeatedly. Stella closed her eyes and held her breath to keep from screaming. He lifted the back of the chair, set down the probe, and picked up the other instrument. He whispered, "She needs to be taught a lesson."

The woman turned on the blowtorch and held it to the end of the brand. Stella couldn't see it, but it looked like a word. She couldn't fathom how anyone could be so sadistic. Although Stella was scared, she wasn't going to give them the satisfaction of showing it.

The man climbed onto the table and began kissing the woman. They manhandled Stella until the man raped her, still kissing his partner. When they were done, he picked up the prod and branded Stella in the middle of her chest. She was thankful the iron had cooled off, but she still felt excruciating pain before she passed out.

When Stella woke up the next morning, she found a bandage on her chest. There was a jar of ointment and gauze pads on her nightstand. Compassion? She got up, peeled back the white gauze, and saw the word "WHORE" branded in the middle of her chest.

Downstairs, the matron called the boss, "Sir, I know you are unavailable, but the new woman, the one they say is frigid, was branded. We need to know what to do."

"This couple is becoming a problem. Have they replaced this *damaged* woman?"

"No, but the conversation they were having in the basement leads me to believe they have a plan."

"Thank you for your attentiveness. I do have a plan. It's early there, do you have time? This needs to go without a hitch…"

Chapter 24

Ben woke up early, having not enjoyed a restful sleep. His dreams were filled with choppy images of inhumane beasts violating an endless line of women. They wore masks—hangman's masks. They laughed and taunted, each one slapping the woman across the face before walking out the door. He couldn't see the women's faces, but he could hear their cries. Each dream was slightly different, but they all ended the same way: someone yelling, "Ben!"

He forced himself to wake up and looked at Merritt, her head resting on his shoulder. Her face was bruised, and her body was covered by a gown. He didn't want to see what they had done to her because he was afraid he would realize his dreams were real and that he had been there, watching the monsters hurt the woman he loved.

He eventually fell asleep again, only to wake a few hours later to blood-curdling screams. Ben looked at Merritt, who was just beginning to stir. He kissed her temple as she moved closer, holding him tighter.

A nurse came in to check their vitals. Ben wondered, "Was that one of the other ladies?"

"Yes and no. It was Maggie's sister. She seems to be more affected by this than the patients."

"That's guilt."

"I don't think I'm breaking any privacy laws by telling you. She called her father last night to tell him Maggie had been found and was in the hospital. She started crying. I'm glad Maggie was sleeping. It sounds like their father is a real bastard."

"Thank you for telling me."

"You look tired."

Ben groaned. "Yes, well, dreams can be a real bastard, too."

"After Doctor Fredericks examines you, he will probably discharge you."

"The ladies too?"

"I'm not sure. I heard him talking about a nurse taking care of the ladies?"

Ben smiled. "That's Hilda. She is the former nanny to Simon and his siblings. Now, she is in charge of Mr. Fredericks' household. She wants to do her part for the ladies."

"Agent Malloy, please find the animals who did this."

Simon came through the door looking rested.

"Did I thank you for the accommodations? I think we both needed to remain close."

"That was my thought as well."

"You look a little better."

"I have learned to turn off my emotions when I'm at work. Sometimes, it's hard, but… anyway, I need to be here. Shaw will be in later. He said he really likes Harry. I guess they had a run-in with Shaw's boss. He wanted to warn me that he may try to insert himself in the investigation. Shaw said Harry told the DA, in no uncertain terms, that the DA's office was to stay away."

"Harry is a force to be reckoned with. We were all thrilled when he was promoted to SAC."

"Thank you, Agent Malloy." The door was open, so Harry walked right in. "I came by to see how you are. I hear Simon has warned you. Doctor, your brother had some very ballsy things to say to his boss."

"Good for him. He's not afraid to speak his mind. He and Abby are alike in that respect."

"She called me. She gave a select list to Phil to check Registry photos. The three people you suspect used aliases, but we know who they are. Both Abby and Phil recognized them."

Simon was writing in a chart, "Ben, how did Merritt sleep?"

"I'd still be sleeping if you hens weren't cackling."

Ben chuckled. "She's better."

"Simon, how are the others? Did I hear screams, or was I dreaming?"

"That was Clara. She was having a nightmare, but she's OK."

"Your father is a sweetheart to have us in his home.

Knock, knock, Beau walked in. "Hi, how are you two?"

Ben's expression didn't change. "We are OK."

"Dad hopes you will stay at the house."

"We will. It is a very generous offer."

"How is Trinity?" Merritt was wary of Beau.

"I haven't been in yet. I just got here. I wanted to thank you both for everything you did. I was talking to Dad, Abby, and some others. We all had the same wish: that you would stay in town. Make Cape Hope your home."

Merritt sat up "We talked about that the night we stayed on the peninsula. I feel like if they hadn't seen us there, if they hadn't threatened us…"

Ben continued, "We left a note telling them to *bring it on.* We think we provoked them."

"Julie hasn't come home yet. She has called a few times. She says she's trying to help. Besides knowing a Federal judge, I'm not sure what she thinks she can do."

"She's OK, you know she's OK?" Merritt was concerned.

"She called to talk to the kids and me. She talked to Kathryn at some point. She feels helpless. I told her about what happened after she left. She seemed, I don't know, scared but angry too."

Ben asked, "Wouldn't you be afraid if you were a woman?"

Beau nodded. "I am scared. Have you seen Billie and Trinity?"

"Beau, I just thought of something. You have access to real estate transactions. Phil couldn't find anything about that house…"

"I will certainly look."

"The man who has taken over for me, he is actually my boss. He and Shaw are working together. You can tell him if you find anything."

"I'll go to the office as soon as I check in on Trinity. She doesn't know anyone but me. I need to be here for her."

Knock, knock, "We were so worried… Beau?" Tim and Lucy came by to see the patients.

"I'm just leaving. I'm glad you two are OK."

Lucy was scared. "I want to hug you, but I don't want to hurt you."

"It's OK." Merritt reached for Lucy. "I'm OK. I watched the video. You and Tim weren't in it."

"Is that why they took you?"

"We think so. Marcus was here yesterday."

Tim sighed "He would have stayed all night if the nurse let him. He and Naomi are more determined than ever."

"Has Matilda been by?"

"No, Lenny told Juice; Matilda was terrified when he told her, but she is relieved everyone is safe."

"Those people let the others go." Merritt was emotional: "They wanted to ruin us. If they see that we are together and more in love than ever…" Merritt cried.

Knock, knock. Beau walked into Trinity's room. He was relieved her eyes were closed because he was still paralyzed by what he saw. Taking a deep breath, he went to her side, gently lowered the bed rail, and laid down next to her. He struggled to hold back his emotions, looking at the ceiling and covering his mouth with his hand.

"Beau?"

He let out a long breath. "I had to go home…"

Trinity put her hand on the side of Beau's head. "You're here now. Kiss me Beau…"

Beau rested his hand behind her neck and kissed her.

"Ahem." Simon stepped into the room and closed the door. "You need to be careful."

Beau rubbed Trinity's head. "Why? Is this contagious?"

Trinity laughed before breaking down in tears. "I missed you so much."

"I hear you met Billie and Maggie?"

"Maggie and her sister are going to stay here."

"Simon, I'll get out of your way. Would you like some coffee?"

"Thank you."

"Trinity, how are you feeling?"

She felt her head. "Fuzzy."

Simon chuckled. "Have you eaten?"

"No, but I'm hungry."

"That's a good sign…"

***

"Do you mind if we talk about our wedding?"

"Sure. What do you have in mind?"

"Tim offered the Pub. What do you think?"

"That is where we met. I can't imagine a better choice."

"I'm not sure I can go back to work there, though."

"You know I will support whatever you decide to do, but maybe you should try to go back first. Don't let those people keep you from being you."

"Oh Lenny." She was still anxious. "Maybe we should go in for dinner."

"I know Tim would love to see you walk through the door."

"OK. I think I should sell my house. I love living here with you."

"We need to visit the ladies at Trip's. They are supposed to be discharged tomorrow. Tilly, I know you are feeling guilty that you didn't talk to those women, but you needed to do what was best for you. You had no idea who they were."

"I know, I know… I think we will need to wait until the fall to get married. I want to ask Billie to be my maid of honor."

"That's perfect honey."

"And I want to ask Telly and Lulu to be our flower girl and ring bearer."

Lenny laughed. "That is perfect, too."

They arrived at the Pub to see Lucy walking toward the door. She saw Lenny and Matilda and waited. "Tim is going to be so happy to see you."

"Is he off tonight?"

"Ya, we were going to eat then decide what to do."

"Have dinner with us. We're talking about wedding plans. Maybe Timmy will be inspired."

"We're good where we are, for now. I will be giving up my apartment, though."

Tim smiled when he saw Lucy. His grin widened when he spotted Matilda and Lenny. Matilda stepped onto the bar rail and leaned in to kiss Tim's cheek. "Hi there, big boy. You and your lady friend are having dinner with us."

"Excellent. Anything on Stella yet."

Naomi had been on the phone with Harry when she heard the question, "No. Everyone in our office wants to be assigned to the case. Ben is convinced that the couple is involved."

"That guy who was manhandling Merritt?" demanded Matilda.

"Yes. Phil came in with his picture, his wife's too. I can't believe they would come back."

"Can we talk about something happy? We want to take you up on your reception offer."

"Yes! Excellent. When?"

"The fall, maybe the beginning of November?"

"Honey, that would be perfect."

Chapter 25

Stella's meal was slid through the door. By the number of meals she had received, she determined that she had been there for three days. The food smelled good; pot roast was her favorite. However, she couldn't stop thinking about what the couple had said regarding giving her drugs. Ecstasy is bitter, and depending on what they mixed it with, she might not notice. Scopolamine has no taste, ketamine is woody, and secobarbital is also bitter. If they concocted some kind of drug cocktail, she might not be able to tell at all. She picked up the tray and set it on the desk. She wasn't going to starve herself, so she ate. Opening the desk drawer, she examined the strips of paper she found inside. She knew the previous occupant's plan had to involve using the liquid soap as decoupage, making letters to spell SOS out of the paper, and affixing it to one of the windows. She recognized the risk but reminded herself that she had already been branded and whipped. Short of killing her, what else could they do?

She left the tray by the door. These people may be barbarians, but they fed her well. She went to the bathroom to brush her teeth, standing in front of the mirror as she lifted her shirt. She was still in shock. *Stop looking at it. You're only making it worse.*

As she paced around her room, she began to feel woozy. She tried to make it to the bed but ended up falling against the side and sliding onto the floor. She started laughing. *Now what?* However, she wasn't laughing when she began to throw up. On her hands and knees, she heaved violently, not noticing when the matron entered the room.

One of the women picked her up from behind while the other held a wastebasket below Stella's mouth. They left her in the bathroom with her head in the toilet. Eventually, the retching stopped, giving way to dry heaves. Confused, dizzy, and nauseous, she realized there was nothing left in her stomach. *Simon, where are you? Please find me.*

She didn't know how long she had been there when she began to feel a little better. The bathroom door was locked, so she pulled a towel off the rack, folded it, and used it as a pillow. As she lay on the floor, she began to shiver. She tried to reach for another towel but became dizzy and fell hard, hitting her head on the bathtub.

After the matrons cleaned and shampooed the rug, they looked in the bathroom. "We're going to get fired." One of them checked Stella's pulse while the other found some bandages. They picked her up and carried her to the basement, where her head was bandaged, and the blood was cleaned from her face. They knew they had to resolve this themselves. Mr. Smith's plan was set for early morning, so they needed to move Stella and get back to the house.

Relocating someone to a semi-remote location was risky, but the matrons knew the area well. They decided on a beach at the end of a town road in a densely wooded part of town. There was a private road that accessed a couple of houses, just long enough to hide until the lights in the nearby homes went out for the night.

Stella had been given a shot of the secobarbital used for abductions. It would keep her unconscious until at least sunrise. They removed the bandages on the off chance there was DNA or fingerprints; after all, most of the employees were ex-cons.

They checked the shoreline to ensure she wasn't in the path of the incoming tide. Being mindful of her injuries and to prevent sand from affecting the wounds, they left her on her side.

The van they were in was left running at the end of the road. As they drove back, they discussed the house and their future there.

***

"Mr. Fredericks, you shouldn't be here."

"I am the closest thing she has to family."

"Nurse, I'm tired anyway. Can he stay until I fall asleep?"

She looked at Beau. "I like your brother. Ten minutes." She closed the door as she left.

Beau laid next to Trinity and kissed her. "I love you."

"I love you too, but I know this can't go on."

"I have done a lot of thinking. I know you would be better off without me, but my heart was broken while you were missing."

"You told your wife about me without really telling her about me. I think you have made your choice, Beau. As much as that hurts, I do understand."

"My wife has a large personal fortune. She would take my kids and disappear."

"I'm sorry."

"I shouldn't have pursued you, but…"

"I told you I was fairly certain you were married. I could have said no." Trinity started crying. "Do you really think staying at your father's house is such a good idea?"

"I am afraid for you and the others, and there, well, there I can visit. You can all be together. Hilda is a great caretaker and an even better chef."

Knock, knock, "Beau?"

Beau got off the bed. "Come in, Simon."

"I was on my way in to say good night. The nurse said you were here. How are you feeling?"

"Better. Simon, Billie and I talked a lot through the vents in the house. We both thought they were drugging us. Today, after Juice left for his shift, Billie came in to see me. Do either of you know what *Gaslighting* is?

"*Gaslight* is Julie's favorite movie. A man is trying to make a woman think she is going insane."

"Essentially. Neither Billie nor I remember what happened before we were found, and we really don't know how long this was going on, but Billie said she was only in the house for a month or so, so we think this *indoctrination* may have only been going on for the last week. We actually talked about it in the house, comparing it to *A Clockwork Orange.* They used devices to keep our eyes open, then showed us images and clips of…" Trinity took a deep breath.

Beau sat on the bed and hugged her. "We get the point. You don't need to relive it."

"They were trying to break us. Billie said she remembered telling me she was looking for Matilda when she was taken. Maybe the people heard us talking and got scared."

"Did you tell Harry?"

"I told Ben and Merritt. They went in to talk to Billie, then they talked to me for a while."

"OK. You two say your goodnights. I'm going to talk to Maggie. I'll see you tomorrow to discharge you."

Knock, knock, "Hello?" Maggie was weeping. "Maggie?"

"My father is an ass."

"Some people, especially some men, don't know how to express their feelings. Most of them don't know how to say they are sorry or admit they were wrong."

"Clara went home to get our stuff and tell our father we are moving here. He told her he would cut us off if we did." She laughed. "We thought about that first and had our trust funds transferred to a different bank. Now he won't have access."

"Do you know why he is so angry?"

"Our mother died a couple of years ago. He's been trying to control us ever since."

"He had no control over your mother dying, so he is trying to make sure he doesn't lose you and Clara too. It doesn't make sense, but it's his way of coping."

"Well, he got the opposite result."

"Dad knows a lot of businessmen. You'll have plenty of time to talk to him after tomorrow. I know he will help you make some connections in Boston."

"Thanks."

"My rotation in Psychiatry taught me that your father is probably regretting his behavior. When you get to the house. Call him."

"If the past ten months have taught me anything, it's that I need to try."

"Our cousin Andy is a priest. He has a great ear."

"I appreciate that. Thanks."

Chapter 26

Sally Hunter was known to the year-round residents as an athlete, a runner who jogged the streets that abutted the beach, meandering through the neighborhoods. On a normal day, she would only run on the streets. But this day was a rarity for her. It was humid and already hot, with no typical breeze coming off the water, so she cut across the beach to head back home. She wanted to get off the soft sand, so she ran straight ahead before turning to run along the wet sand.

As she approached, she saw a figure on her hands and knees. The buttocks looked bare, but a thong bikini wasn't unusual. However, as she got closer, she realized that the woman crawling across the beach was confused and completely naked.

She squatted next to her. "Are you OK?" Then she noticed the gash on the woman's head. Sally had her phone in a pouch on her arm and quickly dialed 911.

"There is a woman bleeding from her head. I'm on the beach at the end of...."

Sally was aware that whatever she said would be on the record. This woman had been battered; she had some kind of burn mark on her chest, and her hair was matted with blood.

The ambulance was there in a few minutes.

When the call came into the station about an injured woman on the beach, Jack and Juice were on duty. As they arrived at the scene, Juice thought it was serendipity that this would be his last call before taking personal time off.

Sally was sitting on the sand, propping Stella's head on her leg. She had a bottle of water that she used to clean the blood off Stella's face. "She is really confused. I hope I didn't do anything wrong."

Jack put a sheet over her "Juice, it's Stella." He lifted her to the gurney and rolled her to the back of the ambulance, as Juice got Sally's contact information "Someone from Cape Hope PD will be contacting you. Thank you for your discretion."

"There is some kind of a burn on her chest. It looks fresh."

Jack wasn't usually emotional, but Molly and Stella were close friends. He wanted to call Kathryn, but he knew he couldn't. "Oh honey, you're safe now." Jack tended to the laceration on Stella's head and then began taking her vitals. He was also concerned about her neck; it looked like she had been strangled.

Juice hopped in the driver's seat. "The woman said there is a burn mark on her chest. Stella, we'll be at the hospital in a jiffy."

Jack had only wanted to cover her up and tend to her head so he didn't see the burn. He pulled the sheet down. "Oh honey, oh honey, I am so sorry…"

"Jack, you're scaring me."

"I'm sorry. You're driving, and this is too, too much. These animals need to…"

"Where am I?" Stella was looking at Jack. "Who are you?"

"Honey, I'm Jack."

"Do I know you?"

"Yes. We're taking you to the hospital."

The tires of the ambulance screeched as Juice turned the corner to the emergency entrance at the hospital. It was just after eight in the morning when Simon ran out of the bay doors. "Hi guys, what do we have?"

Jack grabbed Simon. "You need to sit this one out."

He looked in the back. Even though Stella was strapped to the gurney, she was trying to sit up.

"Get out of my way, Jack!"

Juice went to the back and saw the brand on Stella's chest, stopping Simon before he could see her injuries. "No buddy, no."

Jack had called Shaw, then Lizzy "Shaw and Lizzy are on their way. Please, don't do this to yourself."

"Let go of me, Jack." Simon started crying. "Please…"

Two ER nurses took Stella to a room. While one cleaned the burn with saline, the other called for the doctor, who had just gone for coffee. He set his coffee down at the nurses' station when he saw Simon.

Juice spoke to him. "It has to be the same people, Doc," Juice whispered. "They branded her chest, and she has been strangled."

"Excuse me?" He left his coffee on the desk and went to Stella's side. "Would you call Dr…"

"He's on his way. She is confused. The contusion on her head may have caused some memory loss. The CAT scan will be available in about an hour. Doctor Simon wants to see her. She has a lot of bruising on her upper thighs. Do you want to do a rape kit first?"

"Dear God. She may be more comfortable if you do it. Put her in a johnny. I'll talk to Simon."

Jack and Juice were with Simon in the waiting room. "Hey, Doc. How is she?"

"We have some more tests to run. Simon, there is a laceration on her head. Jack, you said she was confused?"

"Definitely. She knows me. She didn't recognize me…"

Lizzy, Phil and Lenny ran into the ER. "I called Harry. He will be here soon. Simon, are you OK?"

"She's alive, but she has head trauma. They won't let me see her."

Lizzy sat down with his arm around Simon. "You and Stella will get through this."

"I need to take care of her… Where is Dad?"

"He left the house early. He is still trying to call in some favors."

Shaw and Harry met in the parking lot. "Shaw, there is something Juice thought you needed to know. Stella has a brand on her chest. He said it looks like it might have been done right before they released her. Simon hasn't seen it. A plastic surgeon has already been called. It also looks like she was strangled."

"I'm afraid to ask. What was the brand?"

"The word *whore.*"

Shaw looked both heartbroken and outraged at the same time. "There needs to be a special place in hell for these people. Why?"

Harry shook his head. "I agree with you. Your boss knows more about this than he is willing to share. Otherwise, he wouldn't have objected to your father trying to get a Judge to sign off on a warrant."

"Dad passed the bar, and he did practice for a time. He knows a lot of people. I think that's why Ed wanted me on his staff. But he learned quickly that I won't do anything I feel is unethical. I get the job done, so he has never had a reason to let me go. I'm just afraid of what he will do if I decide to leave."

Simon was pacing by the nurse's station. When he saw Shaw, he ran to him, "They won't let me in to see her."

"I seem to remember someone telling me how much he hated family members who insisted on getting in the way while he tried to work."

"How dare you throw my words in my face to make an excellent point… I need to see her."

"You will. Come with me. I want to see Ben and Merritt. They should be told."

Merritt was just waking up, and Ben was already dressed. Simon decided to check her vitals while Shaw nodded at Ben. "Let's talk in the hall… Stella was found this morning. Jack and Juice were on duty. The other doctor won't let Simon see her. Ben, they went above and beyond this time. I think they let her go because she has a head injury, but…" Shaw took a deep breath. "They branded her chest. Simon doesn't know."

"What?… No, I actually don't want to know." Ben looked at Shaw.

"The ladies will all be together. I think they need to be told gently. Stella is very open. She is a sharing person…"

"What kind of obscene thing…"

"One word. Whore."

Ben fumed, "I'm officially off the case, but that won't preclude me from doing my own investigation. Those people think it's OK to abduct women and do ungodly things to them. Merritt was…" Ben took a beat. "She is having nightmares. Shaw, you saw the picture of us together. We are mad about each other. Every time I think about what they did to her…I believe in God, but right now, I'm a little mad at Him."

"Andy is a good listener."

"Phil told me. Simon will need to be told."

"I called Abby. We will tell him together. Ben, I will do everything in my power. You have an advocate in Harry. I offered him one of our guest rooms."

"That is one of the reasons Merritt and I want to live here. Everyone's kindness. Beau actually expressed his wish that we stay."

"He's really not such a bad guy. He has grown up a lot lately."

"Has his wife…"

Abby jogged down the hall. "Julie is on her way home. Hi Ben. How is Merritt?"

"Simon is with her. We need to talk before we talk to Simon…"

Abby was crying when Simon went into the waiting room. As she embraced him, Simon looked at Shaw. "Just tell me. Why can't I see Stella?"

"She has an injury, Simon."

"What can be worse than being raped and terrorized. Please, just tell me."

"She has been strangled. She also has a bad burn on her chest. Jack couldn't let you see it."

"So they called a plastic surgeon."

"Yes. It wasn't just a burn, Simon. She was branded."

Simon sat slowly, Abby next to him, holding his hand. Shaw squatted in front of him. Simon felt numb. "Um… What is it, what… please, I need to know."

Shaw held his other hand and spoke softly. Simon broke down, resting his head on Shaw's shoulder as he cried.

"Simon, Dalton and I invited Harry to stay with us. He is determined to find these people. We will find them."

"The other women. There have to be other women."

"Probably… Simon, for now, taking care of Billie, Trinity, and Merritt is the best way you can help. Let the others do their jobs. You know I'm right."

***

Julie went to Kathryn's office. She was rude to the woman at the desk: "I'm here to see Kathryn."

"Excuse me?" She went in after Julie. "I'm sorry."

Kathryn went to the door and whispered, "Me too." She sat at her desk and watched Julie pace. "Where have you been?"

"I had to do something. Stella was gone. I was scared. Aren't you scared?"

"Julie, what are you up to?"

"I won't give Beau a divorce."

"You need to start making sense."

"Beau was having an affair with that woman."

"He told you?"

"No. I just know."

"I think he has been honest with you about his friendship with her. He didn't have to tell you, Julie. You said your marriage was better than ever."

"It was, it is. I don't want to lose him."

"Then stop being crazy. Have you been home?"

"No."

"Go home. Kiss your kids and have Paulette take them to the beach. Then make passionate love to your husband."

Julie moped for a few minutes, then got up to leave. "Maybe you're right."

"Don't do anything stupid."

Julie drove down the street to Beau's office. "Is he in?"

"Yes."

"Go out, get some breakfast. Beau and I need to talk."

The secretary knew better than to argue with Julie. She put the phones on voicemail and left the office. After a minute, Julie locked the door and walked into Beau's office without knocking. "I've missed you."

"Hi…"

Julie took hold of him. "I've really missed you." She kissed him as she unbuttoned his shirt. "Make love to me right here."

"What has gotten into you?"

"I miss my husband. I told Deborah to get lost. Make love to me, Beau."

Julie was wearing a knee-length tank top dress. She reached down and lifted it off over her head. "I locked the door. No one is going to know."

Beau was surprised, but he didn't stop her. He took off his shoes, socks, and pants. Julie knelt, pulled down his boxers, and then looked up. "Make love to me, Beau."

Beau stepped out of his shorts. "You know what I like." He felt guilty for taking advantage of her, but Julie could easily turn into a seductress when it suited her needs, so he exploited her desire.

"Make love to *me* Beau, *me.*" Julie looked desperate. "Don't make me beg."

Beau got on his knees and kissed his wife, wrapping his arms around her waist as he leaned back…

Julie wouldn't release Beau from her grasp; she needed to feel his body against hers.

Beau lifted himself to look in her eyes. "Honey, what happened? What are you afraid of?"

"Can't we just be here together? I needed you. Isn't that enough?"

"Do you remember when we started dating, and I wanted to have sex, and you kept saying no? Remember what you said?"

"No, not really."

"You said you wanted me to think of you as a friend first. You needed to know that I liked you because you were afraid I liked your money more than I liked you. I actually understood. Once you stopped being closed off and you let me see the scared lonely person you were hiding, I understood. That's when I started to fall in love with you."

"Beau, what is your point?"

"Tell me why you are scared?"

"I'm afraid of losing us."

"Where were you?"

"I needed to find out who was hurting my friends."

"Did you find answers?"

"Well, no... Didn't anyone call you?"

"About what? Why did you come back?"

"Don't be mad at me because no one called you."

"Stella?"

"She's in the hospital. Jack and Juice were on duty…"

Beau wrestled out of her grip. "Why didn't you tell me?" He got off the floor and got dressed. "Why aren't you at the hospital too?"

Julie was sitting on the floor. "Don't be mad at me."

Beau picked up her dress and underwear. "Here, get dressed. Sometimes I really don't understand you… come on, move!" Beau recognized the look on her face. He squatted. "We can talk about this later." He kissed her. "I promise, I'm not mad, but we need to go."

Beau and Julie headed to Stella's room while Ben spoke with Simon in the hallway.

"I just found out. Is she any better today?"

Ben patted Simon's back. "I'll let you talk."

"What do you know?"

"Jack and Juice were on duty yesterday and brought her here. When Kathryn called me, she didn't know much."

"Sit down. This isn't going to be easy…"

Julie was sobbing uncontrollably. "Now, do you understand why I was so scared? These people are monsters. Stella is the nicest, sweetest…" She broke off, got up, and ran out of the room.

"She is terrified."

"She should be. Beau, you have a big problem."

"I know, but right now, that has to be put on the back burner. I've talked to Trinity. She understands. She said she was pretty sure I was married, and she didn't care. I know this will sound awful, but we love each other."

"I know. It sounds like she loves you enough to let you go."

"That is what I am struggling with… Simon, is Stella going to get her memory back?"

"She should, but there is a lot more going on than the head injury. They gave her a number of drugs that affect memory. The doctor that treated her in the ER said she had evidence of excessive vomiting."

"Is she pregnant?"

"No, we're taking precautions, but they checked that anyway. They think the drugs were mixed in the food. Beau, you need to talk to Dad."

"He says he understands. Could he be growing?"

Simon chuckled. "I think Lizzy has been a good influence…" He looked toward the door.

Julie looked defeated. "She doesn't know me."

"She doesn't know anyone, honey."

"The nurse said the rest of the ladies have been discharged?"

"Julie, why do you care? What are you up to."

"I was wondering, that's all."

Beau didn't believe her for a second.

***

The large transport van, disguised as a private vehicle, left the stone house. They carefully scanned the road before departure. Norman, the handyman, reviewed surveillance tapes from the past month, ensuring no workers had been on the road or in the nearby trees. They knew the police couldn't monitor the area 24/7, so they moved the empty rooms the night before, followed by the women, and saved everything else for the final day. Maude and Ellen felt relieved that the move had gone as planned. They were still near the water but now much closer to the interstate.

"Mr. Smith said not to call under any circumstances. I'm glad there weren't any."

"We need to set up the kitchen. Our rooms are bigger." Maude looked in their shared living room. "Look, this is nice too."

"Let's check on the women." They took the elevator to the top floor, where there were three rooms on each side, each with its own bathroom. Large walk-in closets had been renovated into waiting rooms adjacent to each room. Only four women were there, and they were still asleep.

"I wonder if we will be getting two more?"

"I don't know." Ellen had once been capable of empathy before going to prison for involuntary manslaughter due to a patient's accidental death. Tall and solidly built, she quickly learned her place when some of the other inmates asserted their dominance. It was Maude who came to her rescue.

Maude was feared. Though shorter than Ellen, she was a strong, muscular woman whose impressive strength made her stand out. They quickly became friends, but it wasn't until after that bond was established that Ellen revealed she was in for child endangerment. What she didn't share was that she was bisexual and had testified against her then-boyfriend to accept a lesser charge; he was in jail for child abuse, pornography, and pedophilia. Maude also didn't know that Ellen sometimes pursued women. Known for her masculine appearance—partly due to her large hands and a strap-on phallus she used—Ellen could be gentle at times, though on other occasions, she was not.

"The ladies suites are nice, too."

"The clients expect that. They also expect a variety. Do you have any ideas?"

Maude knew where to hunt for women: "I was looking around the Marina in town. I noticed a docked cabin cruiser on the far end, with women on the deck. I've been back to do surveillance. There are two women who seem to live there alone."

"So if we set something up using the mist…"

"Oh, Ellen, I've taught you well."

***

Ben brought Merritt's things to Trip's house. She was taking a nap, so he went out to the back deck. Gazing out over the peninsula, he looked up and thought, *Please don't let what I've been dreaming about be true.*

"Ben, do you need to talk?" Andy had come to the house to lend support.

Ben turned around. "I was actually hoping you'd come by. Do you mind that I'm not Catholic?"

"I am here to listen, but Phil tells me you have faith."

"I feel like a big hypocrite. I'm so mad at Him right now, but I keep remembering my grandmother telling me not to doubt Him."

"Ben, what have you been dreaming about?"

"Those people, torturing Merritt."

"Given that you know that's what they did, it's not surprising you're thinking about it and probably blaming yourself."

"I let my guard down, and now she is hurting."

"Does she blame you?"

"No, she says we will be stronger than ever."

"Have you ever blamed yourself for failing a victim?"

"Not really. I killed someone. He was shooting at us because he kidnapped and raped a girl. I blamed myself until I saw what he did to her."

"Maybe you need to talk to Merritt. Tell her how you are feeling."

"I will, but I know she doesn't blame me. How is Simon?"

"He has an amazing ability to compartmentalize. When he is busy working with a patient, that is the only thing on his mind."

"He blames himself, too."

"Shaw said your boss is determined."

"He has my back… Have you ever felt bad that the advice you gave turned out to be bad?"

"Not really. I do the best I can with the information I am given. Isn't that what you do?"

"I agreed to do something Merritt suggested even though I didn't agree one hundred percent. We poked the bear, and it bit back."

"Shaw told me. Truthfully, it was a good idea. Ben, you need to forgive yourself. I'm sure Merritt can see the guilt when she looks at you. Have you talked to your family?"

"No, and I won't. They don't need to know. Thank you for coming out here. I do feel better."

***

Julie went to Beau's old bedroom, where Trinity stood in her robe, looking out the window. "You must be Trinity," Julie said

Trinity, still self-conscious about her hair, didn't turn around. "You must be Julie."

"We have a problem."

Trinity turned around, and even without hair, she was stunning. Her big brown eyes and long, thick eyelashes were striking. "What can I do for you, Mrs. Fredericks?"

"I have a proposition."

Trinity couldn't contain her sarcastic chuckle. "Oh really. What's that?"

"Tell me where, and I'll buy you a house and set you up with a graphic design business."

"I have a house and a business. I also happen to like it here."

"I'm sorry about what happened, but…"

"Sorry? No, I don't think you are. I think you were happy when I disappeared. I actually wondered if you were behind my abduction."

"That's absurd."

"Mrs. Fredericks, I have decided to stay in Cape Hope. Trip, Lizzy and Hilda have been very kind. I need to make some other decisions, but I have to do that without any outside interference. Trip told me I am welcome here as long as it takes."

"That means he doesn't know about your affair."

Trinity sounded surprised. "What affair?"

"With Beau. I know you had an affair."

"Hmm. Beau and I are friends. Do you have male friends, Mrs. Fredericks? Do their wives assume you are sleeping with their husbands? Your hypothesis is misguided."

"Beau doesn't have female friends."

"I know that's not true. There have been a lot of women here to visit. They have been supportive and kind. I know that they are friends with Beau because they told me."

"Like you said, they were being kind. Beau and I are happy and you are a distraction. You need to leave."

"That is not up to you."

"You will regret it if you stay."

Trinity felt rage. She dropped her robe. She was naked except for her panties. "Look at what those people did to me, to the others. Do you really think your threats scare me?"

Julie was shaken. She turned to leave as Simon came through the door. "Were you eavesdropping?"

Simon didn't answer Julie. He had come by to check on his patients. Trinity stood with her robe at her feet. "Trinity, are you okay?" He picked up her robe and wrapped it around her shoulders. "Julie, get out of here, now!"

Julie stomped out of the room and down the hall.

Simon was worried. "Trinity, did I hear her threaten you?"

Trinity put her arms in her robe but left the front open. "She scared me."

"You sounded pretty confident to me." Simon took her pulse and then placed his stethoscope in his ears. He moved it around her chest as he listened.

"Is your girlfriend really OK?"

"Shh." He put the stethoscope on her back. "She is having memory issues. The nurses are keeping her covered up, and I am respecting her privacy. It scares me to think what they did to her, but I'm doing what is best for Stella."

"Does she remember you?"

"No, but the attending told her who I was. She smiled and said I looked nice. Trinity, I need to ask if you feel your internal injuries are healing."

She chuckled. "You can check yourself if you need to. If I had any modesty before, it is gone now."

Simon squatted in front of her and held her hand. "If you felt any discomfort, I would, but it sounds like you are OK."

"I am. Beau was right about you." Tears welled up in her eyes.

"Julie can be harsh when she gets defensive."

"She wants me out of town. She wants to set me up in another town far away from her husband."

"She is also very possessive." Simon got up and looked down the hall. He then returned and sat next to Trinity on the bed. "I know none of us told her our suspicions. Beau told Abby and our cousin Andy, who is a priest. Dad, Shaw and I told Beau what we suspected. We didn't accuse or lecture. We could see the look on his face. He loves you."

"I know. I'm sorry."

"Don't be…"

Knock. Beau opened the door to find Trinity's robe still open. She didn't seem to notice and ran to embrace him. "You were right about your little brother."

"He's OK." Beau stared at her injuries. "Simon, why didn't you tell me."

"I couldn't."

"Beau, you didn't do this. Please don't blame yourself." She closed her robe.

"Hilda said Julie was here."

Trinity was confused. "I'm sorry Beau."

"Simon, is Trinity OK?"

"I think so. She knows where to find me if anything feels off, right?"

"Yes. Thank you, Simon."

"Beau, may I speak to you in the hall?" Simon whispered, "Trinity is my patient, so I really can't say anything, but you need to talk to Julie."

"Since she got home, she has been overcompensating in the bedroom. She came to my office the other day to seduce me. I know she is upset, but when I was having breakfast, I caught her staring at me. I have to admit, she scared me."

"Don't make any accusations. Innocently ask her if she wants to meet Trinity. Her reaction should tell you all you need to know." Simon paused. "You need to talk to Dad. Shaw will help if you think Julie will take the kids from you. Beau, you have options."

"Thank you. I need to talk to Trinity." Beau went into his old bedroom, where Trinity was looking out the window again. He closed the door and locked it. "I love you," he said.

"I love you too, but I don't know what to do."

"Did Julie threaten you?"

Trinity put her arms around Beau and kissed him. "I do love you. I have a few more weeks before I can get back to my normal activities. Even with everything that has happened to me, I haven't been able to stop thinking about making love to you again."

Beau put his hands on the sides of her head and kissed her again. "Are you ready for a fight?"

She started crying. "I think you need to discuss this with your family first. I wouldn't want to come between you and your kids and your father…"

"I was planning to talk to him. The day they found you, Dad came to me, he knows. I hope he will support whatever I decide to do… I came up here to tell you lunch is ready."

"Am I allowed to eat up here?"

"It's my room, so I say yes."

Trinity caressed the side of his face. "I do love you."

"Hilda will bring something up." Beau kissed her. "I'll be back."

***

Ben was walking in the back door with Andy when Beau asked about Stella.

"She is the same. Michael has been going after work. All the visitors are telling her stories. Simon stays with her as much as he can."

"Beau, did you have time to look at the listings?"

"I can't find anything with that address in the past ten years. It is held by a Trust."

"We took a picture of the back of the house. There was stained glass that looked like a coat of arms. Colt was going to enlarge it for us, but then…"

Julie saw Beau and interrupted, "What are you doing here?"

"I need a reason?"

"No, of course not. Andy, it was nice of you to come by. Have you seen Stella?"

"I have. It is going to be a long recovery."

Beau suggested, "Maybe Simon and Stella should stay here too."

"Beau, I'm not sure there will be enough room. Simon and Stella are family. Maybe that woman Trinity and the other two women we don't know can stay at her house. You said she lives here in town, right?"

Ben suggested, "We can stay at Phil's…"

"No, you were on the job. You should stay here." Julie insisted.

"Julie, I'd like to talk to you outside now." Beau looked at Andy and shook his head.

Julie had the look of a six year old spoiled brat who didn't get what she wanted.

"Explain yourself." Beau was angry.

"I'm sure your father and Hilda didn't expect all these people."

"There are six empty bedrooms in this house. There is plenty of room. Hilda left Simon's room for him because he was staying here before Stella was found. You would have known that if you had been here. What happened to you? You all but begged me to make love to you in my office. You have been frantic in the bedroom like it will be the last time. You are being unreasonable. Dad will not turn those women away."

"You are being intentionally cruel."

"In what way? I need to understand."

Julie held his hands. "Come home with me."

"Dad and I have a meeting after lunch."

Julie reached down toward Beau's pelvis. Beau grabbed her hand. "You need to get a grip."

Julie nuzzled Beau's ear. "What do you think I was trying to do?"

"Knock it off. I'm staying here for lunch. Go to work. I'll be home at the regular time."

Simon saw Julie and Beau's exchange. "You two need to knock it off. The guests here have been through enough."

"Simon is right…"

"You're on her side!"

"Who is her? Julie, I know you're scared, but you need to collect yourself, or you'll have to go home and not come back until you can act like an adult."

"Simon, I'm sorry…"

"I think you should go home. The ladies are here to recuperate. You have to recognize that they have been traumatized. Until you can do that, you need to stay away."

"I didn't mean… this is all too much."

"Julie, You are making this about you. Do you understand Simon has been traumatized, too? He is right; you need to back off."

Abby overheard the conversation and stepped in. "Julie, you know I love you, but Simon and Beau are right. Daddy knew exactly what he was getting into when he invited everyone here. If you can't be supportive, you should stay away."

Julie stared at Simon. "After I leave, are you going to tell them what I did?"

"Oh honey, what did you do?" Abby moaned.

Julie looked at Simon, then lowered her head. "I talked to Trinity."

Beau stayed calm "I was going to suggest you introduce yourself."

"To your mistress?"

Abby knew she was the only person present whom Julie would listen to. "They are friends. What made you think they were having an affair?"

Julie was quiet. She wouldn't make eye contact.

Simon confessed, "OK, now that you let the cat out of the bag, Julie, is that why you were in her room to make accusations?"

"Don't be mad at me."

"Julie, if you really thought I was having an affair, Kathryn would have already served me the papers. Simon, I'm sorry. You have enough on your mind. You don't need this, too."

"Abby, have you met her?"

"No. Hilda said she is having lunch in her room. Julie, what did you say to her?"

"You're on her side too?"

Abby was getting frustrated. "I am on the side of all of those women. They weren't on vacation, Julie. They were abducted and forced to do ungodly things with strangers. Did Stella, Matilda, Billie, and Merritt deserve that?"

Julie scowled, "No."

Simon asked, "Did Trinity?"

She glared at Simon. "Of course not. Now, if you three have finished ganging up on me, I'm going to join everyone for lunch. Are you coming?" Julie went inside.

"She is all over the place. Simon, she needs help."

"Yes, well…"

Abby was surprised. "Did she threaten Trinity?"

"Ya. Trinity was so upset she dropped her robe and asked if she deserved what happened to her. That's when I got there. Julie was really shaken. Beau, this is by no means an endorsement of your friendship, but I understand how you fell in love with her. She is really remarkable."

"I appreciate that."

Abby asked, "Beau, do you mind if I talk to her?"

"I think she'd like that. I told her, you know."

"Simon, what is Stella's prognosis?"

"The plastic surgeon will do a graft, but with her head injury, I'm not sure when. What if she doesn't know what they did to her? What if she wakes up in the morning with her memory and sees…"

Beau grabbed Simon's shoulders. "Don't go there. Believe me, it only makes things worse."

"Beau is right," Abby smirked. "Hmm, I don't think I've ever said that before."

They were all laughing when Dalton stepped outside. "It's so good to see all of you enjoying yourselves. If there's one positive thing that has come from all this, it's that the four of you seem much closer."

Simon agreed. "You're probably right."

Abby asked Dalton, "I'm going up to talk to Trinity after lunch. Do you want to come with me?"

"I know Shaw really likes her, and she told him she will be staying here. Beau, I don't know what has gotten into Julie again, but be careful. She seems a little agitated."

"I don't know what to do. I am worried about Julie, but Trinity needs me."

"You know Abby and I will be discreet."

After lunch, Julie was left alone. She exchanged words with Beau in the driveway. He hugged and kissed her before opening the car door for her. Once she drove away, he went inside, where his father was waiting by the door.

"I saw you and Julie talking before lunch, so I went to your room. Beau, I really like Trinity, but you know how the church feels about divorce."

"Julie is out of control. She was upstairs earlier. Simon heard her threaten Trinity. I cannot…"

"Beau, she is a lovely woman. She tried so hard not to say she loves you, but it is written all over her face. How would you and Julie feel about talking to Andy?"

"I already have. Andy has always had a soft spot for Julie but we need to do something. Dad, you know Julie was different for quite some time. Then I told her about Trinity, about our friendship and her abduction. Things got better; she was happy again. Then everything hit the fan, and Julie left. She said she was trying to help, but when she came back she was different again, frantic. Dad, I don't know what to do."

"I have learned a lot about how a marriage can go bad. Lizzy had a bad marriage, but because her husband was away so much, Lizzy and her kids survived. I cannot tell you what to do, but I know you are concerned about my reaction. You respect me and my opinion. But I feel like this is partially my fault. I pressured you to marry Julie. Harold and I were friends, and he suggested we introduce you. At the time, you needed a push because you had no intentions of settling down, and to me, that wasn't acceptable. Do what is best for you. Don't stay in a bad marriage because of me. I have spent the last ten years in limbo…"

"Dad, I miss Mom so much."

"I've been thinking about what she would say to you. She wouldn't want you to be unhappy."

"I'm afraid Julie will take the kids and disappear. I can't lose my kids."

"Then you need to do this right. We will talk to Shaw and get his advice."

"Dad, I'm sorry I lied to you. I'm going to try to be a better son."

"Go back upstairs. Tell Trinity we talked. Then go home. Have dinner with the kids then talk to Julie. Be honest with her…"

When Beau got to his room, he heard laughter, then Dalton "He helped you move furniture? I hope he didn't break a nail."

Beau opened the door. "All right, all right. You have to watch out for these two. They're mean."

"Oh poor baby."

"They knew I wasn't allowed to hit them, and Dalton always had a crush on Shaw, so they were nice to him."

"I really like your family, Beau," Trinity said with sadness.

"I talked to Dad. He genuinely likes you. I have to talk to Julie. She is acting out again… I'm sorry. I'm going to go home and try to talk to her. I'll be back. OK?"

"Yup."

Beau pointed at Abby and Dalton. "You two be nice."

****

"The house is empty."

Kim thought she misunderstood "Excuse me?"

"The house is empty. The basement has been cleaned out. The rooms still have furniture but no bedclothes or towels."

"Is the tunnel accessible?"

"That was the only way in. We have touched everything in every room. Will Mr. Smith give us up? What about the others? Were they left behind, too?"

"We have to lay low. Maybe that's what they're doing. Did you call the number?"

"Yes. It said to leave a message. They won't be out of service long. The regulars won't stand for it. I wonder what happened? There had to be something big going on."

"Do you think that the woman Sylvie said was an FBI agent recognized her?"

"I didn't think of that. Maybe… but how would they know where the house is? I don't know, honey, but I think we should forget about her, just in case."

"I have an idea, though. Hear me out, but I think you will agree…"

****

Maggie took the house landline phone and went to the back garden. "Hi, Dad, it's Maggie." There was a long silence that worried her. "Dad, we need to talk."

Martin Beckett was conflicted. He missed his daughters and was brokenhearted, but he was a controlling bastard who couldn't admit that maybe, just maybe, he had been wrong. "You sound well, Margaret."

"I'm thankful to be alive."

"What are your plans?"

Maggie knew Clara told him their plans, but she knew not to test him "I would like to stay here. The people here, the people who rescued me, are my friends. I'm sorry, Daddy, but this town feels like home."

Martin sighed. Maggie knew what that meant: "Clara's trip to find you left me in a place I didn't like being. I was alone. I don't want to be alone, Margaret."

"Daddy…"

"Let me finish. You and Clara hurt me…"

Maggie was crying, even though she was trying to contain her feelings. "You hurt us too. This was a mistake."

"Margaret, let me finish. Clara was singing the praises of the family you are staying with. They are respected in the community. I called the DA's office and spoke to Shaw Fredericks. He spoke highly of Clara. He admitted he really didn't know you yet, but his fiancé liked you. He invited me to visit. He thought my presence there would help your recovery."

"Clara was very upset when she got back. Sometimes, you act like you don't care about us. Dad, I have to be honest; when Clara told me what you said, I suggested we make some changes… I'm sorry, Daddy."

"Margaret, I know what you did. You were protecting yourselves. It forced me to reflect. I can't be anyone but the person I am. I am not an emotional person, you know that, but after Clara told me what happened, my heart broke again, just like it did when your mother died. I got angry, and I blamed you for leaving. I'm glad you called. I'm going to pack a bag and be there tomorrow. Shaw gave me the address where you're staying. I'll see you and Clara tomorrow."

Maggie was blubbering, "Bye, Daddy."

Shaw and Ben were in the solarium when they heard Maggie crying "Ben, will you find Clara? I'll go outside."

Shaw put his hand on her back. "Dad said he has the name of a therapist who is willing to come to the house."

"Maybe, I'm not sure. You talked to my father?"

"Yes. He was concerned. I thought I eased his mind."

"You did, you did. He's coming tomorrow."

"I invited him to stay with us."

"Thank you."

"I explained the situation at the house, so I invited him, and he accepted. Dalton and I have plenty of room. Harry is staying with us too. How will your father get along with the head of the FBI's Boston office?"

"I think they have a lot in common."

"Two attorneys from the law firm that will represent you will be here tomorrow afternoon. I'm glad you will have an advocate with you."

Maggie let out a very long breath. "I think that is the first time I have really breathed in a very, very long time."

"I told him how Dad was after Mom died. I'm glad he listened to me…"

Clara was concerned. "Maggie, Ben said you were upset."

"Daddy will be here tomorrow. He didn't actually say he was sorry, but I could tell he was."

"Did you tell him about...?"

"He said he knew, and he understood. He is going to stay with Shaw and Dalton."

"Well, tomorrow will be very interesting."

"You need to tell him about Casey. I know he will like him."

Chapter 27

Beau was sitting on the couch in his bedroom. Julie had been conveniently unavailable to talk. Last night, she had fallen asleep before Beau went to bed, and the night before, she claimed she had dozed off with their daughter—something she had never done before.

Julie walked into the bedroom, not expecting to see Beau. "I've been busy Beau."

"I didn't say a word."

"I'm not going to apologize."

"You and I need to talk."

"So you are in love with her."

"You seem to know a lot about my friendship with Trinity. Did you hire a PI? Did you follow me around? How did you come to the conclusion I was cheating on you?"

"Why are you being so mean, Beau?"

"Oh, you can be rude and cruel to someone who has been through a horrific ordeal, but I can't ask you why?"

"I'm not going to make it easy for you to leave."

"You don't trust me, and that's not acceptable. Your moods have been erratic at best. Everyone has noticed. Don't …"

"Don't what Beau?"

"You will lose a lot more than I will. If you don't trust me, talk to Kathryn. I won't stand in your way. You can keep your money. Just let me move on."

"Is this some kind of passive aggressive way of getting what you want? Why would I make it easy for you to leave me?"

"This is on you, Julie. What you said was malicious and hateful. I don't like that woman, no matter who she was talking to. Did you talk to Billie and Merritt? What about Maggie? Did I have an affair with them too?

I'm going to move into the guest room. We have some things to figure out, but I can't stay here with you."

"How did we get here, Beau? We were happy. What happened? Julie was calm, too calm.

"You were unhappy, sullen. Everyone wondered what was wrong, and don't tell me it was because your father died. This behavior started way before Harold died. The only time I saw you smile was when you were with the kids. Truthfully, I thought you wanted a divorce. You had moved on from me. You were treating me like a stranger. This is on you."

"You said you loved me."

"I loved the woman you were before you left. What happened to you when you were away? I believe you were scared; all the women here were scared, but you left. Where were you?" Beau was desperate. "I called Judge Bradford…"

Julie snapped, "You had no right."

"You left. You said you went to see Becca to talk to her father. I called him. I thought if I impressed him with how important getting a warrant was, he may be able to help. You weren't there Julie. Where were you?"

"I was scared. I ran because the thought of being taken was too much."

Beau believed that, but there was more. "You're going to have to do better than that. Abby, Kathryn, Dalton, and Molly have all been concerned about your unpredictable behavior."

Julie began to get undressed. Beau recognized the look on her face and went to the door. Julie tried to stop him. "Please, please don't leave. I need you." She reached out to embrace him.

"Knock it off. You can't try to seduce me every time you don't get your way."

"I won't let that woman destroy our marriage."

"You are the only woman destroying our marriage, Julie. This is on you."

"Your father won't let you divorce me."

"He knows about your accusations. He thinks we need to see a therapist."

"He won't let you leave me."

"He wants me to be happy. I haven't been happy since you left. Do you understand that the way you treated Trinity is wrong? Do you understand that trying to seduce me, using sex to manipulate me, is sick?"

"You didn't seem to mind."

"I should have stopped you, but I missed you. Can't you see that your actions and your words have made me question your judgment?"

"What happened to you? Why did you have to cheat on me? Why do you love her and not me?"

"I love the Julie I married. The Julie you were before you left to go God knows where. You are out of control. I actually have no idea who you are anymore."

***

Simon stayed with Stella in her room after his shift ended. He brought pictures from their vacation in Bar Harbor and showed her photos of Beau and Julie's wedding, as well as moments from Simon's graduation from medical school.

"We love each other."

Simon was emotional as he held her hand. "We do."

"I'm sorry, I don't remember."

"You and I were at a charity gala to raise money for cancer research."

"Someone told me that."

"You looked beautiful."

"Will you tell me what happened?"

"I'm sorry, sweetheart, I can't. It's best if you remember on your own."

Stella put her hand on her chest. "This is itchy."

"That means it's healing. Try not to touch it."

"When can I leave?"

"Well, are you going to be comfortable coming home with me?"

"Where would I go if I didn't go with you?"

"You have an aunt, Kathleen. Remember, she came to see you with your brother."

"Simon, how can I remember that the medication they are giving me is an antibiotic? I am allergic to lobster, and I keep remembering *antimony, arsenic, aluminum, and selenium.*

"Those are elements. Oh, sweetheart, you're going to remember things but not people or events. If I took you to the pharmacy and handed you a prescription, you would know what to do without even thinking about it. It doesn't make any sense, but that's what happens with head trauma. I want you to remember, but I really can't help you more than reminiscing and showing you pictures."

"Maybe if you kissed me?"

Simon leaned over her and kissed her like he always did.

"Don't look so sad. That was nice."

"Did you have other girlfriends?"

"It's always been you and me."

"Just you and me, no one else?"

"No one else."

"Simon, will you kiss me again?"

"Sweetheart, I could kiss you all day and all night." He kissed her again. "You need rest. I need to sleep, too. I will be back in the morning. I love you."

Chapter 28

"Ben, wake up." Merritt woke up to Ben moaning *no, no, no.*

"Good morning, sweet cheeks." Ben leered. "Did you brush your teeth?"

"It's going to be a few more weeks before we can have a *did you brush your teeth,* morning."

Ben pecked her lips. "How about a make-out session?"

"I know it's only been a week…"

"Six days."

"The doctor says we have to wait." Merritt's chin started quivering. "To make sure…" She couldn't finish the sentence, "I seem to be OK, then, then I'm not."

Ben embraced her. "I love you anyway."

Knock, knock. "Are you two decent?"

"Come in Colt." Merritt sat up in bed.

"Agent Wyatt sent this." He showed Ben and Merritt his phone. "Look familiar?"

"That's a white van," Merritt said sarcastically.

Colt laughed. "Oh, Ben, she's good."

"It doesn't have any plates. I suppose it could be the same one."

"It didn't get on 95, so we're not sure where it went."

"Colt, it could have taken the coast road all the way back here."

He agreed. "That was my thought as well… Molly said Stella is doing well. She doesn't remember anything, but her spirits are better."

"Head trauma can be a bitch. Colt, did Shaw tell you Harry will be staying with them?"

"Yup, I'm going over there now. Do you want to tag along?"

Ben looked at Merritt, who sighed, "Go ahead."

***

Simon arrived at work a little before eight. He needed to complete his duties before he could visit Stella. With a couple of patients waiting, he took care of them, wrote everything up, and crossed his fingers that an ambulance wouldn't come in.

He whispered to the nurse, "Ping me if you need me."

"Is Stella any better?"

"Physically, yes. The rest is slow and frustrating."

"I'll call if we need you."

Simon took the stairs. When he reached the hallway, he saw a doctor and two nurses rushing to Stella's room. He sprinted down the hall, arriving just as one of the nurses opened the door.

"Wow, that was fast. I just…"

"I was on my way up. What happened."

"Go ahead."

The doctor was shining the penlight in Stella's eyes. He looked at the chart "What is your address?"

"Forty-two Essex Place, Cape Hope."

Simon let the doctor finish his exam.

"What is your boyfriend's middle name?"

"Burke, after his maternal grandfather."

Simon walked to the hall and sent a group text: She's back!!!!!! He went back into the room to find Stella crying, "Sweetheart?"

"Simon, what happened to me?"

"Doctor Fredericks, Stella's memory is back, minus details about her injuries."

"Simon?"

"I'll be right back, I promise." Simon went to the hall as the texts on his phone started blowing up.

Simon went back. "Sorry. What happened?"

The attending doctor smirked. "She woke up. She started screaming for you. She said you kissed her goodnight. She thinks you're her Prince Charming."

Simon smiled. "I was reminiscing with her. She asked me to kiss her. We have been living together for years. I didn't see any harm."

"No criticism. I think it worked. But what the hell do I know? I know you may get called back. Go in and reunite."

"When can I take her home?"

"Maybe tomorrow."

"Thank you. Thank you." Simon opened the door. "Hi, sweetheart."

"Maybe if you had kissed me the first day I was here, I'd be home already."

"Look." He showed her his phone. "I texted everyone. Look."

Stella started crying as she read the texts, "Billie and Trinity? Are they all back?"

"Maggie, too. Merritt and Ben were taken Saturday night. It's a long story, but Merritt was found in Kittery. Ben was found with Maggie in a motel."

"Are they OK?"

"They are all at Dad's resting and recuperating. We're going there too."

"Trinity is there?"

"She is so nice. It's so sad. She really loves Beau."

"But Julie and Beau are happy again."

"Julie took off after you were taken. She came back acting worse than before. She said she was scared, but it is more than that. I'm not sure what is going on with her. But Dad essentially told Beau he understood about Trinity. He really likes her."

"Simon, what happened to me?"

"A jogger found you on the beach. Jack and Juice brought you in." He lay on the bed next to her, kissed her, and kissed her again. "What is the last thing you remember?"

"You and I were dancing, and your phone buzzed."

"So nothing about when you were…"

Stella screeched. "In the brothel? That's where I was, Simon!"

Simon was stunned.

"I'm sorry. The doctor told me. I can feel the cruelty. What else did they do to me? I obviously have a laceration on my head, but why is there a bandage on my chest?"

"When the Coast Guard picked up Billie and Trinity, sweetheart, their heads had been shaved."

Stella mumbled something Simon couldn't hear. "Is this your attempt to ease into telling me what's under this bandage? Because…"

"Please… these people, they are cruel. We think you hit your head, and they knew they needed to get rid of you, but they wanted to shatter your self-esteem. You must have really pissed them off."

"I know you're doing your best to lessen the shock for me because I know they are… Simon, please, just tell me."

"Well, it looks like someone strangled you."

"And?"

"I haven't seen it, but they tell me you were branded."

"What?" Stella's eyes filled with tears. "Oh my God. What?"

"The plastic surgeon was in. He can fix it."

"Simon! What does it say!"

He kissed her. "It says *whore.*"

Stella's hands were shaking as she reached to embrace Simon. "Don't tell anyone, please don't tell anyone."

"Jack and Juice saw it. You know how discreet they are…"

"They saw me naked?"

"They did. They are professionals, Stella, just like I am. But the attending was concerned about telling me about the injuries, so Shaw and Abby came, so they know. The only other time I saw Abby cry like that was when Mom died. Sweetheart, it can be fixed. Oh, and a little good news. Dad talked to Dr. Patel, and the rest of my residency will be here. So I'll be much closer and not nearly as busy."

"But you're still learning."

"You are more important to me than anything. I can learn here. Being in Boston has been an incredible learning experience, but I never should have gone in that night."

"Will I ever remember?"

"Honestly, I hope you don't.

Knock, knock… Simon left so Abby and Dalton could see for themselves that Stella's memory was back. They were careful as they embraced her. "Michael will be here later with Lizzy."

"I hope they will let me out soon."

"Your room is all ready for you."

"Simon told me Trip likes Trinity. He said Julie disappeared."

Abby admitted, "She went to the house. She threatened Trinity."

"Is she OK?"

Dalton confessed, "Yes. We really like her."

"Maybe I should talk to Julie. If she can't be supportive, she needs to be told to stay away."

"Honey, she's not being reasonable. She started making accusations. Beau was surprised because he thought they were in a better place. Beau moved into the guestroom."

"I'm sorry, but Julie has always been complicated but Beau has his issues too."

"They both deserve to be happy. I don't think that will happen if they stay together."

"Abby is right. Stella, can we get you anything?"

"Out of here…"

"I heard that." Simon came back in. "You have a CAT scan scheduled for later today. The nurse is going to take you for a walk. The plastic surgeon is coming in, too. I'm hoping I'll be here…"

"No, I don't want you to be here, please."

Simon sighed. "Whatever you want."

***

Ben went to the street and walked toward the stone house. Even though he was off the clock, he would be reprimanded if caught, but he needed to go into that house.

He walked past the gate to the spot where he and Merritt had sat against the tree. Then he walked down the hill to the dock, glancing at the cove side to see if there was any evidence of recent activity.

He stood at the end of the dock, looking at the trap door. Without thinking, he put on gloves, walked to the door, and grasped the handles. He didn't expect it to open, but again, he didn't think as he stepped down the metal grate steps.

Reluctantly, he closed the doors behind him. It was dark, so he turned on his phone's flashlight.

The interior consisted of multiple shipping containers that had been welded together. At first, it was dark, but as he began to move, a small light at the top of the wall illuminated. About every five feet, a light would come on as the one behind it went dark. The tunnel ahead resembled a black hole, absorbing the light.

He counted twenty lights as he walked. When he reached the end, he found a double metal door similar to the back of an eighteen-wheeler. He held the handle and pushed it down, and it opened into a dark room. He reached to his right to find a light switch.

He was surprised to see a room that looked like a reception area. There was an elevator with its door open, and one more door was closed. Inside was a cinderblock room that appeared to be freshly painted. The floor had drag marks—some old and some not so old. He closed the door and approached the elevator. It had three floors, and he pressed the button for the third floor, knowing that was where they had seen the covered windows.

The doors opened to a long hallway with six doors—three on each side. He entered the first room, which had a small anteroom with a single chair. At the very bottom of the inside door, there was a small rectangular opening. *For dinner trays?*

Ben wasn't surprised when he opened the door. Matilda had mentioned that the rooms were very nice, and this one resembled her description. The bed consisted only of a mattress and box spring. The bathroom, while lacking in amenities, was still quite nice.

The spot for the TV was empty, and the laptop Matilda mentioned was not there, but everything else matched her description.

He looked behind one of the paintings but found only the cardboard backing. Before leaving the room, he examined the headboard where Matilda said they cuffed her hands. The brass was scratched, but it also appeared old and recently polished.

He searched the rest of the rooms, taking pictures with his phone. They were all quite similar, except for the paintings and tapestries, which he also photographed. As he approached the end of the hall, he noticed the newel posts of a staircase.

As he tiptoed down the wooden staircase, he noticed an odor. As he neared the bottom step, the smell of ammonia grew stronger. There was an aluminum bucket and a rope mop nearby.

The second floor consisted of an industrial-sized kitchen. Maybe it was a retreat? The refrigerator was empty, as was the storeroom, both featuring shiny shelves that looked recently cleaned.

The cabinets held stacks of disposable plates, cups, and drinking glasses. There were drawers filled with plastic utensils and paper products. Another cabinet contained wire baskets full of small packages of condiments typically used by hotels for room service. To Ben, everything seemed fine and dandy, as his father would say.

He walked down the stairs to the first floor, which featured a suite with four doors. Three were large bedrooms. Again, there was a niche for a TV, just like in the bedrooms on the third floor, but there were no linens or towels. The fourth door was locked. I'm really pushing my luck; I'll just leave that room a mystery.

Ben returned to the basement for one last look around. He pushed the elevator button to bring it back down and closed the door to the cinderblock room.

He made his way back through the tunnel and up the stairs to the trapdoor. Listening intently for whispers or movements, he opened the hatch. He felt relieved when he wasn't met by the barrel of a gun.

It was a windy day, and Ben had to steady himself as a gust of wind hit him hard. He leaned forward while climbing the hill, but something caught his eye in his peripheral vision. It was a small white piece of paper wafting through the air. He moved quickly to intercept it before he lost it.

He immediately recognized Merritt's handwriting on the front: *To Whom It May Concern.*

The envelope was still sealed. *Damn, damn, damn.*

As he walked back to the house, he decided to show Harry the letter. He also planned to visit a nearby office supply store to use a printer. He had photos to print, and after writing a letter, he needed to send it to the State Police anonymously.

A late-model Jaguar sedan with Connecticut plates was parked on the street at the end of the driveway. The man inside had one leg resting on the asphalt. "Hi, may I help you?"

"Do you live here?"

"That's a long story. Are you Maggie and Clara's father?"

"Yes, Martin Beckett."

"Special Agent Ben Malloy. I'll take you inside. My boss, Harry Moran, should be here soon. I was abducted after the Gala Saturday night, so I'm off the case, but I will be here if you have questions."

"Clara said you were undercover at the time. She didn't know much more about the case. She said you and, I believe her name is Merritt, were very kind. I spoke to Shaw Fredericks as well. I knew something was wrong, but I was..."

"Mr. Beckett. We are all back to square one here. The ladies are helping each other. There is no blame. Merritt is Coast Guard Investigative Services. We teamed up for this case. Then we fell in love. We have been upfront with everyone, so that is why I'm telling you."

"I appreciate that. Shaw said the girls have representation?"

"When these people are found, we want to make sure the ladies aren't put on trial. Shaw has been an advocate, but his brother's girlfriend was the latest victim, and this is a Federal case, so he won't be involved in the criminal case."

"Is it possible to see Maggie and Clara privately?"

"Yes. Trip said you can use his office. I can take you there first if you'd rather, or I can take you in to meet everyone."

"I'd appreciate talking to them first. Do you know who is representing them?"

"Yes, I have his card, although I'm not sure who will be here today." Ben handed the business card to Martin.

"Ah, yes." Martin chortled, "He is well known. Thank you."

Ben led Martin through the solarium to Trip's office. "Hilda will be serving a buffet for lunch today. Would you like coffee?"

"Coffee would be nice, thank you."

Martin turned his back to the door, scanning the library shelves lined with books.

"Hi Daddy."

Martin felt a pang of pain as he turned to see Maggie. The bruises and welts from the whip still hurt, making loose clothing her most comfortable option.

"I'm sorry about the way I'm dressed, but I don't have a lot that is comfortable. Two of the other women look worse, so if you'd rather not…"

"It's fine. I understand. Your friend Shaw was quite gentle describing your injuries. I still wish I had been better prepared."

"He didn't want to hurt you. I brought your coffee." Maggie put it on the desk, sat in one of the tufted leather chairs and waited.

Martin eventually sat next to her and picked up the mug. "I'm afraid I don't know what to say to you. I can't change the past. I thought I was right at the time. As angry as I was I never would have wished on anyone what has happened to you."

Maggie was trying hard not to cry, but Martin stood, took her hands in his, gently pulled her closer, and embraced her. Slowly, she wrapped her arms around him and broke into tears.

Ben intercepted Harry before he came into the house. "I took a walk down the street this morning and found myself at the house. I went toward the dock to look around again. On my way back, there was a huge gust of wind, and I saw this floating around. It hasn't been opened."

"So the bear is unprovoked. Well, we're not getting anywhere with the warrant anyway, and you're obviously not behaving yourself. What was on your mind?"

Ben chuckled. "I was bored, so I took a walk. That house was mocking me."

"I'd keep that to yourself when you go in for your psych review."

"There are good reasons law enforcement agencies prohibit interoffice relationships. My judgment is skewed, to say the least. If I hadn't woken up in the hospital next to Merritt, I would have torn that place apart."

"I know you're exaggerating, but I get your point, Ben. Colt told me Billie is going to resign and join Cape Hope PD. Have you talked to Merritt about what you are going to do?"

"We want to live here. We've been looking at some listings Beau sent us. Merritt actually wanted to talk to Skipper about a demotion so she could take Billie's job. She is scared and doubting herself."

"Not a good place to be. Have you met Mr. Beckett?"

"Yes. He is very reserved, a lot like Trip, but anxious to see Maggie again."

"Beau has been visiting Trinity. Was he less than truthful about his relationship?"

"I was pretty sure he was having an affair with her, but there was no evidence that he had anything to do with her disappearance. He must really care for her to jeopardize everything the way he did. His information did bring us into the investigation. Harry, Beau's wife, promised Trinity she would be sorry if she stayed in town."

"The woman scorned making a threat? That's new." Harry smirked. "Shaw filled me in on Mrs. Frederick's history. I can't say it surprises me, but I'm not sure she would follow through."

"Perhaps. Keep her on your radar nonetheless."

***

Beau left the house early to see Trinity before heading to the office. Trip had asked Beau to be careful. Though he liked Trinity, he didn't want Beau to use the living arrangements to his advantage. Beau assured him that he respected Trinity far too much to ever do that. While Trip didn't condone Beau's affair, his strict adherence to church teachings was not only straining his relationship with Lizzy but also affecting Beau's happiness.

Phil had brought Trinity her laptop, and she spent a great deal of time trying to mend business relationships. Unsure of how to explain her absence, she followed Merritt's advice and composed an email, explaining she'd suffered a head injury in an accident and had been out of commission for the past few weeks. Trinity figured this would also help explain her lack of hair. Within a couple of days, most clients responded—some had moved on, but most were happy she was well and looking forward to her return.

Before Beau left for work, he told Trinity, "I moved out of the bedroom. We have some things to decide, but I hope you will be able to wait for me."

"I want to. Your wife scares me, Beau."

"She won't hurt you. I won't let her."

"Beau, I love you…"

"But?"

"You have children. How could they possibly understand."

"They are the only reason I'm still home. If Dad hadn't pushed me, I'd probably still be single. I wasn't a very nice person. I was very selfish; still am. Being a father has helped with that, but when I met you, there was something about you that was irresistible to me."

"You didn't tell me you loved me until you found me in the house."

"I didn't know until you were missing. I will never forgive myself…"

"No, it wasn't your fault. You gave me hope Beau." Trinity opened her robe. "Hold me. I need you to hold me."

He was careful as he put his arms around her and kissed her. "I have to go. But I'm going to plan a vacation for us. Only a few days, but somewhere for you and me, alone."

"I would love that."

"I'll be back later. I love you."

When Trinity arrived at the pool, Ben and Harry were there, along with Maggie and Clara's father and the two lawyers. They discussed various possibilities, though the hope was that the women wouldn't end up needing their assistance.

After lunch, Trip asked to speak to Trinity alone in his office.

"I am worried about your safety. Your house is known to the people who took you. Please allow me to help keep you safe."

"Beau has told me how much honesty means to you. Mr. Fredericks, I love Beau. I don't think I've ever loved someone as much. I was pretty sure he was married, but I was falling hard." Trinity started crying. "I'm sorry. I know how much your faith means to you and your family. I have talked to Andy, Abby, Dalton, and Simon. You have a very forgiving family. I'm sorry that I am causing so many problems." Trinity wept as Trip sat in the chair next to her.

"I'm not accustomed to condoning extra-marital affairs. You are right, my faith is very important, but sometimes exceptions are necessary. The woman I love now is divorced. Getting married in the church may be an issue. I don't like that. I've waited a long time to be happy again. I want Beau to be happy. I own a lot of properties. No one in the family but Beau and Shaw know my personal and business affairs. I have a house in town, it is very nice. I want you to live there. Please don't think of this offer as a place to hide, but a place to live safely and without fear of anyone, including Julie, threatening you."

"Mr. Fredericks, I don't know what to say. I'd like to talk to Beau."

"Of course. Do me a favor. If you feel threatened by Julie, please let me know."

"Thank you."

Trip patted Trinity on the shoulder and left her in his office. She sat, thinking about his offer. *What are you thinking about? Do it.* She stood up and looked out the window to the backyard. She still didn't remember much about her last days before she and Billie were rescued, but she did remember thinking about Beau. She was conflicted because she had always believed that if a person has an affair, nothing stops them from doing it again. *How many affairs have you had, Beau? Don't ask because you probably won't like the answer.*

***

"How long are you going to punish me?" Julie was wearing a short silk robe, barely tied at the waist, with nothing else on.

"Do you even understand…"

Julie moaned, "I was nasty to someone you like, so now I'm the bad guy."

"Now say it like a human being."

"Can you understand why I feel suspicious, Beau?"

"No. You accepted what I told you. You were understanding and compassionate. What happened to that woman?"

"She is scared."

"What happened when you were gone that changed your mind? I need to understand."

"I was scared, Beau. I don't know what else to tell you."

"You weren't mean to Billie or Stella. You didn't accuse Maggie of having an affair with me."

"Trip likes Trinity. He told me to keep my distance."

"He told you if you couldn't play nice to stay away. I agree with him."

"You can't leave me in limbo, Beau; it's not fair."

"No, it isn't fair to anyone. I'm seriously thinking of asking for a legal separation."

"You can't do that. I will claim alienation of affection."

"Are you kidding? Do you even remember how long you wouldn't let me touch you? This is what I have been talking about. You are not the only person in this marriage. I'm never included in a decision. If you decide something, there is no room for conversation. If you get scared, you take off without a word. You left me, Julie."

"What do I have to do?"

"I'm not sure there is anything." Beau paused. "Julie, where were you? Where did you go."

"I went to Nantucket."

"Really? In the middle of the summer, you got a room. Come on. The truth."

Julie wouldn't look at him. She kept her head down as she spun her rings around on her finger. "Forget it; it doesn't matter."

Beau was frustrated. "We need to set up a schedule for the kids."

"Are you moving out?"

"You're not giving me a choice."

"If I apologize. If I tell her how much I love you…"

"You don't get it. You threatened her… I have to go." Beau left the house and drove to Kathryn's office. He needed to explain his intentions.

The assistant wasn't at her desk, so he knocked. "Do you have a minute?"

"Of course."

"I need to make some decisions. Staying in the house isn't working. I don't want to put you in the middle, but Julie has been a yoyo. I don't know what happened."

"I hate representing friends in a divorce." She sat back. "Beau, I haven't had a chance to see Stella. Do you know when she will be home?"

"Maybe today? They will be staying at the house too… May we speak as friends, off the record?"

"Sure."

"I am afraid for Trinity."

"Abby told me. You know Beau, you have a lot of allies. Everyone really likes Trinity. You know I trust Abby and Dalton like sisters. They think you have matured a lot since all of this happened, and they have seen the change in you since Trinity came back."

"Julie is scaring me. The day she came back, she told Deborah to leave, then she practically attacked me in my office. At the time, I had no reason to stop her, but she knew Stella had been found, and she didn't bother to tell me. The next day, she started groping me at my father's house. After I told her to knock it off, she found Trinity and threatened her. The next morning at breakfast, I caught her glaring at me. I am very concerned for Trinity's safety."

"Beau, Julie is a business client and a friend, but you and I have been friends for a long time. No one knows about our *friends with benefits* relationship. You were such a good friend after my parents died. Beau, you never expected anything from me, and you never took advantage."

"I've always liked you. I haven't told anyone."

"Neither have I… OK, I won't say anything, and if Julie does come to me, I will refer her to a colleague. Truthfully, I wouldn't feel comfortable trying to take you to the cleaner."

"I already told her I don't want her money. You know she has much more than me. I think at this point she would be relieved not to lose anything but maybe her pride."

"I'm glad you came to me."

"Trinity wants to meet you. She has heard so much about you; she is curious."

"I'd like that. We're still off the record, Beau so I can tell you; I can see how much you care about her. When Abby told me about Julie's visit, she also told me how much you care about Trinity. I know you, Beau. You wouldn't be talking divorce if you weren't madly in love with her. I can see the sadness in your eyes at the thought of not being with her."

"She loves me, Kathryn. Me, not my status, not my family, or my money. She loves me and believe it or not, Dad is on my side. I can't tell you how much that means. Thank you, Kathryn. Cubby is a lucky guy."

Kathryn got up. "I'm going to walk you out. I need to get something from my car."

Kathryn's office was in a small house, the parking lot in the back. Beau held open the car door for Kathryn and then kissed her. "Thank you."

"My pleasure, Beau."

Julie was driving to Kathryn's office when she saw Beau and Kathryn together. She slowed down, then sped away when she saw them kiss.

Chapter 29

Billie was still sleeping when a dream suddenly woke her. She searched for her notebook and a pen, then began to write furiously.

Juice had gone down to do some laps in the pool. When he came back, Billie was pacing as she read what she had just written. "Shit, you scared me!" She dropped the notebook and embraced Juice's bare torso, her nails digging into his back.

Juice grasped her arms and pried her hands off his back. "Billie, sweetheart…"

"Oh God, I'm sorry. Are you alright?"

"Did you remember something?"

Billie retrieved the book from the floor and handed it to Juice.

He read the last entry, walked Billie to the bed and lay next to her. "Are you sure this wasn't a dream?"

"I can describe him. Can Harry get someone to do a composite?"

"You are still recovering; a defense attorney would tear you to pieces."

"Will you call Shaw?"

"You look scared to death." Juice held her tightly as he made the call… "Shaw Fredericks… Justice Mason… thank you." Juice laughed. "I think he believes I'm a big deal."

"That's because you are."

Shaw was chuckling "Justice Mason, you certainly have a way of making my staff come to attention."

"I'm sure I wouldn't have gotten through if I said *Juice*. Billie has a question."

"Hi, I remembered something, Shaw. Is it too soon to make a statement or do a composite? Juice thinks the defense would think I was dreaming."

"It really depends. Were you sleeping?"

"Yes, but I remember more than what was in the dream. I remember seeing a man. I heard him. I know his face, Shaw."

"I would hesitate to put any of you on the stand. Not only to save you from reliving your ordeal but to save you from being dragged through the mud."

"That's what Juice said. Should I talk to Harry?"

"I have gotten to know Ben and Harry well enough to know they wouldn't conveniently forget something that may hurt the case. I have a lunch meeting with the lawyers that were there yesterday. I will pose a hypothetical to see what they would do. Billie, write it down…"

"I did."

"OK, then wait until after lunch. Don't look at what you wrote after you woke up and write it again."

"OK, but I know what I saw."

"I'm sorry you have to relive this. The Commonwealth is not involved in this case, but I will dispense free advice as long as you ladies and Ben need me."

"I knew there was a reason Dalton liked you."

Shaw laughed. "Call me anytime; I'll get back to you later."

Juice picked up his clothes. "I need to get changed."

"Why? I'll go to the pool with you. I know you enjoy swimming. This is a safe place. No judgment."

"I know I asked you to move in with me. I never got an answer."

"I was a little preoccupied, sweetie… Ben and Merritt are staying here."

"I know. They're looking for a house…"

Billie caressed Juice's face. "I saw that man's face. It wasn't a dream. They knew Matilda's name. The other woman in the house, her name was Harlow. We have to find her."

"You are out of commission, my dear."

"Harlow isn't a common name. It shouldn't be too hard to track down."

"Shaw will let us know what to do after lunch."

"OK… I miss you so much…"

"You need to recover. Look at me." Juice leaned over Billie, her eyes were black and blue "I love you, Billie. I wanted to tell you, but…"

"We knew we were crazy about each other almost right away. I didn't want to scare you off, so I didn't tell you. I love you, too."

"This is where I would make mad, passionate love to you, but right now, I'll just kiss you and look forward to the day we can be together again."

"You are the sweetest man."

Knock, knock… "Billie, it's me, Matilda."

"Come in."

Juice was still lying on Billie. Matilda laughed. "If you two want to finish, I can wait."

"I have missed you." Billie sat up. "You look good."

"What do you mean? I look great."

Billie looked at Matilda's ring and held back her emotions. "It's beautiful."

"Did Juice tell you he will be Lenny's best man?"

Billie slapped his arm. "No, he didn't."

"Will you be my maid of honor?"

Billie rubbed her head. "Could you give me some time to feel a little more human?"

Matilda hugged her, and they both cried. Unfortunately, these weren't happy tears; Matilda still felt responsible for Billie's abduction.

Juice and Billie returned to the pool, where Maggie, Clara, and their father were waiting.

"Mr. Mason, thank you for opening your home to Clara."

"She was a perfect guest. She came to the firehouse and made some delicious meals."

"I made friends there, so win, win."

"Margaret and Clara's mother was a gourmet chef… Mr. Mason, I'm told you were in the Marines. Thank you for your service."

"Thank you, sir. It was an honor… Maggie, Matilda is here with Billie. I know she still feels guilty for not talking to any of you but she was terrified of repercussions."

"I understand. I do want to meet her. I have been worried about a woman named Harlow. She was, at least I think she was very innocent… I'm sorry."

"Billie remembered her this morning. She was concerned too…"

Clara was pacing. "Wait… it can't be… Daddy, there was a girl at Mount Holyoke when I was a senior. I was showing a group of freshmen around the campus. She was very shy, and she was the only one who didn't have a parent with her. So I had her walk with me. That is not a common name…"

"I will call. I know the Provost. Let me make a call."

"Sir, if you don't mind, I think Harry should decide. The less people that know about what is going on, the better. We have seen what they do when they get scared…"

"I will speak to Harry myself." Mr. Mason, thank you for your kindness." He left the patio and went back inside. Trip was coming out of his office. "Martin, good morning. You look like a man on a mission."

"The girls remembered a name. It is unusual, so when Clara said she knew someone from college… Trip, Mr. Mason suggested I wait to call my contact there. He thinks I need to talk to Harry first."

"The fewer people that know about this, the better. Would your connection there be discreet?"

"Absolutely. Time is of the essence."

"Let's go to my office…"

"Dad." Shaw came in with Harry. "I need to talk to you."

"Can it wait? Billie remembered a name, an unusual name. Clara remembers a girl from Mount Holyoke. Martin has a contact there."

Harry spoke up, "Trip, may Martin and I borrow your office while you talk to Shaw?"

"Very well. Shaw, we can go to the solarium."

"Dad, I already talked to Dalton about this, but I need your advice. I had lunch with the lawyers that were here. I guess you sang my praises after I left?"

"I am proud of you. That isn't a secret."

"Dad, his CEO and Vice President were with him. His organization is quite impressive. He grew up in Marblehead, and he loves the area. He has offices…"

"Shaw, I am familiar with his law firm."

"He wants me and Kathryn for a satellite office here. He thought Beau could help find the perfect location."

"You wouldn't be talking to me if it wasn't a good offer."

Shaw handed him a piece of paper. Trip read the entire proposal. "Son, this is a tremendous opportunity."

"Dalton thinks so, too."

"My only concern is what Ed will do."

"I have been assured that Ed will not be a problem."

Trip smirked. "Really? I like this guy. I have heard great things about his organization."

"They are friendly, funny. It didn't seem like an interview Dad. I really like them."

"You've already decided?"

"I wanted to talk to you first, but being close to home, not playing political games…"

"You've made the right decision."

"Thanks, Dad. I'm excited."

Harry and Martin made a couple of calls. "Shaw, we have a name. I called the parents' number. They live in Beacon Hill, but they are gone for the summer. The housekeeper wouldn't share the information, but she assured me she would pass along the message. She did say they haven't heard from her in over six months."

"Harry, this is great."

"I gave them my number as well as Phil's."

"Great, may I talk to you in Dad's office?"

"Harry, I'm leaving the DA's office…" Shaw went on to explain his concerns about the investigations once he gave his notice.

"I'm pretty sure Ed has already warned his buddies."

"Well, I was told that the law firm I am going to has already received the FBI's communication about the brothel."

"Thank you for keeping us in the loop."

"Have you seen Billie and Juice?"

Shaw looked out by the pool and saw Matilda there with the ladies and Juice. After he said hello, Billie and Matilda jumped up, ran toward the door, and embraced Stella, who had just arrived with Simon.

"Maggie, Trinity, this is Stella." Simon had to get back to the hospital. "Ladies, I'm entrusting you to take care of her. Sweetheart, I will be home for dinner."

"Go. You've been spending a lot of time with me. Go."

As soon as Simon left, Stella thanked Juice, "I'm so glad it was you and Jack who found me."

"You had no idea who we were."

Stella put her arms around him. "Thank you, really, thank you."

Juice kissed her forehead. "Just don't make us do it again."

She whispered, "Would you help me later? I'll need to change the bandage before Simon gets back."

"Oh honey, of course." Juice went back to Billie. "She is scared. She didn't say it, but I could hear it in her voice."

"She has a head injury. That will take longer. It will take a while before she is relaxed with us. She will probably be more comfortable without the long sleeves and turtleneck, though."

"There is more going on with her than modesty, Billie. I can't tell you, but maybe with time, she will tell you herself."

Billie put a hand on her head. "What did they do to her? Sorry, that was a rhetorical question."

"Your hair will grow back…"

"Juice, is Stella OK?"

"Ya she'll be OK… Shaw, do you have an answer for us?"

"Well. Let me ask. Did you do what I asked?"

"Right before lunch, I went to the back of the notebook, and I wrote what I remembered about the people who were there. I only saw the man, but there were two women too." Billie went on to describe to Juice and Shaw what happened. She was very clinical and very professional. "Here, you can take it with you."

I am going to resign today. I'll be working for the man who was talking to you the other day. I talked to them about this, and I'll keep it with my notes.

***

Julie was furious with Beau and Kathryn. She had a meeting with a new client yesterday afternoon, so she was busy. Last night, she took the kids to dinner and a movie to avoid the temptation of strangling Beau.

Julie waited until Beau was out of the house to go to Kathryn's office. Her assistant wasn't there. Julie went inside, closed the door behind her, and locked it. She stood in the doorway of Kathryn's office without saying a word.

"Hi honey. How are you?"

"Cut the crap. I have been thinking about what to say to you. I've always considered you one of my best friends…"

"Sit down. Julie, you're going to have to start making sense."

"How long has this affair been going on?"

"You mean Beau and Trinity? I have no proof that Beau has been unfaithful." Kathryn knew better, but Julie was a loose cannon.

"I'm not talking about her; I'm talking about you. How could you do this to me?"

"Everyone is worried about you, Julie, so I will let that pass."

"I saw you and Beau kissing."

"What? Yesterday? Your husband and I have been friends for a very long time."

"You're only friends because of me."

"No, I have known Beau since before my parents died. He was an incredible friend to me at a horrible time in my life, and you would know that if you listened to anything I have ever told you. Get out of here. I can't talk to you right now."

Julie started blubbering, "I'm sorry." She turned around, went to her car and wept.

Kathryn went to the kitchen in the back of the house. She looked out the window as she lifted her phone to her ear. "Hi, Beau."

"Hi, what's up?"

"Apparently, Julie was on her way here yesterday when she saw us in the parking lot."

"Oh… oooh."

"Ya. She thinks we're having an affair."

Beau couldn't stop laughing. "I'm sorry. Kathryn, she is beginning to worry me."

"I got mad Beau. I kicked her out of my office."

"I know you can't tell me anything, but I wish I knew where she was. She said she was at Becca's. I called her father to see if he was able to help with the warrant. Kathryn, she hadn't been there. When I asked her where she was, she said she was in Nantucket. She wouldn't look at me. Kathryn, she has a tell when she is lying."

"Was she turning her rings?"

"Yup. I really don't know what to do."

"I have an idea. Are you still having dinner at home?"

"Uh-huh. We're usually done by seven. Then the kids usually have dessert in front of the TV."

"I'll be there at seven. I need to talk to her, but I want you there. I mean, truthfully, who knows her better?"

"Well, Chip, but who knows where he is."

"I think if he knew his sister was in trouble, he'd come home."

"Kathryn, thank you again."

Beau had planned to visit Trinity after dinner, but instead, he left work early and went to his father's house. He entered through the kitchen door and climbed the back staircase. Tapping on the door, he waited for a response.

"It's open."

"Hi. I missed you." Beau kissed her. "I really missed you."

"I met Matilda and Stella."

"I have to see her." He kissed her again. "I'll be right back." He met Simon in the hall "Trinity said Stella is here."

"Ya. I had to go back to the hospital. There were so many people here…"

"You have to stop feeling guilty."

Simon put his arm around Beau as he opened the door. Juice was inside, having just changed Stella's bandage. She was emotional, crying on Juice's shoulder, who was gentle and caring when Simon walked in.

"Oh, Simon, I was doing so good. I asked Juice to change my bandage, and I kind of fell apart."

"Sweetheart, if I'm not here and you need help, I trust Juice to take care of you."

Juice looked at Stella. "You OK?"

"Yes, thank you."

Beau stayed for a minute. "I wanted to make sure you were OK. I'll leave you two alone."

"I really like Trinity Beau."

Beau kissed her cheek. "Thanks. She is special."

Beau went back to Trinity. "Stella likes you."

"Your family has been wonderful, Beau, but I can't stay here. Your father has a house; he said only you and Shaw know he owns it. I will be safe there. If I were a suspicious person, I would wonder if he is trying to hide me."

"But you're not."

"No, you're right. He also said Julie knows nothing about it. Those people know where I live, Beau. I told him I would talk to you about it."

"It's a beautiful house. It's essentially a summer rental, but the people who reserved it for the last two weeks of August canceled. Have you seen the houses that overlook the ocean on both sides of the downtown area? Well, this house is one of the smaller ones. It is across the street from Tim Edwards's house. His brother is one of Abby's best friends. His girlfriend is a police officer. I don't really know her, but Abby loves her."

"That's good enough for me."

"I have to tell you something I've never shared with anyone. Honestly, I don't think I'd be telling you if I wasn't concerned about Julie's emotional state." Beau went on to explain his friendship with Kathryn.

"So you're not the cad you make yourself out to be?"

"Maybe only to you and Kathryn. We would hook up when we were home for vacation and during the summer. When she went to law school, we lost touch. She spent all her time studying. I spent all my time chasing women. I was at Cornell. Dad thought I should be a lawyer. I wasn't interested in doing the work, so I got my degree and started working for Dad."

"You have a successful business, Beau."

"It was successful because of Dad, not me. I took over for Dad so he could focus on the Foundation. He's on the Board of two hospitals. He is always busy with that. I am lucky I didn't have to look for a job right out of school. I'm not sure I would have lasted being a yes man in the corporate world."

"So why are you telling me this?"

"The reason I told you about Kathryn is because I went to talk to her about Julie. It was the first time we talked about our *secret* since we went our separate ways. Kathryn walked me outside. I kissed her, a thank you kiss, nothing more. Julie was on her way to talk to Kathryn and saw us. She is making ridiculous accusations. We have to do something to rein her in, so Kathryn is coming to the house after dinner. We are going to try to figure out what happened when she left."

"Thank you for telling me. I'd like to meet her. She is obviously important to you."

"Ya, I guess she is."

***

Ben went to his office, where the staff psychologist wanted to speak with him about the case and his abduction. Ben knew what to expect; he had studied pre-law with a minor in psychology in school. His dream had always been to become an FBI profiler. After a few years in the field, he was promoted to Supervisory Special Agent and began studying profiling. His former boss was the best in the field, and he hoped to reach that level someday. However, since meeting Merritt, he wondered if he could be away from her and the family he always wanted.

He arrived at the office early with his personal laptop and a draft of the anonymous letter he had written. It felt like he had read it a hundred times before finally giving in and printing it out. He also printed the pictures from his phone and placed everything in his briefcase.

Ben stayed at his desk, going through his mail and emails until the staff psychologist called him into his office. Although Ben thought he knew what to expect, he was wrong.

"How are the ladies?"

"Mr. Fredericks was right. They needed to be together. They are talking, getting to know each other. Merritt said there hasn't been much talk of their captivity."

"Captivity?"

"There is no other word for it."

"I've talked to Harry, but I wanted to talk to you as well."

"I think the ladies need to talk about what happened. I think that is the only way they will recover. Did Harry tell you what they did to Stella?"

Dr. John Evans was a step up from the last staff psychologist; he was cold and unwavering. John was compassionate and open-minded. The biggest difference was that John always made himself available. "Yes, Ben, how have you been?"

"Angry. Sad. Thankful. Did Harry ask you to talk to me?"

John grinned. "He did. That was when I decided to offer my services. Ben, it hasn't been long enough for a back-to-work evaluation, but do you need to talk? Off the record, of course."

"The drugs they gave me were playing with my memory. I'm really not sure what I remember."

"Nightmares."

"Big time."

"Harry told me about Merritt. Are your dreams about her?"

"Not specifically. I guess they are a fusion of my fears, of what I imagined was happening to her. I know what they did to her. She doesn't remember either, but she had internal injuries that can't be explained any other way…"

"Ben, are you feeling guilty because they didn't batter you like they did the women?"

"I never thought about that, I suppose. I have been wondering if I can be impartial going forward. Can I work a kidnapping or a serial case again without my personal feelings coming into play?"

"Did you feel that way after you shot that man?"

"No, he shot at us. I was brought in because Jeff's partner was on disability, and I was the closest available agent. It was an emergency. I really wasn't as invested as I am now."

"Is there any anxiety being away from Merritt?"

"Knowing where she is, no. May I show you something? It is a video of Merritt and me together. Those people took it as blackmail, I guess. After she saw it…well…"

"Go ahead."

Ben placed his laptop on the desk and pressed the video icon. John watched for a couple of minutes before turning to look at Ben.

"John, Merritt said she knew I loved her. It wasn't until after she saw this that she realized how much. I am scared to death we are going to lose what we had."

"I understand why you're having such a hard time."

"I've never felt like this before. Anyway, I think you should clear your calendar and come to the house. Now that Stella has been discharged, everyone is there."

"Anyone who is struggling?"

"Stella, but Maggie was there for almost a year. She seems to be lost. She's not making eye contact. She was estranged from her father. He is here now, trying to repair their relationship. I think she needs someone like you, not a doctor but a friend, to let her know her life has value."

"I will do my best. You and I can talk again on the record in a couple of weeks."

On his way back to Cape Hope, Ben stopped at an office store. First, he was careful not to leave fingerprints on anything, covering the tips of his fingers with band-aids. If anyone asked, he would say he had burns from a kitchen mishap.

He made copies, bought a large white envelope, and used the address label he had created earlier. He also used stamps he purchased at a local grocery store. Although he knew he had used too many stamps, he didn't want the envelope to end up in the dead letter office. He dropped it in a mailbox next to the grocery store and headed back. He was confident he was doing the right thing. He also knew Harry had asked the area State Police to forward any letters regarding the brothel or abductions to the Boston FBI office, hoping that would keep the DA out of the investigation.

***

Beau talked with his kids about their upcoming activities. The boys were going to spend two weeks in Vermont with Beau's cousin while his daughter was going on vacation with friends.

Beau was concerned that Julie might have something planned for their time alone. He hadn't considered that scenario until the topic of the kids going away arose. He pushed the thought aside when he heard the grandfather clock chime…

"Time for dessert. You don't want to miss Wheel of Fortune."

The kids took their plates to the kitchen, where they met Aunt Kathryn. "I'm here to see your parents. Maybe we can plan something when you get home." She kissed the kids and picked up the tray of coffee. "We'll be in the dining room."

"You do realize you didn't say a word during dinner."

"So." Julie was acting like a child.

Beau saw Kathryn carrying a tray and stood up. He closed the dining room door and asked her to have a seat.

"What is this all about?" Julie looked scared. "Kathryn, I'm sorry."

"You owe both of us an explanation."

"Beau, I don't owe you anything. Were you trying to make Kathryn think I'm crazy and an unfit mother?"

"I may be questioning a lot of things, but you have always loved our children. I have never doubted that."'

"So now you're being nice?"

Kathryn was patient. "Beau is concerned, as am I. When Stella was taken, we were all scared, but none of us left—except you. You said you were scared, but it was more than that. Why did you leave?"

"Aren't you supposed to be on my side?"

"I'm your attorney, Julie, and your friend. Beau and I are worried about you."

"Julie, where did you go?"

"I went to Nantucket."

"Show me your receipts; tell me which credit card you used. Julie, you have to give me something."

"Who else are you sleeping with Beau? Does Trinity know? Does Cubby know?"

"I told you; Beau and I have been friends since High School."

"Beau and Shaw were in private school."

"Julie, we were home every weekend. Kathryn, Brock, Abby and Dalton, we are all friends."

"You never told me."

"That's the thing, Julie: I did tell you, and because it happened before we met, you didn't care. Everything that happened before we met was irrelevant to you. You talked about growing up and everything that was significant to you. But when I tried to tell you about me, you changed the subject. You had to be the center of attention, and my life before you didn't matter."

"You said you loved me, Beau. Was that a lie?"

"I meant it when I said it."

"Then why are you cheating on me?"

Kathryn squatted next to Julie. "Why are you lying to us? You're scared, but it's not because of the abductions."

Julie was quiet. Kathryn and Beau looked at each other. Beau shrugged and sighed. "Well…"

"Beau, do you have a place to live, or are you going to live with Trinity?"

"What?"

"Kathryn, write up a custody agreement. I won't ask for any money, but I'm not giving up custody. I can't lose my kids, too."

Beau was waiting. "But?"

"But nothing. Have your mistress. She will figure out what kind of man you are soon enough."

"Julie, is someone threatening you? Is that why you are so scared?"

"Kathryn, I'm sorry I accused you, but will you tell me why you and Beau were kissing?"

"Beau is worried about you. He was thanking me for listening. He kissed me. That's what friends do. It's not the first time he's kissed me, Julie, and I'm sure it won't be the last. We are friends. You and I are friends. I will not choose sides, so don't make me."

Beau wasn't buying any of it. "I'm staying here until the kids leave. Then I will ask if I can stay at Simon's house since they are at Dad's. Julie, I asked you where you were; Kathryn asked, too. You haven't answered either of us. I don't think we would be sitting here talking about ending our marriage if you had told me where you really were."

"It doesn't matter." Julie left the dining room.

Beau watched as she went up the stairs. "Well, that was fun."

"Let's talk outside… You need to get a lawyer. I talked to a man who will be setting up in town very soon. I like him a lot."

"Text me his name and number."

"Beau, be careful."

"Dad is letting Trinity live in a property on the beach. Shaw and I are the only people who know he owns it. He doesn't want her where those people or Julie can find her."

"If Julie told you the truth about where she was. If she was really with her friend…"

"I've already thought about that. One of the first things Trinity said to me when I saw her in the hospital was she understood I was married. She didn't want to break up my family. She said she loved me, but she didn't want to be the reason my kids didn't have a father. I would have stayed with Julie. It would have broken my heart, but it would have been the right thing to do."

"Beau, you have grown up a lot since the first time we kissed."

"I told Trinity. I'm sorry."

Kathryn laughed. "I told Molly. So we're even."

Chapter 30

Clara was thinking about the day Juice brought her to the station and she met Casey. After that, she visited the station every shift Casey was on. They soon realized they wanted to be together, but she worried about introducing Casey to her father. He was a firefighter on the same squad as Juice and Jack, and Clara was immediately impressed with him. At first, he seemed shy as he watched Juice introduce her to the men and one woman on his crew. When Juice finally approached Casey, he smiled and said, "This must be Clara." He grasped her hand with both of his.

Clara blushed. "I'm afraid; what did Juice tell you?"

"He said there was a lovely lady staying with him while she looked for her sister. I hope you find *everything* you are looking for, Clara."

Jack chuckled as he sat in the back of the ambulance, listening to the conversation. He and Brock had already taken her up on her offer to watch the twins, so they were acquainted. The girls loved her, and he knew Casey wanted a family, so he encouraged them, "You know Casey, Lulu and Telly love Clara."

"Really. They are very discerning. Have you met Molly yet?"

"Not yet. Is she discerning, too?"

Jack and Juice burst out laughing. Jack answered, "In a manner of speaking."

"I'm here to make dinner. I could use some help; that is if you aren't doing anything."

When Clara told her father she was staying in Cape Hope, she didn't mention Casey, certain he would disapprove. Today, however, Casey was in the kitchen having coffee with Juice. Clara decided to seize the moment when she saw her father heading in that direction.

"Daddy, there is someone I want you to meet."

"A suitor?"

"Suitor, really? He works with Juice. He is a firefighter and a Veteran."

"You know how I feel about those who serve this country."

"I do. He didn't go to college. I want you to like him. I want you to be friends. He didn't know his own father."

"Don't worry. I won't interrogate him."

Juice and Casey stood up when Clara walked into the kitchen.

"Hi honey… "

"Casey Thornton, this is my father, Martin Beckett."

"Thank you for your service to this country."

"I was happy to serve…"

***

Shaw set up a meeting with his boss, holding a letter in hand but wanting to speak to Ed in person. His new boss also planned to attend, ensuring the DA didn't make any veiled threats. Shaw had already cleared out the items he deemed important but left his personal belongings to avoid drawing suspicion. He sifted through his mail for the day, took two envelopes to his car, and then returned to his office to wait.

Ed was nothing if not predictable. He got to Shaw's office early. "What is on your mind?"

"Well, I need to speak… oh hello."

Ed's face turned white as he saw the visitor. "Shaw, what is this all about?"

Roger Sparks was well-known in the Boston area. "Hello, Ed. It's been a long time."

Shaw handed Ed his resignation letter. "Ed, I'm leaving the DA's office."

Ed's face went from fear to anger. "And you needed representation because?"

"This was my idea, Ed."

Ed opened the letter, scanned it, and looked back at Shaw. "You know the policy of this office when someone resigns. Shaw, I am very disappointed. Does this have anything to do with the federal matter?"

"Ed, Dalton and I just got engaged. This move will give me more freedom when we start a family. I have done an excellent job for this office and for you."

"That doesn't answer my question."

"Excuse me, Ed. My security company was on duty at the Gala. I feel responsible for what happened to the two agents and Dr. Frederick's girlfriend, so I will be representing the ladies' interests going forward. When the people behind this are caught, their attorneys will try to blame the women. I will not allow that to happen. When I was at the Fredericks home, I met Shaw. He is exactly the kind of attorney I need in my organization."

"What is the status of the ladies?"

"They are recovering."

"Have they found the people behind this enterprise?"

"I'm not privy to the federal investigation. What Harry told you is the truth."

"Shaw. You may take your personal items. I will need to make sure you don't take any case related material."

Shaw picked up a box, then opened his briefcase "You may watch me pack."

Ed looked at both men. "That won't be necessary."

Shaw closed the door. "I talked to Kathryn. She is on board, but she would like to talk to you. She will have her finances ready for you and will be in her office all day."

"Excellent. Is there a place we can meet for lunch after Kathryn and I talk?"

"Yes. There is an excellent pub in town. A friend owns it. He is the brother of Kathryn's boyfriend." Shaw was relieved. "Thank you for coming today. I have a couple of people I'd like to say goodbye to. May I meet you and Kathryn at the pub?"

"If your fiancé is available, please bring her. Your brother, too."

"Thank you, I will."

"Hi Beau, I'm on my way home, can I stop at the office?"

"Sure. Everything OK?"

"Perfect. See you soon."

***

Beau was waiting for Shaw when Molly came into his office.

"You dawg."

"Stop it." Beau chuckled. "Are you here to mock?"

"Why else would I be here?"

"What can I do for you?"

"Julie is off the wall again, Beau. I'm worried about her."

"I am, too. It's those missing hours, Molly; she won't tell me the truth. I get that, but she won't tell Kathryn either."

"Beau, we all love Julie, but we also know how she can be. I wanted to let you know we like you a lot… some a little more than the others…"

"Are you having fun?"

"Yes… Beau, I promised Kathryn I would keep your secret. I'm actually impressed with your discretion. I wasn't around when Kathryn's parents died, but she said you gave her the support Brock couldn't."

"Brock was going through his own stuff back then."

"I know. I know you and Shaw didn't go to school here, but Kathryn said you were sympathetic and told Brock you would listen if he needed to talk. I'm learning all these things about you. It turns out you aren't a bastard at all."

"Well, that's one I haven't heard before." Shaw heard the last comment and had to tease, "Beau, you seem to have a lot of advocates."

"Trinity has been a good influence."

"I went to see Billie. She thought I knew about you two."

"And you still think I'm not a bastard?"

"Like I said, Julie can be difficult, and I know she was distant for a long time. We all knew something was wrong, but she wouldn't talk to us. Anyway… I'll let you two talk. Tootles."

"I need to tell you something before you hear it from someone else."

Beau smirked. "As it turns out, I need to talk to you too. Go ahead."

"I gave my notice at the DA's office today. I'm going to be working for the man who was at Dad's the other day. He is actually talking to Kathryn. He wants me and Kathryn to work here in Cape Hope or Gloucester, wherever you end up finding an office for us."

"You're kidding. That's great."

"Now, what's up with you?"

"I need a lawyer. I guess you're the attorney Kathryn knows that is new to the area."

"You're filing for divorce?"

"Not me. Julie. There is so much she has done. I'm obviously not without blame. She lied about going to Becca's, and she won't tell me where she was. She won't tell Kathryn either. She accused me and Kathryn of having an affair…"

"What? Why?"

"We were talking, that's all. Julie saw us and made assumptions. Kathryn came to the house so we could talk to her. She told Kathryn to draw up a custody agreement. She doesn't want anything from me."

"I actually don't know what she could be doing that she wouldn't at least tell Kathryn about."

"She is hiding something. Before Julie left, I intended to stay with her. As much as it would have hurt Trinity, I would have stayed. Did Dad tell you he wants Trinity to stay in the house on the beach?"

"No, but I think it's a good idea. You're coming with me to meet the new boss. He wants to meet you and Dalton, and we can talk about a new office."

"We're all going to be close to home again. That should make Dad happy."

***

Maude and Ellen took their time surveying the area around the marina. They knew Mr. Smith wanted a full house by the weekend, giving them two days to get the women to the house.

The women were on a boat docked at the far end, where there was little traffic. One boat was absent during the day and returned close to dark, while the other side was empty. Their daytime surveillance was conducted on foot, and when they were ready to execute their plan, they took the boat.

Based on their observations, the ladies had drinks on the deck before moving to the cabin around six-thirty to prepare dinner, which they later ate on the deck.

Maude had a plan: Ellen would dock the boat in the empty slip. After the women went inside, they would fill the cabin with lavender-scented gas. They had two large tent bags, and since the women were both small, Ellen was confident they would fit. They also had chloroform for the trip to the new location, where the women would be held on opposite ends of the house.

They waited near the seawall, where they had a perfect view of the women enjoying their wine. As the hour approached six-thirty, Ellen moved the boat into the empty slip. Maude got out with a gas receptacle that looked like it belonged to an exterminator. She inserted the long hose into the small porthole of the galley, which was always left slightly open. When the gauge pointed to empty, they waited, then went inside the cabin with the bags.

Both women were groggy but not unconscious. Rags soaked with chloroform were placed over their noses and mouths, and the women were stuffed into the duffle bags, which were then carried to their boat. "Let's get out of here," Ellen said.

The trip to the new house didn't take long. It was located on an inlet with a long dock and a wooden path covered by a canvas walkway canopy. A tall wrought iron fence lined the front, flanked by large holly bushes, and a private gated driveway led to the entrance.

Ellen and Maude used a luggage cart to transport the duffle bags. Once inside, they took the elevator to the top floor and deposited the women in their rooms.

Sylvie heard the squeaky wheels of the cart rolling down the hall and started screaming, "I don't belong here!"

Lauren, Harlow, and Macey remained docile. They knew better than to rock the boat.

Ellen whispered, "We have to get rid of her permanently."

"I've actually been thinking about that. Let's get these two settled, and I'll tell you my idea."

***

Steve and Kim had met another woman at their store, a potential partner. They took their time getting to know her and ended up liking her more than Sylvie. Realizing they wanted another rendezvous spot, Steve acquired the space next to the shop. It was quickly renovated and furnished with high-end decor. After abducting a woman at a bar and another sleeping on the beach, they began inviting trusted clients.

They were offered one free hour. If they decided to buy time regularly, they received a discount along with a promise of a choice among the servants.

Though they still wanted Naomi, they knew they shouldn't return there. Instead, they began searching local bars and lounges in upscale hotels. They spotted a woman who looked familiar, recognizing her from previous research trips in the area. They felt she might be worth exploring as a potential option. As they continued their quest, they remained careful to vet each woman thoroughly.

***

Ellen and Maude helped the women settle in. The ladies were a couple, both having previously been in relationships with men but ultimately experimenting with each other after a night of drinking and venting about bad breakups. They had been exclusive for about six months and hadn't yet told their families. Morgan had confided in her parents, but her mother disowned her without hesitation.

Lola was the adventurous one; she owned the boat and was the sailor. Morgan, on the other hand, was reserved and quiet. Neither woman had a job. Lola had an inheritance from her grandfather's estate, while Morgan had been living with her parents—until now, as she was living on the boat, contemplating her next steps.

Maude made the usual call regarding the new ladies. In both cases, the initial encounters went as well as expected. The ladies were animated, which was precisely what the clients were looking for. The man used to a certain type was pleased.

Morgan was convinced her ex had orchestrated her kidnapping. He was furious upon discovering that Morgan had *changed teams* and had been trying to win her back. Lola, meanwhile, didn't quite know what to make of their new environment, but she knew one thing—she couldn't tolerate being with violent men.

Before leaving the house, the man scheduled regular appointments with both Lola and Morgan. Lola seemed more adaptable, while Morgan grew increasingly depressed and began desperately searching for a weapon.

***

Maude and Ellen discussed how to resolve the *Sylvie problem*. Using their knowledge of the area and familiar disposal methods, they devised a new plan.

After a busy Saturday, Sundays were typically quiet. Maude and Ellen left before dawn. Sylvie, dosed with sodium pentothal, was left highly suggestible and willingly provided her ATM PIN. Tied up in the back of the van, she remained unaware as Maude and Ellen—using various disguises—withdrew the maximum amount the bank allowed. Their route led north into New Hampshire, passing through small towns and dense wooded areas. They brought Sylvie to a secluded pond rarely visited by swimmers. At the water's edge, they pushed her forward, and she fell into the swampy pond, thick with cattails and skunk cabbage.

She was flailing, disoriented, and unable to get her bearings as Maude and Ellen walked away.

After a few miles, they passed a pickup truck towing a rowboat. "I was hoping no one would be on the road this early."

"We're in a plain white van. Don't worry about it."

Randy was an avid fisherman who preferred not to visit the same spot twice. He enjoyed being on the water alone, where it was always quiet. With New Hampshire's abundance of lakes and ponds, he had mapped them all out. Today, he was at a small, secluded pond accessible only by a dirt road—just the kind of spot he liked. He backed his rowboat to the pond's edge.

His was the only boat on the water. He hoped for trout, though all he seemed to catch was perch, which he tossed back. As he rowed toward the middle of the pond, something caught his eye in his peripheral vision. He reeled in his line and rowed back toward the shore.

What he saw was the naked body of a woman. At first, he wasn't sure what to do—but then she moved. Quickly, he reached for his phone and called 911.

"Can you get my location? I'm fishing… There is a naked woman. I thought she was dead, but she's moving. What should I do?"

"Give her a blanket if you have one. Tell her an ambulance is on the way."

Randy saw the woman lying on her side, just out of the water. He pulled his boat to shore and hurried to his car, grabbing a canvas tarp from his truck to cover her.

"Help me."

"Help is coming. What is your name?"

"My name?"

Randy spoke with the police as he watched the EMTs tend to Sylvie. They strapped her onto the gurney while a police officer photographed her face and took her fingerprints.

Another officer returned to the cruiser to check the APBs. He recalled seeing a notice from the FBI, so he radioed the captain, who confirmed he would make the necessary call.

"If you could follow me to the station, we need to get your statement. Mr. Harrison, given the woman's condition, your discretion would be appreciated."

"I have daughters. That won't be a problem."

***

Trip wanted to see Beau's kids before they left. Julie was sitting by the pool when he arrived. "May I talk to the kids before they go?"

Julie lifted her sunglasses and rested them on her head. "I never thought you would condone extra-marital affairs."

"I don't. I want my children to be happy. Beau wasn't happy for a long time. He stayed with you, Julie, through all of your mood changes and inexplicable behavior. Beau is not perfect. He never will be, but he talked to you about your marriage and for a time, you two were better. Everyone could see it."

Julie wouldn't look at Trip. "I was scared. I left because I was scared."

"That has been established. Where did you go?"

"Kids! Grandfather is here to say goodbye."

"We'll find out, Julie. It's better if you tell us because the truth coming from a stranger won't look good for you if Beau decides to ask for joint custody."

"He won't."

"Julie, this secrecy of yours started way before Beau had ever heard the name Trinity."

"Kids, come on, we have to get ready to go… Trip, did you know Beau and Kathryn were friends when they were teenagers?"

"Yes. Abby, Dalton, Shaw, Brock. They spent a lot of time at the house. I'm surprised he didn't tell you."

"He says he did."

"Julie, you dug this hole you are in. Is what you were doing while you were gone so awful you can't even tell your attorney?"

"Trip, I'm going to change my clothes. When I come down, I hope you will be gone."

***

Ben and Merritt were sitting on the dock. Merritt was in a funk, and Ben didn't know how to help. He thought that a little time away from the others might do them both some good.

"Tell me what is on your mind, sweet cheeks."

"I was thinking about the look on your face after I fell in the water that day. Confession? I went in on purpose. I thought it might move things along with us."

"Your see through wet blouse didn't leave much to the imagination."

"What's wrong with me, Ben?"

"With you? Nothing, but I think not knowing is worse because you're imagining the worst."

"Colt thinks I need to talk to someone."

"Dr. Evans is coming tomorrow."

"The guy I met at your office? Oh, I liked him."

"I could tell. He's been divorced for about six months, so I worried he might ask you out."

"I only have eyes for you, sweetie. I think the girls will like him. Is Matilda coming?"

"I went by the station to talk to Lenny. He'll make sure she is here. Can we talk about going to St. Louis?"

"Yes, yes. I want your sisters to tell me all your secrets." Her eyes filled with tears. "But please don't tell them mine."

Ben was helpless. "Would you like some alone time with John?"

She laughed. "I don't know, Ben. Do you trust me?"

"I trust *him*."

Merritt pushed Ben in the water. When he popped up, she was laughing. "Don't you dare!"

Ben lifted himself up. "Pull you in? Never! You're laughing—it was worth it."

"Matilda told me when she came home she wanted Lenny to see her; what they did to her. I want to be that brave, but I'm not."

"You aren't Matilda. Simon told me there was no evidence I had sex with Maggie."

"Maggie told me. I didn't ask. She wanted me to know. I think there is a reason we didn't talk about this before now. We trust each other. It doesn't matter what happened that night, Ben… I watched the video of us on the island again. You love me so much."

***

Beau took the boys to his cousin's house, while Julie took their daughter to a friend's home. Before they left, Julie informed Beau about his father's visit.

"I was with a new client. I think their house will be perfect for Ben and Merritt."

"We don't need to have these little chats, Beau. Awkward silence is fine."

"I don't want you to hate me."

"I don't hate you, Beau."

"Good. The kids need us to be civil. They need to know we love them."

"Kathryn told me you were ready to stay with me."

"That's true."

"You love Trinity, Beau. I'm not a naïve schoolgirl. Everyone loves her. I can see that."

"I never wanted to hurt you."

"Then why did you… never mind."

"You left me. About six months before Harold died, you changed. You were distant; you stopped talking to me; Julie, you stopped talking to everyone. You left. You were here for the kids but not for me."

Julie looked dumbfounded. She didn't understand. "What are you talking about?"

"I will get everyone over here, and they will all tell you something happened, and you weren't Julie anymore. But we all loved you, so we left you alone, hoping you would work things out."

"I guess I don't remember."

Beau was puzzled, but knowing that Julie had played mind games before, he chalked it up to that. "I have to go," he said, stopping to look at her.

She was playing with her rings. "I brought my things to Simon's while you were at Mass."

"OK. I'll be fine."

"Do you have plans?"

"I don't know… we were supposed to go away."

"You never talked about a vacation."

"You should have known."

"This is what I'm talking about. How would I know Julie? How? I have to go. I guess I'll see you in a couple of weeks."

Julie's world was falling apart. She would never admit that her marriage troubles were her fault, but she believed her friends should have taken her side. Angry and desperate, she wanted Trinity to disappear. While she knew she wasn't capable of harming her, she felt the need to do something—she couldn't lose Beau.

Chapter 31

Cooper was in his office, reviewing the real estate transactions from the past couple of weeks. Beau had called him about finding an office for Shaw and Kathryn. He thought that if they put their heads together, they could secure the perfect location.

He had his phone in his hand when Abby walked in. "You were up early," she said.

"I like sleeping together every night. Is this a good sign for us?"

"We do need to make some plans."

Coop paused. "You mean us together?"

"Yes, silly, us. Too much has happened. I don't want to miss any time with you."

Coop reached for Abby's waist, pulled her toward him, and sat her on his lap. "I've wanted this for a long time," he said

"You should talk to Daddy."

"I talked to him a long time ago. He knows I want to marry you."

"So, are we official?"

"Not yet. I want to do this right."

"So, a surprise?"

"Maybe."

"I started writing the article. Cubby thinks it should be in at least two parts."

"He's the boss. I'm surprised you didn't announce Cubby's promotion."

"Daddy wants to have a party, but we have a lot of people's feelings to consider. Julie is asking Beau for a divorce."

"That's not how I expected that would go."

"Daddy talked to Andy about marrying Lizzy. Since she's divorced, well, you know… anyway, he is opening his mind, and he likes Trinity."

"She is so different. How is Stella?"

"Struggling. She is having nightmares. She doesn't remember anything after the Gala. She's been talking to Juice and Billie a lot. Ben told me the staff psychologist is coming tomorrow to have a group session."

"Hi you two." Harry was in his car when he called, "May I stop by?"

"Of course."

Abby met him at the front door. "Abby, the State Police received an envelope with a letter about the brothel. I'm going to pick it up. Do you want to keep me company?"

"Yes, yes."

"Off the record, same as before."

***

Tim and Lucy both had the day off, and their plan was to move Lucy's things into storage. Luckily, most of the large furniture belonged to the landlord. While Lucy had a few keepsakes from family, most of her belongings were small pieces. It didn't take long to fill the back of Tim's SUV.

When they got back, Beau was coming out of the neighboring house. He waved and jogged across the street. "Hi! I was hoping you would be here."

"Is this house a new listing?"

"No, it is actually one of Dad's properties. If you could keep that between us, we'd be grateful."

"Sure, Beau." Tim agreed immediately. Beau didn't really know Lucy, but she looked suspicious.

"Dad wants Trinity to stay here. We all agreed she would be safer here. The people who kidnapped her know where she lives. We think Julie does, too, but she hasn't been volunteering information lately. You might hear this from Cubby, but Julie wants a divorce. I'm not without blame, but she has been off the wall."

"That's called *the woman scorned.*"

Tim was surprised. "Sweetheart, Julie has been... Sorry, Beau. It's not my place to say, but there's more to the story, Lucy. Cubby always tries to understand both sides. He and Kathryn have been friends with Julie for a long time, and in this case, Beau isn't completely to blame."

"I'm sorry Beau."

"Me too. Kathryn and I have been trying to figure out what to do. It's not just Trinity; she is keeping secrets from Kathryn. She even accused Kathryn and I of having an affair."

"You're kidding." Tim was stunned.

"I wish I was. I had decided to stay with Julie. Then she threatened Trinity… there is a lot. I'm sorry, but Cubby is your brother, and Kathryn has been a friend for so long. Anyway, as soon as Trinity is comfortable leaving Dad's, she will be here."

Lucy was timid. "Beau, I would like to visit her if you think she won't mind."

"She is a little less self-conscious now that her hair has started growing back. You haven't met, so it won't be a shock. I think she looks beautiful."

Lucy grinned. "Juice said the same thing about Billie."

***

Abby thought it best she remained in the car. Harry went inside, holding his badge in his hand.

The desk Sergeant knew he was coming and took him to the Captain's office.

"Thank you for calling."

"This is weird. There is a letter and pictures of empty rooms. The letter explains that guilt had gotten the better of him, and he had to do something about the activities in the house. When he went back, the house was empty."

"We have tried to keep an eye on the activity of the house where we believe the women are being held. We have no proof the house is being used for anything illegal, but this is puzzling."

"The letter confirms your suspicions about the address."

"For the safety of the women, we aren't sharing this with the press. We will at some point, but the women who have been hurt and released confirm there were more women."

Ring, ring "Excuse me… Where… How long have they been missing… Were there signs of a struggle… If they were taken from a boat… no, I'll take care of it. Thank you."

"That didn't sound good."

"Two women. Their boat is docked. A friend was worried when they missed a dinner date. She went to the boat. There was food on the stove. Their cells are going to voicemail. Technically, the Coast Guard has jurisdiction."

"Let me know if we can help."

"I will. Thank you very much for this information."

"Good Luck."

Harry handed the envelope to Abby.

"He knew where to go?"

"I know. It doesn't fit. I need to speak to Colt."

"I'll call… Hi Colt. I'm with Harry."

"I just got the call. I'm on my way over to the marina."

"Great. Colt, are you still working alone?"

"No. I was going to bring her to Trip's later. She knows Billie. I think it's important for her to see what we're up against. Her name is Daisy."

Ring, ring... "Dear God, what now?" He pulled into a parking lot. "Agent Moran... Where did they take her?... Send me the photo. I'm going to call Jim as soon as I get back. I'll take care of calling in extra Agents. Thank you."

Abby looked scared but didn't ask what was going on. She listened as Harry called Tim. "Hi, this is Harry Moran. How is your staffing situation?... Oh, good. I'll call him. Thanks."

"A woman was found on the shore of a pond in New Hampshire. The officer at the scene remembered the APB. He took her prints and her picture. The prints match the prints found on the Mercedes found in the lot at the Country Club." Harry's phone binged. He looked at the picture and then handed his phone to Abby.

"Oh wow! That's the woman who was flirting with Juice at the Gala. She was with the couple Ben and Merritt met at the Pub. Is she on file for any other reason... Sorry, I shouldn't have asked."

"No, you are cool. When this case is all said and done, I want this story handled right."

"Thank you. May I ask a hypothetical question?"

"Why not."

"How many FBI cases never make it to the news, roughly?"

"A lot."

Abby sighed. "I hope I would have been as understanding if I didn't know so many of the victims. I'm pretty sure I couldn't do that to any woman."

"We see people grieving, mourning, trying to recover from their worst day. You wouldn't be sitting in my car if Ben and I didn't trust you."

"I appreciate that."

***

After Harry dropped Abby off to get her car, he called the Assistant Director. They discussed a plan and decided to pull Marcus from the Pub.

Tim had hired a new server so he wouldn't be shorthanded. They also agreed that they needed Naomi's eyes at the bar.

Marcus headed to the New Hampshire hospital where Sylvie was being taken. He was glad to be back in the field. Harry was sending another agent who would meet Marcus there.

Bellamy Lucchesi was a probie. Harry had her paired with senior agents as she learned the ropes. His intention was always to pair her with Marcus. They had met several times over the past few months, so they were not strangers.

Bellamy walked into the hospital with her badge in hand. "Agent Bellamy Lucchesi. I'm looking for…"

"Hi Bellamy. Do I need to update you?"

"What the hell is going on?" Bellamy was known to speak her mind. That sometimes included rather unladylike language, which she usually toned down until she tested the room.

"This woman was a person of interest. She was at the Gala. Now she's a victim."

"Swell…How is Ben?"

"He is much better. There was no evidence he was injured, but he still doesn't remember."

"What is the plan?"

"She is confused. She was left in a wooded, swampy area, and just like the other women, she was naked."

"The signature is the same?"

"She was injured, but not nearly as bad as the others."

"Could time have been a factor? Maybe they needed to get rid of her fast."

"Definitely a possibility…"

"Agents, you may speak to her, but keep it short."

"Miss, I am FBI Special Agent Marcus Pollard. What is your name?"

"My name? My name is…" Sylvie looked at Bellamy and smiled. "What is your name?"

"Agent Lucchesi."

Bellamy looked at Marcus as she stifled a laugh.

"Miss, would you answer my question? What is your name?"

She looked at the bruising on her wrists. "What happened to me?"

"That's what we are trying to find out."

"What do you remember?"

"About what?"

"Miss, we need to know your name and any details you can give us."

"I don't know."

Bellamy thought the woman was playing games. "Okay, we have your fingerprints, and the doctors are doing blood work. If you are in the system because of your job or anything else, we will find out."

"How long will I be here?"

Marcus replied, "That's up to the doctors."

Bellamy tried to trip her up. "Where will you go?"

"Home, I guess."

"And where is that?"

"Why are you being so mean?"

Marcus was sympathetic. "We can't just let you go if you don't have a safe place to go. Do you remember where you live?"

"No. Can you talk to me? I don't like her."

"She is trying to find out who you are and why you were in the woods last night. Don't you want to know?"

"I'm afraid."

Bellamy sat on the edge of the bed and picked up Sylvie's hand. "You don't have a head injury, so that's good. Your blood work will tell us if you were drugged. Someone did this to you, and we need to find out who it is."

"Where am I?"

"New Hampshire."

Sylvie seemed to be thinking, but she was actually remembering. She needed to get out of there and find Kim and Steve, along with the two women who worked at the brothel. She had to make them pay.

***

After meeting Colt at the marina, Harry went to Trip's to talk to Ben. Even though he wasn't involved in the investigation, he wanted to keep Ben informed.

"I have a few things to share with you. First, Cooper and Abby recognized a name on the real estate transactions. I got two calls. Two more women have been taken at the marina, and the woman who was with the couple at the Gala was dumped and left for dead in a swampy area in New Hampshire. Abby was with me; she confirmed it was the woman who was flirting with Juice. We also got another letter, this time with pictures inside the house. Hopefully now we will be able to get a warrant. Jim is going to do what he can to facilitate that.

Ben looked dumbfounded. "I… maybe I should resign. If I hadn't been so preoccupied with Merritt, I might have done a better job. Maybe Merritt and Stella wouldn't be…" He stood up, feeling guilty about sending the letter. He also wondered if he had been more focused on the case, he might have found the people running the brothel.

"You said you talked to John the other day. Maybe you should talk to him again. Your guilt is understandable, but I also understand how you fell in love with Merritt. She is a remarkable woman, Ben."

"You have no idea…May I see the pictures? Wait. How did he know where it was?"

"That is an excellent question." Harry handed Ben the envelope. "Maybe he followed someone? I'm not going to worry about that right now."

"Maybe it was an employee. They must have a staff."

"Agreed, but I haven't dismissed the possibility it might be a woman. Please tell me if you disagree. The woman from the Gala is dumped the same day the State Police receive an anonymous letter."

"The timing is certainly suspicious. I guess I assumed it was a man, but Maggie mentioned a woman who visited after the client beat her. She said she put cream on her wounds."

"Would you mind talking to Matilda? Maybe she had the same woman visit her. It would certainly explain the person knowing the location."

"I will."

"Marcus has been pulled from the Pub. He is in New Hampshire with Bellamy. Colt has a new partner as well. Her name is Daisy."

"Cool. OK. I do want to feel useful. When John comes tomorrow, I will talk to him too."

"Do me a favor. Sit in with the group. I think if you share your guilt, and you hear that no one blames you, you may feel better."

"You may be right. What is the plan for the woman in the hospital."

"Well, Marcus called. He thinks she might be playing games with them. She says she doesn't remember anything. If she is the sociopath Marcus and Juice described, we need to be careful. If she is trying to deceive us, she will slip up. I worry there is a deeper, darker reason she was left in the woods. Truthfully, I'm stumped."

"She was definitely looking for a hookup that night, and she wasn't shy about it. If she's playing with us, she must have a plan. She can't possibly think we would release her from the hospital without a place to go. If she suddenly remembers where she lives, that will look suspicious. Marcus said Bellamy provoked her but then was kind and supportive. He gathered from that interaction that she was playing games. Marcus agreed that she knows more than she is willing to share and requested that the local police put a guard on the door overnight.

*****

Maude and Ellen thought they had the perfect plan. Before leaving Sylvie in the woods, they selected some devices that the clients liked to use. They wiped everything clean, then placed Sylvie's prints and DNA on the tools and on Ben and Merritt's belongings. They believed Sylvie was dead, so if her DNA or prints were found on the premises, she would be blamed, and the case would be closed.

Their idea was to plant the evidence the night after they left Sylvie in the woods. They watched the news for any reports about finding a woman's body. When the eleven o'clock news didn't report a body being found, they left for the house on the cove.

They parked at the overgrown end of an unused fire road, shielded from the main road. This road connected to the shore, allowing them to access the dock without having to climb the hill. They carried everything in a shopping bag and opened the storage closet that Ben had ignored. They rolled out a cart and emptied the contents of the bag onto it. They were in and out in just fifteen minutes.

Chapter 32

Ben was in the shower when Merritt woke up. The conversation they had on the dock was troubling her. She had never been shy before, and she knew her lack of inhibitions was something Ben admired and respected. She took off her nightie and looked in the mirror. The bruises were fading but were still quite noticeable. "Oh, just do it."

She went to the bathroom and opened the shower door. Ben was rinsing the shampoo out of his hair. "Hello, sweet cheeks."

"Is there room in there for me?"

Ben reached for her hand. "I'll make room."

"I'm sorry I've been such a baby. I don't remember, but I can't stop thinking about it."

Ben's arms were around her. "That's why Dr. Evans is coming today. I'm going to ask the others if they mind if I sit in. I think it may help—me, us."

Merritt kissed him. "Nothing a little copulation won't cure."

"Sex isn't everything. If I've learned anything, it's that I love you no matter what. Yes, the sex is amazing, and at first, it was important, but almost losing you taught me I adore you and want to be with you always."

"You make me happy, Ben Malloy." She reached her hand to his pelvis. "The doctor said no intercourse. She didn't say anything about fooling around."

Ben reached his hands to her butt "Anything for you, sweet cheeks."

***

Harry was on his cell phone. "Thank you, sir. I hope this helps us find what we are looking for."

"I had a little help. You can access the house from the dock entrance. A CSU team will meet you there. Harry, Dr. Evans called. I think talking to the ladies, and Ben may reveal some clues. My sincere hope is you get the same Agent Malloy back."

"Thanks again. I'll let you know what we find."

Shaw was coming down the hall as Harry got off the phone. "That explains this." Shaw handed Harry the warrant.

"The CSU team is bringing a copy as well. I'm going to ask Phil if he will station someone at the dock. I don't want anyone sneaking up on us."

"Not a bad idea. Stella said you arranged for the Agency psychologist to talk to the ladies today. She still doesn't remember. Simon isn't sure he wants her to."

"I can understand that. Did Martin leave?"

"No. He wants to make sure Maggie is comfortable here. He met Clara's boyfriend, who I've known since we were kids. He was very impressed with him, but he is still worried about Maggie. He hoped Dr. Evans might have some time to talk today."

"I'll give him a heads up."

***

Phil was getting ready to meet Harry when Lucy walked in. "Do you think Agent Moran would mind if I tagged along?"

"Thinking of moving up?"

"I'd like to observe the search. I really don't have any experience with that."

"Come with me. You can ask him yourself."

"Are you planning to keep tabs on the women as they leave the Fredericks home?"

"If they are staying in town, yes."

"I hope I'm not breaking a trust, but Mr. Fredericks is letting Trinity stay in a home he owns. Beau saw us and wanted to let us know because it is across the street from us."

"I appreciate your telling me. It's a good idea, I'm not sure she would be safe in her home alone. But you're right, I'd like to know where they are. I will talk to Trip."

Phil and Lucy went to the house together. Colt and Daisy had docked the Coast Guard boat and were talking to Harry "I wanted to introduce Daisy to you, then we are going to the house to see Merritt and Billie."

Phil and Lucy came down the hill alongside the wall. Lucy wasn't shy. "Agent Moran, may I accompany you inside to observe? This would be a great learning experience."

Harry chuckled. "How could I say no to that."

"Thank you, sir."

"Harry is fine."

Harry had transferred the pictures to his tablet. He was glad he did because he noticed a discrepancy as soon as he opened the door to the cinderblock room. "This is wrong. Please take three sixty-degree pictures of this room." Harry showed Lucy the picture on the tablet.

"Harry, that is Merritt's dress." Lucy pointed at the cart. "Someone has obviously been here. May I speculate?"

"Go ahead."

"Maybe the person who sent the letter is screwing with you."

"Or it's a setup."

"These people are sadists. There is more going on here than someone trying to help you find these animals. It's either one person trying to do good. Or two. Maybe the proprietors found out about the first person and came back to try to dispute the pictures..."

"I'm curious to see what we find upstairs."

"Sir." One of the tech's handed Harry Merritt's gun and credentials in evidence bags. "Agent Malloy's weapon and cred's are here too." They also put the dress in a bag. "Sir, the dress was cut and torn. There are also whips and what can only be described as implements of torture."

It was the only room that looked different from the pictures. Harry and Lucy looked in each room and then cleared out so the techs could do their work.

Harry decided to bring everything to the FBI lab in Quantico. He didn't want a defense attorney to have a reason to scream impropriety regarding the handling of the evidence, but he was also concerned about the discrepancy in that one room. He called the Assistant Director with his findings, noted them in his report, and took the next flight to deliver the evidence to preserve the chain of custody.

Before he left for the airport, Harry called Phil, Ben and Colt to Trip's office. "We have a mystery that I want to stay in this room. The State Police received a letter about the house; there were also photos. We finally got a warrant. The technicians are still there. Everything looked the same except for one room which was photographed as being empty. When we went in, there was a metal cart with devices and whips." Harry looked at Ben. "And Merritt's dress."

Ben looked heartbroken. "She loved that dress."

"I'm leaving for Quantico in a few minutes to deliver the evidence. I'll keep you updated as much as I can."

Ben spoke up, "I think we should keep this from the ladies. I will speak to Dr. Evans when he gets here. He can decide what to do with the information."

"That's fine, but from here on in, you need to stay on the sidelines. I know you understand."

"Yes, I do. Thank you for sharing what you've learned so far."

***

Ben waited for Dr. Evans on the concrete bench in the front garden. He was relieved when Harry told him he couldn't be involved anymore. Being careful not to implicate himself had been weighing on him, but not telling Merritt what he had done troubled him more than the lie itself.

"Hello Ben. Where were you?"

"Thinking about that house and if Merritt and I were there."

"What does that accomplish?"

"Not a damn thing, but it's hard not to go there. Up until this morning, I was worried about her. But she decided she wasn't going to let what happened come between us, and she surprised me in the shower."

"How did that go?"

"Being intimate is much more than having intercourse. She didn't want me to see what they did to her, and I respected that, but she has never been modest. It bothered her that those people were messing with her head. She felt shame, which is not her. This morning, she decided to rip off the band-aid. I'm not saying she's over it, but she is better."

"I wish everyone was as open as you."

"Three older sisters. I didn't have a choice."

"How are you, Ben, really?"

"Harry got a warrant for that house. He took a team through there today. They found Merritt's dress and no, I'm not going to tell her. That's what I was thinking about before."

"Why would you do that to yourself? You were both drugged. Why aren't you thinking about what they did to you?"

"Because I wasn't raped and beaten. Harry and I talked about whether I should go into the group meeting with the ladies."

"I think you should."

"OK, good. Maggie's father is here. He would like to speak to you if there's time."

"I'll make time."

"We thought the solarium would be a good place to talk. Stella has been quiet. They all have reason to grieve, but she is taking it much worse."

"The brand?"

"Her boyfriend, Dr. Fredericks, Simon, has been with her since the ER. She is hurting a lot."

Trip met Ben and John inside. "Doctor, thank you for coming. My youngest, Simon, would like to speak to you when you're done."

"I will make time to speak to anyone privately."

The ladies were in the solarium. John noticed Trinity and Billie, but it was Maggie who really stood out. Not because of her looks but because she ran to him, embraced him, and thanked him.

"I haven't done anything yet."

"You didn't have to come. I think we all need this. Thank you."

"I hope I can help."

"Ben, you're staying, right?"

"Yes."

"I'm John Evans. I have been told none of you have really talked. I'd like to help you do that. You all know each other now. You have been through the same experience, but at the same time, each of you has different memories that you are dealing with. Have you talked at all? Have you tried to share?"

Maggie spoke up first, "We really haven't. I was there for almost a year. I had given up. I think the only thing keeping me sane was it was a nice comfortable room. The food was good…" Maggie buried her face in her hands.

John leaned forward. "Maggie?"

"I gave up. I wanted to die. Not just when I was being tortured but when I thought about never falling in love again. Never being a mother. There were days I looked around that room to try to find something so I could end it all."

Matilda grasped her hand. "It's the first time in my life I thought about killing someone. The man who beat me and tortured me first; I will never forget that man's voice."

Billie spoke up. "Maybe it was the same man I saw. I asked if I could do a composite drawing."

John wondered, "How did you manage to see someone?"

"There were times the clients wore masks, and I didn't. There were two women with him who were just as sadistic as he was. They came at me with a device, and I screamed at the top of my lungs. The man stuffed something in my mouth and I pretended to pass out. They took their masks off to talk, and I peeked."

Merritt shared, "It has to be that couple and the gropey girl that was with them."

"I only saw the man's face."

Ben was hopeful "Billie, if you could still describe the man. Merritt and I think we met them."

"Ben, if I do a composite and Billie does one, and they look enough alike, do you think that would help?"

"I will certainly ask Harry. He had to go to Quantico. He should be back tomorrow."

"Ladies, it is understandable why you haven't talked about your experiences, but I think you should try."

Stella surprised everyone. "I still don't remember anything, but I have a constant reminder of what they did. I need to know why they did it. I wasn't there that long. I don't know what I could have done that was so bad…"

Maggie squatted in front of her. "You didn't necessarily do anything wrong. The scar will fade."

"My head? No, it's not that. They, they…" Stella wept.

John suggested, "Stella, would it help if you showed the others what you are talking about?"

"It may help me, but it would make them feel awful, and I don't want to do that."

Matilda looked at everyone. "Maybe we can help you, Stella. None of us remember what happened right before we were found, but you don't remember any of it… Stella, that's a good thing."

"I know, but…"

Maggie squatted in front of Stella as she squeezed her hand. "Stella, you wonder why. There is no answer. If you think showing us what they did to you will help you accept it, please, we may be able to help you, but it is up to you."

Stella unbuttoned her shirt. The bruises around her neck were disturbing enough, but then she lifted the top corners of the bandage and peeled it down. Only Maggie was able to see the brand. Her head dropped to Stella's lap as she cried, "I am so sorry, Stella."

John got up, took Maggie's hand and led her back to the chair.

Matilda, Billie, and Trinity embraced Stella. In return, Stella rubbed Billie and Trinity's heads. "You guys look cute. I will have plastic surgery. I have Simon. I will be OK."

"Juice is worried about you, Stella."

"Billie he is so patient, and he listened even though I know I wasn't making any sense."

John looked at Ben and Merritt, then at Maggie, who was still upset. "Maggie?"

"That puts things in perspective." She placed her hand on John's. "Ben said you know your stuff…"

John chuckled. "I'm glad I could help. Am I right to think you will be there for each other going forward?"

*****

Marcus and Bellamy didn't trust Sylvie. Although her fingerprints weren't on file, and she claimed to have no memory, they remained skeptical.

The doctor assured them she didn't have a head injury. He also explained that, in cases like hers, they categorize the condition as dissociative amnesia. Marcus knew that disproving this diagnosis could be difficult, especially when dealing with Antisocial Personality Disorder.

Bellamy wasn't buying the diagnosis. "Psychopathy, Sociopathy, call it what you will; she is screwing with us. Our Agents have been keeping an eye out for her and two of her friends. They are suspects in the abductions of two Agents and a woman from an event. I would like to call our staff psychologist."

"Absolutely."

*****

After John spoke privately with Martin and Simon, he and Maggie walked down to the dock. John removed his shoes and socks, rolling up his pant legs. "This is a beautiful spot."

"Merritt told me this is where she and Ben like to talk. Dr. Evans, do you think I shared too much earlier?"

"Not at all. What you were feeling was perfectly normal under the circumstances, and you may call me John."

"Thank you."

"Your father is worried about you; after what you said earlier, I am as well, but not for the same reasons. I noticed right away you have a big heart. I'm seeing someone who gives herself completely to a relationship, whether it is a friend or a lover."

Maggie blushed. "I guess."

John didn't react. "You have a lot to give Maggie. Don't let those people take that from you."

"I'm already broken… I'm sorry." She looked down. "Snap out of it, Margaret." She was trying to be detached, but her eyes were sad. "There, all better."

"I hear your sister is staying."

"She is. I think she's in love."

"Being in love is good."

"Oh, are you?"

"Not at the moment." John was taken with Maggie. "Tell me about your father."

"We are in a much better place than we were, but he can be controlling, especially after my mother died. He didn't know how to talk to us. He would have done much better with sons."

"I can see he intimidates you. You have been very open with me. Why"

"Ben said you were easy to talk to." Maggie started kicking her feet in the water. "May I say something totally inappropriate?"

"Why not."

"I really like you."

"You're not my patient Maggie. This case hit close to home when Ben was taken. He came to the office worried about all the women that have been affected. I wanted to get the discussions between you started. You don't need me, but I wanted to at least assess the situation. If any of you feel you need long-term therapy, I will recommend someone close by."

"When I look a little less frightening, may I take you out to dinner?"

"I would like that. Maggie, do you need to talk to someone? I admire your honesty about how you were feeling. It took a lot of courage to admit you were thinking of taking your own life."

"I needed to say it out loud. I heard that is the first step in recovery."

"Admitting your fears? You're not in denial. Try not to go back there. You are stronger than you think. Your sister, and your father, love you. Do you need to talk to someone?"

"I'm not sure. But I promise not to bend your ear while we're having dinner."

"I want to learn about you, and if we must, we can talk about me too."

"We must. I wish I didn't have so much anxiety about going out in public. Maybe I do need to talk to someone."

"How about this? I don't live that far away. Maybe I can come back tomorrow. Maybe we can take a walk?"

Maggie began to weep. "I'd like that. Thank you." She took a deep breath. "My father is leaving in the morning. I think I'm going to miss him."

"That's good. It means you've forgiven him."

"I have."

"Maggie, you were great with Stella today."

"Why would they do that to her?"

"To try to humiliate her. Maggie, do not let those people change the woman you are."

Maggie hugged John's arm. "Thank you for coming today."

Ring, ring ... "Sorry, I need to get this... Sure, text me the address and room number; I'll be there first thing in the morning."

"I'm tired. Daddy bought me a new phone. May I give you my number? If you can't come back tomorrow, would you let me know?"

"I will. Do me a favor; talk to Ben. He is very easy to talk to as an Agent and a friend. He heard what you said; tell him what you told me."

"Sure, I can do that."

"You have put me in a position I have never been in before. I want to help you, but I believe I could help you more as a friend. I don't want to cross a professional line. I want to get to know you because I see someone special behind those eyes, but I don't want to take advantage. I hope you understand."

Maggie smiled. "I like you too."

"I guess subtlety isn't my strong point."

"You're a nice guy, John Evans. Thank you for not being my shrink."

"I hope that either way our relationship goes, we will be friends. It is important to me that you understand how special you are."

"You don't need to say that."

"Even if I meant it?"

"Why hasn't someone scooped you up? Are you one of those high maintenance men?"

John chuckled. "No. To be honest, I've been divorced for about six months."

"It happens. I was in love once. Then his career became more important than me."

"My wife and I grew apart. I learned a lot about what not to do. Next time, I will be a better husband."

"I'm glad to hear you are open to a next time."

***

Trinity was waiting for Beau, looking out the window for his car. Her fears were starting to subside. She had talked to Billie and Merritt, and Abby and Dalton were regular visitors. Although she was feeling safer, she was still scared.

She understood why Maggie felt suicidal; Trinity had begun to feel as if she would never escape alive. But now, Beau was there for her every day. He was patient and understanding. Trinity missed having someone to talk to, and Beau listened. They would lie on the bed in each other's arms and talk. Trinity needed to feel Beau next to her, and he was happy to have her back in his embrace.

Trinity spotted Beau's car as it approached the gate. Taking Merritt's advice, she headed straight to her bathroom. With the door left open, she stepped into the shower. She waited only a few minutes before hearing his voice. "I'm here, sweetheart."

"Beau, would you do me a favor?"

"Anything."

Trinity was covered with suds when she opened the shower door. "Join me?"

"Oh, sweetheart, nothing would make me happier."

"Hold me Beau."

"Did you see your doctor?"

"No, that is still off the table, but I have something else in mind…"

Trinity and Beau were in bed, her head resting on his shoulder. The welts and bruises were gradually fading, and the pain was nearly gone. Beau remained gentle as he caressed her lower back. "If you can wait for me, I am going to marry you."

"As long as we can be together, I don't need a piece of paper."

"I want you to be Mrs. Abbott Fredericks the fourth."

Trinity kissed his neck. "Do you think your father would object if you stayed here with me?"

"I'll talk to him after dinner. I don't want to spend another night away from you."

After dinner, Beau asked to speak with his father. Trinity went outside, where Kathryn was with Abby. "Where is Beau?"

"Talking to your father."

"I have something he needs to sign."

"I'm not sure how long he will be."

"Trinity, I am here as a friend."

"I don't know if I could divide myself like that. You are Julie's lawyer, and you are good friends with Abby. Now, you have to represent her brother's wife. You are a good friend."

Abby got up. "I'll be inside."

"Trinity, nothing that happens here will leave here. Beau has been a wonderful friend for a long time. I am representing Julie because she needs me."

"I fell in love with a man who has been a paradox to me, even now. I know he still loves his wife. I know he has been with her since I've been away. That would make him a cad in most people's eyes, but I love him dearly, and I know he loves me."

"I think there are very few people who have seen Beau's soft, caring side."

"I'm glad he was there for you when you needed him."

"Not just me. Brock was struggling with his sexuality at the time. Beau was a non-judgmental friend when he really needed one. I think he is a better man than you realize."

"I haven't met Brock and Jack. Stella said Jack cared for her on the beach when she was found."

"I know they will love you. Molly too. She is my best friend. She is an artist, too. I'll take you to town to her shop when you're ready."

"Do you know where Beau's wife is? He went home to get some things. He said her big suitcase is gone. I'm a little terrified she is going to hurt me."

"Really? No, I'm sorry I have no idea where she is."

"OK you two. Comparing notes?"

Trinity was unashamed. "It's OK Beau, you were only a teenager."

Beau smiled at Kathryn. "Now, do you understand?"

"I do. I am going to ask Brock, Jack and Molly to come over to meet Trinity. Stella told me she wants to thank Jack."

"Beau, I asked Kathryn about your wife."

"I don't know where she is. Beau, I came over so you could sign these documents. I'll file them in the morning."

Beau looked surprised. "These are divorce papers."

"That's what she wanted."

"Kathryn, I'm glad she isn't going to draw this out, but this makes me very suspicious."

"Like I said…"

Beau looked through the papers. "I suppose I should ask Shaw to look at these."

"Beau!"

"He's kidding. Beau, Shaw and I really like the property. I think it's perfect."

Beau signed the documents, handed them back to Kathryn, and put his arm around Trinity. "Dad said I am always welcome here, day and night."

Trinity started crying. "Oh, I'm sorry. Your father has been so sweet."

"Beau, I'll try to find out where Julie is. I'm really worried about her."

"I am, too. I don't think she believed me when I told her I didn't mean to hurt her."

"I'll let you know if I find her."

Chapter 33

John lifted his badge and then secured it in his belt. "Dr. John Evans."

"Follow me… She has been off the wall, paranoid. She finally fell asleep around three o'clock, so we haven't woken her yet." The nurse opened the door to find the other bed empty. She didn't understand why the privacy curtain was closed. She called out, "Miss?" She then opened the curtain and jogged to the bathroom. "The guard is in here… he has a huge bump on his head."

She ran back to the nurse's station and called a doctor and security. "She didn't have clothes. My guess is she found the storeroom. She's probably in scrubs."

"I need to call this in… "Yes, this is Dr John Evans, out of the Boston office. I need to speak to the Assistant Director…"

"John, I'm here with Harry."

"I'm at the hospital to interview the woman who was found yesterday. She seems to be missing. Security has been called. She knocked out the guard."

"I'm hitching a ride on the Agency jet. I will be there in a couple of hours. We have some information. Do me a favor. Call Marcus and Bellamy. Have them meet you in the office."

"Harry…"

"John, two minutes before you called, we got the DNA results. The unknown DNA gathered after Ben's team found Naomi matches that woman. We need to find her."

Jim assured John they were on top of the situation. "While you and Harry were talking, I sent out a nationwide APB. John, I believe the ladies need to be warned. Truthfully, I'm not worried about them, but they should know. The other couple needs to be found. I know they were at the Gala, so I can't believe they would show their faces in Cape Hope again. Doctor, what do you think?"

"We have no evidence they are involved, only speculation. I did find out that Billie, the Coast Guard officer who was taken, was able to see a man in her room. Matilda remembers the voice of the first man who was in her room. Billie wants to do a composite. If Merritt does one of the men at the Pub and at the Gala, and they match, maybe…"

Jim supposed, "They have all had a chance to talk."

"Sir, that's the thing, they haven't talked about it. When I was with them, they hadn't, and I know Ben suggested not talking about the two women and the man until Harry was back to interview them further."

"John, what about Stella?"

"She finally talked. Maggie got her talking. She didn't want to traumatize the other ladies by showing them her wound, but Maggie spoke to her. She was quite compassionate. Stella took her bandage off. I think it helped Stella realize she wasn't alone. From here on in, I will not be involved. They need to deal with this without interference from me. Sir, honestly, I am quite taken with Maggie. We talked alone after the session was over. I want to try to help her as a friend. She feels broken…"

"I understand her father is there."

"He left. We talked privately, too. I told him I am not her therapist; I am her friend. He was relieved to know she would have someone to talk to, and I assured him I would refer her to a psychologist if I felt she needed professional help."

"Thank you for telling me. Stepping back from a professional association before a connection is established is in everyone's best interest."

"We talked about that too."

"John, I will see you at the office. I called Marcus while you and Jim were talking. Would you go back to Cape Hope? Naomi will need to be told."

"I was going to suggest that. Harry, I will see you soon. Sir, thank you."

"I will keep you apprised of any developments with the DNA. Thank you both."

John decided to talk to Naomi before heading to the office. She was in her room above the pub, so he texted her that he needed to talk.

Naomi opened the door as he was coming up the stairs. "Should I be worried?"

"I just spoke to Harry and the Assistant Director. There have been some developments you need to know about. Do you remember the woman who was with the couple at the Gala?"

"They are people of interest."

"The single woman was found in a New Hampshire pond. Drugged and confused, or so we thought. Naomi, her DNA came back to the unknown DNA found when you were rescued."

She was stunned. "The woman I heard talking. John, I wasn't hallucinating." She started weeping, but only for a few seconds. "John, I think you are the only person besides Ben who knows what this means to me. I really thought I was going crazy."

"Naomi, listen to me. She wasn't at the hospital when I got there this morning. You need to be careful. If she recognized you at the Gala…"

"I'd be dead already. Did you write down all the things I heard her say? She was the mastermind, the evil genius. Matilda told me there was a sadistic woman at the house…"

"Slow down. I have all of your notes. Are you going to be able to work? Should you call in?"

"No, I'm fine. I'm actually relieved. You need to tell Matilda the others."

"I'll be back this afternoon. I have to get to the office. Harry should be back by the time I get there. Marcus and Bellamy will be there too."

Naomi embraced John. "Thank you so much."

"I'm probably going to be here a few times a week if you need to talk."

"Ooh, did you meet someone?"

"At first, I was conflicted because I thought she might need me as a therapist more than a friend. Then, the more we talked, the more I realized I like her."

"She was in the house?"

"For almost a year."

"Are you sure she doesn't need you?"

"She needs a friend. That's where we will start, and if it becomes more, well, we will see."

***

"I know I said you're not allowed in this investigation, but since you're there…"

Harry called Ben from the plane on the way to Boston "…We decided the ladies need to know."

"I don't know. They do need to be prepared. Did you tell Naomi?"

"John did. She is relieved she wasn't crazy."

Harry wanted Simon, Beau, Lenny, and Juice to be present when he informed the ladies about Sylvie. Everyone agreed to meet at four o'clock.

While Harry was at the office, he received a call about the results of the articles found in the house. He was caught off guard when John suddenly ran into the office.

"I just got a text from Maggie. She said she remembered a conversation she had with Harlow. She said there was a woman in Harlow's room before she got there. Her name was Lynn. I asked Missing Persons to look into it."

"Too bad she doesn't know how long ago?"

"Maggie estimates it was about six months ago." Harry looked at John quizzically. "She kept track, anyway…"

"No, I'm sorry, it's good."

"Billie and Merritt are going to do composites."

Harry "I'll meet you at the house. We can tell them together."

***

The search for Lola and Morgan had reached a standstill. There was no evidence found in their boat, and like the other cases, none of the people interviewed had seen anything out of the ordinary. So, Colt and Daisy decided to start over.

They began by speaking to the owners of the boat docked next to Morgan and Lola's. Colt asked innocent questions, focusing on the pontoon boat rather than on Morgan and Lola. They were careful not to cause panic, explaining that a pontoon boat had been stolen in Marblehead and was last seen heading north.

One man, alone on his cabin cruiser, was eager to help. At first, he was like the others: "No, I haven't seen a boat like that." He gladly took one of Colt's cards. "I will keep my eyes open."

Colt and Daisy were walking down the dock when the man shouted, "Wait!" He hopped off his boat. "I saw a boat the week before last. It was close to sundown, and there were only two people on board. One of them was a woman, a very husky woman, wearing a hat. I really don't know about the other person. Man? Woman? It was hard to tell."

"Where was that?"

"Well, that's the thing. It was down there." He pointed north. "Those kinds of boats aren't usually near the marina or that close to shore. It was headed to that house. Agents, it wasn't a pontoon boat; it was a tritoon."

Daisy admitted, "That makes more sense. I don't suppose you remember if the tide was out?"

The man laughed. "It was a lot like tonight. The water was incredibly calm. It was a beautiful night. I stayed out as long as I could."

Daisy was thrilled. "This is great. Thank you so much."

***

Sylvie had stolen a car from the hospital lot, ditching it in the alley behind Kim and Steve's store before stealing another. Eventually, she made it back to her house—a place she inherited from her mother's side of the family. Since the deed hadn't been transferred, there was no way anyone would track her there.

She went straight to her room, into the walk-in closet, and pulled a dress off the hanger. At the far end, where she kept her wigs, she chose a long, curly one. Then, from the drawer where she stored her IDs, she found one that matched the wig. She slipped on some sandals, went to her safe, and selected a .45-caliber gun—untraceable, like the others. She also gathered syringes and vials of sedatives, placing everything in a tote bag before heading to her hidden room. From there, she picked up a few small but painful devices.

In the garage, she had several cars to choose from. Sylvie was set on revenge. She'd start with Steve and Kim; they had betrayed her, and in her mind, that betrayal warranted death—but not before they suffered. After them, she'd go to the Pub to find the FBI agent. That agent needed a lesson, one Sylvie was more than ready to deliver before exacting her revenge.

***

John met with Ben, Juice, Lenny, Beau, and Simon before speaking with the ladies.

"I should have asked Phil and Colt to be here, but Lenny, if you could relay the message… A woman was dumped in New Hampshire. A man was fishing when he found her…"

Ben was anxious. "Juice, it's the woman from the Gala."

John continued, "She left the hospital. When I called Harry at the Assistant Directors office they had just found out about her connection to Naomi's serial killer case."

Harry resumed, "Naomi always believed the man who held her hostage had a female partner. Now we know."

Simon wanted to understand, "So this woman is a serial killer?"

"Her DNA was found when Ben and his team rescued Naomi. Until today, it was listed as *unknown.* This woman has been at the Pub. I agree with Naomi; if this woman knew where Naomi was, she would be dead."

"But they were both at the Gala."

"Naomi is aware and armed…"

"We can't tell the women." Lenny was adamant.

"There is something all of you should know. A photo was taken of Merritt and me. A car that belonged to that woman was seen leaving the photo and a warning for us to back off. It was left in the mailbox here. Shaw was the one who saw the car driving away. That woman believes Merritt and I live here. That was the plan from the beginning, and that is why Molly's boat was brought here. Your father has known the plan from the beginning."

Juice speculated, "You want to tell the ladies the truth?"

John and Harry looked at each other and echoed, "Yes."

Simon objected, "No, absolutely not. Stella is still having nightmares. If you tell her that woman is on the loose, she won't go to sleep at all. I'll quit my job and take her to Montana before I let you do that."

Beau agreed, "Trinity and I will come with you."

Lenny stood up. "You can't do that to them—to us. If Trip will have us, I think we should stay here; otherwise, we need to come up with another solution. I agree with Simon. I'd rather take a leave of absence or quit my job and take Matilda far away before I do that to her. Ben, you understand."

"I do, but Merritt would be furious with me for not telling her. I think Billie would be, too. They are law enforcement. I don't think either one would run."

"Billie would understand my need to protect her, but she would be mad if I didn't let her make up her own mind."

Harry looked at John. "Doctor, it seems we have a stalemate."

Beau cleared his throat. "Dad would want us to stay. He has become quite fond of everyone. I'll call the security company and have them update the system. If any of the ladies ask, we can tell them Dad wanted to do it before they got here, and they were backed up. Tell Merritt and Billie the truth, but please don't tell Stella and Trinity."

John added, "Or Maggie. Gentlemen Billie and Merritt are professionals. They know the importance of withholding information."

Beau continued, "I think keeping them all together makes more sense. Ben, maybe we can call that security firm to have a couple of people at the house. Lenny, Juice?"

They looked at each other. Lenny agreed, "Anything to keep everyone together."

Ben lifted his phone. "Hey Jeff, it's Ben. Looks like we need your services again. Call me back."

***

Ben brought John to Maggie's room. *Knock, knock* ... "Maggie, it's John."

Maggie opened the door "Dr. Evans."

"Oh, OK. Do you need to talk?"

"Too early to kid?"

"No, no. Not at all. I thought maybe I came on too strong."

"No, you're cool. Are we still taking a walk?"

"It's a little warm. You're still recovering. We can talk here. Or Ben said there is a pool house."

"I'm in the house all the time. The pool house sounds nice."

John sat on the day bed, cross-legged next to Maggie. "Your father said you and Clara are going to continue to work for him from here?"

"We are book editors; we can do most of that from here. There are times we need to meet with the author in person. Clara and I thought this would be a good place for our clients to meet."

"I'd like to meet Clara. She seems to be busy at the station a lot."

"She goes to the fire station to cook. She babysits Jack and Brock's twins. She's going to be a really good mother. Do you want kids?"

"Yes. That was one of the issues with my ex. She decided she wanted to wait. Then the wait became longer."

"I would think that the secrecy in your profession might be an issue to some women."

"She is a doctor too. She understood that."

"Where do you live?"

"Peabody…"

The getting to know you conversation went on until Maggie asked, "What if I can't get over what those people did to me?" She got off the bed. "I need to know before I get in too deep."

"So that is a question for John, not Dr. Evans?"

"I'm not sure. How are you at interpreting dreams?"

"There are way too many theories about dreams. In my opinion, it's all guesswork."

"May I tell you the one I had this morning?"

"Sure."

Maggie leaned on the door jamb and looked outside. "I went to the doctor, and she told me I was healthy and she couldn't foresee any issues. When I came back here, you were waiting for me in my room. I sat on the bed. You were at the desk working. You said you needed to finish your thought, and then I would have you all to myself. I got scared because I hoped we were on the same wavelength. You hadn't kissed me up until then, so I wasn't sure. I was sitting against the headboard, and you sat next to me. You leaned toward me, and I woke up. I guess I was dreaming about you because I knew you were coming here. Until I met you, I was in a bad place. I didn't think I would be able to talk to a man about what happened much less have a serious loving relationship. I know I'm jumping the gun John, but I guess Clara being in love so quickly after she met Casey is giving me hope. You've made it easy for me to be able to see a future for myself, even if it isn't with you."

"I don't know what to say." He gave her a peck on the lips.

Until that moment, she hadn't been able to look him in the eye. She put her arms around him and finally looked into his eyes. "Is that the best you've got?"

"In your dream, did I tell you that you are amazing?"

"Nope."

"You are amazing." He kissed her again. "Your honesty is very refreshing. Can we sit?"

John took her hand and sat on the daybed. "Honesty is important, but I won't always be able to talk about what I am doing or where I'm going."

"I understand your job, your profession and who you work for. It's a double whammy. I'm not a suspicious person. I want to get to know you, just you."

"The job is part of who I am, but I don't bring my work home if I can help it."

"I'm curious but not nosey. Does that make sense?"

"It does. Will you tell me about your mother?"

Maggie and John talked for most of the afternoon, losing all sense of time until John's phone buzzed. John laughed. "Ben said Hilda wants to know if I'm staying for dinner."

"Will you?"

"Yes…"

***

Harry was heading to his car when he received a call. He quickly texted Ben, asking him to come outside. "I got a call from Harlow's father's attorney. The housekeeper gave the parents the message. They asked their attorney to handle it. Apparently, they weren't concerned. They said Harlow was a free spirit, and being away, especially during the winter months, wasn't unusual. I asked the attorney if they would contact her so we could confirm her safety. He spent several days trying to contact her to no avail. I am going to his office tomorrow."

Ben reminded Harry, "Ask if his firm received the Agency bulletin."

"I thought of that too."

"Harry, once I'm cleared for duty…"

"I want to talk to you about that. Are you going to be able to leave Merritt if I need you elsewhere?"

"Under normal circumstances, yes. Until these people are found? I can't expect Trip to let her stay here indefinitely, and she won't stand for being cooped up. She wants to go back to work."

"I'll try to keep you close to home, but as you know, I might not have a choice."

"John said he would see me in a couple of weeks."

"OK. Ben, I've been wondering about something. That house is about a mile down the street. You said you walked down there?"

"Yes. I was thinking about, well, everything. I wasn't paying attention."

"The Assistant Director asked me if you could have taken those pictures."

Ben anticipated the question, "I suppose I could have, but I didn't."

"I told him you would never compromise a case. This one is too important to so many people. He said he didn't think you would cross the line, but he had to ask."

"If the roles were reversed, I would have asked too."

"What about Julie Fredericks?" Harry wondered.

"Oh, good. So, it's not just me."

"No."

"She has a way of disappearing at the most opportune times. Should I share a conversation that made me suspicious?"

"That is up to you."

"Kathryn came by with some legal papers for Beau to sign. He was expecting the separation and custody papers, but Julie decided she wanted a divorce. If she is involved somehow and she is afraid, she would want to tie up loose ends before she disappeared."

"Thank you for telling me."

"Does this mean I am listed as an unofficial consultant?"

"Ben, you're a valuable Agent and a good friend. The team wouldn't be the same without you. Do what is best for you. Talk to Merritt. She will understand better than anyone. Ben, I will be back after I talk to Harlow's family attorney." Harry started to leave. He turned back. "Do me a favor. Discreetly do some digging into Julie Fredericks. Go back as far as you can pre-Beau, if possible."

"Anything else."

"Yes, the results of the testing came back on the items found in the room of the stone house. It's the same DNA as the woman in Baltimore."

Chapter 34

Stella was dreaming. The images flashed in distorted, choppy fragments. She was sitting at a table, eating her meal... There was a book with loose pieces of paper... She was hanging from the ceiling... Then, in an elevator... She watched a man's lips move... Her chest hurt... She was crawling on the floor, vomiting... Two large women lifted her up... She felt cold... She stood up... She was on the floor again... Her head hurt... She wanted to cry... "Don't let them see your fear..."

"Sweetheart, wake up. Stella, please wake up."

"Simon..." Stella sat up and let out a blood-curdling scream, "Staawwwwwp!"

Trip knocked and walked right in. "Son?"

"I think she is starting to remember... Sweetheart, I'm here. Dad is here. You're safe."

Beau was standing in the doorway with Trinity. "Simon, may I?"

Simon nodded. Trinity sat on the bed. "Were you dreaming about the house?"

"There was a man. He was saying *ecstasy, scopolamine.* Then they decided they wanted to *try something new.*"

"Were you in a bedroom?"

"No, it was a black room. All black."

"Stella, can you write everything down?" Ben was at the door holding a small notebook.

"Ben..." Simon was abrupt.

"No, it's OK. I remember Simon. I need to write it down. Please. Will you bring me some coffee?"

Ben handed her the notebook and a pen. Everyone quietly stepped away, leaving her alone.

As Ben went back to his bedroom, Lizzy stopped him. "Are you and Merritt still looking for a house?"

"We are."

"I bought a house before I came back, before Trip and I got together. I had some needed renovations done. They are getting ready to do some finishing touches. I thought you might like to take a look."

"Yes. Merritt wants to get out of the house anyway. After breakfast?"

"I'll take us over."

Hilda came upstairs with coffee for Stella, and Ben followed her in. Hilda kissed Stella on the forehead before she left.

Stella looked at Ben. "I read lips, Ben. I remember the man saying, *No, we can't go back there.* I'm sorry I couldn't see the whole conversation. But there were two women who moved me after I hit my head."

"No, Stella, this is great."

***

Colt and Daisy began investigating the homes along the shore north of Cape Hope. Colt steered the boat while Daisy scanned the shore through her binoculars.

"Chief, there is something bothering me. Tell me if I'm wrong. They would have needed a dock, correct?"

"Daisy, there is nothing normal about these people. Billie and Trinity were left in a dinghy, and Merritt was left on a beach in Maine. Matilda was left in a restroom. I think they do what is easiest at the time."

"There is a house with a path covered by an awning. It goes from the rocks to the fence surrounding the house."

Colt shifted into standby, lifted his binoculars, focused, and then reached for his phone. "Hey, it's Colt. Daisy saw a house on the south beach of the point. It is a huge Colonial. Cedar shakes with dark green storm shutters. Can you find the address? Thanks."

Daisy was focused on the house. "We should swing around. Maybe I can get a better view from there."

Colt navigated the cutter to the other side as the tide went out. The only dock was at the house on the point. Daisy set the binoculars aside and brought up the satellite images. "Chief, there is a road. I'm not sure if it is private or not, but I've mapped it from Cape Hope."

"We can't get any closer today. I'll speak to Agent Moran when we get back."

***

Lizzy took Ben and Merritt to her house, where landscapers were planting shrubs outside. Inside, painters were covering the floors with paper before beginning to paint. Walls had been removed, revealing a fireplace with a large, chunky mantle and a spot above for a TV.

Merritt loved the kitchen's proximity to the living room. The kitchen featured a marble island, matching counters, and a backsplash. The hickory cabinets were complemented by black hardware.

Merritt hugged Lizzy. "We'll take it."

"Don't you want to see the rest of the house?"

Ben shook his head. "You're asking the wrong person. May we look upstairs first, sweet cheeks?"

Merritt ran up the stairs, and within a minute, they heard a shriek, "Give her whatever she wants."

Ben was curious. "Is there an office?"

"There is a den over here. Call it a multi-use room."

Merritt came back down. "Please, please, please."

"We should look out back first." Merritt flew out the French doors to the deck in the back.

"Lizzy, this is perfect."

"I wanted to have enough room for my kids when they visit. It really is a home for a family."

"We should go back to the house to talk. Lizzy isn't going to sell it to anyone else. Right?"

"Right." Lizzy laughed. "I'll take you back. I'll be at the station until six."

***

Harry had a meeting in Boston with Harlow's family attorney, Elliott Davis. He was terse. Harry was accustomed to dealing with attorneys, but this man was on the verge of being rude.

"Excuse me, I thought you called me here because you have information."

"Agent Moran, we got the Agency bulletin. What evidence do you have Harlow is in this alleged brothel."

"Alleged? There is nothing alleged about the women who have been brutalized by this organization of animals. They are not imagining the horrific torture they endured. If your client's daughter is there, I would hope they would want to get her out."

"So, you have nothing to confirm that Harlow is, in fact, there?"

"Where is she? I'd like to talk to her. If she isn't the Harlow that was in the house with the other women, I want to meet her."

"Her parents will not allow their family to be dragged through the mud."

"We will not let that happen. The ladies who have been released have representation. He will not allow the press to hurt these women any further." Harry reached into his pocket anticipating the next question.

"I can't imagine any respectable law firm would take on this kind of case."

Harry had the business card in his hand. "I was asked to give a card to anyone who had questions." He handed Mr. Davis the card.

The look on his face was priceless. "Does he know you suspect Harlow is there?"

"He is kept in the loop, yes."

Mr. Davis sighed and rubbed his face.

"If your client asked you to take care of this, as you said, then help us find Harlow. If she is missing, there is a very good chance your client's daughter and the woman in the brothel are the same woman."

"She hasn't been in contact with the family since Christmas. Agent Moran, Harlow has always been different. She has never had focus. She is flighty. More interested in traveling than having a career or settling down."

"They don't care?"

"Truthfully? I don't know."

"We would like to trace her movements. If you have a credit card or…"

"Agent, there has been no activity. I believe her parents think she found a man or she is dead."

"Where was the last place she used her credit card?"

"In Boston. She had tickets to Dubai, but she wasn't on that flight."

"Mr. Davis, I have spent a great deal of time with these women. They are all worried about Harlow. The house they were in was old. They could hear through the air vents. Harlow was frightened. When she was visited by the clients, she begged to be killed. The ladies told us she sounded naïve and scared. Mr. Davis, some of the people who frequented the brothel were sadists. All of the women were severely beaten and brutally raped before they were released. We have resources. Give me what I need so I can notify the other Agencies. If she is alive and living in a castle somewhere in France, we will find her."

Mr. Davis tapped a few keys on his computer and printed a cover sheet with pertinent information: "I'd like to be kept in the loop, too."

"As much as I can. With this, I can send out an APB. We have leads we are following. Mr. Davis, it is imperative this conversation stay between us."

"I read the bulletin. Was this an attempt to scare someone enough to send an anonymous letter?"

"If anyone had a privileged conversation with a client we would hope they would pass the information along anonymously. Mr. Davis, law enforcement and politicians have long been connected to organizations like this. People who think laws don't apply to them. There is a reason the proprietors of this brothel get away with what they do."

***

John visited Maggie again after work. Hilda answered the door and promptly invited him to dinner. "Maggie is in her room."

Maggie wasn't expecting John so soon. She had just gotten out of the shower and was standing in the bathroom, looking at herself in the mirror. She had avoided the full-length mirror until then. Of course, she had seen herself before today, but never in the buff, as her mother would have said. She stared, a little surprised that the bruises and slash marks were still visible. She couldn't look away.

Knock, knock.

"It's open." At first, she thought it was Clara. She always knocked. They weren't modest around each other, but just lately, Clara was letting Maggie know before she came in.

John walked in as Maggie walked out of the bathroom. She didn't try to cover up. "I thought you were Clara."

"I can leave."

"Please don't." Maggie's robe was over the desk chair. She put it on and tied it tightly. "I'm sorry, I think… I actually don't know what I was thinking. John, I'm sorry."

"May I give you a hug? You look like you need a hug."

Maggie crossed the room, wrapped her arms around him, and began to weep. "I didn't want the first time you saw me to be like this, with me looking like this."

John was sensitive. "You have nothing to be sorry about."

"I was hoping to start swimming again, riding a bike, getting some tone back. I used to be in much better shape."

"Maybe Clara can buy you a bathing suit. You can swim here. You know no one will judge."

"She brought one from home. It's a little loose. I tried exercising, and I did for a while. The rooms had satellite TV, so I was able to find exercise shows. But then, I guess it was when they changed the bedspread in my room. I realized it must be Spring, and I got so depressed. That's when I began to give up."

John continued to hold her. "We can talk if you'd like. I hear that's what couples do."

"Can we talk about you? You've already met my family. What about your family?"

John kicked off his shoes and sat on the bed. "Sit next to me."

"I have to get dressed for dinner. Do you mind talking while I dress?"

"Not at all. My parents are Professors at Northwestern. Psychology, and Civil Engineering. I have a sister and two brothers. They are all still in Evanston."

"Please don't tell them what happened to me."

"I don't usually volunteer information about other people, especially someone I have come to care about. That is your story to tell, if and only if you ever decide to share."

"Do you talk to them a lot?"

"I do. I was there in May when my youngest brother graduated. He will be here for his post-grad studies at BU."

"Will he be staying with you?"

"No, he and his partner will be living together in Boston."

"Was that an issue?"

"Not really. They have been together since sophomore year. We knew he was gay. They are both pretty funny. I'm closer to my sister and..." John started laughing. "I guess I should have mentioned I have a twin brother. His name is Joel."

She laughed. "You forgot?" Her facial expression changed. "Did you tell him about me?"

"I told him I met someone. I hope that's OK."

"I suppose." Maggie sat next to John, still in her underwear "Is it weird I feel so comfortable around you?"

"I actually think it is incredible how well you are coping."

"Even the crying?"

"Even the crying. Clara, your father; I think if they hadn't been here, you may be struggling."

"And I suppose you had nothing to do with my recovery?"

"I guess if anything, I was smart enough to step back when I realized I wanted to get to know you. But listening to you is natural for me. I hope I would have had the same understanding and compassion even if I had met you through a dating site."

"I shouldn't trust you, but I do."

"Because I'm a man?"

"Because there is something *too good to be true* about you. I'm actually scared to death about what happens when I have to leave here."

"Trip will not kick you out. If Clara ends up moving in with Casey, I was thinking maybe you could buy Matilda's house. I know she is planning to sell."

"I'm terrified to live alone. If I hadn't met you, I probably would have gone home. You have complicated my life, Dr. Evans."

He held out his hands. "Come here." He held her in his arms. "I like you too, Margaret Beckett."

"What happens if we don't work out? What happens if I can't… John, I want to be able to fall in love again, but I don't know if I can."

"You're getting ahead of yourself. Don't anticipate the worst. Thinking about what may or may not happen will confuse the natural progression of a relationship. Go with the flow, Peaches."

"Peaches?"

John caressed her face. "Peaches are soft and sweet."

"You are too good to be true." Maggie kissed him.

"Not that I'm complaining, but you should probably get dressed."

While Maggie put on a dress, John called Matilda, "May Maggie look at your house?"

"Of course. It has three bedrooms, an office, a nice back yard and a chef's kitchen."

"I can come back in the morning if you're available?"

"I asked Beau to handle it for me."

"That's cool. I like Beau."

***

Kim and Steve were discussing their new venture, which led them to talk about Cape Hope and Matilda.

"Steve, one day, before the Gala, Sylvie and I went to that Pub. There was a woman there Sylvie liked. We followed her to a house in a neighborhood just outside of town. The couple we met there and at the Gala went inside. The woman from the house we saw at the Gala lives there."

"Are you suggesting we get her back?"

"No, that would be reckless, but the day we met at the Pub, there was a woman there who was also at the Gala. I think she was new to town, so she may not be missed."

"There is also the woman I saw in Boston. She was there when I was talking to the Concierge the other day."

"Let's go there for the night. If we can't find her, we can probably find someone."

Steve and Kim went to Boston as planned and decided on an early dinner. The hotel dining room wasn't busy, so Steve spoke to the maître d' to secure a table with the best view of the entrance.

As they enjoyed their meal, they indulged in some people-watching, a pastime they both enjoyed. They were finishing their brandy when Steve's phone rang. It was one of his employees.

"An FBI Agent was here. That car that was left in the alley was stolen. Steve said a woman wanted by the FBI stole it from a hospital. She was a person of interest in *several Federal cases*. He showed me her picture. It was Sylvie. I told him I didn't recognize her. I asked him if I should be worried. He said if she came in, to call immediately. He gave me his card. Harry Moran, FBI."

"Thank you for calling and for your loyalty."

"Anytime boss, anytime."

"Steve?"

Steve sighed. "We can talk about this in the room."

"That woman sitting at the bar, look."

"Huh, what?"

"Focus Steve. That woman at the bar."

"That's her. We need to see if she's meeting someone before we approach her."

"Should I be worried about the call?" Kim whispered.

"I really can't talk about it here. I'm going to the bar. I'll meet you in the room."

"Steve?"

"Do you trust me?"

"Of course. Use our alter ego names. OK? I'll see you in the room." Kim knew from past experience if the hook-up was promising, he would call her. They never met in their room, so she would wait.

Steve leaned toward the woman at the bar. "Are you expecting anyone?"

The woman tried not to smile. "You mean besides you?"

"Hi I'm Bill."

"Zoey. Are you staying at the hotel?"

"I am. Are you here for business or pleasure?" Steve was very charming on the outside. He always made eye contact with his female counterpart, and as soon as he smiled, the woman was usually hooked. Today was no exception.

"At this moment, pleasure." Zoey wasn't oblivious to Steve's charms, but she was careful. When she was in town, she was a different person. On this occasion, she was Zoey, and she told Steve she needed a break from her family: "To be honest, I'm married."

"That's cool." He lifted his hand. "Me too. I don't mind if you don't mind."

"The real question is, will your wife mind?"

"Since we're being truthful, she has been known to join me on occasion."

"Intriguing.' She reached into her purse. "How about this? You and I see how we are together, and if we click, you can invite your wife."

"How could I say no to that…"

Steve knew the hotel well and how to avoid the security cameras. Once they arrived at the suite, Zoey excused herself to the bathroom.

"Make yourself comfortable. I will be out in a few minutes."

Steve pointed at the bed. "I'll be over there, getting comfortable." He removed his shoes and socks, unbuttoned his freshly laundered shirt, and sat on the edge of the bed, being careful not to touch anything that might leave a print.

Zoey came out wearing a short silk robe. She smiled. "Oh, are you shy?"

"Just trying to make the moment last."

Zoey removed his shirt and draped it over the back of a chair. She unbuckled his belt and unzipped his pants. Comfortable taking the lead, she proceeded, and he let her. He stood in his silk boxer shorts as she kneeled, pulling them down slowly. She held his backside as she kissed his belly, moving gently toward his pelvis. Rising, she crawled to the middle of the bed, held out her hand, and waited for him to join her. She then softly pushed him back, straddled his waist, leaned forward, and kissed him.

His hands moved to her buttocks, then to the front of her robe. He tugged at the sash until it fell open, removing her robe and gently cupping her breasts as he kissed her.

They didn't speak. They reveled in each other.

Steve wasn't accustomed to basking in the afterglow with anyone but Kim, but tonight, he was content to remain where he was.

"Maybe I could meet your wife?"

"I think that is an excellent idea…" Steve went to the bathroom to wash up. He got dressed and promised Zoey he would be back with his wife.

Kim was pacing when Steve opened the door. "So?"

"I think you'll be pleased. She suggested I bring you back. She is in a suite right above us."

"I anticipated, so I'm ready." Kim unbuttoned her blouse so Steve could see her lace bra.

He kissed her cleavage softly. "She is going to be a great addition, Kim."

"For us or the house?"

"Why can't she be both?"

Kim smiled. "I love you."

"I love you too."

Steve had a key card to Zoey's room. He knocked before using the card to enter.

Zoey was wearing her robe again, but beneath it, she had on nothing but a thong. She raised her hand. "You must be Monica. I've been looking forward to meeting you."

Kim wasn't shy. "You are perfect."

Zoey reached for the buttons on Kim's blouse. Kim allowed her to remove it before reaching out to touch Zoey's breasts.

Steve sat at the desk, watching as Kim and Zoey got to know each other. He decided they needed to keep her. He didn't want to lose her if she chose to go home. He had a plan, but first, he needed to join the ladies…

Chapter 35

"Mr. Smith, I just received an ABP on your little *mouse*. It was sent by the FBI and forwarded to all the Agencies, including Interpol. They are looking for her. As much as I enjoy her company, you need to cut ties."

"Yes, she was quite popular." Mr. Smith was quiet. "Hmm. The operation has already been moved, but I will take care of this. Thank you. I will comp your next visit."

When a call from Mr. Smith came through on Ellen or Maude's phone, they jumped "Mr. Smith." They both knew not to brown-nose him, so they let him speak.

"I have received a notice about the mousey woman. The FBI is looking for her. Get rid of her."

"Sir? Permanently?"

"I would rather you didn't. I haven't seen any reports on the Feds you took care of. I don't think they want to publicize their ineptitude, so under the circumstances, I have a plan… Find an appropriate dumping ground."

Ellen was next to Harlow, holding a syringe. She looked at Maude. "Are you OK with this plan?"

"It's not up to me. We need to get moving. Make sure it looks like she did it herself. Leave the tourniquet on her arm so it looks like it's been there for a while."

Harlow was already unconscious when Ellen began administering the injections, carefully placing them on various spots on Harlow's arms, using only a drop each time. They monitored her as she regained consciousness. She was disoriented and confused. After a few hours, they repeated the process until her arms were black and blue from the injection sites.

Harlow's arms were already bruised as if she had struggled with an attacker. Her fragile body had been battered, so she had been on a sort of sabbatical. During that time, she hadn't slept. Her mind wouldn't allow it to shut down. The insomnia was taking a toll on her already fragile psyche, and she began to fear what was to come next.

She had a few faded flogging scars, and the track marks on her arms made her appear as though she had lived a hard life. They would wait until the next morning, when the tide was out, to complete their assignment.

Before sunrise, Maude took Harlow on a four-wheeler up the coast. She had scouted the area the previous day to find the perfect spot. Maude injected her one final time before dropping her off in the State Park. By the time breakfast was served, Maude was already back at the house.

Harlow was left on the sea rocks, visible from the water. At the designated time, Maude used a burner phone to call the State Park office. The weather was beginning to cooperate. Standing outside, she noticed the wind picking up. She left a message, claiming that she was on a sailboat and had spotted what appeared to be a body on the rocks. She intentionally cut the call short, implying that the signal had been lost.

When Harlow was found, she was disheveled, looking like a drug addict left for dead. Ellen had dressed her in a dirty shirt, ripped down the front, her shorts stained with urine. She was barefoot. Nearby, the tourniquet and an empty syringe were found.

The ranger didn't see the APB, so when she got the call, she called the State Police, who called Harry. "… we had her sent to Addison."

"Thank you Captain."

Harry was reluctant to call Harlow's attorney, so he waited. If he were a vindictive man, he might have released her name to the press, but he knew that would accomplish nothing. On his way to the hospital, he called John. "The APB worked. Harlow is on her way to the hospital. I think you should tell the ladies."

"I'm free after lunch. I'll drop by."

"How is Maggie?"

"Good, then not so good. Under the circumstances, normal. Matilda is taking her to see her house."

"Please be careful, John."

"We are both using caution, but I need to see this through. She needs me, Harry, and in some ways, I need her too."

"You and Ben seem to be in the same boat. Brought up in the Midwest in close, big families. You are involved with women who are not…"

"Harry, I know… I'm sorry. This is damned frustrating. I spoke to my mother. I asked about a hypothetical situation. She has been doing this a lot longer than me. I promised Maggie I wouldn't tell my family, but I need to be able to give Maggie the best advice possible. Harry, we are talking about a lot of things. I really like her. She is funny, very self-deprecating and then she starts crying. That's when I feel lost."

"My fear is you are falling for a woman who is remarkable because of what she went through. She won't always be that woman, John."

"It's more than that. I liked her from the beginning. That is why I stepped back."

"What did your mother say?"

"She wants to come out here before school starts. I told her she is welcome anytime."

"My guess is she will love Maggie, and when you tell her your mother knows what happened, she may be angry at first, but she will understand."

"Harry, thank you for listening. I'll see you later."

John went to the pool first. Matilda was there talking to Maggie about her house. She saw John and ran into his arms. "The house is perfect."

"I can take you there. That is if you're planning to live there too." Matilda smirked.

"Ben told me to watch out for you."

Maggie was coy. "Yes, John, are you planning to live there too?"

"It depends. Matilda, I need to speak to Maggie, but I need to talk to everyone. Would you rally the troops? Men and women?"

"I can do that."

"Can we go to your room?"

John sat on Maggie's bed. "We need to talk."

"Will I need tissue?"

"I hope not. You understand about doctor-patient confidentiality? That applies if a doctor consults with another doctor."

"You talked about me with someone?"

"Yes." He kissed her. "You confuse the hell out of me, Peaches."

Maggie giggled. "I'm sorry?"

"We've only known each other for a few weeks, but I already know I want you in my life. Maggie, I'm afraid you may hate me when I tell you. I told my mother about you. She is an excellent therapist, and I talk to her anytime I need advice."

Maggie's eyes were filled with tears.

"Please don't be mad at me. I never want to hurt you, but I find myself wanting to help you even though I may end up hurting you more than helping."

Maggie moaned. "That was very convoluted, but I understand. I'm not mad."

"Hold that thought. Mom is coming for a visit next week. She wants to meet you."

"I'm a mess."

"You're beautiful."

"I worried if your family found out that they would think I was damaged goods. But then I thought, if you don't, they won't either. There has to be a reason you're such a nice guy. I also think they should know before I meet them. For the past few weeks, I've only been around people who have been affected by those people. They all understand. I, we, need to get back to normal somehow."

"I told Mom you were amazing. She volunteers at a shelter for battered women a couple of nights a week. She understands."

"I need to tell you what has been in the back of my mind. I had been worried that I had been a special project to you. I know now it's not true."

"I was going to suggest talking to your doctor to get the name of a therapist, just in case. I'm afraid I am a little too biased to give you sound advice."

"Do you mind telling me everything about your brothers and sister?"

"I'd like to skype Joel and introduce you."

Maggie put her arms around John. "As long as you tell him why I look like this before we call."

"I have to tell you something else. I'm here to tell all the ladies that Harlow has been found."

Maggie started crying. "Oh John…"

"We got a photo of her from the family attorney and sent it out to all the Agencies, hoping someone who had been to the house would see it and send a letter. But someone must have told the owner of the house. They dumped her on the rocks on the other side of Cape Hope. Harry was on his way to the hospital. He asked that I come by and tell everyone."

Maggie kissed John. "Thank you for caring about me."

"Oh, Peaches, that is easy. You make me very happy."

Maggie went down to the pool first. John planned to meet everyone a few minutes later. He wanted to speak with his brother first.

"I'd like to skype later. I'm helping with a group of women who were abducted and forced to live in a brothel. I'm not their therapist, but since the FBI is in charge, I have been here to help."

"But?"

"One of the women is amazing; well, they all are, but Maggie was there for almost a year, and I'm falling in love with her."

"Is she going to be able to recover from something like that?"

"She has been very open about her recovery. I want you to meet her. Mom is coming next week. I told Maggie I hoped we could skype tonight."

"My last patient is at four today. I'll stay in the office and expect your call at five."

"She is a little nervous because she and the others were beaten before they were left… I had to talk to Mom."

"I look forward to meeting her. What did she do before she was abducted?"

"Her father is a Publisher in New York. She is one of his editors."

"John, I don't want to see you hurt again."

"I know. I stepped away as her therapist as soon as I knew. She is honest and funny…"

"I look forward to your call."

John went to the patio, where Ben, Lenny, Juice, and all the ladies were already gathered. "Harlow has been found."

Trinity and Matilda hugged John.

"I don't have details except that we had help from her family attorney so we could send out an APB. Someone must have warned the proprietors of the house because she was left on the rocks on the other side of town. Harry is on his way to the hospital. Hopefully, Simon will be taking care of her."

Matilda made a request, "May I visit her?"

"I'll take any of you that want to go tomorrow morning."

Matilda whispered something in Maggie's ear before heading inside.

Maggie hugged Matilda. "I will."

***

Sylvie was growing restless. She watched Kim and Steve's store, but they weren't there. She knew they would eventually show up, but she didn't want to spend her days on stakeout, so today, she decided to head to Cape Hope. Wearing a wig and glasses, she walked into the Pub.

Naomi was alone at the bar. Sylvie ordered a Manhattan, then took the cherry out, popped it in her mouth, and pulled the stem off as she stared at Naomi.

Naomi thought she was being paranoid, remembering the day Kim tied the knot in the cherry stem. She knew Tim was in his office, so she discreetly texted him. Tim then forwarded the message to Phil.

Tim, Phil, and Naomi already had the green light from Harry to set up a sting of sorts. Lucy had recalled Sylvie flirting with her, so they decided that if Sylvie showed up again, Lucy would approach her at the bar. They also agreed that, since Lucy was with Tim at the bar and at the Gala, they would keep things strictly friendly.

Naomi smiled at Lucy when she came in. "Hey girl. How was last night?"

"I don't know…" Lucy saw Sylvie and sat at the bar, leaving a barstool between them. "I didn't get the vibe I'm looking for." Lucy didn't make the first move. She knew if it was the same woman, she would be the aggressor. "May I have a beer?"

Naomi moved to the other side of the bar, opened a bottle of non-alcoholic beer, poured it into a glass, and served it to Lucy. "Hamburger and fries?"

Lucy laughed. "You know me so well."

Tim came out of the office. When he saw Lucy, he asked, "How did the date go?"

"Eh."

Tim laughed. "You'll find someone soon enough, sweetheart, but I'll be your arm candy as long as you need me."

Both Naomi and Lucy laughed. "You are so considerate, so selfless."

"Anything for a friend." Tim returned to the office and texted Lucy and Naomi, "I think it's her." He then texted Harry and Phil.

Sylvie was patient. Naomi tried to avoid making eye contact. This woman was responsible for the worst period of her life. She was angry, but she had to set that anger aside. "May I get you anything to eat?"

"Oysters?"

"Sure." Naomi went to the back. "I'm not sure I can watch this. She wants oysters."

Under normal circumstances, Tim would have laughed, but there was nothing normal about what was happening at his bar. "Can you do this?"

"I have to, Tim. I have to."

Sylvie leaned toward Lucy. "Do you know where the restroom is?"

"Oh sure, over there." Lucy pointed toward the back.

Naomi brought out a plate of four oysters. "Where did she go?"

"Bathroom."

Naomi set the plate down just as the Pub phone rang. Noticing the hostess was away from the podium, she walked over to answer the bar phone. As she picked it up, she heard only a dial tone—and then saw the front door close. Naomi whispered to Lucy, "Will you check the ladies room?"

Lucy went to the back as Phil came in the door. He sat at the bar.

"What can I do for you, stranger?"

Phil shrugged. "You tell me."

"Hey, I just work here…"

Lucy ran to the bar. "She's gone. Cap, that's her glass."

"We must have spooked her. I bet she was the hang-up on the phone." Naomi was annoyed.

Phil called Harry. "She's gone. I think she's playing with us. She left a martini glass. Would you bring an evidence bag?"

Sylvie grew suspicious. She didn't like how Naomi avoided eye contact and seemed unusually abrupt for a bartender, so she left as soon as she could. Keeping the wig on, she added a floppy hat and drove to the house where she and Kim had seen the young couple.

When she reached the house, she slowed down. With no other cars on the road, she idled for a couple of minutes, studying the grounds. An idea was forming...

***

John brought his laptop to Maggie's room while she was in the bathroom. "Do you mind if I put some makeup on?"

"You don't need makeup, but if it will make you feel more comfortable, go for it."

"Did you warn him?"

"I prepared him."

"So, give me some background. Is he married?"

"Yes, no kids yet. Jody is a Microbiologist. Joel is a Psychologist."

Maggie was quiet.

"Did you climb out the window?"

Maggie laughed softly before stepping out of the bathroom "I have always been intimidated around people with advanced degrees. I have an MBA, but everyone has an MBA these days."

"They are regular people, Maggie. Do I intimidate you?"

"No, I know you. I am comfortable with you." Maggie didn't use any makeup. "So, that's why I decided I should be comfortable being myself."

"I'm glad you didn't cover your bruises. It means you are feeling better about yourself."

"I want your brother to see the person you met. I hope he doesn't see how nervous I am."

"I want to talk to you about something. Since you left the house with Matilda, I thought that maybe we could spend the weekend at my place. It would give us time to talk about everything. Clara told me you're a good cook. I like it here, but…"

"Yes, yes. I think it's a great idea. Maybe we can go grocery shopping together?"

"I was going to suggest that."

"Will this be a beta test for our relationship?"

"I guess it would be. It wouldn't be a thorough beta test because all facets of our relationship wouldn't be able to be examined, but I think it's a good start."

Maggie put her arms around him. "Maybe we could take baby steps. Would you mind if we slept in the same bed?"

"Mind? Not at all. It will be a good start. Call it a trial run. You may hate sleeping with me."

"Why? What do you do while you're sleeping?"

"I'm not sure. Do you want to ask my ex?"

"No, that won't be necessary." Maggie seemed agitated. "I'm sorry. I don't want to meet her."

"I'm OK, Maggie. It wasn't a bad marriage or a bad breakup."

"I don't like the thought that someone hurt you."

"I'm in a good place now…" *beep, beep, beep* "It's time, you ready?" John clicked the icon.

"Hello John, how are you?"

"Excellent." John reached out to Maggie to get her in the picture. "Joel, this is Maggie Beckett."

Maggie hugged John's arm. "You don't look like brothers at all." Maggie immediately felt embarrassed, worried she might have said the wrong thing. John kissed her gently on the temple.

Joel laughed. "Thank you! Seriously, I've never understood why people think we look alike."

Maggie suddenly felt overwhelmed, unsure why, but it seemed like she was having a panic attack. "I can't do this…" She ran to the bathroom.

John spoke softly. "Can you give us a minute?"

"Let me talk to her alone."

"Absolutely…" John went into the bathroom. "In through your nose, out through your mouth, slowly." John turned on the water. "Splash some water on your face and come back. Dr. Evans would like to talk to you."

"Um… OK."

"I'll be in the solarium. Text me when you're done." John kissed her. "I have always aspired to be as good as Joel. He will take care of you."

"OK, I'm fine."

John left, and Maggie sat in front of the laptop. "I have no idea where that came from."

"You have been to hell and back, and anxiety can creep up from nowhere. Were you thinking of something in particular?"

"I was thinking I was dreaming again. I would have these dreams. I was with my husband and my kids, and we were having dinner. Then I would wake up, and a horrible evil man would come into my room and do unspeakable things to me…" She took a deep breath. "Now, now, this wonderful, funny, sweet, incredibly understanding man wants to be in my life and I think about him, and I panic because I'm afraid I'm going to wake up."

"Do you think you don't deserve a man like John?"

"I did at first, but I didn't deserve what those people did to me… I did worry that any man would never want me because of what happened… I couldn't imagine saying the words to someone seeing the pity in their eyes. John volunteered his time for us. He talked to my father. I still don't know what they talked about; I didn't ask."

"Maggie, are you afraid your feelings are misplaced? Do you think maybe John was an easy fix to finding a man who would understand what happened to you?" Joel didn't expect Maggie's response.

"I wondered about that. I actually brought it up. Yes, at first, it was easy to talk to him because we didn't talk about details. He saw me when I was a real mess, physically and emotionally. I even asked him if I was a special project. Looking back, I think I wanted to make him mad so he would have an excuse to step away. He didn't. The more time I spend with him, the more I realize I can have a normal life; I can look to the future. I didn't have a future for a long time."

"So why did you panic?"

"Because I was afraid you would think I wasn't good enough. When I was getting ready, I told John I was going to put on makeup. I was embarrassed, but he didn't come out with a bunch of analytical mumbo jumbo to try to tell me what to do."

"Do you usually make a joke when you first meet someone?"

"I wanted you to know I wasn't broken."

"You are incredibly honest."

"I'm not so sure. I did something dishonest. I finally had the courage to look at myself in the full-length mirror. I knew I had to before the bruises faded… anyway, there was a knock on the door. I thought it may be my sister, but then I hoped it would be John. I needed him to see me before we got in too deep. At least, I thought I did. As soon as he came in, I regretted it. I didn't want his first image of me to be of the aftermath of what happened." Maggie was struggling; she didn't want to cry. "I will tell him I lied. I don't want him to think I'm playing games… Joel, I'm sorry you had to listen to my insecurities. It's not the skype call I envisioned."

"Tell me what you thought."

"I thought I would be confident, articulate, funny, and I hoped you wouldn't think John had lost his mind."

Joel laughed. "He lost his mind a long time ago."

Maggie laughed as she wept. "I'm falling in love with him, and no, it's not transference. I know he cares about me, but I'm afraid of what will happen when we are finally able to be together. Will I ever be the Maggie I was before?"

"You can't be. You are who you are now because of what happened in that house. John isn't attracted to the person you were before; he is attracted to the Maggie you are now."

"Was this the real reason he wanted us to meet, so you could talk some sense into me?"

"He wanted me to meet you, no ulterior motives." Joel looked down. "I texted John. Maggie, I want to meet you too. My wife is in the middle of a project, and a colleague owes me some vacation coverage. I'll let you know when I'm available…"

John knocked but walked right in. Maggie put her arms around him.

"Did he tell you all my secrets?"

"Only that you lost your mind a long time ago."

John was gruff. "You promised!!" He smiled at his brother as he kissed the side of her head. "I guess you had nothing to worry about."

"We have a lot to talk about." She looked back at the screen. "Thank you Dr. Evans."

"My pleasure."

***

Kim and Steve had made plans to see Zoey again, wanting to get to know her better before deciding what to do next. Steve had already decided he wanted her but for himself. Kim, however, envisioned Zoey as a partner in a threesome. She didn't consider finding another man for herself; she was in love with Steve and simply wanted what he wanted—nothing more.

Today, Steve used a fleet car. His father's company was immense, handling imports among other ventures, and they maintained a fleet of vehicles for visiting salesmen in need of transportation. Since it was Thursday afternoon, he knew the lot would be mostly full. He signed out a luxury model, picked up Kim at home, and then drove to Boston. Upon arrival, Steve asked Kim to wait for him in the lobby while he spoke to the concierge. Then, he headed into the bar, where Zoey was waiting, sipping a martini.

Steve sat next to her. "I missed you."

"As it happens, I missed you too."

"Maybe we can do something about that. Do you live nearby?"

"That isn't an option."

"I wasn't suggesting that. Monica and I have a retreat. It is quite comfortable. It is a safe place set up for assignations. If you want to meet, we have a text number."

"If I wanted to see you?"

Steve took a cocktail napkin. "Text this number."

"And if I want to see you and Monica?"

"This number…"

"Do you have others you see?"

"We are careful, so no, not at the moment."

"I have my regular room. If I see you both today, would you come back tomorrow alone?"

"Absolutely. Two o'clock? I'll meet you here."

Zoey smiled as she handed Steve her spare key. "I'll see you upstairs."

***

Ben usually didn't enjoy research—it tended to be monotonous—but he was determined to uncover whether Julie Fredericks was hiding something. His initial investigation revealed information about her father's real estate empire and philanthropic activities. Julie had an older brother whose name conspicuously disappeared from articles about the family about eighteen months before her father passed away. In those articles, he was referred to as Harold Jr., but Ben remembered hearing him called Chip.

He decided he needed to go into the office to access the FBI's database. He dug as deeply as possible, sifting through newspaper articles, online reports, blogs, and even local podcasts. He was determined to uncover the reason for the family rift. But more than anything, he needed to find out where Julie had been.

He began to think about the brothel and the methods they used to bring clients to the house. The second letter mentioned a luxury hotel in Boston, each with a concierge desk to handle guest requests.

He was fairly certain a woman wouldn't want to promote a service offering ladies on an hourly basis, so he focused on questioning the men, using one of his alter ego backstories.

He also knew that most hotels were very careful to keep their wealthy, repeat clients discreet and satisfied. Posing as the CEO's executive assistant, he asked the concierge about amenities not listed in their literature. It was Ben's third call when he asked, "Do you offer services for men who would like some companionship?"

"Please hold." When the gentleman came back on the line, he explained, "I needed to change phones. This isn't a subject to be discussed in the lobby. Yes sir, we have access to a service. It is a very discreet location. The proprietors of the house offer transportation. It is cash only. I have a list of prices based on services."

"Excellent. I'd like to come in tomorrow after lunch to talk and set up an account, if possible?"

Ben made the arrangements but needed Harry's approval first. He called, knowing that Harry and John were heading to the hospital with some of the women.

"Harry, I think I found the hotel base for the brothel."

"What happened to the other thing?"

"I was giving my brain a rest when I thought about the letters that were sent. I'll pass on the job to someone else, but I made arrangements to speak to the contact tomorrow. He will give me the details then."

"Ben, Ben, Ben. What am I going to do with you? My concern is someone in the operation may recognize you, and… and I cannot overemphasize this: you are not active at the moment."

"I need to see this through. If I can get an appointment, someone can follow me…"

"Ben, we are about to leave for the hospital. I will speak to John, and I will call you back."

***

Maggie suggested that she should go in to see Harlow first. She planned to explain how they had identified her, and if Harlow remembered, Clara could visit another day.

John went into the room with Maggie. "Harlow, I'm so glad you're OK. We were all so worried about you."

"I'm really confused. Do I know you?"

"I was in the house. I talked to you sometimes. I'm Maggie."

Harlow's hands were shaking. "I remember you." She was numb, having already passed the worst of the drugs. Luckily, they hadn't given her much—just enough to deaden her senses. "Did you find me?"

Maggie looked at John, then turned to see Simon. Maggie whispered, "What should I tell her?"

Simon lifted her wrist to check her pulse. "Remember we talked about the other ladies in the house? Do you remember any of their names?"

"Trinity. Is she here?"

Simon went to the hall.

Trinity went in and held Harlow's hand. "We are all so relieved you are out of there…"

Simon was concerned that Harlow would need inpatient care to recover. John assured him that his mother would be in town and would insist on helping.

"She is welcome to the pool house."

"Maggie and I talked there once. I think Mom would be very comfortable there."

"Shaw talked to Ben and Maggie already. They will be on vacation, so Ben and Merritt will be staying at their house. Harlow can stay with the others at Dad's. I understand her parents are ambivalent."

Harry grunted, "They don't care."

Harry tugged John to the side. "Ben thinks he found the hotel that services the brothel."

"He needs to feel useful, Harry."

"I worry about FBI regs on being out of work."

"I spoke to Ben unofficially. Based on that, I would give the OK for a limited return. He wasn't hurt physically. Not knowing who is behind this enterprise is doing Ben more harm than good."

"Let me think about it."

"I'll talk to Ben when we get back. Maggie and I will be at my place for the weekend if you need me. She wants time for us to talk. We're still getting to know each other. We need the time before my mother arrives."

"I appreciate offering your mother's expertise. I wondered if you would be objective enough to help Harlow."

"I believe she will be better served talking to a woman. Are you going to call the attorney?"

"I'm not obligated to tell him or Harlow's parents anything. I will if your mother thinks I should. If it were up to me, I would never tell them."

"I understand your anger. Some people should never be allowed to have children."

***

Ben stayed in Boston until John called him, "I hear you are misbehaving."

"I'm helping."

"What is your plan?"

"I want to go to the hotel to talk to the Concierge. In luxury hotels like this, a credit check is usually done to create a corporate account. I will give him my backstory information and go from there. If I need to check in, I will do it then. I will call Harry and give him the details. He can follow the car to the brothel."

"I worry that someone will recognize you."

"My hair hasn't been cut in a while. I haven't shaved for a couple of days. I will wear glasses."

"You've thought this through."

"I don't want anyone else to be hurt. I'm sick of these people."

"Do you have your weapon?"

"It's downstairs. Call them! I can get it. John we are closer than we ever have been. "

"Hold on…" John spoke to Harry. They decided Ben needed to see this through: "If you go, call Harry and Ben…"

"I know, I know. Don't do anything stupid."

Ben didn't want Merritt to worry, so he called, "… Do you trust me?"

"Please, please be careful and call me when you're on your way back."

442

"I promise."

***

"Ladies, my sources tell me another establishment has opened in the area. If you could do some discreet research, I'd appreciate it. Also, we need to fill that room. Take your time. We are coming to that lull at the end of the summer. Then, after Labor day, all the conventions and conferences start. The new location will entail another van. We will employ Norman to drive at night and the contact in Boston has someone to drive during the day. I hope these new arrangements will help make the house run more efficiently and ease your responsibilities. Ladies, you have served me well. Thank you."

Ellen looked puzzled. "Served?"

"It's just a word. He is telling us he is pleased with our work." Ellen could be overly sensitive. "Are you unhappy here?"

"This is better than anything I could have imagined, but our time is not our own, and one wrong move, well, you know what could happen."

"Who else would he get to do the things we do? Unless he shuts down the operation, I think he knows we are not replaceable. Besides, I know people."

"What the hell does that mean?"

"It means I'm not worried about leaving here until I want to."

Ellen was anxious about her future, but she had to trust Maude— and that worried her even more.

***

Ben went to the hotel with one task: to gather information about the brothel's operation. He knew the backstory on the corporate account was airtight, but he needed to be cautious not to ask too many questions. Anyone who had used a service like this would recognize questions that might raise alarms.

He spotted the Concierge Desk. The man he needed to speak to was occupied, soothing an irritated woman who appeared to have had too much to drink. Ben checked his watch—quarter to two? He shook his head and moved toward the lounge.

His jaw dropped when he looked into the bar. He almost laughed, ducking behind an artificial tree in the corner between the lounge and the lobby. A column, about six inches from the entryway, provided a perfect vantage point. He looked, scrutinizing the lounge. Holding his phone, he zoomed in and took several pictures of the woman. *I thought I was seeing things. It's her!* Ben felt a surge of encouragement, but suspicion crept in. *This makes no sense.*

He remained in place, keeping an eye on the Concierge, but his focus shifted to the woman at the bar. Standing in the same spot, he kept glancing at his phone. He quickly became adept at peeking over the top of his glasses to survey the scene, snapping pictures of any suspicious characters when needed. To anyone else in the hotel lobby, he looked like just another person absorbed in their phone.

Ben looked up. The man walking toward the lounge wasn't interested in his surroundings. Ben was able to take pictures of him without looking obvious. He watched as the man approached the woman at the bar. The man declined a drink when asked. Instead, he finished the woman's martini, and they both headed toward the elevator. Ben switched to video as they exited the lounge. They went into the elevator alone, but Ben managed to get a shot before the door closed as the woman kissed the man passionately. Ben was in shock as he walked to the lounge. The bartender hadn't taken the martini glass. Ben reached for his credentials and an evidence bag "I need that glass."

"Oh, um." The bartender looked around "OK."

"Have they been here before?"

"A few times."

Ben took out a twenty from his pocket. "Thank you."

Ben stopped at the concierge desk to inform the man that he had been called back to the office and would return later. He then headed to his car "Harry, you may need to sit down…" Ben couldn't believe what he was seeing, but as he told Harry, he scanned the pictures again "I thought I was seeing things… her hair is a different color, but it's her and that man from the Pub and the Gala. Harry, I need to get back to the office, then I'll be home. Could you call…"

"Way ahead of you. Ben be careful coming home. Do not take this as an endorsement to do this kind of thing again, but Ben, this is monumental. I'll see you soon."

***

Maggie and John went grocery shopping. From their conversations, she knew he liked to grill, so they bought steaks and chicken, as well as everything needed for lasagna. While they were putting everything away, Maggie confessed about her fib "…I'm sorry I lied, but as soon as I saw you I regretted what I said. I don't want to play mind games with you."

"Would I be wrong to think you told Joel?"

"No, not at all. Even if I hadn't told him, I had already decided to tell you the truth."

"You will find out soon enough. I am pretty understanding."

Maggie leaned over the stove "I think maybe I needed to give you a reason… whooo, sometimes I think the only thing I'm good for is…" She started to walk away.

"Please finish your thought."

She couldn't look at him. "Yes Doctor, sometimes I think the only thing I'm good for is sex. In my mind, if you saw what those people did to me, you would confirm what I was feeling about myself: that I was a tramp who was only good for one thing, and you would leave before you got in too deep."

"Please look at me. I need you to look at me."

She looked up "I'm sorry. This is not what I wanted to talk about. I want to learn about your childhood, and your other brother and your sister. Your father. Who was your first love? Do you like dogs or cats? Are there any foods you don't like?" She took a deep breath "Dr. Evans, am I ever going to be normal again?"

"Is this because you met Harlow? Or are you trying to convince me I don't want to fall in love with you?"

"Yes." She chuckled "All of the above. John, I'm nervous. We are finally alone, really alone and I'm a nervous wreck."

"I can leave."

Maggie was surprised at first, but then she realized it was a joke and chuckled "I don't want you to ever regret meeting me."

"Maggie, I promise you, that will never happen." He kissed her "How about we eat outside…"

***

Harry and Ben went to Beau's office, where Kathryn was waiting with Beau.

"I asked Kathryn to meet us here. I need to tell you both what has been going on, but I don't think either of you are going to believe me."

Harry continued "We stumbled on some information about the brothel."

Beau sat up in his chair.

"They must have been scared off because they moved the operation. We got a warrant to go into the stone house at the end of the cove. We found Ben and Merritt's guns and credentials and Merritts dress, but everything else had been cleaned out."

Beau grumbled "That house has always been a mystery. It's no wonder I couldn't find anything about its owners."

"We couldn't find anything either, Beau," Ben admitted.

"We've also been investigating the couple Ben and Merritt met at the Pub and at the Gala. We have no idea who they are, but we think they are involved. I asked Ben to do some investigating. Because of the letters we got about the brothel we had some details about how to contact them. Ben found a luxury hotel in Boston with a concierge who may be the go between. While he was waiting to talk to the concierge, he saw someone familiar in the lounge, actually two people, who ended up… well take a look at the video."

Ben had transferred the video to his tablet and handed it to Beau and Kathryn. Beau stood up, looked out the window, and rubbed his face.

Kathryn looked at Ben "Is that the man who was groping Merritt?"

"Uh huh," Ben grunted.

"And you think he has something to do with the brothel?"

Harry continued, "Ben and Merritt had engaged them. They were interested in…"

Ben interrupted "We think they are swingers."

Beau was dumbfounded "I wonder if this man is the reason Julie was so distant for so long?"

"The bartender said they have been in a few times."

Kathryn was furious. "And she had the nerve to accuse us of having an affair?"

"Excuse me?" Ben was surprised.

"We've been friends since we were teenagers. Julie saw us talking and assumed." Beau handed the tablet back to Ben. He looked at Harry "So, what now?"

"I need to read you in on an aspect of the case that I hope Julie isn't involved with, but please, Beau, this is a Federal case…"

"I know how to keep my mouth shut… I'm sorry, this is truly surreal."

"Kathryn, are you comfortable hearing this?"

"No; well yes. Go ahead. We need to know."

"Naomi and I were assigned to a serial case in Baltimore. Her cover was blown and she was taken hostage by a man who drugged her. We believe he was using her for leverage. Naomi believed there was a partner. She remembers hearing a woman who seemed to be in charge. Ben and the team eventually rescued Naomi and the man was arrested."

Kathryn admitted "I don't like where this is going."

"There was a woman with the couple at the Gala. She must have crossed someone because she was found near a pond in a wooded area of New Hampshire, same victimology as the others. Before she was found we had no idea who she was, but her DNA matches the unknown DNA in Naomi's case. It also matches the DNA found on Ben and Merritts belongings. Unfortunately, she is in the wind. She subdued the guard at the hospital and stole a car. We decided not to tell the ladies. We may have to, but for now…"

"You think Julie is involved somehow?"

Harry stressed "We do not know. I have to ask a question though. I know Julie has a brother. What happened?"

Beau confessed "No one really knows. It was between Harold and Chip."

Harry took a deep breath "There is another reason we believe Julie may be involved. The other day when Stella began to remember she told us she saw a man and a woman. She also read the man's lips. She didn't understand everything, but she definitely saw him say *Mr. Smith, Silvie and Chip.*"

"Have any of the other women heard those names?" Kathryn asked.

"Merritt and I haven't been involved in the case. She is still on disability, and her memory is spotty, but I will ask her."

"Kathryn, Beau, it's too much of a coincidence, and since we don't believe in coincidences, we have to ask about Julie's brother."

Beau and Kathryn looked at each other. "Beau and I don't bring up Chip. Julie and Chip were incredibly close…"

"Too close." Beau groaned.

"They always seemed to have secrets. Then something happened. Harold disowned Chip. I mean, he already had his trust fund, so he didn't need anything else, but Harold wouldn't talk about him. Whatever it was, I think it eventually killed him."

"Beau, for someone who is obviously deeply in love with Trinity, you are still worried about Julie. Has there been anything she has done…?"

"Beau, think before you answer that." Kathryn was stern.

"Ben, I never wanted to hurt Julie. We lived in the same house, but she left me. For a year and a half, she was somewhere else, everyone saw it. Then as soon as I told her Trinity was missing, she was the old Julie again… this isn't the first time I have thought about this, but I did think Julie might have had something to do with Trinity's disappearance, but it didn't cross my mind until after Trinity was found and Julie threatened her… Kathryn, I'm sorry, but if she is somehow involved in this don't you want to know?"

"I am in a difficult position. I'm glad you trusted me enough to tell me, but you know there are things I can't say. Shaw and I will be joining a firm…"

"Kathryn, my former boss is good friends with the owner of that law firm. I met him at some social functions. Talk to him. He is known for making himself available."

"I will, thank you. This is very upsetting for me. I actually feel like a fool. Has she been tricking us for the past two years? Is she in business with Chip running a brothel? I am torn between the woman I have known since Harold introduced Julie to Beau and the thought she has an alter ego who would run a business that has hurt so many people. The woman in those photos and that video is not the woman we know."

***

Ben went straight to the bedroom. Merritt was waiting "What's going on?"

"As much as you are going to want to share this with the others, for the time being, it needs to stay between us."

449

"You're wearing your FBI face." Merritt was joking, but Ben's expression remained unchanged.

"Do you know the name of the woman who was with that couple at the Gala?"

"Ya, it's Sylvie. Why?"

Ben took a deep breath. He embraced Merritt "This is going to take a while…"

Merritt's face was pale. "She was here today?"

Phil didn't get there in time. You know as well as I do sociopaths are usually very intelligent. She probably sensed they were on to her. Honey, we are so much closer than we were."

"Honey? What happened to sweet cheeks?"

"They are still here." Ben held her rear end as he kissed her "This woman is dangerous."

"Is Naomi OK?"

"I haven't talked to her, but Harry said she is fine."

"Correct me if I'm wrong, she will not be happy until she kills Naomi because it is her fault her partner is in jail."

"I think she is staking out the Pub. Sylvie will want to kill her, but not before she tortures her."

"What about us?"

"One of the reasons we want to keep everyone together is because of the people behind the brothel. You know it's the best plan."

"You can't be responsible for everyone, Ben."

"John and I talked about that while Naomi was in the hospital. I knew it wasn't my fault she was abducted, but getting her back was my mission, and I may have forgotten to sleep for a week or so."

"You were so guilty when we were taken. You never admitted it but you blame yourself for falling in love with me and being distracted. You put your heart and soul into a case. I'm glad John OK'd you for limited duty, but please remember, you have a woman who loves you deeply. Please don't do anything stupid my love.

"Why does everyone keep saying that to me?"

"Because they know you. I can't lose you Ben."

"You won't lose me, sweet cheeks."

***

John was nervous. He knew he loved Maggie, so sleeping together—just sleeping—would be a challenge. He stripped down to his boxer shorts and sat leaning against the headboard, turning on the TV to watch the early news.

He was also making notes on his tablet for his mother about Harlow. *Based on conversations with the other ladies, Harlow was suicidal, begging to be killed rather than endure further abuse. All the ladies speculated that she might have been a virgin when she was taken.* John had been hopeful when Harlow remembered talking to Maggie and Trinity, but he worried she might have slipped into a fugue state.

When the bathroom door opened, John set the tablet down on the nightstand. He saw Maggie walking toward the bed. A faint ray of light from a streetlamp outside peeked through the shades and crossed her face.

John was speechless. Maggie looked stunning. Her hair, usually pulled back, now cascaded over her shoulders and almost to her waist. He hadn't expected her to be wearing a negligee, and he wasn't prepared for this moment. He had hoped it would happen sooner rather than later, but he had imagined a different scenario for their first time. He wanted to say something, but he didn't want to spoil the moment, so he decided to let her take the lead.

"When you said we could go to the hospital with you, Matilda suggested I call and try to change my appointment."

"Matilda said you went to the ladies room when I asked where you were." John moved to the other side of the bed "I am speechless."

"Clara bought this for me so I would be ready when it was time."

"I've never been in this position before. I am so in awe of you…"

"Please don't make me cry."

"Is this why you were so upset before?"

"I was scared I would disappoint you. John, I need you to know something. Even if this doesn't work out, even if I can't, or it is so awful you hide in the bathroom, I want you to know I love you, but I really like you too and no matter what happens, I need you in my life."

"I'm not going anywhere. Maggie, I love you too."

John and Maggie were kissing. He lay on top of her, his hands resting under her shoulder blades. She had her hands on the sides of his head, fingers laced through his hair. She moved her hands to his face and pulled away, gazing into his eyes "That was awful."

"Give me about twenty minutes. I know I can do better."

Maggie slapped his butt "You mean that wasn't you're A game?"

"I can't show you all my moves all at once."

"I know we bought a lot of food, but would you mind if we stayed right here all weekend?"

"You and I are going to be OK Peaches."

"We have a lot more to talk about."

"More!" John blurted out.

"Oh my God, I love you."

"Good."

***

"You never told me what that phone call was all about yesterday."

"That call was from the store. An FBI Agent came in. There was a stolen car found in the back. You're not going to like this, but Sylvie stole it from a hospital parking lot. He said she is a person of interest in several federal cases."

"Are you worried?"

"No. She doesn't know how to find us."

"OK, I trust you. What have you decided to do with Zoey?"

"We honey, we need to decide."

"She seems perfect, but then Sylvie did too. Did you ask her how long she is in town?"

"At least another week. My biggest concern is she is married so we cannot hold on to her, she would be reported missing, and I've been seen with her at the hotel bar."

"Maybe we need to spell out our concerns and see if we can set up a schedule. We may have to give up on the idea of keeping her for the house." Kim needed to contemplate her options. She had to figure out if Steve planned to keep her for himself. For the first time since they met, she was concerned that Steve's feelings for one of their sexual partners went beyond infatuation.

"Honey, this needs to be a mutual decision." Steve knew how insecure Kim could be, but he needed to find a way to keep Zoey; if not as a threesome, he absolutely had to have her for himself "Can we talk about this later? I love the time we have to ourselves."

Steve and Kim finished dinner and went about their usual routine— having beer and popcorn while watching TV. Lucia and Chuck, their live-in help, occupied the guest house. They always announced when they were retiring for the evening. Steve trusted them, but only because their bedroom suite was monitored. If anyone tried to enter their private space, he would receive a notification. The couple had been in Kim and

Steve's employ for seven years, and the sanctity of their space had never been violated.

"Honey, you have been quiet."

Kim heaved a sigh. "Apparently, your father and my father have been talking again."

"That can't be good. Let me guess. They want to know when we are going to start a family."

"Yup."

"I'm sorry. I'm sure my father was the instigator."

"Maybe just one?..."

***

Beau and Harry decided they needed to confide in Simon. Beau knew it was the only way Simon would allow Harry to speak with Stella. After dinner, Beau asked to see Simon in the solarium, where Harry was already waiting.

"Simon, we have some information we need to share with you before I speak to Stella."

"I don't think that is a very good idea."

"Simon, there are a couple of photos and a video. Stella said she saw a man talking in her room. The rest, you will figure out on your own."

"Beau, you're upset. Why are you telling me this?"

"My emotions are all over the place, but you'll understand soon enough."

"Look at the pictures first, then you can start the video." Harry handed Simon the tablet.

Simon swiped through the pictures. "Julie?"

"Watch the video."

Simon's mouth was hanging open "I didn't think anything could surprise me anymore. I am flabbergasted. Is that the man Merritt was dancing with at the Gala?"

"Yes. We don't know who he is, but we do know Julie has met up with him several times in the hotel bar."

Simon was furious. "Is that where she was after Stella was taken?"

Beau put his arm around Simon. "We don't know."

"Her name doesn't show up on the days after the Gala. Simon, people who have Julie's wealth can buy anything. She probably has more than one set of credentials. Most hotels will always ask for ID at check in."

"But why, I don't understand."

Harry explained "The day Stella remembered; she told us what she saw a man say. It didn't make any sense to her, or us, but it does now. We think Mr. Smith may be a client or even the proprietor. She also said she saw the man say Sylvie and Chip…" Harry stopped when he saw the look on Simon's face.

Simon looked at Beau "Are you freaking kidding me?"

"No. Simon, there is more. The woman we told you about. She is Sylvie.

"Beau, do you think Chip is capable of running something like this?"

"I've thought about that. If Harold found out what he was involved with, it could be the reason Harold disowned Chip."

"And this man Julie is with?" Simon wondered.

Harry was honest "We don't know. Stella saw the couple at the Gala. Having her do a composite of the man she saw talking would raise all kinds of objections."

"But if you show her the video, and without prompting from us, she identifies him as the man she saw…?"

"Simon, since Shaw isn't here. Kathryn is talking with their new boss. We gave her questions to ask him. She is on our side Simon. She was as shocked as any of us, and I believe angrier."

"I know Stella will want to help, but what about Billie? She saw one of them too."

"Billie is going to do a composite at some point."

Chapter 36

Steve was up early but didn't wake Kim. He told Lucia he needed to check on an issue at the warehouse, knowing Kim would believe him, especially after the phone call story the day before. However, Steve went to the hotel instead and texted Zoey that he was on his way up.

When Kim went downstairs for breakfast, she was ready to go out. Lucia told her that Steve was at the office, but Kim didn't buy it. When asked, Lucia said Steve had left an hour ago.

She decided to drive into Boston, making the hotel's garage her first stop. As she slowly drove through, she scanned the cars carefully. There were many black Mercedes, but Steve's had a distinct three-number prefix: SNM.

She stopped behind his car and shifted into park. Unsure of what she was going to do, she knew she couldn't stay there. Finding a spot to park, she headed into the lobby. She grabbed a newspaper and positioned herself on the far side, at an angle where she could still see the elevators.

Kim glanced at her watch and estimated that Steve had already been there for two hours. Her anger was slowly giving way to a deep sadness. At first, she hadn't been the kind of woman Steve wanted. She quickly realized that if she didn't adapt, she would lose him. She didn't want to share him, nor did she want to hurt other women, but if she wanted Steve in her life, she had to adjust—and she did, until Zoey came into the picture. Kim couldn't let Zoey take Steve from her. She needed a plan— one that would get rid of Zoey, permanently.

***

John smelled coffee and reached for Maggie, but she was gone. He had expected her to come through the bedroom door, holding two cups of coffee. He grinned, remembering how he had suggested they spend the weekend together. At first, he wondered if Maggie would fully recover, but despite the rocky start the night before, it had ended better than he could have hoped.

John got out of bed, went to the bathroom, and brushed his teeth. As he walked back to the bed, Maggie returned, holding two mugs of coffee. She was wearing John's shirt, her hair disheveled. In her best southern drawl she said "Good morning darlin' Coffee?"

John took the mugs from her, placed them on the desk, then leaned her back and kissed her with all the passion he could muster…

"Ooh, minty."

John laughed and kissed her again.

Maggie handed John his coffee. "I like your birthday suit."

"It's very comfortable so I hope you won't mind seeing me in it, a lot."

"I'd like that… I never imagined being this happy." She climbed back into the bed with her coffee "Dr. Evans, in the beginning of a relationship is there such a thing as too much sex?"

"It depends on the couple. You and I, too much will never be enough."

"Hmm. What would the other Dr. Evans say?"

"Depends on which one you talk to. My brother, my sister, my mother or my father?"

"Dear God."

"We are just regular people, Peaches."

"Who does your sense of humor come from?"

"Mom. Engineers aren't usually known for their pithy banter."

"Does your father know?"

"That he's not funny? Yes."

Maggie laughed, but quickly looked down and took a deep breath. She then met John's gaze "Any advice as to how I get this under control?" Her eyes were full of tears "I am so overwhelmed with everything that has happened since last night, I'm afraid I'm going to wake up. When will I stop being afraid?"

"When our life together begins to have some order. Right now, there is no order. You have been up in the air living at Trip's. Until last night, you weren't sure about me. Believe me when I tell you there was no hesitation last night. You were the woman I hoped you would be; the woman I knew you could be."

"Our life together? Do you have any idea how happy I am to hear you say that?"

"Sorry Peaches, but you don't look happy."

Maggie placed the coffee cups on the nightstand. John leaned back as Maggie straddled his waist, leaned forward, and kissed him "Oh I am happy darlin'."

***

Abby went to Cubby's office "I haven't heard any updates about the case. Should I ask Harry?"

"Abbs, he's been upfront with us."

"No, Ben was upfront."

"I don't see either of them playing games. They made a deal with you. Trust they will keep that promise… Have you talked to Kathryn in the past couple of days?"

"I know she's busy with the merger, and I've been busy at the house."

Cubby was worried. "Something happened yesterday. You know I don't pry, but she was really distracted."

"I'm sure she is worried about Julie."

"No, she seemed angry. Not at me, but something happened. She said she hopes she will be able to talk about it soon.

"Since Shaw and Dalton are away, Merritt and Ben are going to stay at their house with Harry…"

"Is someone talking about me?" Harry wanted to be honest with Julie and Cubby. "Has anyone spoken about Harlow to either of you?"

"Yes, Clara thought she knew her?"

"She is in the hospital and will be at your father's probably Monday." Harry held his tablet in his hand "You have both been incredibly patient with this story. I need your word that what I'm about to tell you will stay between us, well actually, we told Simon, Beau and Kathryn yesterday."

"We won't hurt the women. They are more important than the story. You have our word."

Harry paced as he told the story. He handed the tablet to Cubby.

Abby's face was flushed "Is it possible she is trying to get back at Beau and being with this guy is a coincidence?"

"We don't believe in coincidences, but we do wonder if when she was gone last time, she was with him too."

"Now I understand why Kathryn was so upset."

"Do you have any pictures of the woman who was with the couple at the Gala?" Harry hoped.

"I will email all of the photos that were taken if that will help?"

"Thank you Cubby, that would be great. Abby, are you OK?"

"Ya. Is Beau all right?"

"He is, I'm not sure there is a word to describe his mood. I think more than anything, he is worried about his kids, and about Trinity's safety."

Abby was concerned "I think all of the ladies are probably in danger."

"They are safe at the house. Between us, I put in a request for security at the house. Your father agreed to ask them to stay with them. Billie will be living with Juice. Phil has gotten the Select Board approval for her to join the department. She will be safe. I hope Trinity stays there. I know Simon is more at ease knowing Stella is there. I have a feeling after this weekend Maggie and John will know if they will be planning a future together…"

"And Harlow? Someone in a government office saw that APB; could there be people shielding the organization?"

"I think Kathryn will be happy I told you, but she spoke to her new boss yesterday about what she can legally tell us about Julie and her business dealings. She wants to help, but she is angry, and I believe hurt. But I also asked her if she would tell him about what happened with Harlow and her attorney. I believe he is the only attorney who will help us decide if we should tell Harlow's attorney we found her. At this point we don't know if we can trust him, but legally?"

"If it is Chip who is running this place he has the funds to secure protection."

"We know, that is why we have to be careful who we tell about Harlow being safe."

Cubby stood up behind his desk "Harry, Julie knows where the ladies are staying. I think it would be reckless to share the news that Harlow was released."

"I agree with you, but as I said, legally?"

***

"May I call your brother? I need him to know how much he did for me."

"Peaches, he knows. I sent him a text with ten red hearts, that's all. He texted back, he could tell you loved me. He is happy for us."

"I'd like to tell him myself."

John reached for his phone on the nightstand, sent a text, then got out of bed to grab his tablet. Meanwhile, Maggie reached down to pick up the shirt she had been wearing "Are you going to put on a shirt or something?"

"He has seen me naked, Peaches."

"Well at least pull up the sheet. Geesh."

Bloop, bloop.

"I didn't expect to hear from either of you this weekend. Maggie, is that your shirt?"

"No. At least I had the decency to put something on." Maggie moved the tablet in front of John.

"Hi there. Maggie wanted to talk to you."

"I wanted to thank you again. John didn't know I saw my doctor yesterday. I didn't want to say anything just in case I couldn't go through with it. Thank you."

"My first thought was to make a joke, but I will be nice. Welcome to the family Maggie."

"Mom will be here on Tuesday. Maggie is nervous. I'm hoping by then she will realize she has nothing to worry about."

"I know I won't be one hundred percent, but I'm getting there. I did want you to know that you helped. Joel, thank you."

"Maggie, Mom is very easy to talk to. You are very open and honest. She admires those qualities. By the way, your hair looks really nice like that."

"You mean a mess? It hasn't been cut since, well, before. I've actually never worn it this long. I like it. Imagine that." Maggie looked down and let out a long breath "How about from now on I apologize to you first, then we can go on to our conversation. I have no idea where the crying comes from. It is really getting on my nerves." Maggie chuckled "Sorry."

"You're using humor to mask your anger, your sadness. If you don't want to talk to John, you can call me. I won't always be able to answer, but I will call you back. But promise me, if your anger takes over, you need to talk about it. Don't be afraid to ask if you want a regular appointment. I want to help if you'll let me."

"You enjoy seeing me cry don't you? I'm still in a place where I don't feel worthy, but not nearly as much since last night. Your brother actually made it possible for me to forget. I'll be OK." Maggie smiled "Thank you again. I'm going to take a shower. Please feel free to talk about me behind my back." She kissed John and jogged to the bathroom.

John waited until the door closed "I've been contemplating whether she needs to see someone. The crying is troubling."

"Have you asked her to start a journal?"

"No, but I will. I'll be off next week while Mom is here. She will be staying in the pool house where Maggie has been staying. There are two women there that really need someone like Mom."

"I am truly happy for you."

"I've never felt like this before."

"You've been in love before."

"Not like this. It's a new feeling for me. I feel like a kid again."

"I'll talk to you soon. I love you."

"I love you too."

John approached the bathroom door and heard Maggie crying. He paused for a moment, took a deep breath, then knocked softly before stepping inside "May I join you?"

Maggie opened the curtain. Her hair in a big bun. Her body covered in soap "As long as you promise to wash my back."

John held her head and kissed her. "I love you."

***

Brock was worried about Kathryn. She usually stopped by to see the girls on Saturday morning, but today she hadn't shown up. Since Jack was on shift, he called Cubby. He admitted he wasn't sure what was going on. After arranging for Clara to babysit, he headed to Beau's office, knowing he was typically there on Saturday mornings.

Brock saw Beau at his desk with his head resting in his hands. "Are you OK?"

Beau looked up "This is a little freaky. I was just thinking about you. Considering how young we were at the time; you and I had some very mature discussions."

"Jack and I are together partly because of your compassion. You and Kathryn were the only friends I had. Tell me what is going on."

"I know I can trust you, but some of this is just too much. I don't want to dump it on you."

"Kathryn is upset. Julie is missing again. I want to help if I can."

"Do you know about me and Trinity?"

"Not really. Beau there is no judgment here."

Beau went to the office door and locked it. "This is going to take a while. I guess I should start with Kathryn and me…"

Brock laughed "That you were more than friends? We lived in the same house. It wasn't my business, but I came home one day and heard you in the den. I went back out and came back later. I don't think anyone else saw the glances between you two. I know her so well and you had become a confidant. It is something I think about on occasion. Your secret has always been safe with me."

"Thanks. Well, we never talked about it until right before Julie went away again. Let me start with Trinity…"

Brock remained patient, keeping his thoughts to himself. Beau was almost finished when both men's phones buzzed at the same time...

Beau got up and unlocked the door. "Did Brock and I say your name too many times?"

"I'm surprised you know that reference Beau."

Brock embraced Kathryn "Honey, I was worried about you."

"Clara told me you were here. What are we talking about?" Kathryn stared at Beau.

"Honey, I wanted to talk to Beau about Julie. I knew your mood had to have something to do with her disappearance. I won't spill the beans, I promise."

"Did you tell him everything?"

"He already knew. He's known all along."

"Of course you did." Kathryn wept on Brock's shoulder "I don't know what to do. How could she do this to her children, to your family Beau, to me?"

"Honey, you need to talk to Cubby; he is worried about you."

"I will. I had a wonderful video call with my new boss. I needed to give him the opportunity to back out of our merger. Given the ramifications of a possible scandal… I am her attorney. I thought she was a good friend. Beau, I'm sorry. I should have known."

"No, none of this is your fault."

Brock wondered, "Honey, what was the outcome of your call?"

"He said he was happy to have Shaw and me in his organization and nothing I had told him would change that. He said he respected me for being upfront with him and he would work with me to handle any repercussions that may develop."

"Kathryn, Harry talked with Abby and Cubby yesterday. They will not let the details get out."

"Beau, what about the kids?"

"Harry needs to find out if Julie is involved first."

"Beau, she is going to have to find another lawyer. I can't represent her anymore."

"Will you hold off on that decision? She is going to need you especially if this is an incredible coincidence. I can't blame her if she needs to get back at me somehow. She started changing before I met Trinity, so my thought was she found out what was going on with Chip and she was caught between him and Harold. I don't know why she didn't think she could talk to me, or you. When Harold died I tried to talk to her, we all did, but she wasn't interested. I'm not going to leave Trinity, not now. Brock, she wants to meet you; Jack and Molly too."

"Brock, she's funny. I have no idea what she's doing with this guy. I'm going to see if I can get Cubby to take a few days off so we can get away. Beau, I won't make a decision about Julie until I know all the facts."

"Thank you."

***

Beau went home to talk to his father. He was concerned about bringing Trinity to the other house, where she would be alone for much of the day, so they decided to stay together at Trip's house.

Trip knew Maggie and Merritt had become friends, and he thought they could all live in the house on the beach. One of the many attractions for vacationing families was the private yard behind the house. He had already arranged for the internet provider to install exterior cameras and a security system. He hoped Ben and John would at least consider it.

"Trip, it's a perfect plan. Thank you."

"When Martin was here, one of his concerns was Maggie's safety. He knew she couldn't stay here forever. Harry, John and I assuaged his fears."

"Dad, there is more to consider now. I don't want to keep anything from you, but I also don't want to have to ask you to keep a confidence. I need to be honest with you about what has been going on. I know I can trust you, but…"

Knock, knock… "Trip, it's Harry. I need to speak to you."

Beau answered, "Come in."

"I'm glad you're here, Beau. I think, under the circumstances, Trip needs to be read in."

"That's a relief. He needs to know. But you also need to know about Dad's idea…"

Harry began by recounting Ben's visit to the hotel for Trip. Beau stood by the window in Trip's office, listening to the story as he had the first time, still in shock. As Harry finished describing what had happened, Beau felt a hand grasp his shoulder from behind.

"I'm sorry Beau. You know I will do whatever I can…"

"Dad, he's not finished. Believe it or not, it gets worse."

Harry shared the details of Stella's memory, and the look on Trip's face broke Beau's heart "I think Harold found out and Julie was caught in the middle, but I also think that was what caused the falling-out."

"Indeed. Beau, again I'm sorry."

"Thank you but you have nothing to be sorry about. Harry, we'd like to ask John and Maggie to live at the beach with Merritt and Ben."

"I cannot assume Julie is going down without a fight. I asked Kathryn to keep an open mind about staying on as Julie's attorney. Just because she is having an affair doesn't mean she is a criminal. I don't want her to be, but if she is I will not allow her to have custody. Trinity will understand if we can't live together for a while. If Julie isn't involved, I have to do what is best for the kids. Her abilities as a mother have never been in doubt."

"Shaw should be back before you need to make a decision. Listen to him Beau, even if you disagree with him, his counsel has always been sound."

***

John watched as Maggie worked in the kitchen, making lasagna—a dish she called laborious "But you'll love it."

John was making notes again, drafting Ben's back-to-work order. He knew Ben was skilled at compartmentalizing—something the best agents had to master to maintain healthy relationships with friends and family. He didn't believe Ben had crossed a line by getting involved with Merritt, so he left their friendship out of his report.

He paused, watching Maggie as she sang softly. He couldn't make out the words, but the tune sounded like *Make You Feel My Love*. He wondered if his love for Maggie was clouding his judgment. He also questioned whether his initial attraction to her stemmed from her need to be loved, paired with his instinct to help her through her nightmare. Her honesty drew him in; though she couldn't look at him directly, he could hear the heartbreaking urgency in her voice. She wanted to move beyond her confinement, yet she needed support. Watching her sing, he felt hopeful. She stopped singing as she placed the bowls and utensils in the sink.

"I have to tell you something. I went into the bathroom earlier. I heard you crying so I stepped back, knocked and went back in."

"I was going to tell you, but I feel like I need to handle the crying jags myself."

"What happened?"

"I heard you and Joel saying *I love you*. It was so sweet hearing that men can open up like that, and I kind of fell apart."

"We're best friends and brothers, and being twins connects us on a spiritual level."

"Triple threat."

"Exactly. I will always know him and love him more than anyone."

"That's cool. Was it a problem before?"

"No. Grace was very busy, very dedicated. Joel noticed how she changed the subject when anyone asked about kids before I would admit it to myself. I think she was a little bothered by my friendship with Joel. I will tend to talk to him about things. I don't think that will ever change."

"How does his wife feel about you two?"

"We tended to mess with her. We were in some of the same classes. She was attracted to Joel. After a while we decided to play with her. She is so smart. She caught on right away and turned the tables on us. They hadn't slept together yet, so one day, she grabbed me after class and took me to her room. She pinned me in the corner, and as she was about to kiss me, she started laughing. She said *You two are evil, but I can't do this to Joel.*"

"I will like her?"

"You will love her."

"We need to talk about our living arrangements."

"I know. I… I'm not in a position to ask you to move for me. It's too much to ask."

"You liked Matilda's house."

"It's perfect for a family, and being near everyone, especially Clara is important."

"I agree, but I thought you might like to be closer to town."

"Did you have something in mind?"

"Beau has a house near Juice and Lenny's."

Maggie was trying very hard not to cry.

"It's OK to cry. I love you. I love Cape Hope. Ben and Merritt are buying a house. I know we will be happy there."

"This is happening so fast. Are you sure you want to get mixed up with the likes of me?"

"Not really, but I'm willing to give you a shot."

***

When Julie became Zoey, it was a complete transformation; Julie ceased to exist.

She discovered her brother's preferences before their father did. At first, she was appalled, but her love for her brother won out, and when he suggested she meet with a friend, she went along with it.

Julie had attended Catholic girls' schools and was naïve. Chip's friend introduced her to a new lifestyle, one that Beau never suspected. He would never have believed she was leading a double life.

Soon after their first meeting, Julie and Chip began making weekly trips to the house, but these visits grew increasingly time-consuming. During their travels, they often discussed a property near Cape Hope—a house that had once belonged to their mother. The home, held in a trust to be split between Chip and Julie, was one they had no interest in restoring, so it sat untouched at the end of the cove, gathering dust. The trust's attorney managed the property, covering its taxes from quarterly dividends. Julie hadn't thought much about it until they considered using another location.

Julie contacted the trust attorney, had her share transferred to Chip, and helped him renovate the house, thinking it was the right thing to do. That was until Harold stumbled upon their enterprise. They never found out how he learned about the house, but since the deed was in his wife's great-grandmother's name, he made assumptions about who was running the business. Chip had no desire to implicate Julie, so the secret stayed between them, leaving Julie with mounting guilt.

They rarely discussed the business side of the operation, but Chip was her closest confidant. When Julie noticed Beau's car parked in Trinity's garage, she confided her suspicions of an affair to Chip. He reassured her that Beau would never do such a thing, and since she worshiped her brother, she believed him—at least until Beau mentioned his friend who seemed to be missing. Julie had asked Chip to handle Trinity, knowing her brother had a hand in her disappearance. With her husband back, Julie didn't care what became of Trinity. But when Stella disappeared, panic set in, and she sought refuge in the one place she felt safe and cared for. She and Chip went to the South Shore.

Chip stayed with her for several days, then disappeared without warning. Julie returned home a day later, only to find her world unraveling. Unable to reach Chip, she decided to go to Boston, knowing he owned a hotel where she could hide. When she met the man she'd come to know as Bill, she thought he looked familiar but brushed it off, captivated by his charm.

He was unlike anyone she'd known before. In past relationships, she'd lose herself in the moment, then go home and leave the experience behind. But Steve lingered in her thoughts; she knew she was falling for him. When he texted that he'd see her in the morning, she went shopping for special undergarments—something she'd never done for Beau. She needed her time with him to feel different, to last.

Julie knew she had to tell Bill she needed to go home; it was time to pick up her kids. School would be starting again, and she'd return to the life that wasn't entirely her own. Though she no longer felt beholden to Beau, her kids needed their mother. But Julie also needed Bill and was determined to find a way to keep him in her life.

***

Harry went to Phil's office to update him on the case. Phil already knew about Harlow, but Harry needed to fill him in on everything "We have decided that, except for Merritt and Billie, we won't be telling the ladies." Harry had to ask a difficult question. Phil could feel the tension "Lenny; will he…"

"Lenny will not do anything to prevent these people from being captured and prosecuted. He will not compromise the case."

"I had to ask, but I would still like him to stay on the periphery."

"I understand. He will as well."

"I will be posting someone at Trip's."

"What about Naomi? What about Matilda?"

Harry understood Phil's concern. "It's hard to know what to do in this case because we don't know if Julie is involved."

"I would think she would be home when her kids get home."

"That is Saturday. We will see. If she doesn't come home, I will be forced to put out an APB."

"This man; did you check facial rec?"

"He either doesn't have a license or… I really don't know. I believe he is connected enough to do whatever he wants. I really detest people who believe they are above the law."

"Since we have the photo of the man Tim labeled a misogynist and this man, we would need a photo of Julie's brother. Then we can set up a photo array for Billie and Stella."

"You know Simon better than I do, but he is making unilateral decisions for Stella. I understand his need to protect her, but she's a big girl, Phil."

"We all thought they were too young to be so serious. They were always together. They both went to school in Boston and after surviving dorm life freshman year, they got an apartment together. You know how intense pre-med can be. In some ways, Pharmacology is harder. They both maintained three point eight averages. Most kids wouldn't have lasted through that. They are the epitome of the word *soulmates.*"

"Phil, thank you for telling me. Will I be looked upon as a monster if I sidestep Simon and go straight to Stella?"

"No, not at all, but I would ask that you have John there too."

"Good enough."

***

Maggie was packing her bag. "I'm going to miss you."

"I think this will be a good test for you."

"Just me?"

"I won't always be able to take time off. You need to learn to fill your day without me."

"I know. This weekend has been perfect, but I am scared. I'm actually screaming inside. I think I trust you more than any man, but I am truly frightened that this weekend is ending."

"Don't think of it as the weekend. Think of it as two consecutive days I didn't have to work."

Maggie chuckled "You are a very weird man. Maybe I could stay here. I'm sorry I don't know why I'm feeling so insecure."

"Your dreams have been screwing with your reality." John was worried as Maggie held him tighter "Maybe I can stay with you tonight. Trip already told me I am welcome to stay."

Maggie looked hopeful. "Are you staying at the house while your mother is here?"

"That was the next topic on my list."

"You have a list?"

He tapped his temple "In here." *Bing* "I have to get this… Hi." John walked away.

Maggie worried that her fears might come between her and John. He was incredibly understanding and loving, and she knew she had to do everything possible to keep from pushing him away.

"Hey Peaches. Harry wants me at Trip's in the morning. I guess I'll be staying with you after all… Maggie?"

"The screaming inside stopped as soon as you said you were staying with me. John, I think I need to talk to someone. I can't dump all of my fears on you. It's not fair."

"Let me call Joel. You've already made a connection, and he wants to help."

Maggie's hands were shaking as she reached for John's cheek "Thank you. I'm not going to say I'm sorry. This isn't my fault. I would forget everything if I could. I mostly put it out of my mind after we got here. I feel so safe with you, but I… I don't understand why I'm still so scared."

"Finish packing and I'll call." John kissed her "I'll be right back."

Maggie sat on the bed, listening to the sound of John's voice, though she couldn't make out his words. When he returned to the bedroom, he was smiling "He's coming next week, but he will call later to talk."

Maggie started crying, but stopped herself "Whoo, that was relief. I feel like a bottle of champagne that just popped its cork."

"That's quite an analogy. You can talk to me, Maggie. Please don't feel like you are bothering me. If I'm here, if I'm at work and available, if you need me I am here for you."

"I'm not going to say I don't deserve you, because I do. But what about Harlow? Who is she going to lean on? I think she is going to need more that we can provide."

"Mom knows. I told her what you and the other ladies heard. She will spend as much time with her as she wants."

"But what if she doesn't want help? You didn't hear her. It was heartbreaking."

"This may sound harsh, but you need to concentrate on you. You can talk to Harlow, be her friend. Don't talk about the house; talk about her. Helping her realize there is life beyond that house is what she needs, Maggie; it's what both of you need…"

"I love you so much."

"I am torn between my clinical side, who knows you need to regain your sense of self and the side who loves you. Both you and Harlow will never be the same again. Don't look at that as a bad thing. Right now, you are in mourning. That will fade with time if you let it. Don't hold on to your anger, your fear. Look forward to the wonderful life we will have. Can you do that?"

"Maybe I don't need Joel at all."

"I think you will be surprised what you tell him. He wants you to be whole again, too."

"He said I will never be the Maggie I was before."

"Your experiences mold who you are. Some people revel in their misfortune. You do not. You are trying so hard to put it behind you. Let Joel help you."

Maggie smirked. "Aren't you afraid I will fall in love with him?"

John caressed her face. "No."

"It doesn't bother you that I might be able to discuss things with him that I can't with you?"

"No. I'm hoping that will happen. You need an outlet."

"Will your mother want to talk?"

"That is up to you, but she is incredibly easy to talk to."

***

"Abby, what were you planning to do with that small room? It seems like it is the only one without a purpose."

"Maybe a nursery?"

"Don't mess with me, lady."

"We both know we want kids. We might as well get it ready, so we won't have to later."

Abby hated keeping secrets from Coop, but to preserve her sanity, she knew she had to tell him about Julie "I need to tell you something, but you need to pinky swear."

"Wow. It must be big."

Abby began to pace, "Promise me, Coop."

"Of course."

"You may need a drink…" Abby was heartbroken for her family, especially for Beau's kids. She and Cubby had already decided that, for the sake of the children, they wouldn't print certain aspects of the story unless forced to by falsehoods published by competing outlets.

Abby needed to remember everything Harry had told her. Her mind was overwhelmed, but nearly everything he said made the past couple of years fall into place. Suddenly, everything became very clear.

"Are you OK?"

"Not really. I know Beau is not without blame, but all of her weird behavior started before he met Trinity. I know I shouldn't, but I feel betrayed."

"You have been her biggest advocate. You should feel betrayed."

"Can we talk about something else?"

"On my way home tomorrow, I'm going to stop to get some paint samples. What color were you thinking for that room?"

"I suppose it depends on what we have." Abby had a sly look on her face.

"Are you?"

"I don't know. I haven't checked. This past month has been so crazy I thought it was nerves, but I've never been this late before. Even when Mom died, I was only a few days late."

"Do you have a test?"

"Yup. I'll go check, but I need to say something first. Cooper Matthews, will you make an honest woman of me?"

"Even if?"

"Even if." She kissed him "I'll go check. I'll be back in a few minutes."

Coop knew he wanted to marry Abby after their first date. Most people considered it a disaster, but Coop was thrilled to have finally met a woman who was genuine, who didn't put on airs.

By all accounts, they were perfect for each other. But something went terribly wrong—or really right, depending on how you looked at it.

They still argue about who first brought up political affiliations. Although Abby had always considered herself a moderate and Coop a conservative, they ended up on opposing sides of an argument. Neither of them remembers exactly what they were arguing about, but by the end of the night, they both knew they wanted to see each other again.

Coop was taking something out of his desk when Abby came back. "So, you never answered my question."

Coop jumped "Don't do that!" Coop held Abby's hand "You know I want to marry you. I have known since that first night. Abby Fredericks, will you be my wife?"

"Yes, of course, yes."

"And the mother of my child?"

"In about seven and a half months."

Coop took her left hand and slipped on a radiant-cut diamond, flanked by smaller ones on each side.

"How long have you had this?"

"Since the day after you told me you loved me."

"We need to tell Daddy. Do you mind having a small affair at the house, in the backyard, maybe in the fall?"

"That sounds perfect, but we need to do something before we leave."

"You are reading my mind."

***

Simon spent his breaks at the hospital with Harlow. He told her about Stella and what had happened to her, as well as about his family and where she would be staying.

"I don't know why you would want to help me."

"All of us have been affected by everything that happened there. Maggie was there the longest, as far as we know."

"I remember her sister. She lives in your father's house, too?"

"No. She met a firefighter after she came to Cape Hope. I believe they are living together, but Maggie is staying at the house. Everyone will be there tomorrow. Is that OK with you?"

"Of course. It must be a big house."

"You will be comfortable. Do you want to call anyone?"

"No! Sorry, the Agent said I don't have to call my parents. They really don't care."

"None of us want you to go through this alone. A woman will be here on Tuesday. Her son was here the other day. She is a Professor and a therapist. She wants to help if you'll let her."

"I'm not sure anyone can help. I don't know if I'll ever be OK…"

Knock, knock ... "Harlow?"

"It's Dr. Evans. His mother is the therapist." Simon said quietly.

"You can come in."

John and Maggie decided to stop and see Harlow on their way back to Cape Hope. Maggie walked past Simon and took Harlow's hand "How are you feeling?"

"Physically, much better, but my dreams are disturbing."

John stepped forward "I have time if you want to talk?"

Harlow looked at Maggie.

"I brought a book, just in case." Maggie implored, "Please, talk to him."

Harlow sighed. "I don't know; I think I'm a lost cause."

"Please, for me? He's not my therapist, but he has helped me a lot."

"You two are in love; I can tell."

"I didn't think any man would ever want me. I was wrong."

"Harlow, would you rather talk to Maggie?" John asked softly.

"How does talking help? I would think it would make it worse."

Maggie squeezed Harlow's hand "If you don't let out the grief you are feeling it will only get worse. All of us are together in Mr. Frederick's house. We all had similar experiences. At first, we didn't talk about it but being together made all of us feel better. Please, we will all help."

"Excuse me." Simon was ready to leave for the day "If Maggie wants to come home with me, Dr. Evans will stay here with you for as long as you need."

"Yes, I want to hear what you have to say, or I can talk, and you can listen but I would feel awful if I didn't try to help."

"Ah, guilt." Harlow tried not to smile "I've been in therapy before. My parents thought I needed it because I was quiet. The doctor I talked to was an ass…"

John sat in the chair next to the bed "There are parents who are too busy or simply ill-equipped to raise a child. Without knowing your family's history, I would be negligent to comment. Some believe therapy is a cure-all. Just because you were shy doesn't mean there is something wrong with you."

"My parents don't care…"

Simon and Maggie left the room without saying goodbye.

Maggie put her arm around Simon. "He really knows his stuff."

"You have an air of confidence you didn't have before; you seem more at ease."

"I saw my doctor on Friday when we were here. Simon, thank you for talking to her. She told me you sang my praises. She said you called me brave."

"You are. John's friendship has helped you a lot. He said he has learned a lot from his mother. My hope is she will be able to help Stella."

"I have talked to John's brother a few times this weekend. I am going to video chat with him. Simon, sometimes I don't feel very brave. Sometimes I want to scream at the top of my lungs."

"You have admitted you need help, that is half the battle." Simon opened the car door for Maggie "I think you would be a great counselor."

"You mean like addicts become counselors?"

"Sometimes it works that way. I've heard you talking to the others. Talk to John's mother, I have a feeling John is a little biased."

"I love him, Simon. I keep thinking I wouldn't have met him if I hadn't been abducted. I thought that would make me feel better, but it doesn't."

"What did John's brother say when you told him?"

 "He said it's natural to wonder." Maggie chuckled "He said *I can sympathize. You go through a horrific experience, and what is your reward? John. I understand, I really do.*"

***

Abby and Cooper arrived at Trip's house about an hour before dinner. The driveway was full "It sounds like everyone is out back. We can talk to Trip in his office."

Abby looked in the office "Coop, Daddy is in here." She ran to Trip "Hi, Daddy."

"Hello Trip. Abby and I would like to talk to you about something."

Trip sat behind his desk. "Shoot."

"Sometime at the end of September, beginning of October, we'd like to get married in the backyard."

"Will you give me away, Daddy?"

Trip was very solemn as he hugged his daughter. "When are you due?"

Coop burst out laughing.

Abby slapped his chest "Daddy!"

"April? Sometime in the Spring." Coop's grin was ear to ear "We'd like to keep it small. I'm not sure how my mother will feel about that, though."

"Cooper, this is your wedding to plan with Abby. Your mother has no say in the matter."

Coop grunted. "Would you mind telling her that?"

Trip embraced Coop and whispered, "Thank you, son."

"I'd like to call Kathryn and Cubby. I want Dalton, Kathryn and Stella as bridesmaids."

"Honey, have you absolutely decided Julie is guilty?"

"Nothing is absolute, Daddy, but she lied to us. She pretended to be the woman scorned and…"

"Abbs, maybe only Dalton and Kathryn, and I'll ask Cubby and Shaw. We're keeping it small, remember? Besides, you may not want to put Stella on the spot."

"Can I ask Jack and Brock if the girls can be flower girls?"

"I'm sure they would love that."

Chapter 37

Julie didn't want to tell Bill she had to go home at the end of the week, but she hoped that by doing so, he would make time to see her every day.

She knew he would be stopping by, likely arriving sometime after nine, depending on the traffic. She dressed in her new, barely-there teddy and, while she waited, called her kids. She called them every day. They were the only reason she was going back to Cape Hope.

Julie had planned her stay in Boston carefully. Not wanting to be found, she used the ID her brother had obtained for her and made a reservation in Boston. She also searched online for a luxury hotel with an available room and found one on the coast of Maine. She checked in without a suitcase, telling the staff she would return for her belongings later.

Afterward, she went to Boston, where she visited a salon to have her hair dyed. She also scheduled an appointment at a different salon to have it dyed back to its original color before returning home. Finally, she checked into the hotel as Zoey.

Julie thought she had all her bases covered. Her plan was to return to Cape Hope as the grief-stricken wife who had made the mistake of asking for a divorce. She decided she couldn't let Beau keep his mistress without a fight. She rehearsed the plan in her mind, but she knew she needed her brother's help.

Chip agreed to get her receipts from a friend who owned a bed and breakfast on Nantucket—a friend who owed him several favors. He had the man email the receipt to Julie's work account. She was confident the plan would work.

Julie heard a click from the door. She had given Bill a key and had the "Do Not Disturb" sign hanging from the knob, so she knew it had to be him. She sat on the bed, waiting until she saw Bill "I know I keep saying this, but I missed you."

"I assure you the feelings are the same."

***

Merritt and Ben were staying at Shaw and Dalton's house. Harry had gone home for the weekend and wouldn't be back until morning. Ben was scheduled to meet with John for his return-to-work evaluation.

"John, thanks for meeting me here."

"I stayed at Trip's last night. Maggie saw her doctor on Friday. It was a very pleasant surprise."

"She needed a compassionate man. Did she tell you we talked in the hospital?"

"I know she was embarrassed."

"Even though we can't remember, she was, yes. I almost wish she hadn't been told. Just one more thing to make her feel ashamed. It's hard not to imagine when you don't know."

"How is Merritt?"

"Better. Once she decided not to let the experience control her thoughts, she was able to move on. As soon as she decided that intimacy would be enough during our celibacy, she was able to be the free spirit she was before. Merritt and modesty was not a good combination. I'm happy for her sake she was able to come to that conclusion on her own."

"My brother will be here later in the week."

Ben chuckled. "Does Maggie know?"

"He has taken her on as a patient, so yes. Keep it to yourself. I want to see the reaction when he comes to the house."

"Your secret is safe with me."

"I'd like to talk to you about something. Off the record. Friend to friend."

Ben had a bad feeling, but he agreed, "I wouldn't want to talk about anything that may make you question my ability as an Agent or hurt a case."

"Off the record, completely, totally, everything you say; off the record."

"Is it that obvious?"

"You and I were friends before I talked to you professionally the first time. Friends first, Ben."

"What do you want to know?"

"What were you thinking? If that house had security, you'd not only be out of a job, but you'd be in jail. Did you think about any of that?"

"It was the only way. I had to do it for all of the women. Have you talked to Harlow? I was thinking about her, Stella, Matilda, Trinity and Billie. Merritt and I were in that room, John. I woke up in the room and only remember a minute or so. The room was black cinder blocks. It looked like Frankenstein's lab. Metal tables, a chair that looked like an electric chair in a prison. There was a cart. There was a car battery on the bottom shelf and things I thought only existed in the movies. I heard two men talking about *taking care of the woman*. I don't remember any more." Ben was looking John in the eye as he explained what happened "And before you ask, the reason I didn't tell Harry was because I had been dosed with something in the parking lot. Who would believe that what I saw was really what I saw."

"I didn't understand why you did it until this past weekend. If I had known Maggie before she was taken, I probably would have done the same thing. Harry asked me if I thought you were capable of going there. I told him you would never compromise a case. I believed it at the time. I actually still do. Ben, my only concern is if you slip."

"John, I have put the incident behind me for the sake of my relationship with Merritt."

"I hope you can." John took out his mini tape recorder and pressed record "Ben…"

***

Billie, Merritt, and Trinity went to the hospital for their follow-up appointments. After receiving a clean bill of health, they visited Harlow's room. She was standing by the window, wearing a dress that Simon had brought from Stella's closet. Though Stella didn't know

Harlow, Simon said they were about the same size, and Stella had insisted on lending her some clothes.

"Harlow, are you ready?" Trinity wondered.

"Is Maggie OK?"

"She is. We all had appointments, so she stayed at the house."

"Dr. Evans was here for a long time yesterday. I wanted to thank her for giving up her time with him."

"Did he help?" Merritt asked.

"He actually did."

"Maggie knows John's time is not always his own. He wanted to be here to talk to you. She hoped he would help."

"What am I going to do now?" Harlow was melancholy.

Trinity and Billie looked at each other, "Recuperate." Trinity walked Harlow to the bed and sat down. "You need to talk. John's mother will be here tomorrow. Talk to her."

"I don't want to go home."

"Do you live with your parents?"

"I live in their house on Beacon Hill. They are never there, so I basically live alone."

"Did you finish school?"

"Yes. I have a master's in art history. I've never worked. I have no idea what I want to do with my life."

"I have a graphic design company. Do you draw or paint?"

"I paint. I can draw, but I haven't for a long time."

"I'm doing work for the family who owns the house we have been staying…"

Knock, knock … "Are you ready to go home?" Simon had come up to see Harlow before she left.

"The doctor examined me. She said to be celibate until I come back. I got mad at her. I screamed. *You obviously haven't looked at my chart. Sex is the last thing on my mind.*"

"Did you agree to talk to Dr. Evans when she gets here?"

"I did. Dr. Evans said she does counseling for people like me."

"Harlow, she volunteered to come. John told her what has been happening here."

"Thank you for helping me, Dr. Fredericks. I really don't remember how I got here, but you have been very kind and sensitive."

"You'll meet Stella when you get to the house."

"You are sure those people won't find me?"

"Harry is the head of the Boston FBI office. He has had Agents there since we were all found. They must have done some cleaning house because they moved the operation."

"They did. I woke up in a different room one day."

Billie had been quiet so far. "I'm going to be working for the Cape Hope Police. I will keep an eye on you, I promise."

"Thank you all. You didn't need to do this for me." Harlow wept. "I'm never going to be the same again. I guess I will need to talk about it."

***

Harry called Marcus and Bellamy into his office. "Starting tomorrow you will be on protection at the Fredericks home. The primary reason is that the victims who are law enforcement will be going home today. But there will be a new addition. Her name is Harlow. She was released by the brothel after we sent an APB with her picture to all the Agencies, including Interpol. Someone was scared. That is the only reason they would have let her go."

"Sir, that can only mean someone high up saw the photo and warned the proprietor."

"That is exactly what that means. Bellamy, Marcus has already met the Captain and his officers. I will be there when I'm available." Harry handed Bellamy a piece of paper. "This is the Captain's cell number."

"Sir, what about Ben?"

"As soon as he's cleared for duty, he will be at the office. He can't be involved in this case."

Marcus was worried about Ben. "Have we been read in on everything?"

"No. Watch this, then I will explain."

Neither Marcus nor Bellamy knew Julie, but Marcus knew about Beau through Ben. "So that's Beau's wife with the guy from the Gala and the Pub?"

"Yes. As far as we know, they didn't know each other at the Gala. No one remembers seeing them talking."

"What will we be doing?"

"Harlow, Trinity and Stella will still be at the house. But as I said, because Harlow was released only a couple of days after the APB we are worried whoever it was that recognized her might try to silence her."

Bellamy was direct, "Then why didn't they kill her?"

"Who the hell knows? There is also a BOLO out on Sylvie. We know that is the name she has been using. Marcus has seen her at the Pub and at the Gala. She is dangerous, Agent Lucchesi. She will not hesitate to kill."

"Sounds like she is also arrogant." Bellamy thought.

"She went into the Pub the other day, but she slipped out before the police got there. Naomi didn't want to spook her because the lunch crowd was there. They were hoping to apprehend her without a scene, but she is very smart. She must have been spooked. She was wearing a short brown wig and glasses. Naomi did a composite I sent to your phones. Since Marcus is known at the Pub, Bellamy, I would like you to go there to familiarize yourself. Tim Edwards knows you're coming. He will introduce you to Captain Landry, Detective Lenny Clarke, and Officer Lucy Finneran."

***

Steve had been with Julie all morning. Neither of them wanted to admit what was happening between them, but Julie knew she had to tell him she would need to go home at the end of the week.

"I have to go home. If it were just me, I'd stay here, but I love my children."

"I make my own schedule, so I'll be back, but my wife wants to see you again."

"I enjoyed my time with her."

"How about this? We have a shop on the North Shore…"

"Well, well, that is very convenient. Go on."

"I will have her meet you there. She can show you what we have to offer; then I will meet you both at our home, which is a few miles north."

"I like what I'm hearing."

"Will that be easier for you? Because it would be easier for me? I would certainly like to see you on a regular basis."

"Then it's a date. Will you let me know if you can come back tomorrow?"

"I will come by for lunch. How is one o'clock?"

***

John reached for the tape recorder and turned it off "Ben, I am going to recommend you be reinstated to full duty. But I want to talk to you at least once a week. We can do it casually, but I need to know you are OK."

"I appreciate your concern, but I think you know I would come to you if I was questioning myself. I'm not going to do something stupid. Merritt and I are buying Lizzy's house. We're talking about a family. I won't do anything to stand in the way of our happiness."

"What are Merritt's plans?"

"She wants to take Billie's job, but truthfully, I think she would rather work at Cape Hope PD."

"She should ask. Maybe she could job share with Billie. The Captain may allow for that so Billie can have the same schedule as Juice."

"Does Maggie know how smart you are?"

John smirked "She thinks I'm wonderful, so yes, I guess she does."

"Have you talked about living arrangements?

"Maggie wants to live near Clara, but she said she would move in with me. I think she would be lonely there. Right now, she needs interaction. After Mom and Joel are gone, she is going to realize I am right. Her father is going to have her car shipped here, so she will have more freedom, but I don't think braving the 128 traffic every day to come up here is something she will want to do."

"Did you tell Trip you'd like your mother and brother to stay at the house? It certainly will be easier to have everyone together. It will give Maggie a chance to know them better too."

"He said there is room for everyone. It should be fun. I should warn you though, Joel and I get our sense of humor from Mom."

"I'm sure Trip will be happy to have his house back. Harlow should be there now. Is she OK?"

"I was surprised at how frank she was. She is very smart. I hope I never have to meet her parents because I would give them a piece of my mind."

"I'd be right behind you."

"I'm sorry about the other thing. I contemplated talking to you about it. I think you needed to talk about it as much as I did."

***

Ben spoke to Merritt about John's idea. She went to Trip's to talk to Billie… "So, what do you think? I think it could be the answer to coverage during the summer and for vacations."

Billie paused her packing and went to the station with Merritt. When Phil saw them at the desk, he waved them into his office.

"You two look like the cat that swallowed the canary."

"Phil, John came up with the solution to all of your staffing woes."

"Woes you say, hmm. I'm intrigued."

Merritt and Billie eagerly explained John's idea.

Phil leaned back in his chair. "I'll have to speak to the Chair of the Selectboard, but the money has been approved. I think they will be happy to have two experienced officers coming on board. Will you be in charge of your schedule?"

Billie handed Phil a piece of paper. "We basically work a schedule, so I will be off when Juice is off. We clearly won't be on twenty-four-hour shifts, but we came up with this on the fly. It will obviously need to be tweaked. What do you think?"

"I love it. I wish I had known Merritt was leaving the Guard; I would have suggested it myself."

"We won't let you down."

"You are both dedicated to law enforcement, and you're good friends to boot. Give me a few days. What are the living arrangements going to be? I'd like to keep tabs on the ladies as they try to get back to normal."

"Ben and I will be living with John and Maggie at the beach house while we wait for Lizzy's place to be done. Stella, Trinity and Harlow will be at Trip's, and well, I'll be with Juice. We will be safe Phil."

"That is my main concern. Marcus will be at Trip's today. He and Bellamy decided on a two on two off-schedule. Ben and Dr. Evans know Bellamy. Harry said she is a spitfire."

"I like her already." Billie chuckled. "We would both like to thank you for this opportunity, Captain."

"It is really a perfect fit for both of us. We're excited."

Phil handed Billie the APB. "I may as well show you this now. Billie, Merritt knows this woman. She is a person of interest in an FBI case."

"I've seen her." Billie sat down slowly. "I saw her… Merritt, she was in my room. Captain, I told Harry about an encounter I had with some people in my room. They were sick. I saw this woman. They wore masks, and I wasn't blindfolded. This woman came at me with a…" Billie wept as her head dropped.

Phil left the office and called Ben, "Hi, can you get in touch with Dr. Evans? Billie needs him. We're at my office. Juice is on shift, so I'm going to have Merritt take her to their house."

"What happened?"

"Billie just identified Sylvie as a visitor to her room."

"John is with me. We'll be right there."

Phil whispered to Merritt, "Can you take her home? Ben and Dr. Evans will meet you there."

"Billie has had a setback. Phil showed her the ABP. She said Sylvie was in her room. All Phil said was Billie identified her and that she needed you."

"I was afraid of something like this. PTS is sneaky. Granted Billie wasn't there as long, but she and Trinity were subjected to brainwashing as well as the physical torture."

They took John's car "Take the next left. The house is the Gothic Victorian duplex."

"Wow, look at that."

"I'm told it was neglected and Lenny and Juice restored it. Matilda said the work was cathartic for both of them."

"After being overseas. Yes, I imagine it was…"

Merritt came to the porch and waved. She ran to the car "John go in. She is expecting you. She just fell apart when she saw the APB."

"Thank you. Will you tell Maggie I'll pick her up at Trip's? We want to thank him together."

John went inside to find Billie pacing in the kitchen "Billie?"

"Juice told me this might happen. He said PTS can be a bitch if you don't talk about it. He and Lenny have a group at the VFW…"

John put his hands on her upper arms. "Billie, look at me."

She took a deep breath. "John, that woman is evil."

"Have you told Juice any of the details?"

"No. Today was supposed to be…" She began to cry "We haven't been together. I had the whole evening planned. I hadn't thought about that woman. I didn't want to tell Juice because I didn't want him to think about it. It's an awful image. I can't do that to him."

"He never talks to you about Afghanistan?"

"No, and I didn't ask. Is that awful?"

"Not at all. He seems very introspective."

"He is, but he is kind and he has a very dry wit… Stella told me about the first time he changed her bandage. She was embarrassed because her injury is *strategically placed,* and she can't wear a bra. She couldn't look at him. He had to put ointment on the burn, which was painful. She said he was so compassionate. When he was done she cried on his shoulder. He didn't say anything, he just let her cry."

"Are you afraid he will be disappointed?"

"I'm afraid of that woman. Juice wouldn't hurt a fly. He doesn't know we went to the doctor. I wanted to have a romantic evening and make love all night."

"I know it's simplistic to say *you can't let those people win.* Billie, they wanted to break you. People like that revel in causing pain. Don't let them take you from Juice again. Maggie and I will be living here. Even if I am in Boston during the day I will make sure I am available for you. If you think talking about what the woman did will help you, my mother will be here tomorrow. She counsels abused women. Please, if you can't talk to me, talk to her."

"What do I do tonight?"

"Have you talked at all about being intimate again?"

"We have been intimate, and it has been wonderful, but…" Billie buried her face in her hands. "I have to get through this first time. It's been a long time since the man I love has made love to me."

"Can you clear your mind of everything except you and Juice?"

Billie took a deep breath. "I have to. Can you give me some advice? Maggie is very happy."

"She is. You can be too, Billie. Trust Juice; trust your love."

"If you don't hear from me tomorrow, well, how about I thank you now? Thank you Dr. Evans."

***

Sylvie was restless. She had been idle too long, and her craving to inflict pain needed to be satisfied. She needed to find another outlet, but the location of the conduit she sought remained elusive. She wanted Kim and Steve—and she wanted them to pay.

Sitting at her desk, she stared at the pictures she had taken at the gala. She had been careful not to let anyone see her as she moved around the room. Her decision to save them to the cloud made her smile. She chuckled as her illicitly purchased facial recognition software proved useful.

She was able to identify several people. She remembered Justice Mason as the man she wanted for herself "Hmm, he's a firefighter. Big and strong, but he would be missed. Shaw Fredericks, Assistant DA? No thank you." Shaw's former boss had neglected to remove his name from the public record, a task he planned to complete once a replacement was found.

"Let's see, Lenny Clarke, Cape Hope PD, nope. Wait a minute, he's with that woman from the house… She works for the school department… Kathryn Ellis, an attorney, not gonna happen. OK, are any of these people nobodies? The FBI bitch isn't listed, interesting. OK I'm getting nowhere. I'm just going to have to go back to Kim and Steve's shop."

Sylvie decided that calling the store to confirm Kim and Steve's schedules was the best course of action. She also needed to track down the brothel's new location, as she had some unfinished business with them. Eager to find not only the proprietor of the brothel but possibly a new victim or two, she chose to tour the streets of Cape Hope.

***

Billie waited in the bedroom, wearing one of Juice's work shirts. She rolled up the cuffs and sat on the bed.

Juice was predictable. After his shift ended, he went straight home. Billie's car was parked outside. He entered through the back door and dropped his laundry on the washer. "I'm home!"

"I'm up here."

Juice smiled when he saw Billie sitting on the bed, his shirt left unbuttoned. They had been intimate, but he hoped her demeanor meant she had seen the doctor. "Are all your clothes dirty?"

"I contemplated sitting here in the buff. Then I saw this and…"

"Honey, are you ready?"

"I talked to John. I am nervous, but I have been looking forward to this since…" She took a deep breath and let it out slowly. "I love you so much."

Juice laid on the bed "Come next to me. Let's talk." Juice kissed her "Do you need to tell me about what happened in that house?"

"Need? No… I don't know… Merritt and I are going to job share. Captain Landry…"

"Honey, honey you don't have to talk about it. You may want to at some point, but right now, I can hold you. How does that sound?"

"Do you have any idea how much I love you?"

"I think I do. When I first saw you at the Pub, I just knew."

Billie grinned. "Me too." She straddled his waist as she began to unbutton his shirt. "You are a little overdressed, don't you think?"

***

"Trip, thank you for opening your home to all of us. It was just what the doctor ordered."

"Your help with the ladies is thanks enough. Maggie, did your father tell you he was coming at the end of the week?"

"He did. Thank you for offering to have him. I know he wants to meet Harlow."

"He was thrilled when Clara called to say she was safe."

"My mother will drop her things off at the house then we will be over in the morning."

"Your mother has made quite a name for herself with her charity work. We are looking forward to meeting her."

"Speaking of charities." John handed Trip an envelope: "For your wife's charity."

Beau came home just as John and Maggie were leaving "Thanks for going to the beach house. I feel more comfortable having Trinity here." Beau glanced at John, then Trip.

John looked at Maggie. "Meet me in the car?"

Harry and John decided that disclosing the latest revelations about the case to the ladies would be reckless.

"Beau, Ben and I are friends. Having my mother and brother with us will make for a more laid-back atmosphere. Maggie is looking forward to our time with them."

"It does make more sense, but I'm worried because that woman knows this house."

"That is for Marcus and Bellamy to worry about. The updated security will monitor the first floor and ping their phones if there are any unwanted visitors. Beau, we understand your anxiety. Stay aware of your surroundings when you're not here. If you have to go home, speak to Phil so someone can go with you. We suspect Julie will be home to pick up your kids. If she's not, Harry has a plan for that scenario too."

"Aren't you worried about Maggie?"

"I'm concerned about all the women. Beau, we have a plan. If Julie calls you, please let Harry know right away."

"I was going to wait for her at the house on Saturday."

"Son, Harry needs to know as soon as she arrives."

"I know Dad. Trinity and I…"

"She already thanked me. I want her to be safe too, son."

"Thanks Dad."

Beau went to the bedroom. "Sweetheart?" The bathroom door was open. "Trinity?"

She came out of the bathroom, her robe loosely tied around the waist. "I went to the doctor today, Beau. She said I'm fit as a fiddle."

Beau put his arms around her "And ready for love?" Beau stepped back "I'm sorry, that was really insensitive."

"No Beau. I need you. I need to know I can be the woman I was before. The woman you…" Trinity was emotional.

"The woman I fell in love with? I would have waited as long as it took if it meant you were safe and healthy."

"We never talked about the second time you came to the house. Why didn't you make love to me then?"

"Not the way you were." Beau sighed. "I wanted to, but I couldn't disrespect you like that," Beau grunted. "Kind of hypocritical considering the first time I saw you there."

"I don't care about that. I love you. Besides, I knew you were married and I didn't care."

Beau kissed her. "So it seems we were made for each other."

"It seems…" Beau lifted her into his arms and kissed her as he gently laid her on the bed…

"Are you crying?"

"I'm happy Beau. That morning in the hospital, when I saw you, I was just thinking about that. In spite of everything, you make me very happy."

"It was like I was with you for the first time."

"For a long time I didn't think I would ever feel like that again. Thank you Beau."

"I hope you will always be as happy as you are now."

"Where do we go from here, Beau? It would be dangerous for me to go home. What should I do?"

"Shaw will be home today. Kathryn already left the papers for him to look over, but you know I trust her."

"You surprised me Beau. Kathryn is a beautiful, smart woman. Why did you keep your affair a secret? She is perfect for you."

"We were in high school. Shaw and I were in a private school, so our vacation week was different. Kathryn and Molly were at a private school nearby but Molly really wasn't a friend yet. Anyway, Shaw was out, and Kathryn came to the house to see Abby, who had some after school activity. We were there alone. We started talking, and one thing led to another. It was actually the first time for both of us. She wanted to get it over with." Beau laughed "She said *I'd rather lose my virginity to you than some guy who will dump me after it's all over.* I said something like *Ooh, how could any man resist a proposition like that.* Going to a girls school she didn't meet a lot of guys. I was kind of a jerk. I was a little full of myself, but with Kathryn, we knew each other already, we were already friends, so I could be me. We thought being mysterious was mature, so we didn't tell anyone."

"I want us to be friends."

"Abby, Kathryn, Molly, Dalton, they all want that."

"Why am I still afraid?"

"Because we're still up in the air. Trinity, I meant it when I said I want you to marry me."

"I don't want to make any plans until I know. I trust you. I don't trust your wife."

"I don't trust her either. There is a reason Harry wants you and Stella to stay here. Since all the law enforcement is gone, you still need to be protected. After some talks about what will be safest for everyone, Harry and Dad come up with the new plan. I'm staying here with you if you don't mind being here."

"I have become very fond of your father, Lizzy and Hilda. I'll stay as long as needed. I'd actually like to finish the project you and I started and give you my time for the charity and any other projects your family may support. I owe all of you so much."

"I heard Harlow say she had an art degree and paints."

"We talked at the hospital today. She seems very lonely. I'd like to have her help me. She doesn't appear to have a purpose. That's a dangerous place to be. Does Abby have an Art Department?"

"Ask her tonight. Dad wants the family here for dinner. I'm sure she will love to talk to you and Harlow. We are supposed to be out back for cocktails at six." Beau leaned over Trinity to look at the time "It's only four o'clock. Was there anything you wanted to do before then?"

***

Colt and Daisy had spent the day in plain clothes, paying special attention to the water surrounding the property, which was suspected to be the new location for the brothel. On land, Phil had a car patrol there every night, but so far, there had been no reason to stop any of the vehicles coming in and out.

Colt hadn't seen any boats near the house or dock either, so he decided to explore the water near the cove. From Ben, he knew that the house could easily be accessed from the ocean side of the peninsula, so he decided to investigate there as well.

It was nearly six o'clock, and they were preparing to go off shift when Colt piloted the cutter around the tip of the headland.

Daisy was on the bow. "Chief, Is that the tritoon the man told us about?"

Colt eased back on the throttle and moved back out of the sightline of the other boat.

"Chief, should we call the Captain?"

Colt had his phone in his hand. "Way ahead of you."

"Chief, how are you?"

"It's been relatively quiet."

"Daisy thinks the tritoon is headed toward the peninsula."

"Can she jump to shore and investigate?"

"I wanted to check with you first."

"Go. I'll take my car to Trip's; you can pick me up on the dock."

The Fredericks family was gathering for cocktails by the pool. Shaw and Dalton were back from vacation, and Simon had just returned from work and was taking a shower. As soon as he joined the party, Trip clinked his glass.

"Everyone. Thank you for coming on such short notice, but I have a very happy announcement to make. On the first Saturday of October, we will meet here for Abby and Coopers nuptials…"

Dalton screamed "Are you pregnant?"

Coop's smile said it all, but Abby nodded "You'll be my maid of honor, right?"

As the family congratulated Abby and Coop, Trinity and Harlow lingered in the background.

"Are you doing better now that you're here?"

"You're right, this is a beautiful home. My room is very comfortable. Have you met Marcus, the FBI agent?"

"No. Beau and I were getting reacquainted."

"Weren't you scared?"

"No, I love Beau. I know you will find a gentle, loving man."

"I'm not so sure about that. He would have to be very understanding. I don't know."

"May I ask a very personal question that is none of my business?" Trinity asked reluctantly.

"Sure."

"When they took you to the house, were you a virgin?"

Harlow chuckled "No, but I had only been with one man. I was always very timid. I have never been very comfortable with my body. I just wanted to die."

"We could hear you. We were afraid for you. Clara really saved your life."

"I know. She is coming by tomorrow. Trinity, I talked to Dr. Evans yesterday. I'm going to talk to his mother when she gets here. I need to be able to take this experience and help myself be a stronger person."

"Are you going to call your parents?"

"No. I asked Dr. Evans to tell me the truth about how they found me. They were never very interested in being parents, especially to a shy, mousey girl."

"You're not mousey, Harlow."

"I'm going to work on my confidence."

"Beau and I thought you might want to help me with my business. Trip owns a newspaper. Beau and I thought Abby might be able to use you in the Art Department."

"Dr. Evans did say I need an outlet."

"Tomorrow I'll show you what I do. Maybe you'll have some ideas…" Trinity saw the Coast Guard boat slowing at the dock.

Harlow pointed toward the cove "Should we be concerned?"

Trinity looked toward the family group "They don't look worried.

Marcus walked to the back and whispered to Trip. He laughed. "As you young people would say "He's cool."

Beau laughed. "Dad? Did I hear you right?"

"Don't be a fuddy-duddy Beau."

Phil came to the back to say hello, then headed to the dock.

Beau saw Trinity standing alone after Harlow went inside. "Beau, that is so exciting. Coop seems over the moon."

"He has wanted to marry Abby for a long time and a baby to boot. He is beyond happy."

"Beau, I should have told you something earlier. I was caught up in the moment, but I really should have told you. I'm sorry."

"You're talking in riddles. I don't think there is anything you could say that would upset me."

"OK, here goes. When the doctor asked me about birth control, I said I'd have to talk to you about it. I really meant to, I'm sorry. I was so happy to see you and…"

Beau was smiling "Shh. It's up to you, but I would be happier than Coop is now if you had our child. But it's your decision."

"Your cousin…"

"Andy is cool."

"But you would want to raise our children in the church…"

Andy heard Beau and Trinity's conversation: "Children are innocents, Trinity. They will not be judged."

"I was baptized in the Catholic church, I had my first communion, but I wasn't confirmed. My parents divorced, and the priest said I couldn't be in the church anymore."

Andy shook his head "There are clergy who are unyielding." Andy looked at Beau "I hope I am more open minded than the priest who refused to confirm you."

"Julie filed for divorce. I'm not going to contest it. Then Trinity and I are going to get married."

"Father, thank you for listening to Beau after I was abducted."

"As much as I oppose what he did, I could tell how much he loves you."

Trinity threw her arms around Andy. "Thank you."

***

Colt went to the end of the cove to the stone house "You can get off here. Daisy is staying inside the perimeter. I'm going back to the point."

Phil wasn't in uniform. He pulled his shirttail out of his pants and tucked his gun into his belt. Staying behind the trees, he had a clear view of the water. There were sailboats, cabin cruisers, and other vessels, but the tritoon they had seen on the other point wasn't there. Phil texted Colt: *Do you have any DO NOT CROSS tape?* He wanted to use it on the hatch door.

I'll be right back.

Phil was concerned that the stone house was still being accessed by the owners. "Can you dock at Trip's? I have an idea.".

I can't reach Daisy.

502

Phil called Harry, who had just arrived at Trip's, to talk to Marcus.

"Colt dropped Daisy at the peninsula. They saw the mysterious tritoon boat. Colt tried to contact her. I am going to ask Lizzy to keep an eye on everyone here; Colt is going to pick us up."

Harry called Ben. "When you and Merritt explored the peninsula, did you find any access from the far side?"

"It looks like there may have been an old access road. I'm not sure if it connects to the ocean or not. Can you tell me…"

"Daisy was searching the peninsula. She's not answering."

"Can Merritt and I help? Please?"

"Sure."

Phil called Lenny and Lucy. As soon as Ben and Merritt arrived, they parked across the street and headed to the spot where Ben had seen the road. They spotted Colt's cutter docked near the stone house. Ben then received a text from Harry, asking them to search as close to the water as possible.

There was a clear swath for a vehicle that led down to a path. At the end, a well-defined trail cut through the beach grass. Merritt spotted something in the grass. She slipped on a latex glove and tugged at the metal ring she saw poking through the grass "Wow, that's really in there." Merritt squatted "Ben, do you think this could be used to secure a boat?"

"I can't imagine another reason it would be there."

Ben and Merritt carefully combed through the grass. Just as it seemed like there was nothing unusual, something shimmered in Merritt's peripheral vision.

"Ben, Ben, look…" Merritt didn't pick up the item she found "Ben, no one is going to believe I found this here."

Ben looked through the grass. Hidden in the tall beach grass was one of Merritt's earrings, the one she had worn on the night of the Gala.

Ben walked toward the water and called Harry,… "I know how it will look, but it is still evidence. Did you bring any bags?"

"Ya, I have a couple. We'll head to the station after we finish." Ben headed back to Merritt, who was kneeling on the sand sobbing.

"They belonged to my grandmother. She was the only person who really understood me, Ben. Everyone called me Merrie. I really hated it. Grammie was the only person who called me Merritt. She was the only one who really cared."

"Maybe we can go back to the Country Club and look around?" Ben held his hand out to Merritt "I'm sorry you're hurting."

"We have to find Daisy Ben. We can continue my pity party later." Merritt held his hand as they walked along the edge of the woods. Colt and Harry, Phil and Billie, Lenny and Lucy were all searching for Daisy, each searching without communication. Colt had already determined the tritoon wasn't in visual range and was sure she was either hurt or missing.

Merritt shielded her eyes as the sun began to set behind the trees. She gently pulled Ben away from the beam of light. She smiled as she whispered, "Ben, look. Our spot…"

Ben put his forefinger to his lips and pointed toward the formation of rocks. They had both drawn their weapons when they heard, "Is somebody there?"

Merritt ran to the clearing as Ben called it in.

"Daisy!" Merritt took off her shirt, balled it up and held it on Daisy's head. "What happened?"

"I was hit from behind. I heard them talking. They were going to take me until they saw my gun. Then *whack!* I was woozy, but I saw them as they walked away. Two large women. One six feet, the other maybe five ten. My head is killing me. I think I need stitches."

Ben had come back "Colt is on his way with a medical sled. Phil called an ambulance. Do you want my shirt, sweet cheeks?"

Merritt took Ben's shirt from him "Thanks. Daisy, can you remember anything else?"

"One of them had a syringe in her hand. For two large women, they were very light on their feet. I didn't hear them coming."

"They are very experienced. Daisy, are you sure about everything you heard?"

"Positive. Right before they left, one of them said "Come on, Maudie, let's get out of here. Then I crawled over here to hide."

"Daisy!" Colt put down the sled.

"I'm OK Chief. I can walk."

Merritt helped her up and put her arm around her "Tell me if you need to stop."

"I'm OK, but my head hurts." Daisy handed Merritt her shirt "Thanks."

Simon was waiting at the dock with Phil and Billie. "Dad told me what happened." He looked into Daisy's eyes, then looked at the cut on the back of her head. "I'll meet you at the hospital."

The EMTs came down the hill and then carried Daisy to the ambulance.

Harry met them on the dock. "Ben, what the hell happened?"

"Two big women. One named Maude. They didn't kidnap her when they saw her gun. One of them was holding a syringe."

"Well, that's more than we had. Thanks for your help. Ben, may we meet in the morning? Marcus is staying in the pool house. He said we could meet there. Ten o'clock?"

"That's good."

Merritt and Ben went back to his car.

"Ben, I went to the doctor today."

"Is everything OK?"

"She said I'm as good as new. Why do these people keep screwing with us?"

"Is this because of Billie?"

"She was so upset Ben. What happens if I am working and I see these people? Am I going to fall apart too? Am I going to be able to be a good police officer?"

"Oh honey… are you still good staying with John and Maggie?"

"Yes. I like them, Ben."

"I never had much use, or respect, for that matter, for psychologists. John is great at what he does, and he is a good friend."

"I hoped I could talk to his mother since you already talk to John." Merritt looked sad.

"I do talk to him. I've been worried about you, honey, but I'm worried about a lot of things. My confidence as an Agent, my ability to keep you safe. Those people messed with my head, too."

"I love you so much. Don't let what happened to us come between us."

"Not going to happen. Merritt, tell me about your grandmother."

Chapter 38

"Good morning, very, very Special Agent Ben Malloy." Merritt had been lying in his arms all night, her head on his shoulder and one leg resting across his waist.

Ben kissed her forehead. "Is it OK that I'm not so worried about you now?"

"Knowing how much you love me makes all the difference. I couldn't have gone through any of that if I was still alone." Merritt laid on top of him "We're buying a house Ben. We're going to be a family. Before I met you, that dynamic never crossed my mind."

"After we talked last night, I could see the load you were carrying lift right off. One thing I learned from being in a big family has been sharing emotions, both good and bad is very liberating."

"John told me you are one of the most open and principled people he knows."

"He's being kind."

"You are being modest."

"When I meet with Harry today, I am going to ask him if you and I can go back to where we found the earring. I think if we search the path to the dock, we might find the other one."

"I wanted to be able to give them to our daughter."

"We're having a daughter?"

"After we have a boy."

Ben's hands rested on her rear end before moving up her back to her head, where he gently brushed the hair from her face. "Will you marry me first?"

Merritt grinned. "Absolutely."

***

Dr. Charlotte Evans arrived in Boston on an early flight from Chicago. She informed John that she would rent a car and meet him and Maggie at the house.

John had an appointment with Harlow, and Ben was meeting with Harry, so Merritt went to visit Billie to discuss their work schedules.

When Charlotte arrived at the house, Maggie offered her hand. "Welcome, Dr. Evans."

"You are lovely." She kissed her on one cheek and then on the other, "Please call me Charlie."

"Thank you so much. John and Joel have been lifesavers. They both sang your praises."

"This is a beautiful location."

"John and I will be staying here until we figure out where we want to live." Maggie reached for Charlie's suitcase "Let me take that for you."

"Dear, your hand is shaking."

"I've been fine. One of the Coast Guard Agents was attacked yesterday on the peninsula near the house where I… I was fine until Ben and Merritt got back last night."

"Maggie, what were you going to say? Near the house where you?"

"I was going to say *lived,* but that word is blatantly deceptive." Maggie rolled the suitcase to the bedroom with a Jack and Jill bath. "You and Joel will share a bathroom."

"Thank you. Maggie, can you look at me?"

"It is so hard because you know what happened."

"Can you explain?"

"I feel like you can see into my soul. I feel like you see me in that place and everything those people did. I know it's irrational… John and I went grocery shopping. I thought everyone was looking at me. I felt like everyone knew what I had been doing for the past year. When we got to his house, I asked if we could call Joel. I made a dumb joke about them not looking alike. I felt foolish and started to panic. John left me alone to talk to Joel. You have two wonderful caring, compassionate sons, Dr. Evans, um, Charlie."

"Maggie, the fact you have opened up to John and Joel…"

The expression on Maggie's face changed.

"No, dear, they didn't tell me anything. I know where you were, but neither John or Joel went into any detail, and they won't."

"How do women do that for a living?"

"Necessity. But there is a big difference. You and the others were being held prisoner. There is no other way to describe it."

Maggie looked down "We had good food, clean clothes, a beautiful room, books, satellite TV. It was confusing. They took care of us. When we were whipped a woman came in to put salve on the wounds. It was all very confusing."

"Maggie, can you look at me?"

She breathed deeply, then looked up "I told myself I was going to be strong and confident. John loves me. I don't want to disappoint him… I made coffee, would you like a cup?"

"Yes, thank you. Maggie, I think you are doing very well, considering how long you were there. John said you are incredibly honest about your state of mind. What did he mean?"

"They changed the bed linens in my room. The bedspread was flowery and bright. That was when I realized it must be Spring. I began to look for ways to kill myself. I couldn't imagine a life without a husband or children. The first day John came to the house to talk to all of us, I ran to him and hugged him. I thanked him for coming. Up until then none of us had really talked about what happened. I told them I wanted to end my life. Then Dr. Fredericks' girlfriend talked. She was only in the house for a few days. They branded her chest. How can people be so cruel." Maggie had tears in her eyes as she looked at Charlie.

"John said you were a remarkable woman. I'm glad you agreed to talk to Joel."

"Trip; Mr. Fredericks wants to have everyone at the house for cocktails after Joel gets here. My father will be here too. Daddy already liked John, so that was half the battle."

"Helloooo, is my Mommy here?"

Charlie laughed and kissed her son. "You look well. Maggie, I can see how happy he is."

"You were right about your mother. How is Harlow?"

"Looking forward to meeting Mom."

"We were all so worried about her. It was heartbreaking hearing her cries for help. I'm sorry. This is supposed to be a happy meeting. May we take you to lunch in town?"

"Yes. I'm looking forward to some fresh seafood. Oh, Joseph and A.J. will be here on Saturday. I asked them if we could meet for lunch before we go back."

"John said he is going to school for engineering, but he has always wanted to be a writer."

"Dear, he is looking forward to meeting you. He wants to pick your brain."

Maggie chuckled then kissed John "I'll let you two talk. I'll be in the back."

***

Harlow found Marcus in the small study off the front hall. He had a large monitor on the desk, displaying ten or twelve squares of pictures. Harlow was curious "Are those rooms in this house?"

"Oh hi. Yes, but just the first floor. Hi, I don't think we were properly introduced. My name is Marcus Pollard."

"I'm Harlow. Thank you for protecting us. May I sit next to you?"

"Sure, but I have to watch the monitor, so I really can't look at you while we talk."

"That's OK. I'm not sure what I would say anyway."

Marcus was very friendly and could also be quite charming when motivated. "Do you know how long you will be here?"

"At least until I have my follow-up appointment with my doctor."

"Dr. Fredericks is staying here with Stella. I'm sure he would be available if you need him."

"No. I'm OK." Harlow felt self-conscious but had resolved to make the best of her time there. She liked the women she had met. Before she was taken, she had mingled with the social crowd, attending parties and charity events. While in the hospital, she borrowed Simon's phone to check her voicemail and email. Aside from a message from the family attorney, there was nothing of a personal nature. She had been feeling positive about moving on with her life—until then. She talked to John about that more than her time in the house. He encouraged her to be open with the other women and suggested she ask Simon to introduce her to Abby.

"So, are you allowed to sleep?"

Marcus laughed. "If I'm good."

Harlow saw a glint in his eye. "You are what my grandfather would have called a rascal. May I ask, where did you get those beautiful blue eyes?"

"They are my fathers. My mother gave me the Latin swarthiness."

Harlow's face lit up. "You are a rascal. Did Special Agent Moran tell you about my family?"

"Only that they are not in the picture. He only told me what I needed to know… I'm sorry that sounded insensitive. There is something they teach in the Academy: do not make a judgment until you have all the facts."

"How do you know when you have all the facts?"

Marcus looked surprised. "Were you a fly on the wall that day?"

"That depends. How long were you at the Academy? My incarnation as a house fly only lasted for about three weeks."

Marcus sat back, folding his arms. He took his eyes off the monitor and marveled at Harlow's positive attitude.

She grinned. "Agent, the screen?"

"Oh yes. The day the instructor talked about that, I asked the same question."

"So, do you sleep here?"

"The love seat pulls out. If there is a breach a hand comes up from under the mattress and shakes me until I wake up."

"A fairly efficient arrangement. Sounds like an episode of the Three Stooges where the hands wash the baby…"

Marcus looked away from the screen again. "On the conveyor belt. You like the Stooges?"

"They were comic geniuses… Agent, the screen?"

Marcus laughed. "You are one of a kind."

Harlow laughed. "I'm sure we will bump into each other again. I'll let you get back to work."

***

"Ben, John said you are ready for work. I know you are friends, but I also know he would never give a back to work order for you if he had the tiniest concern, probably because of that friendship. Are you ready?"

"I am. Is there any way I can help…"

"I talked to Jim about that. You have created quite the conundrum for yourself and for me as your boss. You are an excellent Agent, but your involvement with this case should have ended with your abduction. I think to keep you on the sidelines would be a mistake, but you need someone to keep you in line. Jim is sending Toni Wyatt."

"She's cool."

"And she will be in charge."

"That's cool too."

"I didn't think you would object. I mentioned to Jim you had let your hair and beard grow. Keeping that would be a stipulation. When you are out with Toni, you need to wear your eyeglasses. We believe the people running the brothel are still hunting for women. That was confirmed yesterday. Jim and I believe there will be scouts in the area. Sylvie was seen at the Pub. We know Julie is at the hotel. We thought you could start there tonight."

"Where will Toni be staying?"

"At Phil's. Have you moved everything?"

"Yes. I hope she likes kids?"

"She is talking to Connie now. She will meet you at the Pub for lunch where you will *meet*. Then tomorrow, you will go to the hotel bar."

"I'd like to tell Merritt."

"Of course. She and Billie will be a great addition to the department."

"We're talking about family. She wants a boy and a girl. It's not officially official, but she said she would marry me."

"Congratulations."

"She asked if we could look for her other earring. They belonged to her grandmother."

"I'll send Bellamy."

"Thank you, Harry. This means a lot. Will you thank Jim for me?"

***

"You have become an addiction, my lady." Steve wasn't being hyperbolic.

"I don't want this to end. I have a big problem."

"We have a big problem. I love my wife, but you, you have stolen a part of my heart. I know that sounds corny, but it is how I feel."

"No, it's how I feel too. I have to go home for my kids, you already know that, but I will meet you wherever, whenever."

"You don't want more?"

"What I want is irrelevant at this point. I am usually a very selfish person, except when it comes to my kids. I need them as much as they need me."

"Have you made plans for tomorrow?"

"Monica is meeting me here and taking me to your store. She said she hoped the three of us could get together. She thought the addition would be done?"

"Yes, it's done. There is a space next to our fine leather shop. We have converted it to accommodate our clients preferences. You will be our first guest. I have to get to a meeting. I look forward to seeing you tomorrow."

Julie walked him to the door. "I miss you already."

***

Bellamy was sitting at the bar when Maggie, Charlie, and John arrived. "Excuse me," John said as he leaned on the end of the bar, looking at his phone. Bellamy, sitting two barstools away, was focused on the menu. "Does the menu look good?"

"Yes, I've heard the fish and chips is excellent. Are you here on vacation?"

John smirked. "In a manner of speaking." He whispered, "I'll be at Trip's on and off this week."

"I am here for work. I have no idea how long I will be here."

John continued to look at his phone "Please be careful. These people are dangerous and without conscience."

Bellamy slid the menu to John. "Here you go."

"Your mother is telling me what a handful you and Joel were."

"We were delightful; still are."

"They are also quite modest."

"John told me Joel is his best friend and will always love him more than anyone."

"That didn't worry you."

"It's a different kind of love."

"It is. I'm impressed you can see that."

"We have a lot of things to figure out. His love for his family and for me isn't one of them."

"Thank you, Peaches."

"Peaches?"

"I am soft and sweet."

John kissed the side of her head and smiled at his mother. "I told you Maggie was an extraordinary woman."

"May I ask, what would be the best time for us to visit Chicago? I went there once and was completely overwhelmed. That was one of the reasons I didn't like going into New York every day. My mind felt like it was about to overload. I prefer towns like this."

"Probably during breaks. Where did you grow up?"

"Darien. Growing up in a town like that leaves a child without the wherewithal to survive on their own."

"Your mother must have shaped you. John said your father was strict."

"Our mother only wanted to be a wife and mother. Daddy was lost when she died… Can we talk about something else?"

"Martin admitted to me he was too rigid. He regrets his part in your disappearance."

"I know. We're good now…" Maggie stood up. "Oh, Clara, we're over here."

John stood up. "Clara, this is my mother, Charlie."

"Your son has been a lifesaver to so many people. He said you are the reason he became a therapist. Thank you."

Ben entered the pub. Harry had already spoken to Tim and Naomi, neither of whom had seen Ben since he grew his hair and beard. Tim didn't recognize him, and neither did Bellamy—until he sat next to her.

Ben spoke in a hushed tone, "I'm told you are looking for a good time." He lowered his glasses and grinned.

"You should be so lucky."

Ben sat sideways on the barstool, leaning on the bar "I'm meeting Toni Wyatt. Harry said you would be here flirting with the barfly's."

"I am a little out of my element. I used the facial software to try different hair and glasses for the woman we are looking for. I hope it didn't screw me up."

"That was a good idea. She is really dangerous, Belly."

She glared at him. Ben's charm allowed him to get away with a lot "Don't worry *Benny*, I have Siggy here to protect me." As she put her hand on her handbag, she saw a familiar face walk in "I believe your real conquest has just arrived."

Ben had met Toni at a conference in D.C. the previous year. He was happy to see her again.

The bar was filling up so she sat next to Bellamy "Hi."

Ben leaned toward her "Hi."

Toni was snarky. "I wasn't talking to you."

Ben tried not to laugh. "Thank you for taking care of Merritt."

"How is she?"

"Perfect."

"Do you two want to sit together?" Bellamy said seriously.

Toni looked at Ben, then at Bellamy. "Do you mind?"

"Far be it for me to get in the way of whatever this is."

Bellamy moved to an empty seat on the other side. Tim, having overheard the conversation, went over to introduce himself. "I'm Tim. I'm usually here if you need anything."

"How is Naomi?"

"She is great. I wish I could keep her."

"Well, you can't!"

"Ben told me to watch out for you."

"I'm harmless… now."

Tim laughed. "You need to meet Lucy and Lenny."

"I'm sure I will. I'll be at the Fredericks pool house when I'm not on protection inside."

"Good to know." Tim leaned forward "Please be careful. These people are without conscience."

***

Sylvie stood outside across the street, waiting for someone she recognized to come out of the pub. She needed a backup plan in case tomorrow's scheme backfired.

She had stopped by the leather shop earlier to figure out when Kim and Steve would be there. After flirting with the man who worked there, he told her the appointment book was marked off for Wednesday between noon and three. Sylvie knew that meant at least one of them would be there. She was hopeful, though desperate to begin torturing and killing again.

She was growing bored when a group came outside. She recognized one of the women from when she and Kim were there before the Gala. The other young woman looked more familiar—she had been in the house. Sylvie never got the thrill she wanted from her, but she decided to follow them anyway. She walked down the street, then crossed to the parking lot. She felt pleased with herself when Maggie, Charlie, and John got into his car. The other woman continued walking down the street.

Sylvie followed the car at a safe distance, beginning to recognize the neighborhood. When the turn signal blinked on, she chuckled to herself. She slowed down and drove around John's car as it waited for the gate to open.

She went two houses down and turned into the driveway, stopping across the road from Trip's house. With a pair of opera glasses, she began watching the house, curious about what made it so alluring. Unable to see much, she pulled up closer. The house was well protected, so she eventually left, hoping to discover who owned the property.

John, Maggie, and Charlie entered through the front door, where Marcus greeted them in the hall. "Marcus Pollard. Your son has been a Godsend to a lot of us in the Bureau."

"Thank you Marcus. How goes the battle?"

"I hope it stays as quiet as it has been since I arrived… Marcus looked up to see Harlow coming down the staircase. "How was your nap?"

"Good. I'd rather sleep through the night and skip the after-lunch naps. Hi Maggie, Dr. Evans."

"Harlow, this is Dr. Charlotte Evans."

"Hello. Thank you for coming. Your son is the only therapist I have ever talked to that actually cared about me. Apathy is not a quality a therapist should embrace… sorry. Nice meeting you." Harlow ran back up the stairs.

John exhaled. His mother recognized his concern. "I think everyone is probably out back."

Harlow waited until the foyer was empty before coming back down "Are you allowed to eat?"

"Hilda brought me something. Are you OK, you kind of ran away."

"Sometimes I'm too forthright with strangers. I heard myself but I couldn't stop talking, so I did what I do best: I ran."

"I like your honesty. It's refreshing."

"I'm going to hold that over your head the first time I piss you off because I'm too honest."

"Come sit next to me. I obviously don't know you very well, but maybe the reason you do that is because you want to give people a reason not to like you. Maybe?" Marcus grinned.

"How long have you been doing this?"

"A few years. I hope to be a profiler. The man who recruited me for the Boston office was the best in the Bureau. I hope to be that good."

"He's gone?"

"He fell in love and retired."

"Maybe I can be your inspiration... I'm sorry, that was really presumptuous." She stood and ran up the stairs.

 Marcus went to the door and called out "Harlow..." Marcus knew Bellamy was at the Pub. He texted her *If you're all moved in, I could use a break.*

You got it.

Bellamy and Marcus had opted to stay in town while on protection— Bellamy at the pool house and Marcus inside. When Bellamy was on duty, they switched. They also agreed to give each other a break if needed. Marcus had been there since the night before, and he felt the need to stretch his legs. He also wanted to let Harlow know she was welcome to talk to him anytime.

Bellamy entered through the back, eager to introduce herself to everyone. John's mother wasn't there; she had taken the ladies to the solarium for a group session, which they all agreed would be helpful. Trinity went to Harlow's room, but when she wasn't there, the ladies started without her.

Harlow didn't want to talk to anyone. She felt overwhelmed and as though she didn't belong. *Am I trying too hard?* Yup, probably. *You don't have to connect with these women if you don't want to... Keep that to yourself, dopey.*

She went outside and down to a small building she assumed was a cabana. She knocked on the door, but no one answered, so she tried the doorknob. It opened, and she went inside, feeling a real sense of relief. John had told her that if she felt anxious, she should take cleansing breaths. They had done it together a few times, and it helped her feel better.

Harlow sat on the floor, breathing in deeply before slowly exhaling a long breath. She repeated this several times before opening her eyes. Marcus was standing in the doorway "Better?"

"Who is tending the flock?"

"Bellamy is here." He sat on the floor "Bellamy and I are sharing this room. While I work, she stays here and vice versa. You are welcome to use it as your refuge anytime you need it."

"Admitting I need help is really not in my skill set. If John hadn't come into my room at the hospital I don't think I would have sought him out. He is very kind."

"He is here. His mother is talking to the ladies. Do you need to talk? I can get him."

"No. I feel very comfortable talking to you. Truthfully, if my parents saw me talking to you, they would be horrified."

"I really don't care. I like you. I'm not interested in anyone's approval but yours."

"I like you too. You are funny. I wondered why you were talking to me before. At first, I thought you felt sorry for me, but then, well I don't believe that anymore."

"You went through something. I don't need to know the details, but you were strong enough to survive. I admire that."

"Oh Marcus. I'm a good actor. I'm a mess. I'm not sure I will ever be able to have a normal relationship again. You are so easy to talk to. You're not trying to get something from me. You're a nice guy Marcus. Thank you for making me feel like a person again." She was sobbing "I'm sorry. This comes and goes."

"Do you need John? Or I could take you to the solarium. Try talking to the others. For me?"

Marcus smirked when Harlow looked at him "Oh you're good. OK, for you."

They went to the house. Marcus knocked. "Excuse me, ladies, Harlow would like to join you."

***

Shaw and Kathryn met with Beau and Trinity at the house "Shaw, we decided not to say anything the other night because you really have to see this yourself. It can't be explained."

Beau had the video and pictures on his tablet "Hit play. This part requires no explanation. But there is more."

Shaw watched it. Then he watched it again. "I suppose if I watch it again, it will be the same?"

Kathryn rubbed his back "It gets worse. When Stella was in the house, she was able to read a man's lips. She saw him say *Mr. Smith* and *Sylvie,* who we now know is wanted for kidnapping and serial murder. But she also saw another word, *Chip. "*

"Julie's brother?"

Beau nodded. "We think he owns the house. We also think Harold found out and that is why there was a falling out. But I also think Julie found out about my affair with Trinity, and she had Chip kidnap her."

Kathryn had her arm around Trinity "We went back and forth about whether to say anything about what Ben found. Merritt and Billie are the only ones who know."

"We were all in with John's mother yesterday. Billie and Merritt are going to be job sharing for Phil. Billie said she is afraid of what will happen if someone sees her in uniform. She's afraid what will happen if someone leaks the information to the press that she was a prostitute."

Kathryn promised, "I will happily sue any publication that prints something like that."

"I've been thinking about what this will do to my kids if Julie is involved. She has always been an excellent mother, at least I thought she was. I have no idea what I will say to them."

Kathryn leaned toward Beau "We will speak to John; we will all take care of it together. We will protect them."

"Shaw, did you look at the divorce papers?"

"I did. I think they should be revised. Beau, Harold bought you that house for a wedding present, it is half yours. Don't give that away. You didn't have a prenup, you deserve more."

Kathryn was quiet. She knew Shaw was right "Maybe we can put that discussion on the back burner until Julie gets back. I am going to talk to her. Then I will speak to Shaw. We will figure this out between us. But I think she is doing this to prove something to herself. I know I sound like I'm making excuses for her but… she has been all over the place. I'm sorry Beau, Trinity, I am worried about her state of mind."

Chapter 39

Ben and Toni decided to meet at the diner. Phil was there with Lenny, Lucy, and Tim. When he saw them, Phil stood up and pulled a small table over to their booth. "Over here," he said.

"Phil, Lenny and Lucy, this is Toni. Portsmouth field office."

Lucy smiled and winked. "And who might you be, stranger?"

Tim piled on, "Ya, who are you?"

"I thought you said you knew these people."

Ben laughed "Lenny, how is Matilda?"

"Getting ready for school to start. She was very relieved her principal didn't say anything to the staff about her hospital stay. Matilda told her she had an accident and they left it at that."

Lucy added, "She is making wedding plans too."

Ben nudged "Lenny, is that a smile?"

"Lizzy is planning a shower. We don't need anything, but Lizzy wants Tilly to have the full wedding experience. She deserves the best."

"May I ask? Is she one hundred percent?" Toni wondered.

"Depends on the day. Most of the time she is. When she heard about Daisy she was understandably upset. Ben, do you know how she is doing?"

"She has a concussion and six stitches, but she will be fine. I am so sick of these people."

"Toni, what is your assignment?"

"I'm supposed to make sure Ben doesn't do anything foolish. But I understand his passion to end this before anyone else gets hurt. I'd like to say hello to Colt. He was in full-blown protection mode up in Kittery. He had taken off his shirt and had Merritt covered with it when I got there."

"I hadn't heard that." Ben sighed "OK, we should get going."

Phil stood up "We should all be at Trip's on Friday, see you then."

***

Kim arrived at the hotel early to surprise Julie. She went straight to the room from the basement garage, but Julie wasn't ready to go to the leather shop yet "I'm not ready yet. Come in. I'll be quick."

Kim stopped her and kissed her. "We have time."

Julie hesitated. Kim was unashamed. "I was hoping for some alone time."

"Oh. Give me a few minutes. I'd like to shower first." Julie closed the bathroom door behind her and stepped into the large glass enclosure. As she rinsed off, she saw a figure through the steamy glass.

Kim opened the door and walked in…

Julie was confused. She was beginning to feel in over her head but didn't want to disappoint Bill. She questioned her decision to get involved with a married couple, unsure why, but she knew she needed to find out where the leather shop was located "Where is your shop?"

Kim didn't like revealing too much "Witch City."

"Which city? Where is your shop? What town is it in?"

Kim laughed "Witch City, you know, the North Shore. Come on. Bill is waiting."

Julie felt rushed but didn't want to disappoint Bill. "Hold on." She picked up the small pad of paper from the desk and took a cosmetic bag from her suitcase. Heading to the bathroom, she turned on the faucet and wrote a note. After applying a little lip gloss, she returned to the room, leaving the note in the cosmetic bag before putting it back in her suitcase. "There, all set."

"We'll take my car. Bill has a meeting here later so he will bring you back."

Julie was feeling better about the excursion to the shop "Thank you. I've enjoyed our time together."

Kim had asked Steve to meet them at one o'clock. They arrived at the shop a little after noon.

"I'd really like to see what your shop has to offer."

"We took our love for fine leather and mixed it with our penchant for hard-to-find leather items."

Julie had no idea what she was talking about but she grinned and nodded "I'm intrigued."

As they neared the shop, it finally dawned on Julie "Oh, Witch City, you meant Salem. I feel like such a dope."

Kim chuckled. "I'm going to park in the back."

The ladies entered through the back door. After a few minutes of looking around, Sylvie calmly slipped inside. She moved quietly, watching as Kim and the woman examined the merchandise. Sylvie's anger flared when Kim kissed Julie. She raised her gun and cleared her throat.

"Ahem."

Sylvie gagged them, duct-taped their wrists, and forced them at gunpoint into the cargo space of her Range Rover. Once in the car, she blindfolded them and threw a blanket over their bodies.

She drove them to her house, undecided about whether she would let one of them go. To create a false sense of time, she drove around for fifteen minutes. She expected Steve to be there, intending to torture him as Kim watched. But now, she had a mysterious woman with them. As she killed time, Sylvie considered what to do with her two victims. She didn't care about money—her only focus was revenge. The plan she settled on was depraved. She wouldn't kill the women, but she would make sure they wished she did.

Sylvie's house, located just south of the store, was protected by tall stone walls and a code-secured iron gate. She drove toward the back, where the six-stall garage was obscured from the view of the house.

Once parked, Sylvie opened the hatch, grabbed Kim and Julie by their feet, and pulled them until they could stand. She then grasped the front of their dresses and led them to a door. Inside, she removed their blindfolds. The steps led down into a small, dungeon-like room. One corner held a king-sized bed. The rest of the room was disturbing—tables typical of doctor's offices, metal storage cabinets filled with bottles and vials, a wall covered with handcuffs and various restraints, two birthing chairs, and on another wall, an array of whips and chains.

There were also two Lally columns in the middle of the room, about six feet apart, with large carabiners hanging at different heights on the beams between the posts. Sylvie cuffed Kim, cut off the duct tape, and attached her cuffs to the carabiner above her head. She repeated the process with Julie.

Standing in front of them, Sylvie held a large pair of tailor's scissors. She grabbed the front of Kim's dress and cut it down the middle, then snipped the fabric at the shoulders. The dress fell to the floor.

She was about to do the same to Julie when she saw she was crying "Oh poor baby. I bet you thought Kim and Steve were nice deviants."

Julie looked at Kim. Her fear had changed to anger.

"What's the matter sweetheart? Did they tell you a fib? Well honey, that's what they do. They lie. Isn't that right Kim?"

Kim was furious. Julie seemed defeated.

"What did Steve tell you? Did he make you believe he was in love with you?"

Sylvie cut off Julie's dress too "Ooh, nice. Were you expecting some hanky panky honey? Did you tell her about me? No? I didn't think so. Steve and Kim used me then threw me to the wolves. But I got away. You won't be going anywhere. I am going to keep you here and I am going to play with you and I'm going to hurt you and make you sorry you were ever born."

Sylvie left them hanging in the basement, gagged and in the dark.

***

Ben and Toni discussed the plan for approaching Julie at the hotel.

"You are assuming she will be at the bar. What if she isn't?"

"Then we wait. Harry spoke to the bartender. He said she had been there every day."

"He cooperated?"

"Apparently, his grandfather was a cop. He wanted to help."

"Cool. So, are we a couple?"

"I will approach her, distinguish her mood, then if I think she is agreeable, I will lift my glasses with my thumb and forefinger."

"Are we interested in a threesome?"

"We know the man Julie was with was in the house with another woman and the woman who abducted Naomi. We don't have confirmation on the other woman's identity but we are operating under the belief that she is the man's wife. We don't know if Julie knew the man before their meeting here. We cannot assume they did."

"And if she is only interested in you?"

"I will take my phone out of my pocket, look at it and put it right back."

"Sounds good to me. So we stay in the lobby, close enough to communicate, but not close enough to look like we are together. You will go to the bar after you see Mrs. Fredericks. I will go to a table a few minutes later."

"Pretty simple."

"Special Agent Moran suggested I listen to your ideas. He said you are tuned into these people, but because of what happened to Merritt you are too eager to close this case. I questioned your ability to be objective. That is when he told me I would be lead on this assignment. Are you going to be able to take orders from a woman?" She smirked.

"I have three older sisters. You tell me."

Toni laughed "Agent Moran said you were going to talk to the Concierge."

"Harry and I talked about it. If I'm able to make an appointment at the new location of the brothel, we can set up a sting."

"For the sake of all the women, I hope this works."

Ben parked on the lobby level of the hotel's garage, where Toni got out. He then drove down to the basement level and took the elevator.

Ben knew the procedure for the brothel. The same man was at the desk, so he approached in the executive assistant persona he had created "I spoke to someone here about ten days ago about my boss. He asked me to find a five star hotel in Boston where he would be able to find a companion. The day I came in you were trying to placate an inebriated woman. Then, I was called away. This is the first chance I've had to come back."

The man at the desk averted his gaze "Yes, I think I talked to you. I will need to run a credit check, then I will be able to give you the information your boss will need."

Ben handed the man a sheet with the backstory information "I will wait in the lobby."

Toni sat on the couch, reading a newspaper, while Ben sat in a chair to her right, looking at his phone. They had a clear view of both the reception desk and the bar. It was nearly an hour before the man left his desk and walked toward them.

Ben stood up as the man approached "This looks good. I've included the information your employer requested and also my private number. This is the credit limit for the account. I hope it will be more than adequate."

"Excellent." Harry had given Ben some petty cash for food and tips, suggesting he provide the concierge with an incentive to ensure future loyalty. Following the advice, Ben discreetly slipped the man a fifty-dollar bill as they shook hands. The concierge returned to his desk, glancing at his hand only after parting ways. A few minutes later, Ben received a text. *Thank you sir. If you need anything at all, you may text me.*

Ben texted back a thumbs-up. He looked at Toni "You and I need to start talking so I have a reason to stay here."

Toni reached out her hand "Hi, Toni."

"Ben."

They sat in the lobby for a couple of hours, talking as if they were on their first date. Since they didn't really know each other, the conversation flowed easily as they shared everything. Toni mentioned that she had a boyfriend who lived in Portsmouth and expressed her hope that they could see each other on weekends. Ben reassured her, explaining that Harry was very laid-back about his agents' personal relationships, and Phil and Connie were the same.

Ben noticed the sun beginning to peek through the office building across the street from the hotel. Glancing at his watch, he checked the time "We've been here all day. I'd like to talk to the bartender before he leaves. I'll be right back."

Toni observed the guest relations staff attending to a large group of people checking in. She noticed the Concierge speaking with a well-dressed man who wasn't wearing a name tag, leading her to assume he must be a guest. A sense of paranoia crept in as she became convinced both men were watching her while they talked. Curious and uneasy, she headed toward the gift shop, hoping to overhear their conversation.

Ben struck up a conversation with the bartender, who mentioned that the woman hadn't been in that day—a first since she had checked in, as she typically came by for at least one drink. This made Ben wonder if she had checked out. The bartender offered his thoughts, but Ben remained lost in speculation "Let me take a look. Zoey Smith. She hasn't charged anything to her room today. That is another first, and she hasn't checked out."

"Can you tell if her room has been cleaned?"

The man walked to the end of the bar, picked up the house phone, and had a brief conversation "No maid service. That is three."

Ben put a twenty on the bar as he leaned in. "The Bureau appreciates your cooperation."

"Anything I can do to help."

Ben returned to the lobby, but Toni wasn't on the couch. He chose a different chair, still keeping an eye on the elevator and the bar. He had to stay composed, but after about ten minutes, worry began to creep in. He couldn't let on that he knew the woman, but he needed to find out if anyone had seen her.

Ben went to the gift shop, but she wasn't there. He bought some gum and then asked the clerk if she had seen a tall blonde woman wearing a suit. The clerk wasn't very helpful. Ben noticed the Concierge was alone and mumbled, "Let's see how far fifty dollars goes.". He opened the package of gum, put a piece in his mouth then asked, "Do you have a wastebasket?"

"Of course."

Ben threw the paper in the bin. "I guess I must have come on too strong with that woman. I thought I was going to get lucky tonight."

"I'm sorry I didn't see her. It got really busy. Check-ins, you know."

"Oh well."

"You have the information."

"Oh, I couldn't do that. I'm a bit of a germaphobe."

The Concierge laughed "I'm right there with you. Well, good luck."

"Thanks." Ben got into the elevator, where there were two people, so he couldn't make a call. Once he reached the basement level, he jogged to his car and called Toni while scanning the garage. He heard a dinging sound—ding, ding, ding. He continued searching until the sound seemed to be coming from the trash. Putting on gloves, he reached in, pulling out debris as he searched for the phone. Eventually, he had to dump the entire trash bin over. Inside, he found her pocketbook. He looked through it, finding some cash, her ID, and her gun. He dialed the number again. Still on his hands and knees, moving the trash around, he finally found it. On the screen, the name *Ben* appeared.

He felt desperate as he waited for Harry to answer the phone. Finally, he yelled, "Answer the fucking phone!"

"Whoa, Ben."

"She's gone. Harry, Toni's gone…"

***

Beau and Trinity were lying on the bed. Beau always became lost in the moment when he made love to her. They both savored their time together. Trinity's eyes were filled with tears again, and Beau knew it was because she was happy. He held her tightly, as if it were their last time together. He felt like he was in paradise, but he knew the dream might end when Julie returned. He couldn't shake the worry about the motive behind Julie's willingness to let him go.

He had talked to his kids every day, just as Julie did. Each time he called, he asked if they had spoken to Mommy. Without fail, they always answered, "Yes, Daddy." He always called at the same time, from Trip's office. But today, the boys said Mommy hadn't called yet. He didn't ask his daughter, figuring she was having fun, so he let it go. Both he and Kathryn had tried calling Julie, but the phone always went to voicemail.

"Beau, we have to talk about what happens when your kids come home."

"I wish I could say I have a plan, but I don't. I'm supposed to pick up the boys. Julie is supposed to pick up Annie."

"Will they like me, Beau?"

"How could they not? Julie wouldn't try to poison their minds. She has always been a positive influence. Her parenting approach does not involve negativity in any way, shape or form."

"Kathryn is a good friend. She is right. You shouldn't walk away without any compensation… I'm sorry, that's the wrong word."

"I wanted the marriage to end, I wasn't thinking about me. I was thinking about you, but you're right, we need to decide where we will live. I will show you the properties that are available. I will find a contractor to finish your house. We will be together."

"We can look at the properties together. I love old architecture. I hope that's OK."

"You can have anything you want."

***

Ben was despondent. After Harry and all available agents arrived at the hotel, they searched every nook and cranny of the parking structure. Harry instructed the team not to wear their jackets or Kevlar vests, wanting the search to be as covert as possible to avoid tipping off the hotel management.

Harry contacted his best computer tech and ordered him to hack into the hotel's security system. The tech, who trusted Harry, followed the instructions. It took some time, but he finally found the man standing behind Toni. The man was obviously a professional, his face obscured. The van was white, with stolen plates. Harry immediately called Phil, asking him to send a car to the house they suspected was operating as a brothel. However, there was no activity there.

Harry also called Colt, who was understandably upset, "I'll stay out here all night if I have to."

Ben sat in his car, talking to Merritt. She didn't try to cheer him up; she just listened.

When the team was finished, Harry got into Ben's car. Ben handed him his gun and credentials. "I'm a failure. I told her I was going to talk to the bartender."

"Did she try to stop you?"

"No."

"So, why is this your fault? If she didn't want to be left alone, she should have gone with you."

532

"I should have insisted she go with me."

"You weren't in charge, Ben. She should have stayed in the lobby to watch for Julie."

"I did get information from the bartender, but at Toni's expense."

"Ben, go home. Talk to John. He will tell you what I told you. This isn't your fault."

"I have the brothel information. Someone needs to make an appointment." Ben handed Harry the information.

"I'm going to do that. Ben, go home, and please be careful."

The traffic was light going back to Cape Hope. When he got home, John's mother was sitting on the porch. "I hear you had a bad day."

"I feel like a failure," Ben told Charlie about what stood out in his mind before Toni disappeared.

"Can you close your eyes and think about what you were seeing before you went into the bar?"

Ben closed his eyes. "I was watching the area around the elevator, waiting for Julie to get off."

"What was happening?"

"Nothing unusual. It was around three-thirty, four o'clock. There were a lot of people at the front desk checking in. The Concierge was talking to a man."

"Was he an employee, a guest?"

"He wasn't wearing a name tag. Maybe the Manager, but he could have been a guest. He was looking in my direction as he was talking."

"Did you walk by them when you left to look for Toni?"

Ben concentrated. "He was taller than me, maybe six-three, thirty-five, forty. Brown hair. His suit was expensive, impeccable. Navy blue, white shirt, blue and red striped tie, with brown shoes. He had a gold watch and a pinky ring on his right hand."

"Can you describe his face?"

Ben focused on the man's face. "Clean cut… Dear God… it's the misogynist."

"You know him?"

Ben opened his eyes. "I haven't looked at the picture recently, but Tim has it hanging in his office at the Pub. He is a nasty man. He frequented the Pub. Tim suggested he may be a misogynist. Because Matilda is such a flirt, he warned her to stay away from him. She did, and Tim said it seemed to piss him off. It wasn't too long after that Matilda disappeared. Doctor, thank you. I need to tell Harry and Phil." Ben was overwhelmed as his head hung down. "Toni…I shouldn't have left her alone. If anything happens to her…"

"If she saw Julie or the couple from the Pub, would you expect her to wait for you?"

"Not necessarily. If it was an immediate situation, she would investigate, but as I said, the lobby was full. For a civilian, that scenario might not seem optimal for an abduction. But in the mind of a criminal, it would be the perfect circumstance."

"I agree. Ben, John has told me you are the first real friend he had at the Bureau. I know he believes you are a good friend and an excellent Agent. He said he would be very surprised if you didn't blame yourself. After you called, Merritt told John and I what happened. Merritt asked if I would talk to you."

"I tried to fight off that guy at the Gala. I had him; then I saw he had his gun on Merritt's temple. I had to fall back. I had to…"

"You did the right thing, Ben. You and Merritt should visit your family. I think that would be the best prescription for how you are feeling."

"Charlie, as much as I need my family right now, I need to be here more. Even if I can't be involved, I need to be here."

"It doesn't surprise me to hear you say that. Do me a favor. When Joel gets here tomorrow, talk to him. He has a unique perspective. He is the best of Joel and me."

"John said his sister is a doctor, too, but I haven't heard much about her."

"Jill. The boys call her Jillie. She is a Special Needs specialist, but she sees kids up until age eighteen. John and Joel talk to her a lot. They actually bounce ideas off each other when they are stuck."

"Maggie told us Joel is a lifesaver."

"Ben, if you have any doubts about your ability as an Agent ask Maggie. She was singing your praises earlier."

"Did she tell you how they found us?"

"John did. Are you feeling guilty about that, too?"

"I worried that something happened, but Simon assured me my DNA wasn't found…" Ben sighed. "I guess I was a little embarrassed. Even though neither one of us were responsible for the situation, sometimes, when I see her talking to Merritt, I feel like I cheated on her. I know it's irrational, but I've been beating myself up about a lot of things since Merritt and I were taken."

"Maggie made dinner. She kept some in the oven for you. Please eat, you'll feel better."

***

Sylvie went back downstairs after having dinner and a few drinks. It was almost ten at night. By then, both Kim and Julie had been there for nearly eight hours and had both wet themselves. Sylvie had expected this and brought paper towels, a plastic bag, and disinfectant spray. She let them down from the pole and made them clean up the urine from the floor.

Julie was crying again as Sylvie cut off their panties. "Put them in the bag!" She held her gun in one hand, then ordered Kim and Julie, "In here. You two smell like a litter box."

The bathroom consisted of a toilet and an open-stall shower. Instead of a typical shower head, there was a hose with a spray nozzle. Sylvie took a small switchblade from her pocket and cut off their bras before turning on the cold water, spraying them both.

They tried to shield themselves from the freezing water. "Oh, poor babies. Too cold?" Sylvie said mockingly as she switched the water to hot. She continued spraying them until the scalding water turned their skin bright red.

Sylvie was laughing. "What was I thinking?" She removed their gags and repeated the process, laughing as the women screamed.

She eventually grew bored. Picking up two towels, she ordered... "Clean up that floor."

Sylvie watched as they mopped the floor. They stood up. Julie hung the towel on a hook, but Kim did not.

"Well, it seems your friend has some manners." Sylvie escorted them back to the room, where she ordered Julie to sit on the floor. After her cuffs were attached to the pole, she grabbed Kim by the hair, faced her toward the column and locked her arms over her head. Sylvie went to the wall, chose a whip and proceeded to whip Kim's backside until it bled.

"That is what happens if you don't behave."

Sylvie then gagged both women again, turned off the light and left them in the dark.

Epilogue

The FBI was out in full force scouring the hotel and the surrounding area, but Boston was hard to navigate even for the most seasoned Agent.

Harry and his team were determined, but the case was about to get darker and much more convoluted. Even the most experienced Profiler couldn't have predicted the maze of complications the Bureau was about to encounter.

The Story Of Cape Hope
Book Two
The Revenge

"…Oh dear God, what a baby. What the hell are you doing with the likes of Steve and Kim anyway? Hmm, let me see if Steve is worried about you yet." She had taken both phones and turned them off. She turned them on to hear *Bing, Bing, Bing, Bing…* "Well, it seems Steve has been trying to find both of you. Huh, seems he texted you, missy, more than he texted wifey." Sylvie let out a maniacal cackle. "Oh dear. Was that supposed to be a secret?"